Love's Lonely Pursuits

Marina Sonkina

Love's Lonely Pursuits

BOOKS

Cover artwork by Włodzimierz Milewski

Note for libraries: A catalogue record for this book is available from Library and Archives Canada at www.collectionscanada.gc.ca

ISBN: 978-1-0695346-0-6

BOOKS

MW Books
Garden Bay, BC
Canada
mwbooks.ca

10 9 8 7 6 5 4 3 2 1

Contents

"Great are the mysteries of human life and love is the greatest of them all."

- Ivan Turgenev

Philosophy Lessons

For Sasha

1

When I was a student reading German mystics, I came across the folio of an alchemist and physician named Balthasar von Reinstüsser in early fifteenth century Marburg. Reinstüsser spent his life searching for an explanation of that strange phenomenon, which is the human heart. What forces, he asked, set in motion that tiny lump of flesh in the womb? What makes the fetus's newly formed heart produce its first beat and begin the long journey of keeping, for years, its owner alive? In Balthasar's view, Divine Providence made the heart beat the same way a clockmaker sets a pendulum in motion, with a tap or a nudge. But exactly how did that happen? With a touch of God's finger? A sudden descent of divine afflatus? Or was the sheer energy of Divine Reason enough by itself to give to the new life its impetus? In order to respond to God's call, to God's command, the alchemist believed the heart needs be tender and yielding, exactly the kind of heart that everybody is born with.

Many years later, I found in some medical treatise a confirmation of the alchemist's conjecture. The delicate nature of the heart's tissue is necessary for it to be able to react easily to tiny electrical impulses, a fact that may also make it vulnerable to electromagnetic or even sonic effects, either one a possible stimulus for that first beat. And in the same way, a strong enough external physical impact may be enough for the heart to suddenly stop. If the blow of a ball or a stone should happen to coincide with the amplitude of the heart's own rhythm, it may end in a disaster. Could an emotional trauma have the same effect as a physical one, unexpectedly leading to death?

I'm now seventy-six and just as curious about these things as I ever was. I still like to learn, even though the names of books and their authors are sometimes slipping away. I often forget what I've read, which for me is the most distressing part. I suppose I can still pun the way I used to and tell a funny story to a point, if I had somebody to tell it to, that is (by the way, my late wife, Priscilla, was never bothered by her lapses of memory, which were more pronounced than mine).

Half in jest, I comfort myself with the idea that my brain is trying to return to Aristotle's tabula rasa, to its primordial state of pure potentiality, when all the neural pathways were still uncluttered and it was possible to inscribe...But what, exactly, at this point...what fresh insights could I inscribe on my own aged wax tablet? Could it be (as I follow my own logic) that obliviousness to the physical world is a necessary step for recovering the true knowledge that, as Plato supposed, we had in full measure before we were born? The knowledge that will be revealed to us once again after we die? I can't resist one of my favourite quotes here: "If no pure knowledge is possible in the company of the body, then either it is completely impossible to acquire it, or it is possible only after death." That's Socrates, of course, in the days before taking his own life. Must be the *Phaedo,* yes, or...is it?

I have no doubt that my memory got worse after I retired, and I'm sorry that I ever did. The college where I taught for nearly forty years would have let me stay on. Of course, teaching ancient philosophy to eighteen-year-old ninnies, most of them anyway, was a waste of time. Rarely did they put down their electronic devices to gaze in my direction. Standing before them, I often felt like some disinterred fuddy-duddy whose time had long since passed and whose interests had no connection whatsoever to their young lives. If you think I'm grumbling like an old geezer, wait till you get to be my age.

Although I'm no great fan of contemporary technology, I did consult the Internet about my memory lapses. Let's suppose, some neurologist wrote there, that you completely forget about a medical appointment. They call to remind you. Glasses, wallet, keys, a spare battery for your hearing, all finally stuffed into your pockets, you hurry out the door. Fine. But now suppose you hang up but stay put since the call itself is something you're no longer aware of. The first scenario is part of the normal aging process; the second is death in life, the beginning of Alzheimer's. If I'm to trust the good Internet doctor, I really don't have anything to worry about. All the same, I decided to make my life a little easier by writing notes to myself about one thing or another.

Now before going to the store, I jot down whatever I need – no more than a few items, usually, since I don't eat much. I never used to rely on shopping lists, regarding people who wander through supermarkets with slips of paper in their hands as feeble-minded at best. My prejudices are strong, and I'm still reluctant to get out my own slip of paper. But usually a finger's touch in my pocket is enough to bolster my confidence. From grocery lists, I've moved on to copying down, for no special reason, fragments from books and articles that catch my attention. Well, I've always done that, just more so today.

Recently, for example, I recorded the following. The thirteenth century Holy Roman Emperor and King of Sicily and Jerusalem Frederick II was a man of insatiable but cruel scientific curiosity. He once ordered the complete isolation of several infants from any human speech to see if on their own they would start speaking the language of Adam and Eve instead of their parent's native tongue, whether Hebrew or Greek or Latin or Arabic or any of the other possibilities. He's also said to have had a man sealed inside a barrel to find out if his soul could be observed leaving the container after the poor victim suffocated...

As I was writing all that down, a light snow started to fall. Outside my study window, I could see snowflakes sliding down the shiny dark green leaves of the rhododendron next to our house. Years ago, Priss had planted a shrub there that, at the time, scarcely reached my windowsill, although now it's a small tree. Priss loved the fluffy crimson spume of its flowers. But I find that bacchanal of colour excessive, and in its papery artificiality even the gorgeous inflorescence itself looks lifeless to me. The red maple growing behind the fence in our backyard is much more to my liking. It retains its modest rust-brown leaves until the beginning of winter. Then they all seem to drop off at once. I enjoy the way they slowly spin in the air before settling on the driveway's damp cheek with what look like open hands. The day it snowed, they were cold, and that made them curl their fingers like living hands – or so it looked to me.

2

Ever since Priss died two years ago, I've felt in my dreams an exhilarating sense of liberation (we had tried to separate several times during our long life together). But as soon as I awake, a heavy boulder of guilt collapses on me, pressing down on my chest. The stillness of the empty rooms at night is a particular torment, and every morning I look for an excuse to get out of the house. I don't do volunteer work. I dislike clubs. That usually means merely wandering around the city, something that also frees me from having to answer the phone, rare though these calls are.

My walks usually take me away from home for as much as three or four hours. I make my way across the rumbling Burrard Bridge, which connects Vancouver's business district, on a peninsula, with Kitsilano, where my house stands on a steep slope above English Bay. Across the bay to the left, I can see the shoreline of Stanley Park and the dense, almost black stand of evergreens that occupies the peninsula's western tip.

There might seem to be no good reason for an old man with a cane (more for security than need) to be walking across that enormous bridge, but I'm stubborn. Although the bridge is defended on both sides by masses of steel (it was built in the 1930s), I still can't bring myself to look at the water far below. My gaze soars aloft to follow the bridge's heavy, dirty-yellow arches down to where they end on the north side in paired but strangely confused art-nouveau Roman sarcophagi with Egyptian wings. Bicycle riders, those sleek greyhounds, separated from the bridge traffic by large concrete blocks, seem to be the only people in Vancouver who actually care about their looks: nylon tights, bright jerseys and jackets, matching fingerless gloves. What a sharp contrast to the sloppy blouses, drab untucked-in oversized shirts, and khaki pants slipping off the hips of the bipeds walking around. I have many regrets in life: some big, some small. I regret, for example, that the so-called hounds started to abandon their old brightly coloured, streamlined helmets: they called to mind, my mind anyway, wing-footed Hermes, the ancient god of travellers and guide to the Underworld. The new ones, those dull-green round things of quasi-military design...well, whoever decreed them fashionable must be nostalgic for World War II.

What is it that draws me to False Creek? After all, if I wanted to see English Bay and the Coast Mountains, I could go out the back gate of my house and down the path to the water for an unobstructed view. Perhaps it's the proximity to other people, the bustle that I used to dislike but that now has become such a welcome contrast to the atmosphere of my own home, to its mute clutter, now that Priss is no longer there.

She was superstitiously afraid of empty spaces, and over the course of our life together she gradually dragged into our home half the inventories of the musty second-hand furniture shops on Fraser Street. All the rooms (except for my study) are now crammed with chiffoniers, dressers, étagères with elaborate inlays, useless standing lamps, card tables with fake Tiffany lamps, Chinese jade figurines, little porcelain elephants on lace doilies, and similar junk. After Priss died, I considered getting rid of it all, but then I decided against it, afraid it would only aggravate my lingering guilt. When she was alive, I silently struggled against her whole being, so unlike my own. But now that the struggle has ended, I'm unable to find any peace with myself. Somehow, I've been turned into an old cranky pants, into a Grumpasaurus. I always resented the pedestrian materiality of my wife's world. But now, without her, I'm turning into some contrived, abstract creature akin to the barren high-rises of the False Creek quayside.

3

After the effort of the bridge crossing, I need to rest. I continue east along my usual route past the moored yachts and powerboats until I come to my favourite bench facing the harbour. I get out of my jacket the little chess set I usually carry with me. There was a time when I could play against myself in my mind, but now I need to have a board and pieces.

Absorbed in the game, I didn't notice a little boy climb up onto the bench beside me, but here he is, and evidently he's been watching me play for some time. He looks around five or six years old. Curly chestnut hair frames the healthy glow of his round, dark-peach face and cherub cheeks. His bright red lips, full like a girl's, kept witching as if he was trying to keep from smiling. Taking a closer look, I realize that his face combines European and Asian features: a small nose, dark, wide-spaced eyes, and prominent cheek bones. The combination of slightly slanted eyes and curly hair is unusual, but what's most striking about him is something more elusively tender, something reservedly affectionate in his demeanor. He tells me that his name is Giovanni, and the Italian inflection only adds to his mystery.

"Can I play too?" he finally asks, as if he's been working up the courage.

"Do you really know how to?" I skeptically reply.

"My papa taught me. But we have a real chess set. Papa made it out of wood."

"This is a real chess set too, only it's small, so I can carry it around in my pocket."

"Can I touch it?"

Giovanni picks up a queen from the little board, carefully looks it over from every side, and then puts it back. He examines the king the same way, and then, evidently having satisfied himself that they are indeed real despite being small, he moves closer on the bench, sighs, and is briefly silent.

"Are you Santa Claus?" he suddenly asks, looking at my face with a sly grin.

"Do I look like him, you think?"

"You have a white beard and a cane just like Santa Claus. Can I touch the cane?"

He carefully examines my walking stick, which I bought in India. He's especially intrigued by its intricately carved boxwood handle shaped like the head of a snake.

"Can it bite?"

"Well, no, of course it can't. It's made of wood."

"Can I feel your beard too?" he asks.

Apparently without considering that a stranger might object to such a request, he moves his head closer to mine and, with a squint, starts to examine the long strands of my untrimmed beard. And I'm again struck by the gentleness emanating from his touch, his whole being.

"Why is it so white?"

"Because I'm old. Old people's beards turn white."

"When I have a beard will it turn white too? My papa's young. His mustache is black," Giovanni notes.

He tells me that his father is a "security guard" who goes around a "campus" making sure "everything's all right." That sometimes he rides a bicycle and sometimes a motor scooter. That he always picks Giovanni up after school and takes him home. And when it isn't raining, he likes to jog along the quayside while Giovanni waits, swinging his legs on a bench and playing video games on an iPod he keeps in his pocket. But this time, he's put the device away. "Better to play chess with you," he concludes.

I also learn that besides his papa, Giovanni has a green parakeet named Po-Po with clipped wings, so it can't fly. At night, Po-Po calls out, "*Voglio dormire, voglio dormire!*" meaning that it wants to be put in its cage with a cover over it. And then, when it wakes up the next morning and wants to be fed, it says, "*Mangiare, mangiare!*" Like Po-Po, Giovanni speaks Italian at home. His grandmother, who lives in Perugia, doesn't understand English at all, he informs me. Extending his lips like the bell of a tiny trumpet and rolling the *r*, Giovanni pronounces it *Per-r-r-o-o-ja*. His mama, however, lives far away in Hong Kong. She has a new papa there and a new baby, Giovanni's half-sister, although he's never seen her and misses his mama very much, but his papa says that he won't be able to visit her there just yet – he needs to get bigger first. Giovanni makes a little roof over his head with his hand to show how much bigger he needs to be before he can go to Hong Kong by himself, since his papa will have to work and won't be able to come with him.

We start to play chess. I'm struck by his ability to concentrate, unusual in children his age.

"Should I go easy on you?" he impishly asks after I've made a few moves.

"No allowances, please," I say.

Giovanni looks at me with a serious, studying gaze before taking one of my pawns. Then I give him a knight too. He looks at me again, this time puzzled.

"You can take the move back, if you want," he generously offers. "I'll go easy on you." He's apparently just learned the expression and enjoys repeating it.

About ten minutes later, a solidly built young man with curly hair like Giovanni's and a dark mustache comes jogging over to us. Even though it's late November, he's wearing only a tank top and shorts. This is Giovanni's father – Giovanni senior. Jogging in place, he says something in rapid and brusque Italian. The boy nods like an adult while nervously twitching.

"Well, we thought we might play a game," I say with a smile, hoping to lighten the atmosphere. "Your son's a great kid! He plays like a grown-up and is about to get the better of me."

Delighted by the praise, which is clearly very important to

him, Giovanni jumps down from the bench and starts to hop around.

His father takes a water bottle from his waistband and tosses his head back, drinking greedily.

"You want some?" he asked his son. "No? Well, that's it, then. We still have grocery shopping to do, and he has to practise his recorder."

Giovanni stops hopping, and his mobile face, which seems to register the slightest shifts of mood, immediately becomes sad. He sighs.

"Papa, can we come back tomorrow?" he asks.

"It depends on the weather. If it's raining, there will be no jog."

As they leave, Giovanni keeps looking back at me and waving. And then, as they climb the slope from the quayside to the street above, he either squats in an amusing way or hops like a rabbit, meaning, I suppose, to leave me with a final entertaining impression.

4

The next day is sunny, and I go back to the quayside again. There's a piercing west wind, and as I wait, hoping for Giovanni to turn up, I shiver from the wind and the bench's cold steel slats. But the boy doesn't come, and the day, for all its brilliantly glistening blue water and peacefully clinking yachts, has lost its charm. But I stay even so, waiting and watching people pass by. Tumbling over each other, a flock of loudly quacking mallards emerges from the water and skirts my bench before continuing up the green slope. The birds aren't at all intimidated by my presence and silently began to forage behind me.

Many birds pass through Vancouver in the fall and early winter on their way south. Some of them remain, and in the fall and winter you can see wood ducks, white-winged scoters, harlequin ducks, and many other interesting species. Rocking like little painted boats on the water, they occupy a fairly wide expanse of it, and as they move forward in it, they arrange themselves in much the same way they do in group flight. But today, the birds' extravagant plumage gives me no pleasure, as if in Giovanni's absence, nature's bounty has been wasted on me.

Suddenly, I realize that I'm hungry. The idea of having a light meal at Giardino on the Marina side Crescent, my usual haunt, comforts me for a moment. A section of outdoor tables extends from the restaurant out to the quayside walkway but is separated from it by a low fence of stacked steel tubes. Above the tables is a sort of tinted-glass awning to shield the restaurant's patrons from winter rain and summer sun. Even if it's cold, I usually take a table outside, where the restaurant's relentless music is less audible. The bridge's low rumble can still be heard, but it's somehow just another part of the whole alien, impersonal landscape. The outdoor tables are mostly empty on the weekdays I go there. Covering my knees with a burgundy Afghan provided for that purpose (they're draped over the stainless-steel backs of all the empty chairs), I'm at last able to catch my breath.

On the other side of the fence, not much more than an arm's length away, a woman walks by talking to herself – or so it seems, since she has nothing in her hands. But from her animated tone I realize that she's talking on the phone through a device I can't see. As if my own fate somehow depends on it, I strain to capture the tip of her conversation. "By customizing and personalizing the interface...You'll get loads of options that way. "Disappointed, I turn away to look at the blue-green mountains and the cloud shadows running along their flank.

A very young waitress (almost a girl) takes my order. Her name is either June or Julia – I can never remember which. She stands with her hands diffidently clasped in front of her starched white apron, and the meticulous care of her appearance is exceptionally pleasing to me: the precise part of her chestnut, smoothly combed hair, the gleam in her green eyes edged with dark, lightly mascaraed lashes, and especially her little turned-down Peter Pan collar that surely nobody has worn for decades. Could it be that I have really been taking this route to the dragonfly quayside for the sake of this young woman?

The first time we met, Julia (that really does suit her best) introduced herself to me as an "actor." The word jarred. A world in which actresses have all turned into "actors" has lost a good deal of its charm, becoming as bland as oatmeal. And maybe for that reason I didn't ask her where and in what she had performed, silently deciding that she hadn't performed in anything anywhere and that the unhappy word "actor" was really more an expression of her ideal sense of self, of her Platonic essence, as opposed to her temporary instantiation as a waitress on the dragonfly quayside.

But today, for some reason, I'm especially glad to see her.

"A pizza, as usual?"

"Yes. Mushrooms, bell pepper – well, all the regular stuff. And please bring me a small salad too. I'm famished."

"Would you like me to bring the pizza first or the salad?"

"Which one is faster?"

"The pizza only needs to be heated."

"Excellent, the pizza, then." I rub my chilled hands together, pleased with the effect my old-fashioned politesse always has on her.

"And a Grandville ale, as usual?"

She remembers, sweet girl! Something is loosened and warmed in me by her response, and it even seems to me that I'm entitled to the ale and to Julia's care and friendly green eyes as a compensation of sorts for Giovanni. After I finish the pizza and start on the firm, slightly crunchy green leaves of my *verdura mista* salad, I realized that Chinese white radish – daikon – has been added to it. Whatever for? It's completely out of place, and it has ruined the excellent Italian recipe.

As I'm getting ready to pay, Julia suddenly announces that it's her last day. She's moving to London! London?! Has somebody offered her a job there or given her a part? No, there's no part yet, but she has a friend in London, and the friend has a friend, and the friend of her friend said there are more opportunities there...Opportunities?

"Well, certainly there will be more opportunities in London," I mutter, although I want to shout, "Wake up! Don't go to any London! You're very pretty, that's true, but you don't know how many pretty little mugs are already knocking on the doors of London theatres. And is Vancouver really so much worse? We have spectacular views. Hollywood shoots ten or more pictures here a year, since it's cheaper.

All you have to do is find a way to sort through it, to make some useful contacts...But London – what do you need London for? The grass is always greener on the other side, in this case, the other side of a whole continent and then an ocean!"

Obviously, I don't say any of that. What right do I have to meddle in her life? Who am I to her? Nor did I mention that I have a friend there with whom I studied at University College London. For what help could an old professor of history in London possibly be to a waitress from the Giardino in Vancouver? A waitress, moreover, who wants to be an "actor"?

We say our farewells, and I leave her a big tip, but I feel even more despondent – my day has been irrevocably ruined.

As I make my way back along the quayside, my legs start to feel heavy, and my heart begins to pound. But I carry on, anxiously listening to the thumping in my chest. It's something I've experienced for a long time when I'm anxious. But what, this time, is the cause? Julia, with her naive ideas? What business is that of mine? The cold wind that prevented Giovanni from coming back? Or is it my last conversation with Brigid? Yes, that must be it. But what did she say? Nothing special, as usual, it was just the tone of her voice... My old girlfriend, Brigid, calls several times a day. I'll hear her loud breathing for a moment, since she no longer bothers to leave messages, knowing that I rarely check them. Of course, I could just unplug the phone, but I don't, subconsciously hoping, I suppose, for an unexpected call, God knows from whom, or else for some bit of happy news, some unexpected joy. But this time she got me, not my answering machine, just as I was leaving the house.

I've known Brigid for well over thirty-five years, almost as long as Priss. Our relationship is a mouldy, ramshackle thing now. The quick, easy laughter and inner glow that attracted me to that red-haired, grey-eyed woman vanished with our youth. She's faded now, and her flesh is starting to droop, and when her head is tipped at a certain angle, she looks amazingly like Priss. If I should ever happen to wake up in her bed (a complete impossibility), I would be met by the same slack, vacant look I never could get used to in Priss; the same shuffling slippers and complaints about being tired after a "hard" night; the same grumbling about high prices and the rudeness and vulgarity of life in our glass city, which has been metastasizing like an aggressive melanoma; and about the razing of beautiful old Victorian homes. Oh, yes, there are the traffic jams from the endless street repair, the tattoos disfiguring backs and arms and legs and I shudder to think where else of most Vancouverites, both young and old.

Priss suffered from migraines and couldn't tolerate the sun; Brigid suffers from nightmares and complains about the rain. I don't rule out that Priss found out about Brigid at some point (how could she not have in thirty-five years!), and it's even possible that the women met and, organizing a cabal of two, had a good deal of hearty giggling at my expense.

Even though Priss eventually accepted my refusal to have children, the fact that she had to leave England when I was offered a job in Canada was something she never could forgive. And because of me, too, Brigid never got married. She hoped for my emancipation, waiting for years in the wings, so it's not in the least surprising that now she wants to be the sole manager of what remains of my life. Dear Brigid! We have fond memories of the past, but you know very well that your wish has zero chance of fulfillment!

5

It rains continuously for the next three days, and the quayside trek makes little sense. But then it's sunny again, and I'm hurrying along my usual route. And this time, I'm lucky. I have barely reached the cube with the rusty car on top - modern urban sculpture - when I see Giovanni. He's running toward me as fast as he can, radiant with joy.

"Let's play chess until Papa comes back, okay?"

We head for our old bench, but it's occupied.

"We'll find another," I say, but Giovanni hesitates.

"No, it's better to wait here for a while. Papa said not to leave the dog park."

The "dog park" is Giovanni's name for a small grassy area with large rocks placed here and there and a steel sculpture in the centre that looks like an asymmetrical jawbone. Dogs are running around the sculpture and rocks while their owners brandish red plastic throwers, tossing balls to them. The park is bright, with a strong breeze. The yachts sway at their moorings. The hardware attached to their masts clinks like crystal goblets in the cold air.

"What if there's a big windstorm?" Giovanni asks."Then all the ships will sink!"

"Don't worry, we don't have storms like that here."

"Why not?"

"Well, for one thing, it's a harbour, and for another, we're protected by mountains. See!"

I take him in my hands and carefully, so I won't lose my balance, lift him up so he can get a better look at the mountains. It was the first time his eyes are at the same level as mine. But instead of looking at the mountains, he carefully examines my face, and especially my beard, touching it with his small gentle fingers.

"You see, mountains all around. On the right and the left, each one higher than the one in front of it, as far as you can see. And that one over there looks like a sleeping auntie with her arms folded across her breast."

"What's the auntie mountain's name?" Giovanni puts his arm around my neck and, finally, turns to look.

"It's called Grouse Mountain, after a kind of bird."

"If Grouse Mountain wasn't there, could there be a big windstorm?

"Perhaps."

"And all the ships would sink?"

"What makes you think that? If they took the ships farther out to sea, they wouldn't sink. The most dangerous storm waves are near the shore, but out on the ocean, it isn't so bad."

The expression on his face suddenly changes, and his little eyebrows twitch. He's thinking about something else.

"Then I'll go on a big ship to visit my mama in Hong Kong. I'll go by myself with Po-Po."

"But Hong Kong's very, very far away! It would be much

easier to go on an airplane!"

"But if I go on a ship, I might see a big fish."

"You mean a whale?"

"No, a very big fish," he mysteriously replies.

Suddenly he sticks his nose in my beard, awkwardly making a kissing sound, and starts to laugh at his prank. Enveloped by a milky smell, I realize his chin is smeared with something. I put him down and reached in my pocket for my handkerchief.

"Were you eating something?"

"An ice cream at school. They only had vanilla. My favourite is chocolate."

"Do you like school?

Giovanni nods.

"What do you like best about it?

"I like drawing and music. I like everything the best."

"And the teachers?"

"I like Miss MacGregor and Miss Sherwood and Miss Giompuolis. I like all the teachers the best."

"I used to be a teacher too. I taught philosophy." For some reason, I want to test him, to surprise him with an unfamiliar word.

"When I grow up, I'll also...also...I'll also...teach *philostrophy*!" Clearly he wants to say something that pleases me.

"Do you know what it is?"

"Yip!" He pauses for a second, then impishly replies, "I knew yesterday."

"Let me see if I can explain it. Well, one way to think about it is that philosophy teaches us how to be good so we'll be happy.

How to think and do the right things...You see?"

"Are you good?" Giovanni asks.

The question trips me up.

"Well...I'm not sure. Probably not very. Probably I'm good sometimes, and sometimes I'm not, depending on the circumstances. But I always try to be good."

"Santa Claus is always good."

"Do you really think I'm Santa Claus?"

Giovanni smiles and nods.

"Really? So that's it! That must mean that I didn't really know who I was until I met you. Maybe I'm Santa Claus after all!"

"Why didn't you know who you are?" He's obviously perplexed by the idea.

"Do you know who you are?"

"I'm me!" Giovanni exclaims, apparently amazed that such a simple truth isn't obvious to everyone.

"That's certainly true! You, little friend, couldn't possibly be mixed up with anybody else. But with other things, it isn't always so easy. Sometimes, it's clear what a thing is, and sometimes it isn't. Take chess, for example. There are chess pieces, right? And there are the game's rules. But is it so clear that either could exist without the other? On the one hand, they could exist, but on the other, maybe they couldn't. And which came first, the chess pieces or the rules, is hard to say."

Why on Earth am I trying to explain such a conundrum to a young child? But it's too late. Giovanni stares at me, dumbstruck, or rather at the opening in my beard from which fly sounds that have no meaning for him.

I get out my little chess set, open it, and pick up a knight.

"You see this knight? It's small. But at home, you have a bigger chess set, and the knights are bigger too. Maybe they even look different. And they're made of wood instead of plastic like this one. Chess sets can look different, but we can still play with them if we know the rules. With big sets and little ones and wooden ones and plastic ones, right?"

"Yes," Giovanni says, continuing, with unwavering attention, to study my mouth.

"And if we took away the board and hid all the pieces and decided to play the game in our heads, with an invisible set, would that be something we could do?"

With a slight frown, Giovanni skeptically tips his head to the side.

"Why not, then?"

"Because I never tried it. I never tried to play in...invisibly."

I laugh and gave him a quick hug. The precocious quickness and receptivity of his mind has endeared him to me. I start to think that, in his own way, he can probably understand Plato's cave parable as well as some of my eighteen-year-old students had. And it even seems to me that I might be able to hint to him in some way that I'm often overwhelmed by a feeling of the unreality, the insubstantiality of the world, a feeling that has grown more pronounced since Priss died.

6

Teaching Plato for many years and talking about the world of Forms and the reflection of that Platonic world in our material, physical one, I made every effort to convince my students of the grandeur of Plato's conception. Being invisible and inaccessible to us, the world of Forms is nevertheless the only true world! I passionately defended Plato's position as if it were my own. Did I in fact believe in it? The truth is I would be able to grasp it only if I could summon the spiritual strength, the spiritual daring to do so. But the longer I've lived and the weaker my powers have become, the more inaccessible that ideal has seemed.

But today, with Giovanni, it suddenly strikes me that I have at last found the until-now elusive point of contact between the blessedly heavenly and the merely earthly. Trite though it will sound, it's concentrated in the palm of Giovanni's hand lying on top of my own and in the searching gaze of his dark, wide-spaced eyes. He, too, has apparently sensed something, and taking hold of my jacket, he becomes still, pressing his curly little head against my chest. My throat tightens, I can't speak, and I just lightly smooth his dark curls.

Then he lets go of my hand and says, "Okay, now it's my turn to ask a riddle. It's, it's um..." And he suddenly breaks free of me, jumps down, and runs after a large glaucous gull. The startled bird immediately takes flight, flashing the snow-white underside of its wings. Giovanni follows it with his eyes. "I know! Guess this! Why... hmm, why do birds have two wings?"

I think about it for a moment. How should I answer?

Because they couldn't fly with just one? They wouldn't be able to keep themselves aloft? I would think that such a thing would already be obvious to perceptive little Giovanni and that he must have something else in mind. And trying to explain the nature of bird flight would be much too complicated anyway.

"I give up," I say.

"You give up?! You do?!" He spins in happy excitement, like a top. "But I know! I know why! Because only one wing would be ugly!"

How extraordinary! The little boy has placed symmetry, balance, the equipoise of the world at the apex of his triangle. Does he see it as the first cause and the indispensable condition of all the world's arrangements? But what if the symmetry of double wings only seems beautiful to us because it satisfies the laws of physics?

"You didn't guess, so it's my turn again!" Giovanni exclaims, taking my silence for agreement and pleased with what he must regard as his obvious superiority. "Can you guess what my favourite number is?"

"Well, that certainly is a hard question even harder than the first one! Probably something large! A hundred, or a thousand, or a million?"

"You didn't guess! You didn't!" Giovanni keeps jumping up and down. "My favourite number is six!"

"Six? So little?" I make an astonished face.

"Tomorrow I'll be six! That's why!" He holds up one hand, his five fingers splayed, and the other hand with his index finger extended. "That many!"

"Well, then you really are a big boy! Happy birthday!"

"And will you come to my birthday party tomorrow? Please come! Please!" Giovanni tips his head to the side and looks at me with an affectionate grin.

"I'd be glad to," I say with hesitation. "Only we'll have to ask your papa first."

"He won't mind! He won't mind! Samantha and Peter and Douglas will be there. Douglas is my best friend. There he is, there's Papa!"

7

Farther down the knoll, near the water's edge, a crowd has gathered to look at something on the ground. Giovanni pulls me after him. His father is standing with his back to us, bent over with his hands on his knees. In the centre of the crowd kneels a man of about forty, with an impassive face. In his hands is a black box with buttons, but his attention is fixed instead on what looks like a large mechanical spider. It quietly hums and flashes tiny lights, sticks out four steel legs, and then, gently swaying, begins to rise straight up into the air. It describes two wide circles over the marina, and then, responding to the console in its owner's hands, it returns to its original spot. Giovanni watches, transfixed, as it retracts its legs, turns off its lights, and falls still.

"How much does that thing cost?" Giovanni senior asks the machine's impassive owner.

Without taking his eyes off his toy, the latter mumbles

something in reply.

And then he tucks it under his arm and quickly sets off along the quayside in the direction of Burrard Bridge. The crowd disperses.

Giovanni senior wipes invisible sweat from his brow with the back of his hand and shakes his head."Two grand!" he exclaims."Some toy!" And then he adds, "I see that you've become buddies with my son."

"Yes, we've been asking each other riddles. Giovanni asked why a bird has two wings. I wanted to say that otherwise it couldn't fly, but now I see that I was wrong. That thing could fly very well without any wings at all."

"Papa, can we buy one too?"

"What do you think?"

"That we won't." Giovanni sighs. "Papa, can I invite this Santa Claus to my birthday party?"

Giovanni senior gives me a policeman's once-over. "Santa Claus? Hmm, I thought Santa Claus only comes on Christmas. It's still the end of November, I believe. And wouldn't it be pretty boring for your Santa Claus friend with all your little friends?"

"Please, Papa, please," Giovanni pleads, twisting his comical little mug.

"You see what a sociable little guy I have. He starts up friendships right on the street. By the way, would you mind staying with him another ten or fifteen minutes so I can do another run? Down to the bridge and back? And I actually have no objection to the birthday party, if you really want to come."

I tell him he can jog as long as he likes, that Giovanni and

I have been having a good time and that there's nothing for him to worry about.

The birthday party is to take place tomorrow, Saturday, at noon. Vaguely gesturing toward the high-rises beyond the knoll, Giovanni senior gives me their address and trots away.

"Let's walk around a little and then play chess," I say to Giovanni.

Giovanni pulls me away from the direction his father has gone.

"What kind of present are you going to give me?" he asks.

"I don't know. I'll have to think about it."

8

I gaze at the marina with its yachts and boats, and I remember the splendid model of the Swedish galleon *Vasa* that I bought on a visit to Stockholm many years before. Made of different kinds of wood, the model replicated, with masterful precision, all the details of the famous seventeenth century warship that had foundered just as it was leaving Stockholm harbour on its maiden voyage. I imagine the interest Giovanni's little fingers would take in the decorations of its high flat stern, the intricate carving of its bowsprit, its square-rigged sails...I imagine how I might linger on some pretext, and then, after the Samanthas and Peters and Douglases all leave, how Giovanni and I will sit down on a sofa somewhere in a corner and I'll tell him everything I know about the ship: what a beautiful vessel it was; how, in order to amaze the world, the builders added an additional deck of bronze cannons, which very likely made the ship so top heavy that it keeled over and sank from the first strong breeze even before it reached the open sea. I'll tell him how three hundred years later, at great risk to themselves, divers helped bring it up from the bottom after removing the remaining cannons and freeing the ship from the mud into which it had sunk.

"Well, have you thought of anything?" Giovanni asks, apparently deciding that he's given me enough time.

"But if I tell you now, it won't be a surprise."

"You tell me a little bit. Please!"

"A little bit? Well, all right. My present's something that floats."

"A seagull?"

"No, you haven't guessed."

"A boat?"

"You're getting warm. Okay, I'll tell you. Not a boat but a ship."

"A real one?"

"No, a model, only it's so perfect that it's just like a real one."

Giovanni falls silent, the ends of his little mouth drooping.

"Don't worry, it's a very beautiful model. You've never seen anything like it. You can look at it from every angle and inside and out, something you can't do with a real ship."

But he still didn't say anything. And then his chin suddenly starts to tremble, his bottom lip creeping over his upper. He is about to start crying, and my heart skips a beat.

"What is it? What's the matter, sweetheart?"

"I don't need a ship because...because I lost my recorder."

He can't help himself and starts to sob inconsolably.

At first, I don't understand what he means, but then, from his disjointed account, I'm able to piece together the catastrophe that has befallen my little friend in the four days since I've seen him. He and his father went to IKEA to buy a little table on rollers, and first they went to the different floors together and his papa picked out what he wanted, but when they got back downstairs, his papa remembered that they needed some bathroom hooks too, and he left Giovanni in the play area while he went to look for them. Giovanni started to play with another little boy there and got a Transformer out of his backpack to show him, and his recorder was in the backpack too, since they had gone to IKEA directly after his music lesson, and maybe he didn't put the recorder back in the backpack after he got the Transformer out, or maybe he did put it back, but when they got home it wasn't there anymore.

His papa still doesn't know about it, but when he finds out, he'll yell at Giovanni, since the recorder was expensive and his papa is very strict.

I draw the little boy toward me and smooth his hair.

"I'll buy you a new one. Don't cry, little friend. Don't cry, kiddo."

"But Papa will ask where it is, and I...I don't know."

"I'll talk to your papa. Everything will be all right, I promise."

He presses himself against me, quietly whimpering. It breaks my heart to see my happy, sunny little Giovanni in tears.

I get home in a mild panic, but there's still enough time. I drink a quick cup of coffee and, barely catching my breath, drive to a music store. The clerk shows me a shiny black soprano recorder for $35 that he thinks is appropriate for a six-year-old. I, of course, have no idea what kind of recorder Giovanni lost, but it doesn't matter. I have no doubt that I'll be able to smooth things with his father, whatever kind it was. The model ship is in a special glass case in my study. This morning, it would never have occurred to me to part with it, but now everything has changed. Giovanni will get both the model and the recorder. I can't find a suitable box for the model, which is almost a metre long and bulky even with its masts and sails removed, so I empty three smaller boxes and use their cardboard to make another box of the required size, which keeps me busy for quite a while. Tired, but with a feeling of having accomplished something worthwhile, I finally go to bed.

The next morning, I get up early. After breakfast, I take a shower, trim my beard, even out the shaggy bristles of my eyebrows, and put on my best three-piece suit and a bowtie. I grin at my reflection in the mirror. When was the last time I wore a bow tie? The Seattle Opera brought *Parsifal* to town, and I got tickets to celebrate Brigid's sixty-fifth birthday. That was just after Priss died, probably.

I splash on some cologne, put on my black, rather old-fashioned but still excellent cashmere overcoat, and, cradling the model in its large box, head out to the garage. Then, realizing that I've forgotten the recorder, I run to get it after placing the box in the back seat.

I look for a parking space near the quayside a long time, and

then, when I do find one and put ten dollars in the metre, I see that
I've made a mistake. This is an area where the spaces are reserved
for the exclusive use of the nearby yacht club. I circle around
another twenty minutes or so under the bridge, under its branching
off-ramps and crossings, afraid I'll be late. Finally, in desperation, I
place Priss's handicapped sign on the dashboard and park in the first
such space I come to.

I put the recorder in my overcoat pocket and get the big
box with the model out of the back seat. As I'm trying to manage
all that, I suddenly started sweating, even though it's cold. And then
with the box at last cradled in my arms and the recorder sticking
out of my pocket, I start to climb the knoll toward the high-rises
where my little friend lives. I don't remember his address, but I
have it written on a piece of paper, somewhere. I put the box down
on the grass and go through all the pockets of my coat, my jacket,
my vest, my pants, but still I can't find that piece of paper. I start
to sweat again. Where did I put it? In the hallway? On my desk? In
the kitchen? Should I go back and look for it? If I miss his birthday
party, Giovanni might think I've let him down, but there's nothing
else I can do.

Picking up the box, I hurry back to the car. But after I've
already driven halfway over the bridge toward home, I suddenly
remember that there never was a piece of paper with the address to
begin with: Giovanni senior had simply called the street and number
out as we were parting. Something about the address struck me at
the time, but what? Oh, yes! The street name! *Homer*! For there
is, in our city, a street that runs through the centre from north to

south and that was very likely named for the owner of a mine or a sawmill, like everything else in Vancouver. But I prefer not to think about mines or sawmills now. I chuckle to myself. Forget about the mines and sawmills! My Giovanni could only live on a street named after the real Homer who wrote that Poseidon...well, never mind, never mind, Poseidon has nothing to do with it!

As soon as I get across the bridge, I turn around again and drive back to the quayside. This time, I'm able to find a parking place right away. I almost run to the high-rises. Who lives in these buildings, blank glassy blue, like the vacant eyes of a dragonfly? Must be some creatures with reticulated wings, free of routine and domestic life. I see them flitting out onto the quayside individually, some jogging, some hurtling past on bikes or roller skates, a few of the joggers pushing infants in three-wheeled strollers. And hidden among these buildings inhabited by these people is the one human soul I need! But how will I be able to tell which of the buildings is his? And even if I do somehow recognize the building number, how will I identify the apartment, since I don't even know his last name?

After I get back to the car a second time, sweating even more profusely and completely exhausted, a light rain starts to fall. I put the gifts back in the car and try not to despair, comforting myself with the thought that I can go to the quayside tomorrow and explain to Giovanni what happened and that everything will be the same as it was before. I even leave the gifts in the back seat when I got home, so sure am I that I'll see him the day after.

Once home, I'm overcome with such enormous fatigue that I can't even brush my teeth or pull back the covers on my bed.

41

Without undressing, I lie down in the darkness, listening to the loud, irregular thumping of my heart. For no reason, I'm in a cold sweat again and overcome with unbearable anxiety. I clench my teeth to keep from being completely overwhelmed by it, but then an agonizing pain suddenly grips my jaw and quickly spreads to my neck and shoulders. When it let go, I can't catch my breath.

I don't remember calling an ambulance or being taken to the hospital. From the long weeks of recovery, I remember only Brigid's broad face, hovering over me and again moving away, dissipating in a fog.

It's not until the beginning of March that I'm able to go to quayside again. The sharp light reflects off the white concrete and stainless-steel, hurting my eyes. As usual, a motley, busy crowd moves along the quayside in a continuous stream. Everything around me seems to be running or flying, with the bicycle riders hurtling toward me like a moving wall.

But I never see Giovanni again.

Later on, I do encounter him twice in my dreams. He's standing on the bow of a magnificent old galleon with a parrot on his shoulder. I understand that he's on his way to visit his mother in Hong Kong. But the second time, we're sailing together, and I feel with my whole broken, damaged heart that we will never part again, that we are one. He has returned to me from the depths of my own childhood, a shy little boy with dark, curly hair and a recorder, and I am Giovanni and he is me. And my mother, and Priscilla, and everyone, all the other people in my long life, are alive, and loved by me the way they had not been in my real past, and the lapping of a matte-white wave merges with the gentle modulations of the innocent, childlike music Giovanni and I make together. In that sublime world of eternal Forms, of which I'm now certain.

Translated by Judson Rosengrant

The Knight of Melancholic

Countenance

"All the rivers run into the sea; yet the sea is not full; unto the place from whence the rivers come, thither they return again."

- Ecclesiastes

1

I had enough money for about three months and no more. Overcome with a strange apathy, I sat all day on deserted Jericho Beach counting the barges in English Bay and gazing at the mountain landscape across the water.

As the sun set behind Vancouver Island on my left, the peaks to the north and northwest turned into stark silhouettes against the rapidly fading sky with torn patches of fog slowly creeping down the nearer slopes toward the dimming water. The prisms of the skyscrapers across the bay began to light up from within like luminescent, deep-dwelling ocean creatures. The mountains and water seemed to merge and then dissolve in the darkness until it was impossible to make out anything except the lights of the pulsing human anthill on the opposite shore and those of the barges, their glimmering reflections in the motionless water suggesting a beautiful, enticingly magical life within.

I had joined my boyfriend, Umberto Perreira, in Vancouver after he was offered the position of resident choreographer with Ballet BC. I have to admit, however, that it was more than a wish to follow him that led me to abandon the life I'd made for myself in Montreal. My wanderlust has always searched for a pretext. Every transposition in space tears from the temporal continuum a stretch of no-man's land. There comes a point when the past suddenly loses its grip, while the future shimmers at the horizon in a shape of some wondrous land fashioned out of nothing by the hunger of your imagination.

What bold thoughts, what adventurous plans swarm in your head as you sit on your suitcase at the crossroads! How fresh life feels, as you've parted with the past and have not yet ventured so much as a step into the future.

It was with good reason that Umberto had called me a "tumbleweed." He used to say there could be no making a home with me, since because of my weight – forty-two kilos, the same as my age at the time – gravity had no effect on me. My combative, explosive character was another culprit, he said. The slight proved a source of particular grief when I learned that the position of *répétiteur* at Ballet BC that I thought had been promised to me had been given instead to a cousin of the company's artistic director.

The mutual reproaches had begun to rock the already wobbly tent of our union. Umberto's affair with a teenager in the corps de ballet brought it to an end – the tent collapsed. Fine, I said. Fine. I'm free.

As my separation share, I received this glass-and-stainless-steel city nestled in the midst of, I admit it, rare natural beauty.

With almost no vacancies in the city, a small studio apartment on the top floor of a prefabricated building was my next piece of luck. The Venetian blind with its cheap plastic slats reached only partway down the window, exposing the room to an oppressive gleam reflected from the corrugated steel of a newly installed roof on the opposite building.

I retired from professional ballet performance at the age of thirty-five, but I never abandoned the barre. In my new lodging, I did pliés, tendus battements, and vertical jumps, my eyes covered with a scarf like in Blind Man's Bluff to avoid the tin glare from the roof across.

After an early breakfast (a cup of black coffee and half a banana) I would wander through Stanley Park without purpose, thinking nostalgically – the irony of that! – of the life in the city I've just abandoned.

Maybe I was simply lucky. In spite of the fact that people were leaving Montreal in droves, I had some success there: I taught in a ballet academy, supplementing my income with reviews of ballet and theatre. The best known European ballet companies came to visit. Boston and New York weren't very far away, so it wasn't especially hard to go to either for a show and then write a review of it.

In Vancouver, deprived of connections and sources of income, I had to start from scratch – and quickly. But instead, I sat on the beach for days, gripped by a strange lack of will.

On one of those long, hollow days, Umberto's sister, Manuela, called me from Montreal. She knew about the breakup, but we maintained our friendship, and she wanted to help. Through her Chilean husband, she was acquainted with the entire Chilean community on both sides of the continent. One of her husband's friends in Vancouver, a "real gentleman," as she put it, was looking for people to contribute to a new magazine. What he was doing in

Vancouver, she wasn't exactly sure, but he used to be a big cheese
in the Chilean government, she informed me. "He needs somebody
who can write about art," Manuela said. "Call him and find out."

And that's how I met Laureano Santalone.

2

The doorman of a ten-storey building on a quiet Alberni Street let
me into the lobby, decorated with a big pot of orchids and several
Chinese vases with blue dragons, each reflected in the mirrors in
marble frames.

Compared to my own unsettled circumstances, Santalone's
apartment seemed to be the epitome of bourgeois comfort. Heavy
velvet drapes darkened my host's study, and the reflected glow of
a fireplace played peacefully on the gilded bindings in a bookcase.
With his aristocratic bearing, refined manners, and old-fashioned
courtesy, the man who greeted me seemed to have stepped out of a
world long since vanished. Laureano looked about sixty. The fine
features of his narrow face, with its pointed but well-shaped beard,
his lean figure, and tall stature – all reminded me of classic portraits
of Spanish aristocracy. Castilian blood did in fact flow in his veins,
as I later learned from our long conversations. His ancestors had
come to the New World from Spain in the eighteenth century.

The cut of his dark suit was impeccable; his manners very
cordial yet reserved. Gracious hospitality and solicitude are natural
features of good breeding. Much like rain, they spread evenly
on everybody who happens to be outdoors at the moment. Now

I'm embarrassed to think how eagerly I took Laureano's genteel benevolence for the signs of personal attention. But who hasn't taken something desired as real? I'm sure I wasn't the only one who felt more intelligent, kinder, and gentler in the presence of this man.

On that first visit, my host placed before me a small silver tray holding two crystal goblets. As I was sipping a cocktail of brandy and white crème de menthe, a woman in a short skirt tightly stretched over fat thighs looked in on us. Strings of red coral beads lay upon her powerful, semi-naked bosom. "What a vulgar maid he has!" I involuntarily thought. The woman gave my slight figure a once-over, then said something rapidly and vehemently to Laureano in Spanish. "Let me introduce my wife, Rosalia," he said smiling. I got up to shake her hand, but she didn't extend hers, leaving mine awkwardly hanging. And then she quickly left.

Laureano envisaged his new bilingual (Spanish–English) magazine primarily for the city's Latin American diaspora.

"My Spanish is really poor," I pointed out.

"Oh not to worry!" he said making himself comfortable in the armchair across me."Please write in English, and I'll translate it. So far, you and I are the only ones on the staff."

Laureano intended to write a political overview for the first issue and offered cultural coverage to me. It was 1998, the centenary of Eisenstein's birth, and he wanted an article about the unfinished documentary *¡Que viva Mexico!*

As it turned out, a great deal in Laureano's life was tied to Mexico. The fall of Allende in 1973 had forced him into exile, and that's where he met his second wife, Rosalia.

I'd never written about films, but I kept my qualms to myself: I needed money. Besides, Eisenstein had interested me ever since I was a young dancer with the Omsk State Music Theatre in Siberia. The theatre's artistic director was from Almaty in Kazakhstan, where he had met the supervisor of the magnificent dances in the second part of Eisenstein's Ivan the Terrible, and his stories about it were something I'll always remember. When Laureano heard that, he became quite excited.

"Wonderful! Wonderful!" he said, splaying his pale, slender fingers like two fans to make a pyramid with their tips – a habit of his, as I would learn. "You see what kind of coincidences there are! Well, my dear friend, you already have the cards in hand and will very likely be interested in the things I can provide. As you certainly know, two communist artists, David Siqueiros and Diego Rivera, became acquainted with Eisenstein in Mexico and accompanied him on his travels around the country in 1931. I myself knew Siqueiros. I even have two letters from him and one from Eisenstein. Wouldn't that help you with your article?"

He knew Siqueiros, I thought. The same Siqueiros who took part in the first attempt on Trotsky's life. How extraordinary!

"I think it was two years before he died that I met him," said Laureano. "He was already an old man then...had aged a lot during his time in prison, but he remained unbroken. See, I myself dabbled in painting in my youth. Like other young left-leaning artists, I'd been impressed by Siqueiros's iconoclasm. His Barcelona Manifesto for new revolutionary art was famous. I don't know which one was greater in him: his artistic or his revolutionary passion." Laureano shot an intense gaze at me."Siqueiros was a man of radical views, and a confirmed Stalinist. His Stalinist sympathies were not, it goes without saying, something I shared."

He fell silent for a moment, making sure his words registered, then picked up his pipe.

"Do you mind if I smoke? I can go out onto the balcony. My wife always chases me out there, so I'm used to it." He chuckled.

"Oh no, it won't bother me," I lied, startled at the same time by how easily I did. "Did Stalin offer him protection in Moscow after the attempt on Trotsky?"

"No. Though Siqueiros's connections with Moscow and the NKVD were very strong." Laureano waved a cloud of smoke away from me. "Perhaps because of that, after the attempt on Trotsky, he didn't suffer any harm. Pablo Neruda was the Chilean ambassador to Mexico at the time and helped Siqueiros with the move to Chile. But Siqueiros's radical views were too dangerous for the Chilean government to allow him in the capital, you see. So he and his family settled in Chillán, a little provincial town. It's famous now, thanks to Siqueiros's *Muerte al Invasor.* An enormous mural he painted on the walls of the local school library."

"But how did you meet him?"

"At the thirtieth anniversary of *Muerte al Invasor*. It fell to me to arrange the celebration."

"How interesting!"

"Just one of my bureaucratic responsibilities. I organized festivities in Chillán, and Siqueiros was touched by the attention he received and wrote me two letters. He also gave me a copy of

another one he'd received from Eisenstein. The one I mentioned...
May I refill your glass, Magda?"

"When would you like the article?" I asked, more and more
intrigued by the unusual person to whom fate had led me.

"There's no hurry. The magazine's only in the organizational
stage, with the financial question still unresolved."

That slightly alarming news about funding didn't discourage
me. I wouldn't want to disappoint Laureano, that much was clear to
me.

I enthusiastically began to research everything connected
with Eisenstein and his time in Mexico.

The story of *¡Que viva Mexico!* is one of the more tragic in
Eisenstein's biography. Already a world-famous director thanks
to *Battleship Potemkin* and *October*, he'd been sent by Stalin to
Hollywood in 1930 to study the new technique of talking cinema.
After cordial meetings there (Douglas Fairbanks and Mary
Pickford entertained him at their Beverly Hills mansion) and a
contract for financing with Upton Sinclair and his wife, Eisenstein
set off for Mexico. His cameraman, Eduard Tisse, and assistant
director, Grigory Alexandrov, accompanied him. Stalin personally
monitored every film production in the USSR, and making a
documentary about the recent Mexican revolution served his
propaganda purposes. Eisenstein had a different vision in mind and
embarked on filming the country's colourful present and enigmatic
past as witnessed by magnificent and terrifying monuments of
its vanished civilizations. The filming, however, encountered

difficulties. Eisenstein was unable to keep either to the budget or the deadline, and in the end, Stalin ordered Eisenstein to return home. The director had, in the meantime, sent well over fifty thousand metres of exposed film to Hollywood for processing, the last he would ever see of it, despite attempts to send it to Russia. Eisenstein viewed that separation from the fruits of his labour as a personal catastrophe, one that he was unable to get over for many years. It was only in 1979, thirty-one years after his death, that a version edited by his assistant director Alexandrov was finally shown – a pale shadow of the grand plan Eisenstein appeared to have in mind.

Laureano was pleased with the finished article but couldn't pay for it. Since the magazine's sponsors were still delaying its funding, the business was stalled, and our collaboration therefore came to an end. When I realized I'd no longer have any reason to see him, I was gripped by panic. But I knew he gave private lessons in Spanish in his home. Might he take me on as a student? To my amazement, he agreed, although he wouldn't accept any money.

"I am in your debt, Magda. Permit me in this way to express my gratitude to you. Please."

Since I'd picked up quite a bit of Spanish from Umberto, I thought I might be able to start speaking it in a few months. But to take advantage of Laureano's services that long without payment wasn't something I could bring myself to do. We wrangled over our mutual generosity, assuring each other that for both of us, "the ideals of art and culture were higher than any material considerations." In the end, we agreed to trade languages. Laureano would teach me

Spanish grammar, and I would work on his English, which he could understand well but spoke with difficulty.

What did we talk about? Laureano had arrived in Vancouver the year before I did, and so naturally we compared our impressions of the city. Could a refined aesthete raised in the tradition of European culture, despite his own deep New World origins, really like a young, Americanized metropolis on the Pacific coast of Canada? Or was he praising Vancouver out of politeness, having set himself the rule of criticizing neither the cities into which fate deposited him, nor any of their inhabitants either? By training, he was a historian and jurist, but not a single university in Vancouver took any interest in him, his English being quite poor.

Left with nothing meaningful to do, he'd come up with the idea of a magazine. For lack of connections or business skills, Laureano's noble project never got off the ground. Perhaps that wasn't the first attempt of its kind, for, as far as I could tell, any reference to the magazine got from Rosalia only a skeptical smirk. She seemed to regard her husband's ventures with disdain: the magazine was just another of his pipe dreams.

I saw Rosalia only occasionally, each time struck by something crude, even vulgar, in her face and mode of dress that was in stark contrast to Laureano's aristocratic elegance. He was unhurriedly courteous, while his wife was hasty, brusque, and peremptory. What connected those two, I wondered. And Rosalia was suspicious of me too. She had no time to stand on ceremony or waste it with us on chitchat – that she conveyed with every one of her gestures.

As it turned out, Rosalia Merandelos was a cultural attaché in the Mexican consulate in Vancouver. I've never met anyone who less resembled her profession than she did. Yet she knew languages, was evidently a capable administrator, and must have had other qualities that ensured her success in the Mexican diplomatic service. Before Canada, she'd served in several other consulates, including ones in Argentina, Spain, and the United States.

An unemployed husband of a diplomat wife, very likely fifteen years younger than he was, Laureano kept moving with her from country to country.

3

I had no idea how to teach English. A second-hand grammar book provided me with some convoluted explanations about the way reality looked like from the point of view of sixteen English verb tenses.

"Not to worry, *querida* Magda. *¡No se preocupe en absoluto!* We are in the same boat, no?" Laureano's generosity quickly put me at ease. "Why don't we each choose an object in the room and then try to describe it? *Mujeres primero*."

I looked around. A small pencil sketch in a wooden frame sitting on a bookshelf attracted my attention. Don Quixote with Laureano's face, his thin, caricatured legs spread wide apart, was wearing a breastplate and pantaloons fastened at the knee. In his extended left hand, he held a book. Squinting through spectacles about to slide off his thin, hooked nose, the Knight of Doleful Countenance was struggling to make out what the book contained. In his right hand were the halter of a skinny nag with a little guy of about ten astride it. The boy's narrow face and sharp chin were just like his father's, as he stared from the picture with wide-set unsmiling eyes. Perched on his curly head was a black kitten with its back arched. The drawing's grace and economy of line were those of an exceptional artist.

"*¿Quien es este?*" I asked.

"My son, Emilio," Laureano said softly.

"*El se parece a ti.* He looks like you."

"Is good, no? Maybe no. My son loves cats! My son never without Patroclus."

"*¿Un gato Patroclus?*"

"*Si, si.*"

We both laughed at our baby talk: obviously, we were too curious about each other and the world to continue with it. And so it came about that we slid to our previous mode: I was talking to my "teacher" in English, and he to me in Spanish.

"Gilberto was a good friend of mine and a talented caricaturist," Laureano said examining the drawing. "I visited him in prison, and he gave me this as a farewell gift before I left Chile." Evidently overwhelmed with emotion, Laureano fell silent. "Would you like a cookie or perhaps some chocolate, Magda?"

"Oh no, no, thanks!"

"Ballet dancers don't eat that sort of thing. I forgot."

"If you don't mind my asking, does your son still live in Chile?"

"Yes, a grown up man now. The last time I saw him he was

ten, like in this picture. I couldn't take him into exile then."

4

During one of our sessions, five minutes before it ended, Laureano
said he'd have to cancel the next one: he and his wife had a reception
planned for the same day.

"How am I going to manage without him for two whole
weeks?" I asked myself as I went back down in the elevator, for the
first time confronting clearly what I'd been unable to admit to before.

From the start of our classes, my week was divided into two
parts: before seeing Laureano on Wednesday, and all the days after.
My energies always ran high in the anticipation of our meeting.
I applied myself to my barre exercises with double vigour (more
than ever I wanted to be in good shape). I looked for some English
books that might interest Laureano; I designed grammar drills that
we'd never end up using. But after Wednesday, it all went downhill:
useless Thursdays, followed by empty weekends, would give me a
physical sense of falling, as if the earth under my feet were ready to
give at any moment. I would eat indiscriminately, massive amounts
of food I'd normally never touch, then feel heavy and disgusted with
myself. But on Monday, my body and spirit would soar again, the
path now going upward, and in two more days it would bring me to
Alberni Street.

But now I thought with distressed clarity about the succession
of monotonous days, a gap in time the length of two weeks. Gripped
by profound misery, I couldn't bring myself to return to my empty

apartment. Instead, I went to the English Bay Beach, only a fifteen-minute walk from Alberni street.

A scavenger was waving the wand of a metal detector over the damp sand. Fog had obscured the mountains to the north, merging the water with the milky whiteness of the sky. A listless wave slapped against a log, first rolling it toward the shore, then drawing it back out into the bay. Logs of the same kind were spread in parallel rows along the whole length of the beach, where they served as benches. I sat down on one. A large gull fearlessly alit at the other end, its yellow bill, with a reddish spot at the tip, and black rings around its yellow corneas plainly visible.

I began to shiver as if the temperature had suddenly fallen. The solitary log continued to beat against the sand, trying to move back up onto dry ground like a living thing. Useless, useless attempts. I, too, should stop beating against the shore of somebody else's life. This two-week break was godsent. I should turn it into a permanent farewell. An excuse? Busy, got a new job, it didn't matter...

How deserted this beach was. To warm myself up, I got up and took a few carefully measured steps, then some more; then rose on point and did several écartés, and before I knew I was dancing... What was it? Some movements from "The Eternal Idol," a ballet set to Chopin. I used to teach it to my students in Montreal. We had a lot of fun then. I'd bring a small model of Rodin's sculpture that had inspired the ballet. Look at it carefully, I'd say. A naked man kneeling at a naked woman's feet, his head buried in her breasts, his arms behind his back, as if somebody had handcuffed him.

Is he consumed, is he enslaved by his passion? And the woman? Seemingly detached, withdrawing, bending her leg behind her back and nonchalantly catching her own toe. What was she feeling? Did she even care? Could it be that she pitied him while letting him kiss her breast and humbly worship her? Interpret it as your wish, I'd instruct my students, and weave your interpretations into your own dance. Then we'll look at existing choreography. But now, on this deserted beach, I myself danced this woman, then the man kneeling in his worship...then both of them together. The more I danced, the more I felt relieved, my brooding loneliness replaced by a feeling of sudden ease and contentment. And then I stopped as something struck me from within. Laureano was standing next to me, watching me and gazing, from time to time, at the smooth grey surface of the water.

"What do you see over there?" I asked without turning around, lest I frighten the vision away.

"That log, reddish-orange inside," Laureano said. "Look how the waves are burnishing it."

"It's a Western red cedar," I told my apparition. "Do you have anything like that in Chile?"

"I don't remember anymore, it's been so long." His voice was muffled. "The sea seems lifeless. An enormous watery desert."

"I want to show you something."

I took Laureano by the hand and led him to the tennis courts in Stanley Park. I pointed to a cluster of tall, still-naked trees with shaggy clumps of nests in them that looked like huge worn-out Russian fur caps.

"A colony of nesting great blue herons," I said. "They return. Every year at the same time, around February, herons return."

"To the place they were born in?"

"Yes. They repair their nests to begin a new cycle of life... fighting for females, laying eggs, incubating them, males by day, females by night. Blue shawls with fringes they wear, see those?"

Nobody answered me. Something changed in the air. The darkness fell. My back felt cold. I knew I was alone again.

5

In spite of my own decision, two weeks later I again found myself on Alberni Street. Even though Laureano couldn't have had the slightest inkling about my imaginary adventures with him in Stanley Park, I felt awkward, as if I'd committed some secret crime. I didn't know how to start the conversation, but he came to my rescue.

"Tell me, Magda, more about your life in Siberia and the theatre in Omsk where you worked." He smiled. "I've always been interested in Russia. I even wrote a whole book about Lenin. His grand experiment didn't work out, I'm sorry to say. We had such hopes, all of us, that it would."

I couldn't conceal my astonishment – a book about Lenin?

"You never expected such a thing from me? Well, for many years, Lenin was my idol. And not only mine. Everything progressive in Latin America was inspired by his ideas. Lenin was the trailblazer. The first to show the path to a better, more just society. What a daring experiment! It wasn't his fault that mankind couldn't take advantage of his insights!"

I was stunned. I'd never taken any interest in politics, but even so, I couldn't grasp how a man of his intelligence could've been captivated by the ideology of a dictator responsible for the brutal deaths of millions of people.

But Laureano no doubt spoke the truth: the majority of leftist Latin Americans were confirmed Marxists who admired the Soviet Union and accused Americans of supporting and instigating the many military coups on their continent. Thanks to Umberto, I'd known people among the Latin American diaspora in Montreal. They were of the most varied kind and origin: Argentinians like Umberto, Chileans, Colombians, but they all agreed on one thing: if the Americans had not grabbed all the natural resources and put dictators on the throne, there would be socialism, equality, fraternity, and prosperity in their countries.

"Allende was my friend. If Pinochet hadn't seized power, he'd still be alive."

"Was he a communist?"

"Allende? He was the leader of the socialist party, the Unidad Popular, but that isn't the point. You see, he was one of those rare people who remain faithful to the ideals of their youth and hold onto them in full measure. That requires courage. Some accused him of having committed suicide. Is that cowardice or an act of heroism? You know that after Pinochet's coup a plane was put at Allende's disposal for him and his family to leave the country. But he was worth his salt – *digna de talnombre* – and he refused."

"I thought he was killed."

"This can't be ruled out either. One day we may find out. But much of what Allende had wanted to do, he managed to achieve. He built schools and introduced free education for the poor. Have you ever been to Chile? Tens of thousands of its citizens were living in terrible poverty. Allende gave those people hope."

"I see. But tell me, it is true that you held a high position in Allende's government?"

"I was a deputy minister of culture. When Pinochet came to power, I had to flee."

6

After the fall of the socialist government in 1973, some two hundred thousand of Allende's supporters fled Chile. Could I argue about such things with someone who'd lost his homeland and family? Whose price for freedom and probably life was exile? His friends and colleagues had been tortured in Pinochet's chambers. Thousands more perished in concentration camps for political prisoners. The infamous Caravana de la Muerte, as the army officers invested by Pinochet with unlimited authority called themselves, tortured with exquisite sadism both imagined and real enemies of the regime who'd already been sentenced to death. When the Caravana arranged public executions at the Santiago stadium, Laureano had already fled to southern Chile.

Skirting Lake Maihue and crossing the mountains, he eventually reached Argentina. But Pinochet's secret service had a long reach. The car of General Carlos Prats, a minister in Allende's government and commander-in-chief of the Chilean army, was blown up in the centre of Buenos Aires a year after the coup, killing the general and his wife. Clearly, it was unsafe to remain in Argentina, and Laureano made his way to Mexico, as did many other Chilean refugees.

Laureano shared all that with me only in the most general way. The details I got later from Manuela. And when in his hallway that day he was helping me on with my coat, I couldn't help asking, "If you liked Lenin so much in theory, I mean enough to write a book about him, how come you never went to the Soviet Union to see how it worked in practice?"

"Call me a limousine liberal! But more seriously, I realized that your country would disappoint me, that I wouldn't find there what I had hoped to, inasmuch as Stalin had completely perverted Lenin's ideas. I'm sure that without Stalin, your country would've taken a completely different path. It would have flourished!" Laureano smiled apologetically.

"Paradise on Earth," I mumbled to myself as we parted.

7

It seemed to me that after Laureano shared some of the details of his biography, we might grow closer. What happened was the opposite. At our next meeting, he was aloof and coldly formal. Our conversation stalled.

"What shall we talk about? Something remote from politics?" He paused. "Well, all right," he said at last, "you still haven't told me very much about yourself, Magda. You were born in Omsk, in Siberia, I understand. Until you, I'd never met anyone from that part of Russia. The only thing I know about Siberia is the enormous scale of nature there, its splendid evergreen forests..." He was sitting comfortably in his usual armchair, cradling a glass of wine.

"Yes, my grandfather took his life in those splendid forests," I was about to say but cut myself short swallowing my growing irritation. He sounded like he was quoting an advertising prospectus extolling the natural beauties of some exotic land.

"If I'm not mistaken, the Yenisei flows through Omsk, one of the longest rivers in the world. We have beautiful rivers in Chile too, but they're comparatively short."

"Omsk is on the Irtysh, not the Yenisei. And the river's water was always a murky yellow. That's what I remember from my childhood. Silty loam. I'm not really attached to the place, even though I was born there."

Laureano gave me a surprised look. "Oh? I may be old-fashioned, and forgive me if it sounds trite, but a feeling of native rootedness, the ground beneath one's feet, seems extraordinarily important to me. It gives one a sense of oneself. As long as that feeling exists, one can travel, or even live for a long time in foreign lands, without...how shall I put it?... without losing one's deep essence. Our inner essence, if you will, is to a large extent determined by our connection to the soil into which we were born, no? The call of that homeland, sometimes powerful, sometimes barely heard, will sustain a person in difficult times, don't you think?"

I shrugged my shoulders. "Possibly. For some people." I stared at the fireplace. "Siberia has always been foreign to me, even though I was born and grew up there. We Poles had been expelled from our home and tossed into wilderness! And besides, if they keep reminding you your whole life that you're aliens, then what kind of connection could there be? What kind of call? Didn't we agree not to talk about politics though?"

Laureano got up, came over to me, and put his hand on my shoulder. It was so unexpected that I recoiled.

"Do you know that you have dancing arms?"

"What? What do you mean?"

"I mean when you talk, Magda, your arms, your hands dance. And it's beautiful. You have very beautiful gestures, Magda, even when you're angry, which happens a lot, doesn't it? I wish I could've seen you on stage. Our conversation was difficult last time, and it seemed to me then that I offended you. Forgive me if I did. Believe me, it wasn't my intention at all. Let's speak freely, just as we did before! Shall we? And if it's disagreeable for you to recall your life in Siberia, then I ask you again to forgive me."

He smiled with just his eyes, charming me with their velvety affectionateness. I immediately relented. Again, as many times before, it seemed to me that he could see into my soul like few others.

"No, I wasn't offended. I could tell you about Siberia, if you wish. Only, my family's story is a pretty ordinary one."

My grandfather was a professor at the University of Lvov in what had been eastern Poland. After the Soviet Union and Germany divided up the country in 1939 and the city became part of Soviet Ukraine, he was sentenced to ten years in the camps, as were many other Polish intellectuals in the annexed territory. His wife and son – my future father – were also exiled to Siberia. My grandfather felled trees in the camps, eventually managing to get two years off his sentence. When he was finally released and allowed to return to his family, they were all sent to a tiny settlement near Omsk. But it was too late for my grandfather. He was a broken man and took his own life. My father was five when they were sent into exile and thirteen when my grandfather died. My mother was half-Polish and half-Ukrainian, and she and her people had been exiled from Lvov too. My parents met in Siberia.

Laureano was now sitting in his armchair with his hand over his eye, as if overcome by sudden fatigue. "Stalin's crimes rivalled Hitler's," he said slowly. "That, in fact, was what I meant when you asked me why I hadn't visited the Soviet Union."

"That mercilessness didn't just come from Stalin – he had died in 1953. It also came from the people themselves. It was in their blood – the envy, the cruelty. There's a Russian saying: it doesn't matter if my own eye is poked out, as long as my neighbour loses both of his."

Laureano gave me a quick glance and then looked away. "Well," he interjected while continuing to avoid my gaze, "envy isn't only Russian – it's a universal human characteristic. Take that portrait of my son, over there on the bookshelf. My friend Gilberto gave it to me. He was a talented and bold caricaturist, thus a threat to the regime. When Pinochet came to power, Gilberto

was arrested. Since I still had some connections, I tried to obtain
his release. I acted through another artist, an old school friend of
Pinochet's. The artist didn't have a scintilla of Gilberto's talent and
was terribly envious of him. He said he couldn't help, although I
knew that he had only to say a word and Gilberto would be freed.
Don't get involved, he warned me, but when he saw that none of that
was of any avail, he started to openly undercut my efforts."

"So you never managed to free your friend?"

"No. He died in prison. I learned it later, when I was already
in Mexico." Laureano abruptly stood up and went over to the
window. He was seemingly upset.

"I didn't mean to pry," I said.

"It's all right, all right," he repeated with some distraction.
"But what were we talking about? Oh, yes...envy...I only meant that
envy is the most widespread human quality. You know what Marcus
Aurelius said? I think it goes like this: When you wake up in the
morning, tell yourself, 'The people I'll deal with will be meddling,
ungrateful, arrogant, dishonest, jealous, and surly. They're like
that because they can't tell good from evil.' But I say to myself,
'Today a miracle awaits me, for nothing is foretold and everything is
possible.'"

Laureano parted the curtains, letting sombre January light
into the room. A drizzle was falling, the cold, unpleasant kind so
common in Vancouver in the winter.

"Look out the window. Even this grey day has its charm.
The raindrops on the branches like crystal – isn't that a miracle? You
know, during the junta, despite the terror, blood, and violence, people

would risk their own lives to save their neighbours. We shouldn't write people off, not yet!"

He took a handkerchief from his pants pocket and patted his brow with it. The starched white triangle in his breast pocket remained undisturbed.

"Do you mind if I take off my jacket? It's getting hot in here. Perhaps we should turn off the fireplace."

He flicked a switch, and the flame licked the pile of artificial logs one last time.

"Loving your neighbour, someone near at hand, is the most difficult thing," Laureano said, lighting his pipe. "If the 'other' is completely unlike you, he might be tolerated, but if the difference is small, then atavistic laws of the cave take over. To root out that gene of rejection, people need to be trained, educated."

I thought it was obvious, what he was saying, and too often, education had little to do with it. I was disappointed in him, and at the same time unhappy with myself for being disappointed. But didn't he suggest that we speak our minds freely?

8

I hadn't allowed myself to think about the Omsk ballerina Shpalikova for the longest time, but something shifted in me: I felt an indiscriminate pity for myself, and, perhaps unconsciously, wanted Laureano to pity me too. Remembering it now, I'm embarrassed. For the person in whom I was taking such delight could easily have suspected me of being craven or petty.

Shpalikova was the company's prima ballerina, while I
merely danced in the corps de ballet. The Omsk Dramatic Theatre,
although a provincial company, was by no means the least among
them. The population of the city was over a million, and directors
and performers visited from capital cities. At the time we were
staging *Esmeralda* based on *The Hunchback of Notre Dame.* The
great Bolshoi star Maya Plisetskaya came from Moscow to supervise
it. She was asked whom she would recommend for the title role.
The celebrated ballerina silently tipped her head in my direction.
Naturally, the theatre's management was not pleased. It was the early
1980s, the years of Polish solidarity, when the position of people
of Polish descent like me was even more precarious. Magdalena
Czewolska, a girl with such a name, could not dance the lead. But
who could dare argue with Plisetskaya?

The dress rehearsal arrived. I was dancing the solo in the
square in front of Notre Dame, when my legs suddenly gave way and
I collapsed from sharp pain in my feet. We ballerinas are accustomed
to pain. Sprained ligaments and chronic toe pains are ordinary things,
but this was different. I untied and removed my toe shoes, blood-
stained inside, and shook a handful of ground glass from each one.
An investigation was begun, but as usual no guilty party was found,
although they didn't look very hard either. Eventually, the business
was dropped. When a month later I was able to dance again, the role
of Esmeralda was no longer available. Shpalikova was the one to
dance *my* Esmeralda in the years to come. And then around four years
afterward, as I was about to leave the theatre and Siberia, she stopped
me in the hallway and said, as if in passing, "How's life? You learned

your lesson, didn't you?"

"If you mean that episode," I said, looking her in the eye. "I haven't forgotten. I've known all along who did it."

"Did what?"

"You know damn well what I'm talking about. Aren't you afraid I'll report you?"

I read mock astonishment in her watery grey eyes. "Me, scared? Nobody would believe you anyway. But if you do take it into your head to complain, I'll deny everything."

What made her confess? Certainly not remorse or a bad conscience. She had no other purpose than to humiliate me – that was obvious. She knew I was leaving the theatre and couldn't file a complaint.

My subconscious calculation had been right. Laureano took my story to heart.

He paced back and forth, puffing on his pipe, visibly agitated. "What happened to you is deplorable! But can we judge a whole people by individual instances? Yes, many are prejudiced, narrow minded, butt here will always be ten, five, even one! One good person who will restore harmony. To forgive an insult and especially an injustice is extremely hard, but trust me! It's the only way to make peace with yourself. Forgive this lady, if you can."

I, too, got up and started pacing the room.

Where had that Christian forgiveness come from, I wondered in astonishment, since I regarded Marxism and Christianity as incompatible. "Excuse me for being so blunt! But let me ask you: You yourself, have you been able to forgive? The death and torture of your friends, your own exile? Have you forgiven that?"

I felt the blood rushing into my face. As before, I immediately regretted my outburst. Who was I to disabuse him?

"I'm sorry," I muttered."I have no right to judge you. I haven't been through what you went through."

"You, Magda, you had your own share of suffering. I know it's difficult to forgive. All I'm saying is just because the ideal is difficult to achieve doesn't mean we shouldn't stop trying."

"My life wasn't that hard. But I saw the humiliation of the Poles in our settlement. And I also saw that many forgave their tormentors. 'Chop down a forest and chips will fly!' they'd say; that is, since the Russians were building world communism, we might suffer for that righteous cause as well! Why, they justified their tormentors! Why? That's what's incomprehensible."

I don't remember all that was said that day, but never before had I been able to elicit such emotions from my teacher. He was visibly upset, and for the first time, I noticed that his hands were slightly shaking.

If I had known what I know now, I would've never tested him the way I did.

In the mid 1980s, around the time Gorbachev came to power, my father's long-held dream of returning to Poland was partly realized: we were allowed to move back to Lvov, a former Polish city, now part of the USSR. People on my mother's side had remained there all along, although she'd already passed away. The move was a lucky one for me. I was hired by the celebrated Lvov National Opera and Ballet Theatre.

I remember my six years there as the best of my life. My father, however, still wanted to return to Poland proper, even though, as I mentioned, he was only five when the country's eastern part was annexed by the Soviet Union. I don't think he was doing it for his own sake as much as to honour the memory of his father, long dead. I was apprehensive all along about his intentions: He hardly even remembered the language. Starting all over again at his age? He would be an outsider in Poland, much more then he had been in Soviet Russia. Too proud to ask for my help, he was counting on it anyway. My refusal to quit Lvov Ballet Company and come to Poland with him devastated him. It led to a complete break between us.

"Very sad indeed," commented Laureano after I told him about my father. "But I empathize with him. In my dreams, I still see Santiago the way it was in my youth. I know it has changed, but here it stays intact. "He pointed to his heart.

And then he broke the news. I remember every detail of that day. His pacing the room, trying to smoke and then putting down the pipe unlit.

Rosalia had been offered the post of cultural attaché at the embassy in Santiago. The offer had come suddenly. They were supposed to stay in Vancouver another year, but the vacancy opened up sooner, and now they were packing. After a long exile, he was finally coming back home.

"When are you leaving?" I asked, feeling a light pinch in

my heart.

"In two weeks. It's been quarter of a century since I've seen my homeland. I believe I can be of use to my country. What do you think?"

I'd never seen him so agitated before.

10

Once mentioned, the theme of returning home never left us. Every conversation ultimately led to Laureano's departure and new life in Chili. Now he had one goal, to be of use to his fatherland.

"Of course, there's a whole new generation now," he mused out loud. But he still had connections there! He had helped a lot of people in his day, some because of his position, others out of friendship. Professors, writers, lawyers and judges, movie directors, and journalists used to be among his friends. The children of those friends were now in the government and universities, so he wouldn't be forgotten!

In the depths of his dark eyes lit a sparkle I hadn't seen before.

At the beginning of our acquaintance, I had tried to lessen the distance between us, to become a close friend and confidante rather than just a student. But now that he was leaving, it seemed to me that I had at last achieved that goal. He was asking for my advice. He was sharing his hopes and plans as if I'd become a family member and were packing my bags along with him.

A week before their departure, the Santalones threw a party.

They were saying farewell to Canada, to their diplomatic colleagues and friends, while Laureano was saying goodbye to his students.

Their furniture was to be sold or given away. I got a chair and the small side table, the one on which Laureano had always put a silver tray with chilled drinks. Without the dark-blue tablecloth that reached down to the floor, it turned out to be an ordinary rattan thing from a cheap Indian imports store. Under Rosalia's watchful eye, somebody helped me load two rattan items into a minivan taxi, and then I handed her a hundred dollar bill.

11

Seven years passed. I often recalled Laureano, trying to picture his life in remote Santiago: important events, interesting encounters...

Never having visited Chile even once, I could imagine the setting any way I liked: majestic mountains with waterfalls, icy lakes, and respectable cafes in the capital like the ones I'd seen in Vienna during the Lvov Ballet's tour there, with plush upholstery, newspapers on wooden rods, large chandeliers, and, moving among marble columns, attentive waiters in black vests with snow-white napkins draped over their forearms. I imagined Laureano shining with intellect and wit at diplomatic soirees and easily eclipsing his boorish, ill-mannered wife; or in a circle of writers and poets discussing the problems of Chilean literature; or among political figures proposing a new constitutional project.

And, my goodness, what a contrast to my own bland life and its daily routine! Thousands of kilometres away here in Vancouver,

I worked as a subcontractor on advertising brochures, and in the evenings, I went to a community centre to teach ballet to ladies of retirement age!

It would be nice to get a note from Laureano, however short, I sometimes mused. But there'd been and would be no note. Who was I to him? A chance acquaintance at one of the numerous stops placed by fate along his exile's path.

Once, in early spring, I went for a walk in Stanley Park. It was after a hard rain, and the forest had a pungent, earthy smell, with still-wet pine needles gleaming in the sun and the cedar trunks exhibiting their velvety sides. Even the lichen hanging in pale grey tufts from the dead branches seemed to have perked up and taken on an almost greenish hue, with small pearls of rain nestled in their folds. The deciduous trees, still bare, were dotted with the Russian fur caps of heron nests. For the last twenty-five years, blue herons continually returned to this same colony, fixing their old nests and hatching their chicks. High up above your head, you could see males and females bob up and down, clapping their rapier beaks together and showing off their long, skinny chest feathers in a ritual of courtship. Males flew with the sticks in their long beaks for females to inspect, and then to weave the best new sticks into the old nests. Males brought food: you could see them along the edge of the park lagoon, standing still on one leg waiting for fish to splash.

I remembered the imaginary but never-taken hike with Laureano to Stanley Park, and either from the fresh spring air or because everything around was again young with rhododendrons already bursting into bloom, it suddenly seemed possible for me to realize my fantasy. I would arrive to Santiago and call him from the airport. "It's Magda. Do you remember? The Eisenstein article, our English and Spanish lessons?" If Rosalia answered, I'd say I was on a magazine assignment in Chile for a few days. I wanted to take them both out to lunch. If they could spare an hour, that is.

When I got home, I called Manuela to get the Santalones's address in Santiago. She cautiously told me that Umberto had recently married. I hardly paid any attention to that news and turned the conversation in the direction I needed.

"The Santalones's address? But..."

"I'm going to be in Chile on business," I rushed to explain."I thought I'd visit them. Why not? Laureano was such a wonderful man, right? We became friends, thanks to you."

"Oh yes!" Manuela chirped."My husband and I miss him terribly."

"Of course, we all miss him – his students, I mean. There was something very special about him, right? But how time flies! Can't believe it's been seven years! Have you heard anything about him? How has he been doing?"

There was a long pause.

"Magda, did you really not know?

"Know what?"

"Laureano died."

"What do you mean, died? Died how? When?"

"The way people do...about three years ago."

"Oh. I...I...had no idea. But he wasn't even that old!"

"Seventy, if that. An aggressive form of cancer. Enrico and I saw him in Santiago about a year before he passed away. He was still healthy. We invited him out to a cafe, and he was delighted but complained about being totally alone. Spent whole days without exchanging a word with anyone."

"Wait? How could that be? His wife was a diplomat. They often had receptions, interesting people to entertain."

"Ah, you really aren't in the know. They divorced after they got to Chile. We didn't pry about the details, but I think Rosalia was the one who initiated it. Laureano was left with no money and nowhere to go. His son took him in. Emilio is, by the way, a very successful doctor, according to his father anyway, but unfortunately, he didn't get along with his father."

"The son wasn't Rosalia's?"

"No, from his first wife. But I mean, it's unheard of! His father stays in the same apartment and the son barely talks to him, barely offers him food. You remember what a dandy Laureano was – but when we saw him – that really broke my heart, Magda. That worn-out sweater he was wearing! A pair of beaten shoes. As I said, we invited him to a nice cafe for lunch. And he was so grateful. He was obviously hungry! Can you imagine? But then he cheered up and remembered Vancouver, his friends there. He especially asked about you."

"About me? Well, I'm grateful...what am I saying...he's dead now. What I don't understand...he told me he had lots of friends in Chile, lots of connections! Or had the country changed so much in the twenty-five years he was away?"

"Oh, that's for sure, but that isn't the point. A scandalous story came out. Only, it's not to be passed on."

"There's nobody I could tell. Except for your brother, I don't know anybody you know here."

"That story caught up with him when he returned. A long time ago, when the junta seized power, a friend of his had been arrested, an artist. And while his friend was in jail, Laureano had an affair with his wife! This artist eventually died in prison. But that was after Laureano had fled. Everybody knew about the affair, and when Laureano returned to Santiago, the people of his generation did not forgive him. He became a pariah, you know, like an untouchable."

So that's how it was, I thought after finally hanging up. This cartoonist he said he tried to get out of jail. While sleeping with his wife at the same time. But what difference did it make now that Laureano was gone?

My face burned, but my hands were ice cold. I couldn't bring myself to turn on the light. As if someone had slapped me, and in the dark the blow wasn't so painful or shameful.

I recalled my father saying that cancer settles – that's the word he used: "settles" – on those who find themselves of no use to life anymore. Nothing to apply themselves to, and nobody left who would in any way need them. Life pushes them out of service, and death, like a wave, obligingly washes them away. That belief was firmly held by Siberian exiles.

I went to the kitchen to splash my face with cold water, to see things more clearly. Then I returned to the living room and sat at

Lauriano's table, with his empty armchair across me.

"See, your friends didn't forgive you. Nor their children. None had the generosity of spirit you've preached and counted on. Who was that woman, the wife of your friend? You must've loved her with extraordinary passion, didn't you? The kind I danced so many times on stage, the only place it can survive...till the tragic denouement of the last act. Tell me, did you really try to save your friend, at least initially? The harder, the more you wanted to escape temptation? But love proved stronger than all the obstacles, the conventions of family and marriage, and the laws of honour. Is that how you justified it to yourself, Laureano? And if you loved her so, why didn't you take her with you, into exile? Or did she refuse to leave her jailed husband? What happened to her, after her man had died, perhaps tortured and killed, with you having fled? Who could protect her? But you, you found a safe haven by marrying Rosalia, the Mexican diplomat, a marriage of convenience? Was it an act of desperation? An attempt to hoodwink the fate? And your son, that little boy with a cat on his head, was he taking revenge on you for your transgressions that might have included his own mother, an untold early chapter of your life? The son is no judge to his parent. But should I forgive him for what he has done to you, or should I hate him, the way my own father must have hated me till his last day? Should we all be forgiven for our past? For our present and our future, once and for all?"

That night, I couldn't fall asleep.

The milky darkness of dawn was already creeping over the city. I opened the window and leaned against the frame. The Japanese plum trees planted in rows along both sides of the street were in the full glory of their ephemeral brilliance, and their dull wine-red leaves were barely distinguishable through the froth of the pale-pink bloom. The street lights had been still turned on and their halos were pink. A subtle, sweetish fragrance filled the air. The central hospital wasn't far from my building. The sound of a siren cut through the air and the gentle fragrance of the blossoming trees: someone in an ambulance was in a race with death.

"As he came forth of his mother's womb, naked shall he return to go as he came, and shall take nothing of his labour, which he may carry away in his hand."

And I do hope that you, the Knight of Doleful Countenance, you don't suffer any more. This I will take as my small but only consolation.

Translated by J. Rosengrant

The Eyes Of Santa Lucia

1

Not just once did Anton hear from the adults about an all-round orphan. And when they exhaled – *o-o-o-r-phan* – their stiff, fist-collected faces softened and went limp. So Anton decided that to be a round orphan was good. No angles, no bumps. A circle. While everybody else huddled in communal apartments, in the corners or on narrow cots, a round orphan could fittingly live inside a circle.

It took Anton several weeks to perfect circles without a compass. To trace the line with an unfaltering hand was painstakingly difficult, given his circumstances. And when the cuckoo over a dresser called the hour, or neighbours behind the wall got into their screaming matches, Anton's fingers would lose the imagined trajectory, and he would have to begin all over again. But Anton was stubborn. He practised on old blotting papers, on reverse sides of the drafts covered with his father's minute handwriting. And by spring, he was able to make – with one sweep – a perfect circle of any diameter and then fit an all-round orphan inside: two dots for the eyes, a dash for the mouth.

Anton didn't have much use for bodies. They were a nuisance. So the sketch allowed for no more than a head and a neck hinted at by two insignificant lines that led nowhere. Just like Anton's, the boy's head was shaven; the round orphan must also have had lice.

Anton hid the drawing under his pillow next to a piece of pink chalk that he had found on a pavement just barely freed from snow.

Pink chalk was a rare find, a treasure.

While his father examined caterpillars, spiders, and grasshoppers through a magnifying glass, Anton was not allowed to ask any questions or show any signs of life. He was supposed to be asleep, period.

Eyes half-closed, Anton watched the manoeuvres of troops. The night, conspiring with a corner street lamp, threw across the wall whole armies: lanced warriors dashed forward, then vanished under the baseboard, engulfed by shadows. And sometimes, if the streetcar passed, the dissipated warriors grew antlers and emerged from under the floor in the shape of a deer; another shift, and the deer would morph into a sharp-elbowed man leaning over the desk. Pointed head, chin, and nose elongating monstrously.

The wire mesh of the bed squeaked as the boy crept deeper under the old, cotton-filled quilt to hide from the night reshaping his father into a monster who stretched across the wall. For sure it wasn't his real father. It couldn't be.

His true father is now sailing on the icebreaker *Lenin*. Or on the submarine *Nautilus* together with Captain Nemo. Or perusing the tropics on a ship with magnificent scarlet sails! Here he is! Standing on the captain's bridge, he notices a typhoon ahead; he conquers that typhoon. He is young, courageous, tall, good looking. Not sullen, old, and bald, forever stooped over his typewriter, clearing his throat at monotonously predictable intervals. He is a captain, not an entomologist and geneticist – the two words that make people's brows go up: "He is a who, you said?"

Anton imagined his Captain Father and himself catching

a dangerous spy; then extinguishing the taiga fires. They see the Ussurian tiger trapped in flames; they save the tiger, making a way for him in the wall of fire. Next to his Captain Father, Anton is never short winded; nothing compresses his breast, he can stand erect.

Now his Captain father is bravely drifting on an ice floe toward the North Pole. He promised Comrade Stalin he'd be the first to reach the apex of Earth solo! But then spring comes, the ice is breaking off, bit by bit, like pieces of a watermelon, one tiny slice is left, his father balancing on one foot! He taps out a secret code on the radio that Anton had assembled for him under his bed, specially for this ice-floating adventure. In the whole world, only two of them know the code. Anton should ask Comrade Stalin – Father taps – to send a plane out for his rescue. And now he, Anton, together with another pilot, is perusing the hostile deserts of the Arctic. After hours of desperate search, they discover a tiny speck in the blinding white infinity...And then...no, not like that...Somebody else, not his father, is a minute helpless speck. His father is cut out for heroic deeds: he's the one rescuing that dot, the someone else who has risked his life on an ice floe. The two of them – he never leaves Anton behind – are flying the polar plane and Anton shouts: "I see him, I see him!"

"We're descending!" declaims his Father. "Anton, prepare the rope ladder! Throw the rope through the hatch!" But the rope is frozen stiff to the floor. Then Father orders: "You, Anton, fly the plane! I'll manage the ladder!" Anton is now alone at the controls. He pulls and pushes all kinds of levers, and the plane descends. Father hacks the ladder free with an axe and releases it. Anton knows he has to go in lower and lower circles till the man can catch the rope. Anton has never piloted the plane, but he is his father's son. He can do anything! One circle, two, three, closer and closer to the treacherous slab of ice! How small it is and how lonely is the figure of the stranded man...Finally! Together they pull him in.

The man is frost bitten and can hardly talk, but the first words to crunch like broken ice from his mouth are: "Dear Comrades, Father and Son, I owe you my life."

"Don't mention it," replies the Father Captain. "We could do it again."

"Any time," adds the son, and they take a course right to Red Square. There Comrade Stalin is waiting on top of the Mausoleum, the red carpet is plush under their feet. Leaflets, flowers, mountains of flowers, a wind orchestra, jubilant smiles...

Anton knows that someday he will run away to meet up with his authentic father. But one thing is preventing him right now: an awkward but deep sense of connection with the grotesque shadow that is leaning over the table. He was first aware of it while examining, through a lens, sharp-kneed grasshoppers, triangular-armed spiders, dragon flies with whispering-glass wings, caterpillars with ugly protrusions, twenty-legged centipedes. Unlike his Insect Father, he detests bugs. He is sure that because his fraudulent father was constantly dawdling over these knobby creatures, he, Anton, ended up with a hump on his back. The hump, though not that big, grows to one side: it gives him a grotesque look in any clothing he wears. Anton has adjusted to his deformity, though breathing is never easy: the hump compresses his lungs, and he can't run like other kids; when he tries, he becomes a laughing stock.

Anton can only lie on one side, but the good thing is that it is the side from which he can see his mother. Mother lives in a small wooden frame on a chest of drawers. When Auntie Luba had moved into their flat and Father removed the portrait, Mother died again. But somehow Anton knew that Mother would come back and didn't worry for her, not as much as he worried for his Captain Father.

It was Captain Father who needed to be taken constant care of, for whom new adventures had to be invented daily.

2

Auntie Luba arrived with a nest on her head. It was made up of transparent braids that reminded Anton of a particularly wonderful batch of challah he once saw in a bread store. What a huge line gathered for this challah on that day! The legless beggars, plenty of them after the war, got together for a fun ride near the bread store – back and forth, back and forth – on their low, make-shift platforms with ball-bearings for wheels. But when the rumour of challah came, they went crazy from the smell of the freshly baked bread and rode right into the crowd! But vertical people formed an impenetrable wall, and the roller-boarding cripples didn't get a crumb! Auntie Luba, on the other hand, had a whole loaf of it on her head!

Auntie Luba produced all kinds of sounds when she moved, and it took a while for Anton to figure out how she did it. A starched blouse with a ruff said *"tracsk-tracsk"* when she raised her arms. Her black skirt stridulated as she mounted herself onto a chair, and her high heels were strict and stern like a pointer at school. Every time

Anton heard their tap-tap-tap, he'd pull his head into his shoulders.

When Auntie Luba moved in with them, Father put a screen in front of the boy's bed, and Anton couldn't watch the great battles on the wall anymore. Instead, he listened to the rustles and whispers of the night. Aunt Luba giggled as if somebody was tickling her. But who would make their way to their home at night to tickle Auntie Luba? That, Anton could never figure out.

Every morning, Aunt Luba made Anton do *hygienic exercises*. She flapped her arms in front of him like signal flags while he had to squat twenty or thirty times. "Up, down! Up, down!" she ordered. "You want to remain a hunchback forever? Then keep you back straight!" What was amazing was that in the morning she had no nest on her head, but a short sparse growth instead, of an indefinable colour. However, the white blouse with the ruff and black skirt stayed.

After hygienic exercises, Anton wasn't allowed to have breakfast yet. First, he had to clean up the mess under his bed. His hump prevented him from crawling beneath the hanging metal-net belly, so Aunt Luba gave him a broom on a long handle and watched, arms to her hips, him poking with that broom here and there to fish out his meagre treasures: a slingshot, an old cartridge case, some charcoal for drawing, a pen-knife, and pieces of bark he needed to carve things; and all sorts of springs and rusted parts to assemble the radio one day. These he imperceptibly drove away with the broom to the very corner, and Aunt Luba didn't notice. "A real garbage pile, this place is, no air to breathe," she sniffed.

Aunt Luba lived with them for about three weeks, but Anton

knew from their first meal together that she would soon be gone. He knew that and, for the time, followed her orders.

On the first day of Aunt Luba's arrival, Anton entered the room when the table was already set. He'd never seen white napkins with red cockerels before.

"A present from Auntie Luba." said Insect Father.

He stopped short, afraid to look up at their new guest.

"Is he always late for dinner, your son?"

The Insect Father withdrew his head into his shoulders, exactly the way Anton did, but said nothing.

"Come over, sit down," Auntie Luba said, patting her hand on the seat next to her.

Anton hesitated. Instead of climbing into the chair, he first dragged it away from her and tried to straddle it, all the while facing their guest to hide his deformity.

Aunt Luba squinted her eyes, examining the boy.

Then she put her knife and her fork down.

"Oh, that's what it is...kyphosis!"

The Insect Father looked away, then drew Anton to his side. And by the way he did it, hand dallying on the left shoulder, Anton knew Aunt Luba was a goner. Intuiting the day of her disappearance, he returned his mother to her old place. And by the time Auntie departed, and the screen was removed, Mother was back home.

3

Anton didn't like to go outside much. But the Insect Father insisted: fresh air was essential for the development of a healthy mind and body.

Boys from the courtyard teased Anton: "Give us a humpity-bumpity ride, eh? What's in your hump, camel?"

When he approached them, they didn't beat him but simply gave him a chase and shooed him away like a cat. Hobbling off, he groped for air – a fish out of water – so funny to watch. Anton would find refuge in the shoemaker's workshop, the man's huge arms covered with thickets of curly hair, his black beard concealing half his chest. Leo the Kike looked like the pirate Barmaley from the famous children's story. He always wore an old mariner's shirt, smeared with blacking, so you couldn't tell anymore the black stripes from the white ones. Topping this off was a greasy leather apron with two enormous pockets. Leo the Kike mangled all thirty-three letters of Russian alphabet, as they say.

"So, Antosha! Are they mishtrating you again?"

"Nah, they are just teasing."

"Boorhish people. Bachbarians. Teach their childhren bad zings." Leo the Kike extracted a chocolate nugget from his pocket: The Bear of the North. The outer wrapper showed a bear climbing a diagonally fallen log up to the azure sky."Have a bite!" urged the shoemaker.

But Anton carefully unwrapped the treat, examining first the outer layer, then the shiny foil and, finally, the transparent waxy coating. Having made sure that everything was in place, he wrapped it all back and hid the bear in his pocket.

"Saving it for your dad, eh?"

"No, for Lusya," said Anton, climbing onto a high stool next to the polish caldron, his usual post. He peeked over the pot edge to better see the bubbles gurgling in the black slop.

Lusya's real name was Lucia. When she was only two years old, she had arrived, together with three thousand civil war children, from Spain. Her parents were real, true Spaniards, and they never learned to speak Russian properly. Lusya, on the other hand, was only a little bit Spanish, not much really, because she spoke exactly like Anton. Yet everything about her was extraordinary. She was always dressed festively, not like other girls. Her ironed skirt had many neat folds, and her little lacquered belts looked so tender on her waist. She smelled sweetly, as did a cinnamon bun that Anton had seen once but never tried. And she had a deep cleft in her chin he found irresistible.

Boys teased Lusya in a dirty way. "Lussy, Lussy, show me your pussy." But Lusya passed by as a queen, without so much as twitching her shoulder. Yes, she was very proud, in a quiet way. She smiled shyly, into her palm. And when she adjusted a polka-dot satin ribbon in her hair, she kept her emerald-green eyes cast down.

On a boot tree, Leo the Kike placed a wreck of a shoe, and the magic began. With one precise movement he freed the shoe out of its old shell, a worn-out sole that had given away its last breath to the toils of the roads. Now the shoe looked like a pallid skeleton: too naked, too fragile to come into contact with even a road paved with feathers.

Anton liked the astringent smell of turpentine. He liked the way Leo the Kike turned the shoe this way and that, then put it away for a moment. On the shelf, he kept different pieces of leather. He took one piece, cut out a new sole, attached it with the small shiny tacks fanning out of his mouth, then cut off overlaps with a knife and adroitly rounded all the edges with a special tool. Anton watched a leather ribbon coiling down to the floor in a neat stack. Leo the Kike dipped a flat stick into the bubbling cauldron – the moment Anton held his breath for – and traced the join between the sole and upper with a shiny border. Now the shoe was ready for new adventures, its second life.

Anton climbed down from the stool to collect the leather snake and all the rubber shavings left on the floor from other jobs.

"Father promised to buy me a talking parrot," he said, dawdling a little, shifting his weight from one leg to the other. It was a lie, but he wanted to thank Leo the Kike for his gifts. And the only way of doing it, in his mind, was to tell him something extraordinary. Anton's cheeks flushed. After all, it wasn't a total lie: He'd simply blended two fathers together. Couldn't his Captain Father one day bring the parrot from some tropical country? And couldn't his Insect Father, who knew so much about every creature, teach that parrot to talk? "I must go now," declared Anton. "So much business to do!"

"You'll have to show me your parhot one day," Leo the Kike said, laughing. "When you get some frhee time, busy man."

"I will," promised the boy.

Indeed, he was in a rush. He had to peel potatoes before Insect Father came home from work, and had to mend his father's socks and do his own homework. But first he had to get over to Uncle Tolya, all the way across the yard, before Uncle Tolya closed his *edemption* shack for the day. The sign outside once read "Empties Redemption Centre." The letter *R* had disappeared, and until the previous year, Anton still had thought *edemption* was some kind of transparent, invisible rat poison that people were bringing to Uncle Tolya in different-size bottles.

To avoid the gang of boys flicking pen knives against the wall, he took a longer route past the back side of the grocery store. But he found the path blocked by a refrigerator truck. The man in a padded jacket was heaving frozen cow carcasses out of the vehicle, dragging them by a rope over the ground to the zinc chute, then barrelling them into the opening. "Thump, thump, thump." Anton counted each hulk thudding onto the still-frozen ground. Crash! Bang! At the other end of the chute, underground workers shouted and swore. Anton peeped inside the truck filled with carcasses. By the time they unloaded, Uncle Tolya would have already closed.

Anton bent over to measure the distance from the ground to the truck's underbelly, then dipped below. Crawling clumsily, he reached the front wheels; waited till the man with carcasses turned away, then dived out at the other end.

4

Inside a long shack, Uncle Tolya was sitting on a wooden crate puffing on his cigarette. Black inside and out, as if built from planks pulled out of fire, the shack didn't have one single window. It smelled of fungus and mildew. Emaciated mice darted about, paying no attention to an obscure bulb clinging to its twisted cord. Uncle

Tolya was picky: some poisons suited him, and some he rejected. But he must have tried *edemption* on his shack's little inhabitants. They looked so thin, and altogether unhealthy. That's what Anton thought before he even went to school. But now, a first grader, he was big and knew better: *edemption* simply meant empty bottles.

Uncle Tolya was wearing grey coverall with black oversleeves. There was something ratty in him, some kinship with the rotting wood, with the decay of the underworld. He flicked his cigarette butt onto the dirt floor, then poked his head out a hole in the side wall to serve his waiting customers: grey and black coats, mostly women and children in oversized garb; and a couple of men in urgent need of cash for the "morning after." On the ground, a little to one side, a glassy snail of string bags bulged with *edemptions.*

"I'm not taking sour-cream jars on Tuesdays! How many times do I have to tell you?" "Uncle Tolya shouted to an old woman in a grey woollen headscarf.

But she held her ground, as if frozen, with a jar in each mittened hand extended out to him."Two hours in line, please have mercy."

"Fuck your mother!" barked Uncle Tolya."Don't you understand plain Russian, old hag? Next!"

Anton sighed in disbelief. Such an old *babushka,* really ancient, still had a mother, while he had none.

With unexpected agility, the so-called hag bent to one side over her sacks, extracting new bottles."How about some beer empties? Will you take these? Left from my son."

Uncle Tolya shot a stern glance at the bags."Who's going to

wash the labels off? Me? You know the rules: get them off, then come back."

"But you'd be closed by then, I stood for two hours already."

"What about milk bottles? You take them?" A young woman with a baby in her arms was elbowing her way forward to take the hag's spot.

"Depends what kind," snapped Uncle Tolya without looking at the young mother. "One litre – maybe; others no."

Taking advantage of the woman's hesitation, a hunk of a man struggled forward.

Several women in the crowd mumbled variations of "Don't cut in line, you shameless scum bag!"

"No queue for vodka bottles, comrade citizens!" snarled the man.

"Who said so? Since when? And you woman, yes, you – with the baby – standing there counting crows in the sky! Letting crooks in!"

The crowd started a commotion, closing ranks in an attempt to squeeze out the offender and that gawk of a girl with a baby. Anton felt sorry for these two women. He didn't like Uncle Tolya at all. He'd gladly avoid this shop, never show up here; but the *edemption* shack was the only place he hoped to get what he was looking for: bottle shards. Not the ordinary green pieces of glass strewing the dirt floor inside, but the rare, smoky-blue ones, from foreign bottles.

He had already put by several valuable things for Lusya: a pink chalk to draw the hopscotch, the leather garland for her necklace, and the Bear of the North. She could eat the chocolate and use the wraps for her *secretik*. What he needed was a suitable piece of glass to cover the *secretik*. A lot depended on his find: a beautiful glass could turn the *secretik* into magic; an ordinary one would make it look like any other girl's.

While Uncle Tolya was fighting the *edemption* people, Anton examined the shack's floor more carefully: cigarette butts, broken glass – nothing special. It was getting late; his Insect Father would soon come back from work. The boy picked up a green splinter, just in case, and hobbled out.

Convulsively, Anton gulped in the prickly, crisp air of early spring, partaking of the great work of earth unfolding in front of his eyes. He felt the snowdrift's secret sorrow, how it couldn't help itself anymore: the loosening of its shape and dignity, first imperceptibly, then into open nakedness. The treachery of melting had begun underneath, in the snow's deep bowels, where it first touched the earth; then the yielding sprawled through the snowdrift's spine and blackened it with soot, remorse, and desperation. The snow cried and bemoaned its fate, its memories of lost power, its grip on the earth. And now sobbing, it was retreating into nothingness, pulling its arms away like white flames. Anton bent down. On the strip of dirt freed from the shackles of winter, there wallowed a magnificent shard of red glass. It wasn't just red, it was ruby red, with dark green veins pulsating inside. Sealed in its depth was the flame of its foreign blood: the bliss of the hot beaches under a never-setting sun, the ecstasy of the festive, care-free existence nobody in the observable world could fathom. Anton's dexterous fingers grabbed the ruby. He would examine it later; now he had to go, before somebody snatched the treasure away from him.

5

It had been almost five months since he'd fallen in love with
Lusya. Five months of fear that she would get weary of him. He
camouflaged that fear and his thirst for her presence by rapid talk
and little gifts he spent most of his time looking for. Lusya must be
finished with her homework by now and would soon go out, so he
ran to her house. Socks and potatoes would have to wait.

He stopped at the foyer leading to her complex of apartments.
He never shouted like other kids, hands cupped to their mouths –
"Lusya, when are you coming out?" – till Lusya's mother showed up
on the balcony and broadcast in broken Russian, her unbent arms on
the railings: "Please stop to shout! Lusya, he is busy now. He make
the homework."

No, he, Anton, always waited.

Anton was mesmerized by the shadows from Lusya's
eyelashes, the way they seemed to cover half her face. They flew
to him in his dreams. The polka-dot ribbon and the matching socks
rising up from the lacquered shoes collected Anton's shimmering
happiness like a prism. Lusya never teased him, and if there was
nobody else around to play with, she agreed to play with him.

He was sitting now on a bench next to her entryway, waiting
patiently. From time to time, he checked his treasure, hidden in his
pocket, felt its delightful smoothness. Spring bloomed, and dripping
icicles sang their arias. Neither his deformity nor the encroaching
evening with his Insect Father bothered the boy right now. The
air thickened in the premonition of almost intolerable happiness.

Anton's heart pushed against the bars of its cage. Lusya stood in the entrance doorway. She stiffened, evaluating the situation.

"Lusya," Anton whispered, rising from the bench. "Will you play with me a little?"

The girl looked dreamingly over his head (she was a year older and almost a head taller.) "All right." She paused. "Did you bring me the boat?"

Now her eyes were pouring steady calm light over him. Anton's feet wobbled; words rough and dry like last year's leaves stuck in his throat.

"It isn't ready yet. Tomorrow, for sure."

"You promise?"

"Yes, you'll see!"

At the end of March, when the snow, firmly packed by months of blizzards, finally yielded to the sun and gushed down the pavement in torrents of water, the kids came out to launch their boats. They'd slapped them together out of litter released by the melting snow: woodchips, fragments of plywood, even scraps of newspaper. But Lusya had to have a real boat, carved out of wood, with masts and sails and all the rigging and even a crew to boot. Anton began to work on her boat before the snow fell. Throughout the whole winter, he'd been collecting cork bottles at Uncle Tolya's and rubber cuttings from Leo the Kike. It was the sailors he got stuck on: he made two of them, then ran out of plasticene.

"Do you mind if I make sailors out of acorns?"

"Acorns?" Lusya chuckled. "Won't it look funny?"

Anton quickly calculated. He had already removed all the

saddles and the spurs from the plasticene cavalry he'd built two months before. Of course, he could pinch off riders' legs too – after all, these were cavalry men, not foot soldiers – but legs are thin. There wouldn't be enough for a whole crew of sailors. Besides, the cavalry was sitting right on his father's desk on a piece of plywood. Father would notice and ask questions.

"I don't have any plasticene left," Anton finally confessed.

Lusya cocked her head to the side, smiling enticingly. "I got a whole new box for a birthday present. You can use any colour you want."

From constant use, his own plasticene was crumpled and crimpled into balls of indiscernible colour: something brownish, with impregnations of green and dirt-yellow. He imagined untouched sticks, with even, machine-made grooves, each piece nestled into a separate cardboard compartment according to its shade, like a rainbow, from light green to intense purple to tender pink. He sensed the marvellous, industrial smell of this rainbow and ardently wanted to become its owner.

"Look what I've got for you." He reached for the ruby, but his hand hesitated, then pulled out the candy. He wanted the ruby to be a splash of surprise; he'd give it to her last, and see how her face bloomed.

Lusya unwrapped the Bear of the North, then sent the chocolate into her mouth as she surveyed Anton dreamingly with her languid eyes, the bow of her lips moving rhythmically. A starched white handkerchief appeared from the pocket of her blue coat. She gently blotted her mouth.

"It's not because of the plasticene," he said."Please don't get the wrong idea." The very thought that she might suspect the chocolate bar as a payment for her generosity was unbearable.

"Of course not," said Lusya, chewing calmly.

Anton scratched his head under his cap; when he was nervous, the stubble made him itchy.

"Thank you," Lusya said. "You're a kind boy."

Nobody in the radius of his acquaintance ever talked like that: "He's a good boy. She's a good girl." That's how her parents must carry on at home, Anton thought, his afternoon quietly lighting up.

Meanwhile, Lusya was examining the wrapper against the sun."This is the best. Even Tankya doesn't have wrappers like this. Come on, I'll show you something."

Shuffling rather than skipping along the way as Lusya did, Anton followed her to the courtyard fountain, dry ever since it was made. Along the outside of its round cement wall, the girls had dug small depressions in the earth. The bottom of each hollow was laid with foil. Shiny trinkets were placed on top: candy wrappers, shards of glass, pieces of coloured ribbon. A piece of plain glass covered the cache. A layer of soil made the *secretik* invisible.

Late autumn was the best time for *secretiky*. Fallen leaves camouflaged the spot; then snow fell, and in spring you removed the layer of earth and dug till you hit the glass, a window revealing the treasure, forgotten over the long winter. If somebody else found your cache, fights would erupt, in spite of the rules that you'd have to relinquish all your rights.

"You hid it here?" Anton asked, bending over next to Lusya.

"Anyone can find it."

"I'm not that dumb! This one's fake. The real one's over there." As she continued to dig, she waved her head away from the fountain. Under the ordinary green bottle glass, finally emerging from beneath the layers of last year's litter, was nothing but dirt. The real *secretik* was some distance away from the fake one. And it was splendid: golden and silver candy wrappers, white pigeon feathers, and coloured glass beads forming a star.

"You're the only one who's seen it," whispered Lusya putting her arm around Anton's neck and pulling him closer. Her eyelashes almost touched his cheek. "Give your Pinky Swear that you won't tell anybody."

"I give my Pinky Swear."

Lusya let him go. "Where is the glass you said you'd bring?"

Anton dipped into his pocket, feeling for the ruby.

"Lucia, come home!" Shouted her mother from the balcony. "The teacher for piano is arrived!"

"*Estoy viniendo!*" Lusya called to her mother. Already skipping away, she called to Anton over her shoulder: "I have to go now."

"Will you come out later?" he shouted after her.

"Don't know! Maybe!"

With a light shrug of her shoulders, she flitted out of his world, immediately turning his treasure into a useless trinket. Anton's day died in his hands. Nothing was left of it, except the persistent croaking of the crows in the tops of the naked trees. He rolled his shoulders restlessly, snivelling, then slowly walked toward his home.

6

The first thing Anton needed to do was darn his father's socks.
Otherwise, what would Father wear to work? The boy had learned
the skill by watching old ladies on the bench. One of them gave him
a cracked wooden darning mushroom she no longer needed. Not for
nothing did Anton have long, pale, and adroit fingers that he could
almost braid together. He could sew and mend all kinds of clothing,
his Insect father being hopeless when it came to any housework. And
Anton could peel a potato in two seconds. As for school homework,
there was Lusya's "maybe" hanging by a silvery thread, and his
father never checked his homework anyway. Even still, he had a
bushel of things to do while she was running her gentle fingers across
the keyboard of her piano.

Once, he visited her flat and now could see clearly the dining
room, the brightly glazed vase on a table, and Lusya's straight back
at the piano, in something airily, delightfully pink. Her parents never
allowed her to invite anybody up from the "street." The fact that
Lusya had broken this rule was Anton's greatest reward for his awful
humiliation a month before.

On that day, he'd gone out into the courtyard to confront a
frightening scene. Lusya was sitting right on the dirty pavement,
smearing tears over her cheeks, her hair dishevelled, the ribbon
and the coat lying in the dirt, the laced hem of her dress torn, one
foot bare. Girls were volleying her shoe to each other, laughing and
grimacing; then, bored with it, bean-pole Tankya scooped up some
snow with that shoe and poked it under Lusya's nose: "Go ahead,

eat it." That was a signal for the bashing to begin. The girls crushed Lusya under their fists and took turns kicking her. Lusya made no attempt to defend herself.

Watching this, the sun grew black in Anton's eyes. Without thinking about it, he attacked Tankya, the beanpole, twisting his tenacious fingers into her hair. She jumped away, screaming. Then he tried to peel the other girls off Lusya, working his elbows like hatchets.

"Look," screamed Tankya."He's going crazy! The creep!"

But Anton thrashed left and right. He was alone against a whole swarm of girls, each of them taller and older than him. They crushed him under and sucked him in. They mauled him and lashed him over the face with slimy, rotting flowers out of the garbage. Then they pushed him inside the iron garbage container, the size of a giant's coffin, threw a dead cat on top of him, and slammed the iron lid. Anton shouted, beating against the lid, but to no avail. Much later, Leo the Kike, who went to throw away his cuttings, pulled Anton out. The boy was barely alive.

After this mishap, Lucia bestowed a great honour on Anton. For the first and only time, she invited him to her place. He took off his shoes and gingerly stepped on the mirror of the parquet in the living room. The sweet smell – the same smell he sensed around his idol – enveloped him. The grand piano watched him in dark silence as he tiptoed after Lusya to her room. Two ornate black-lace mobiles on a carved table bowed their heads, catching the light breeze that moved the curtains.

"We're going to make theatre," announced Lusya, closing the

door behind them. "Do you want to be my page? And I'll be your Princess." Without waiting for him to respond, she cried: "Let's begin!"

Out of the lacquered drawer came a Spanish grandee in a soft hat of black velvet with a red feather, black cloak, a toy sword dangling at his side. Anton was dazzled.

"And who is this?" he asked holding his breath as his princess pulled the second puppet out of the same drawer.

"This is Matador," she said. "It belonged to my grandmother. That's what we got out of Spain, these two. Touch it, gently."

"What does Matador do?" Anton asked, stroking the golden brocade, the silk embroidered jacket, the coloured waistband of the puppet.

"He fights a bull. Like this, I'll show you."

Lusya spoke rapidly in Spanish, manipulating the matador and the grandee. Both of them attacked the cat, Marcela, who served as a bull, and finally emitted a heart-breaking mew before escaping under the bed.

"Enough," Lusya declared. "My mother doesn't allow me to handle the puppets for too long. They're too old for that. Marcela, you were a good bull. Come out, I'll give you some milk." She looked at Anton meaningfully. "Well, my page, let's go do something else. Ready?"

She climbed up on a chair and pulled down a folio with gold-embossed covers from a high shelf. Straining with its weight, she nestled on a sofa next to Anton. Interspersed with rice papers were pictures by old masters. Lusya traced them with her finger, reading the names of artists in unfamiliar script: El Greco, Goya, Surbaran. Anton could already easily read in Russian, but that his princess could make sense out of these strange letters so effortlessly! A bird of paradise flitting from one exotic flower to the next!

They were sitting close to each other, Lusya leafing through pages, making sure the rice paper didn't crease. Suddenly, he stopped her leafing hand, stunned by the strangeness of a portrait they came to. A young woman in a bright dress – half of her face sharply lit, half still consumed by darkness – stood tall, gazing impartially at the spectator. Her dark hair was decorated with a wreath of roses. In her left hand, she held something long and sharp, like an unusually long branch, or a feather, the likes of which Anton had never seen. But it was the object in her other hand that startled him. On a platter floated two liquid, transparent eyes. Alive, they were staring at Anton.

"What is it?" he whispered.

"This is Saint Lucia, the martyr. I was named after her."

"Why is she carrying...these...on a tray?"

"They tore her eyes out because she was a Christian. But she didn't die. She grew another pair, instead."

"For real?" Anton rubbed his own eyes as if to make sure they were all right. "You mean, she could see with them? With the ones in her face and on the tray?"

"Yes, but the eyes on the platter are magic. They see hidden things. For example, if you lose something, you ask Santa Lucia's eyes, and they'll tell you where it's hiding. Or if you're lost in the woods, her eyes can show you the path out."

"How do you know?"

"Everybody does."

"Can I copy them?" asked Anton timidly.

"I can't loan you the book, but my mother won't allow it."

"Do you have any watercolours?"

Lusya hesitated, looking over Anton's head at the closed door. "My parents are coming home soon. There's no time."

"I'll be fast, you'll see."

She thought for a moment, then returned with a glass of water and an unopened box of paints. Anton dipped a brush into water, then scooped some dark brown pigment, then green and brown again. Several strokes, and there appeared a platter resembling the one in the painting. He kept painting, forgetting to breathe normally, a bizarre whistle coming out of his chest with each exhalation, his lower lip now sticking out, a thin thread of saliva beginning its journey toward his chest. And finally, there appeared a pair of bulging eyes floating on the platter.

"I didn't know you could paint so well." Lusya patted him on the nape of his neck.

She was looking at the picture from some distance away, and, becoming aware of his saliva he inched back a bit farther so he didn't wind up drooling on her.

"You made them not look scary at all," she said. *Son blandos.* Tender and a little sad." She leaned toward him, looking more closely. "But Santa Lucia's eyes are brown, not green."

Anton looked at her gravely. "These are magic eyes. And green. Like yours."

"You like my eyes?" She opened them even wider. "Here's a handkerchief. Wipe your chin."

Then she covered Santa Lucia with rice paper, closed the book, and put it away on the shelf.

Since that day, Anton had been carrying the Magic Eyes in his pocket. But at night, he had to hide behind his bed, slipping the painting beneath a loose flap of wallpaper. When he stumbled onto the red ruby glass, he knew right away who helped him to find it, directing his steps.

7

But for the next two days, Lusya didn't come out to play. When Anton finally saw her, she looked so forlorn that his heart grew heavy with pity.

"I'm having my wart burnt," she murmured, looking down at the tips of her shoes, her skipping rope hanging listlessly in her hand. "My mother is taking me to the doctor's."

"Just don't go," Anton blurted out, himself suddenly overcome with a pang of pain.

"How?"

"Why do they have to burn it? Look what I've got." He closed his hand into a fist. On the right knuckle sat a small rough mound. "I played with the frogs last summer, and that's what happened. But I'll never have mine burnt." Anton was embarrassed by his own words. How could he compare himself to his princess? She was perfect. No wart could make her any less beautiful, whereas he could always be uglier."

"Well, it's not really a wart. It's just ugly. It's actually a birthmark, and if I don't get it burned off, nobody will marry me. That's what my mother says."

"I . . I will!"

Lusya laughed. Anton cast his eyes down.

"Is it big, your thing?"

Lusya rolled down the white round collar of her dress: a brown spot covered with black hairs sprawled down toward her chest.

"Mine is not from frogs. I was born like this."

Anton was baffled. In his mind, he was the only one to have any deformities, by virtue of his indefinable but certain affinity with dead insects. But Lusya, his enchantress, the light of his life, couldn't possibly have anything like what he'd just seen.

"You know what they'll do? They'll fasten me to the table and then burn me with a red-hot iron. *Pssh, pssh, pshhh,* like that." She cocked her head to one side to see the effect.

Anton shuddered. Burn her with a red-hot iron? That would never stand. No, he couldn't allow it to happen. He had to prevent it, to undertake an urgent course of action.

"Let's run away, then!" he whispered, glancing furtively from side to side.

"Run away to where?" she scoffed, flicking the tip of her tongue around her lips.

"To my father. He's the captain of a big ship. He's in charge of everybody. He'll give an order, and they'll sail to Spain, to your relatives."

"All my relatives are finished. Done with, in the war."

She spoke matter-of-factly, raising her head. Anton followed her gaze: the pigeons had taken off from the dovecote on the roof and were now circling in the sky.

"Your father isn't a ship captain. You're just making things up. Your father studies insects. You told me so yourself."

"This is my father for here. But I have another father over there. Honestly!"

Lusya chuckled. "You're silly! There's no such thing. Understand? I know that for certain."

"But what about Kolya?" retorted Anton. "He had a brother in Kiev. He himself told me. And this brother has another mother. So Kolya has two mothers, right? I have no mother, but maybe I have two fathers instead, see?"

"Yes, I see. That you're still a little boy." She sighed and thought of something. "All right. If you have another father, how do we get to him? Where's his ship? Tell me."

Anton hesitated for a second. "First, we take a train. We ask the auntie conductress to take us to the boats. We get off at the seashore, and there, everybody will know my father's ship."

Lusya unfolded her rope and began to skip. "Su-ppose, su-ppose – there's a ship some-somewhere. We still need an exact address, silly!"

"There is no address on the water. Addresses are on land."

By now she was skipping away, and he was losing her.

"Lusya, wait, wait! We don't need to go to the ship, we can hide at Burnt Man Barren. They won't find us there, I promise!"

Burnt Man Barren was a scary place: muggings, assaults, rapes, even murders. Children believed that, before the war, a man was tied to a tree and burnt alive. They said you could still see his

silhouette on a scorched trunk. Burnt Man Barren was adjacent to the
railway track, separated from it by two fences. The endless freight
trains swished by at full speed, and nobody ever saw one stop. It took
your breath away when you counted the cars – on a bet – ten, twenty,
thirty, and soon Anton would run out of breath and lose the count,
shivering in the brutal blasts and swirls of wind that could knock him
over and suck him under the wheels any moment.

8

The day he finally managed to talk Lusya into going to Burnt Man
Barren, they climbed, as he usually did, over the first fence only to
realize they were trapped. The hole in the second, much higher fence,
standing a metre or so from the first one, was now hammered tight
with planks. Anton scratched his head trying to figure what to do.

"Let's turn back," Lusya declared.

"Wait, I know another path, through Motovka Depot!"

"But it's going to get late! I'm not allowed to come home after
dark."

"There'll be another break in the fence. It can't be too far, you'll
see! Let's go. Please."

Lusya stepped away and looked hard at Anton. "Why have you
dragged me here anyway? Why? I don't want to count your trains!"

"I thought if they force you to have this thing burnt...if we
needed to hide someday...we could come here, but if you really don't
want to..."

Lusya sniffed. She was a big girl, after all; he, but a little hunchback. She made a step forward with proud, regal reluctance. Squeezed by jagged, sooty walls on both sides, they now continued to walk carefully, avoiding the snowy slush mixed up with human and dog excrement. As if locked in a prison cell with the ceiling taken off, the only thing they could see was the fading eggshell of the sky. But Anton didn't mind. He loved enclosed spaces, preferred them to open, unprotected vistas. And now he felt a strange exaltation being so close to her, watching her making these tentative, cautious steps in the sludge. His senses were sharp: he could see and smell and hear better than other people. He noticed the transparency of the huge pale disk hanging over his head – no more than a sketch of a moon in the dark blueness of the sky. And beneath was snow mixed with dirt and her small footprints filling with water the moment she lifted her foot.

Minutes later, the moon had already come fully into its body, all luminescence. It transformed everything around – darkening and expanding the walls on both sides, snatching the half-belt on the back of Lusya's coat and sculpting it into a furry living thing. Anton was happy: he wanted nothing else from life, nothing but this moment, a page following his princess into eternity.

And then the glad monotony of the inner wall suddenly faltered: here it was, the other break Anton had hoped for. He looked up at it. The hole was way above his head.

"I know what to do. You climb on my shoulders, and I'll hold you tight. See that plank up there? You grab it and then jump down on the other side and wait for me."

Lusya glanced at Anton, her eyes frosted. "And you? How will you get over?"

"Don't you worry. I can climb better than a monkey. Come on, Lusya, let's go!"

And he stretched his arms toward the girl.

Lusya stepped back.

"No," she whispered. "No."

What he read in her eyes was not just fear, it was also disgust – disgust with him; disgust with the very idea that she would have to touch and even rely on somebody so pathetically deformed yet wanting to play the role of a strong and healthy, grown-up man.

"No," she repeated. "Never."

"Okay. Whatever you say." He felt a dry lump in his throat.

And again they walked, locked between the two walls, Anton gasping, struggling for air and lagging behind in the hope she wouldn't hear the forced, pathetic sound his lungs were making. But then the fence abruptly came to an end, and they found themselves at large again. Warehouses, sheds, piles of lumber, heaps of coal. In the dark, the railway tracks glittered.

The high beams of an oncoming train suddenly blinded them: a freight. And then something extraordinary happened. They heard the screeching of its brakes, the hissing of the locomotive, and the train shuddering to a stop. The children waited in total silence, their eyes wide open. Anton had never before seen a train stopping here. What they thought was a cattle car turned out to have barred windows. Behind them were faces. Emaciated, spectral, they stared into the darkness, and the two children stared back at them. Into this suspense, a folded piece of paper flew through the bars; then another one. White doves were alighting at their feet, some falling between the wheels. And immediately, without warning, dogs appeared out of nowhere, their ferocious barking shattering the silence. Taut leashes, the guards straining on them, searchlights dissecting the sky. Then the train hiccupped, as if choking, the wheels moved, and a minute later, the vision was gone.

All that was left were the tracks glittering in the dark, the blinking eye of a semaphore down the line, and pieces of paper scattered white on the ground. Anton picked one up.

"Leave it! Don't touch!" shouted Lusya.

In the light of the moon, her face was deadly pale. But Anton had already stuffed the paper into his pocket, as he always did with almost anything his sharp eyes noticed, just in case. She stood there dumbfounded, and then a terrible scream split the air. Anton never imagined anything like that could come from anybody's throat.

He slouched against her, covering her with his arms:"Don't, please Lusya! It's over! These were bad people, in the train. But we're safe. Nobody saw us, I swear!"

"How can I go home now? What will I say? If my parents find out, they'll lock me up! They'll..."

"Nobody will know. Tell them you played at my place."

"I will never, never lie to my mother! It's all your fault! Your country is terrible! My mother hates it! Why do we have to stay here? The war is over, and I want to go back home to Barcelona!" The words spattered out of her, more and more coloured with an exotic foreign flavour.

"You will go home one day, I promise! My Honest Word."

He pulled a tattered rag out of his pocket and held it out to her.

As he watched her wiping away tears with her own handkerchief, he didn't dare to touch her anymore.

9

That night, Anton couldn't fall asleep. As soon as he closed his eyes, the searchlights were disembowelling the black sky, German shepherds tore off their leashes, and Lusya screamed at the top of her lungs. He remembered he still hadn't given her the ruby and thought he should find a way of doing it; the ruby and the boat. Spring was coming; the girls would be opening their *sekretiky* soon, and launching their boats. Even if she never forgave him for the disgrace he'd brought upon her, even if neither the ruby nor the boat could mend the harm he'd inflicted, she still had to have the best. He'd make sure she lacked nothing; she could depend on him no matter what. The thought comforted him, and he was finally able to fall asleep. In his dream, the ruby caught fire and burned through his pocket, the flames reaching higher and higher, all the way to his heart. He was trying to grab the ruby, scorching his fingers, throwing it to Lusya. Soldiers with dogs came to extinguish the flame.

Their appearance woke Anton up; the soldiers proved to be real. They were searching the flat, looking for something. Father's books and papers were scattered on the floor, and a huge Brazilian butterfly, the pride of his father's collection, lay smitten out of her glass case, tipped over onto one wing like a crashed airplane. The ceiling light illuminated sharply the dishevelled figure of his father. With no colour in his face, he was barefoot, in his underwear. He tried and couldn't get his leg into his trousers.

"It's nothing, nothing, Antosha. Keep your spirits up. T'-w-will all end well." These were the last words his father said as he kept fumbling and failing to insert the buttons of his fly into the holes. Then one stranger took away his father's typewriter; the other picked up all his insects; and the third one took Insect Father himself.

All of the next day, Anton stayed at home listening for sounds from the staircase: quick tramping, then silence, a thump, and silence again. He boiled himself a potato and ate some bread, then crouched in the corner. The sound of his own breath, short whistling exhalations escaping from his breast, now scared him. Night fell. Shadows thickened, intensifying his fears: he expected *those men* to come back any minute. But more than anything, he worried about Insect Father. Where did *they* take him? He was a helpless man, unable to as much as darn his own socks; without Anton, he would perish, that much was clear. Under the dishevelled desk, something was glistering in the dark. Anton crawled across the room, afraid to make any noise. His father's microscope lay on its side amid shards of glass. He tried to unscrew the lid, and his whole body throbbed with soundless sobs. Daddy, my Daddy, my wonderful Daddy! He managed to dismantle other parts and stuff them in his pants pocket. When he found his daddy, they'd reassemble it together and put it back on the desk, and everything would be as it had always been: the light of the lamp snapping his daddy's bent back out of darkness; the projection of his head on a wall, stretching upward or shrinking, or moving sideways at the eerie will of the streetcar headlights.

Anton tried to comfort himself by thinking of his other, heroic

father, but nothing came of it. The captain proved to be no more than
a shadow, easily yielding to the quiver of his daddy's hands, lips
unable to form a word. It was up to the son to find the father, then; to
return him to the life they'd had before. Anton waited till the timid
spring dawn diluted the sky into liquid grey; then he soundlessly
opened the door, looked around, and tiptoed down the stairs.

It was early. The yard was still empty. Leo the Kike and Uncle
Tolya were closed. Anton climbed inside the dead fountain and
squatted, protected by its round cement wall. Chilled to the bone,
he hugged himself with his long arms and stiffened, half-dozing yet
alert. When neighbours began to emerge from their houses, Anton
scrambled up to his feet and, half-crouching, went to the vaulted gate
separating their building from the street. That would be the best place
to encounter people, to inquire about Father.

Anton loathed these gates. He could smell the stench at a
distance: at night drunks relieved themselves under the protection of
the thick arches, swaying like ghosts back and forth against the wall.
By morning, yellowish stalagmites grew on every vertical surface,
and you had to jump over streams of frozen urine to make it into the
street.

Anton waited. Finally he saw the first familiar face. It was
a neighbour, and he eagerly hobbled forward. But the young man
hurried away: Did he not recognize Anton? A woman approached
the archway. She glanced at the boy, but when he intercepted her
gaze, she turned away too. He was used to it: people were often
embarrassed at the sight of his infirmity. Yet he sensed there was
something different here; though he didn't know what it was.

Without strategizing any longer, he let his legs carry him wherever they wished, and they brought him to his usual outpost, on the bench near Lusya's entryway. Sooner or later, she'd show up, on her way to school. He waited. Then the air swelled and pushed into his chest with a familiar hot wave. Lusya, his enchantress, was standing on the porch. Red beret, red mittens to match, dark blue coat. In the dismal light of early morning, her face was pallid, her eyes looking vacantly at the world around her. His tender joy; the anchor of his life, the sweet breath of his bitter days – what happened to you at home? Did they find out? But he couldn't tell by the look of her.

And then she saw him. Her face changed into a singular expression of concentrated pain. "What are you doing here? Go, go away! My mother is coming!"

"I wanted to tell you, I'm sorry about yesterday, and also, my father...they took my father away."

"I can't play with you anymore. Go, Antosha, get lost."

"But why?"

"My mother said you dragged me to the Barren because your father is an enemy of the people and he ordered you to kill me!" Lusya quickly turned around, her voice now a whisper.

"You believe that I...?"

But at that moment her mother appeared on the porch. The woman flicked a startled glance at Anton, jabbered something in abrupt Spanish,then pulled Lusya away. Anton stood motionless, but then he struggled after them, flushed from the strain of trying to walk straighter than he possibly could. He had to rectify the injustice, to kill the lie.

"Come, Lucia," her mother said. "Come. We're getting late." She spoke in Russian, apparently for Anton's ears.

Lusya responded to her mother in Spanish, then freed her hand and stopped for a second, cocking her head.

"Lusya," Anton pleaded, "it's not true about my father. Honest Pioneer Word!"

She continued to look at the boy with a shy, vague smile. "Where is the piece of glass you promised? And the boat?"

"The boat I'll finish tomorrow. And the glass is here." Anton fumbled in his pockets. In one there were pieces of the microscope; in the other, there was nothing but a hole. His heart dropped. He was done for! What a fool he was for letting that hole in his pocket grow till it engulfed everything precious he had, ruining him, destroying his life! He swallowed. "I...I...must have left it at home."

"Oh, I see." Her face took on a dull, indifferent expression. "Figures."

His lips trembled, forming almost no sound. "I'll bring it to you tomorrow. And my father, he's not an enemy of the people. Please don't believe that."

But Lusya had already turned around, catching up with her mother.

Anton froze, nailed to the ground, then waved.

She didn't turn back.

He wandered aimlessly around the courtyard. He had lost the ruby out of his own negligence. And his father...Anton hadn't looked after him well enough. That's why it had happened. Many a time he was ready to exchange him for a more adventurous and glamorous version, so they came and took the meek one away. Clearly, it was all his fault.

Heavy adult despair descended onto the boy. He was doomed: nobody and nothing could help him now. He looked at the sky; it was all aflame, the greyness melted away, replaced with a blissful azure. Bright morning light turned the tiny icicles adorning each tree branch, each cornice, into translucent, scintillating jewels.

And suddenly he remembered. The eyes of Santa Lucia! They alone could save his father! People are useless, but the Magic Eyes had found him the ruby glass once; they'd help him again, they'd find his father! That's what he'd ask for first. *Magic Eyes! I'll look after you! I'll fold you ever so carefully. I won't smear your paint. Tell me where they took my father!*

Anton turned around and ran awkwardly, sagging to one side, toward home. He mumbled on the way something that came to his mind, a prayer, a supplication. He believed he had to ask the Eyes in really, really special way – he had to ask in verse, with all the power of his heart, for the miracle to happen.

Magic eyes of Saint Lucia,
Show me paths, far and near;
In the sky, or on the plain,
Put me on my father's trail.

The door of the apartment was wide open, and two men were dragging Father's desk to the staircase landing. He stole past them to the place where his mother had lived before. But her photo was gone, together with the chest of drawers, her home.

Then he knew it was now his turn. His bed stood alone, exposed. He dashed to it and plunged underneath: there, in the little cache formed by the covering unstuck from the wall at the baseboard, he saw the edge of the paper with the Eyes of Santa Lucia, still intact, still unsmeared. But in the urgency of his desperation, forgetting his hump, he got stuck under the bed and had to lie flat on his belly, unable to reach the Eyes.

"So that's where we're hiding, a drifter!" said the man who looked exactly like one of the guards in Anton's dream. "Comrade Petrov, can you lift the other end of the bed? There is this dwarf hunchback here. Stand up. Stand up straight! What's in your pockets? Get this shit out! If you try to run away, we'll shoot."

For the first time in his life, Anton was setting out on a real orphan voyage. He was going to an orphanage, to this perfect circle where – he knew with all his vast, eight-year-long experience, with the whole length of his crooked, hunched spine – there would be no *secretiky,* no Bear of the North, no boat with rigging made out of cork and leather shavings; no father, no mother, no Lusya, no Leo the Kike, no Uncle Tolya, the master and lord of mice and his empty *edemptions.*

They were taking him into a new home, a circle he had so many times tried and finally succeeded in drawing without any compass.

He fumbled in his pocket. There, instead of Santa Lucia's eyes, was an unfamiliar piece of paper. Under the light flickering into the Black Maria at intersections Anton managed to make out uneven scribbles:

My Beloved Olechka! Please do not send me parcels anymore. I won't need anything here. Take care of our boys. If you meet a good man who can help you raise them, do marry him. I will love you into eternity and will forever remember how

The truck suddenly lurched up to the curb, and Anton dropped the paper. As he bent down to pick it up, someone nudged him out of the Black Maria and onto the street. He would never know what the letter writer would forever remember.

Bird's Milk

These were shiny rivets on the edge of the fibre suitcase. They gleamed under the lamp like lightning bugs about to fly through the irregular spaces between the crocheted snowflakes of the doily that covered the lid. The suitcase belonged to the confined rooms of my childhood as solidly the long massive oak kitchen table, old and warped and hiding a secret under its faded vinyl tablecloth. That secret was the round dent resulting from my grandparents' years of cracking walnuts with a hammer; then carefully separating pieces of shells from the kernel and bitter papery membrane, then giving me some of the edible bits if I happened to be nearby.

With time, the suitcase itself became furniture: first a TV stand, then a night table next to my grandparents' bed sporting an assortment of disparate objects, most of which had nothing to do with sleeping or waking up: a darning mushroom, a sugar-bin, and a china ballerina on one gilded foot.

"When are they coming? We've run out of sugar," said my grandmother, inspecting the empty bowl on top of the suitcase. "You know Liza has a sweet tooth."

"Won't hurt them if they use sliced apples instead, like I do,"replied my grandfather. A severe diabetic, he had no use for sugar and was convinced that his own strange tea drinking ritual would suit everybody just fine.

A prolonged silence would follow, interrupted only by the

sound of a spoon rattling in a glass. My grandfather never drank tea out of cups but preferred a glass in a simple metal holder. Why he needed to stir slices of apple into his tea was a mystery to me; perhaps he liked to watch them whirl in the water, chasing each other. Or perhaps, the chime of the spoon reminded him of the morning tea trays rattling glass on metal, on the long distance trains when he was the chief railways inspector before the war.

The Levins, my grandparent were waiting for, were an elderly couple, always dressed in dark baggy coats. They would remove their galoshes from their felt boots and put them side by side – one pair small, another big – in the hallway, leaving two muddy puddles of melting snow on a threadbare mat. The knock of their knuckles on my grandparents' door was purely symbolic: hardly a sound at all. The Levins sat without ever changing their postures, and no chairs ever cracked under their weightlessness. Auntie Liza, with her prominent Jewish nose and heavy half-closed eyelids, resembled a small tired bird. It was impossible to imagine this woman ever being young or vivacious. Her husband, whom everybody, including his wife, called simply Levin, was tall and emaciated, with a mass of black hair that sharply contrasted with his crumpled face and pale lifeless lips. Levin rarely spoke, but when he did it was always in the same monotone: "Joseph, if your son goes to Minsk to get the papers, I'll wait in Moscow till he returns. You know it's my last chance."

"Where are you going to stay in the meantime?"asked my grandfather, without lifting his eyes from the round dance of apple slices.

"Why do you ask?" grumbled my grandmother. "You know

they have no place to stay." She looked hesitatingly around the room. "Well, maybe,"she said in a quieter tone, "maybe they could stay with us while they wait."

"Oh no, we don't want to inconvenience you," said Aunt Liza, eyes downcast. "We were planning to leave tomorrow for Ryazan. Levin already has six orders from there. I'm sure there'll be more, once we arrive and people hear about us."

"Going without a passport? Ryazan isn't a small place."

"I'm telling Levin, small villages are much better: out of sight, out of mind. But he won't listen to me." Aunt Liza sighed sorrowfully.

"I'll take a risk,"said Levin."It's only three or four days, you see. I'll make a good buck and pay Gromov for the passport."

"I wouldn't count on three days,"said my grandfather, stirring his tea again."It can be a week, two weeks, you never know. As for Vladimir...you know my son. He doesn't always knock at the right door. I wish I could go with you, but, you know, I can't. People might recognize me."

"You?"Levin balked."That's out of the question, Joseph, that's understood. But I don't want to put your son at risk either, not on my account. Though I think it's safe. I was told by people I trust."

"You think so? What if it's a trap?"

"Look," said Levin. "Gromov knows the guy. He's Aaron's relative, completely reliable."

"And where's Aaron?" asked my grandfather, putting his glass aside and settling both hands on the table. "Please tell me." He pointed to the suitcase in the corner. "This has been waiting for him for eight years."

"He'll come back," said Levin calmly. "You'll see. But you should've opened the suitcase and looked inside."

"If he's coming back, why would I open it? It's your brother's. You should take it."

"Where would I put it, Joseph? I have no home. Besides, it was entrusted to you. You should keep it till he returns."

My grandfather bent toward Levin."He isn't coming back. Let's not fool ourselves."

There was silence.

"There's a difference between fooling yourself and having hope," said Levin finally. "Without hope, where would I be now, Joseph?"

Again there was a pause. My grandmother brought out two more glasses in metal sleeves. She put a plain saucer with a small heap of round crackers on the table. Then she poured pale tea into both glasses. Auntie Liza took one cracker, soaked it in her tea, and bit into it with her few remaining front teeth. Levin held the glass without drinking, warming his transparent fingers with its heat. I was afraid to look at his mutilated right hand, with its missing index finger and thumb.

It was only recently that the Levins found each other after twelve years in the labour camps. In 1936, Levin, a biologist and the director of a research institute, had confessed that he was a paid Trotskyite agent, a tool of the American intelligence services assigned to drown the conquests of the socialist revolution in its own blood by growing a deadly virus in his institute's lab. The virus killed 1,470 horses, 3,304 pigs, and 1,900 cows in one district alone. His wife Liza confessed that, as her husband's accomplice, she dreamt up a "smoke tax" and personally collected it from all the peasants who had chimneys in the nearby villages to finance her husband's subversive activities.

Miraculously, they survived the camps, Levin by felling trees in Solovki, 150 kilometres from the Arctic Circle, and Liza in Siberia, half a continent away, near Turukhansk. She turned out to be a fine calligrapher and painter, and instead of building the Salekhard railway road – the Death Road, as women in the camp nicknamed it – she painted murals for the Red Corners, the official rooms outfitted with Lenin's busts and red banners. She also designed *Lightnings*, the Gulag propaganda bulletins.

When they reunited, they beat the odds again – only to discover that the miracle of their reunion was marred: their son Leonid was nowhere to be found.

The day after his parents' arrest, men in civilian clothes took the five-year-old into an orphanage, where both his first and last name were changed. That was, no doubt, a manifestation of justice but also mercy, aimed at removing the shameful stains from the boy's biography by the simple act of severing any links to his parents, the accursed enemies of the people. As Comrade Stalin had pointed out, no son should be held responsible for the crimes of his father.

When all their efforts to find Leonid led to nothing, Auntie Liza gently slipped into another world. She would tilt her bird's head to one side, listening intently to God's divine lisp, which she alone could discern. Aunt Liza never doubted God's benevolent intercession into her family's affairs: it was only a question of time, and of all people, Liza knew everything there was to know about time. She also knew that God, in His infinite mercy, after munching some sounds in His ancient mouth, would dictate to her the initial letter, then the first and second syllables of her child's assumed name, and finally, He would reveal all, first, the patronymic name and then the last name. None of it would be as sweet as the boy's real name: Leonid Lvovich Levin. No, it would be a rough name, in itself a guarantor of its bearer's survival. Something like Boris Petrovich Stepin or Petr Andreevich Drozdov, a name with sharp corners, more palatable to this world.

The moment would always come when Aunt Liza would quietly move her tea glass to the side, get a pencil stub out of her purse, and make some quick notes in her tiny, elegant writing on a scrap of paper buried in her threadbare bag. She anticipated the revelation of the secret with humility, that moment when she'd see the name appear on paper, the right one, and then fill her mouth with its new sounds, savour them, sing them quietly to herself, and finally carry them to the Central Information Bureau in her open palm, so that in a month, at most two or three, her little boy, now grown up, still pale and scraggy but all right, would run out of the piles of stamped and signed papers right into her arms, leaving behind the jumble of metal orphanage beds, lice-infested shaven heads, steel mugs and plates, railway stations guarded with dogs, forlorn locomotive hoots, abandoned construction sites, entangled wire, fallen electrical poles, frozen dirt, and coal piles soiling virgin snow across the indifferent white expanses of her land, joyfully hollering,"Mama, Mamoshka, I'm here! I knew you would find me!"

"Sonia," my grandfather turned to me. "Go out and play. Go."

"Where will the child go? It's late," said my grandmother, closing the curtains and shutting out the night, another silent witness of their private conversations.

"Come, come over here, then," my grandfather motioned. "What's today, Sonia, Monday? Check if the candies in my pocket grew all right. Give me your hand. Right there, see? Now, which one do you want? A Bear in the North or a Golden Rooster?"

"Bird's Milk," I said firmly. "I want Bird's Milk."

"No, that one doesn't grow on Mondays."

"Tuesdays, then?"

"I'm afraid not."

"How about Thursdays?"

"Well...maybe this Friday. We'll check again on Friday."

"Ah, you're cheating!" I shouted in a blitz of an insight, violently shaking my head from side to side."Candies don't grow in pockets. You buy them in the store!"

"Who told you that? Have you ever seen any candies in the store?"

My grandfather was right. Years after the war had ended, there were still no candies or apples to be bought, but as a former secretary of the regional party committee and a war hero, my grandfather was entitled to a special food ration from the party's internal food distribution centre.

"Look," he said."Here's the Bear in the North. Did you see

it yesterday? No. So what happened overnight?"He pointed to his pocket again."It just grew."

I pulled a face at him."I want Bird's Milk."

"But birds don't make milk, didn't you know?"

"If you say candies grow in your pocket, then birds make milk too. And besides, I just had Bird's Milk yesterday. They're the best in the world."

"Where did you get them?" asked Aunt Liza, awakening from her trance. She scooped the scraps of paper into her purse and gazed into my face.

"Tanya," I said innocently.

"Tanya? Who's Tanya?" Aunt Liza's eyes seemed alight. "And where did she get them? Up North, that's what I craved for most: chocolate, candy..."

"Her father brings Bird's Milk from work," I said quietly, looking away.

Years later, I found out that Tanya's father was a prosecutor at Lubyanka. He called Lubyanka "the organs." I felt guilty having tasted Bird's Milk while Aunt Liza hadn't and now wanted it as badly as a little girl.

"Aren't there lots and lots of chocolates and candies, up North, Aunt Liza?" I asked."Don't Bears from the North live there?"

"No, my sweetheart, there were none at all. But what does Bird's Milk taste like? Tell me."

"Like...like...like chocolate waffles."

"Chocolate waffles," Aunt Liza repeated the words and looked away. She turned back to me. "If Tanya ever gives you another one, will you treat me to some?"

"I promise. When I grow up and earn a lot of money, I'll buy you a whole box of Bird's Milk!"

I felt sorry for Aunt Liza. Her eyelids looked so heavy. I wanted to hold them open with my fingers.

"Joseph," said Levin. "Let's open Aaron's suitcase and see what's inside. Maybe there are some papers, or some clothing Vladimir can use if he goes to Minsk."

"Now go and play with your dolls, Sonia," said my grandfather.

"I don't want dolls," I said. "I want to see what's in the suitcase."

Without the doily, the suitcase looked naked, ominous as if a stranger had suddenly appeared in the room. It wasn't new. Cuts and scars traced diagonals across its surface. My grandfather pressed hard on the metal buttons. The two clasps popped up, and the lid fell open. The women held their breath. On the top lay yellowed newspapers with washed-out print in an unfamiliar script. My grandfather took them out, and I could smell tobacco and the faint odour of eau-de-cologne. We all stared at the clothes: canvas tennis shoes; striped, foreign-looking shirts; a belt with a bright gold buckle; turtleneck sweaters the likes of which none of us had ever seen. None of it seemed to interest my grandfather at all. He rummaged. He was looking for papers about the fate of his vanished friend Aaron Levin.

There were none. Instead, from underneath the heap of clothes, a piece of fabric emerged, a print of tiny, shimmering pink and purple flowers in a pale blue meadow. It was a woman's scarf that must have somehow lost its way on the roads of war before finding this unlikely shelter. My grandmother admiringly stroked it, then handed it to Aunt Liza, who examined it against the light and then pressed it to her face with small whimpering sounds.

But the scarf was only a prelude. My grandfather's excavation had unearthed the edge of a photograph at the bottom of the suitcase. I wondered, as we pulled it out, whether the young woman owned the scarf. It was an exotic face, not Russian, framed with thick black curls. The face of a beauty. She wasn't smiling, but her dark eyes were all sparks. Her lips were parted slightly with a hint of mischief, as if she was gazing at a marvel no one else saw.

"I didn't know he had a woman in Spain," said my grandfather, examining the picture.

"Aaron's fiancée," replied Levin. "They met in 1939 in Barcelona, shortly before it fell to the Nationalists. He was going to bring her to Moscow and marry her here."

My grandfather looked at Levin but said nothing. Then, in reverse order, he started putting clothing back in the suitcase: the photograph on the bottom, sweaters, shirts, tennis shoes, and, finally, the newspaper. He locked the suitcase and carried it back to the bed.

"Yes," he said after a pause. "I hope Aaron comes back."

Aaron was born to a Jewish family in Lithuania. Together with his elder brother, Lev Levin, he came to Moscow to help make the revolution. That's where the two brothers met my grandfather, then an aspiring Komsomol leader. The three friends became inseparable. But the revolution was soon over, replaced by the civil war. "All men are brothers! Down with the rotting corpse of the bourgeoisie! Labour will rule the world!" These were exciting times. You could feel the air crackling with euphoria. Aaron was good with horses, and with his sabre in hand, he galloped from the Western to the Eastern fronts, cleansing capitalist filth from the world, protecting the oppressed, summarily executing the enemy, all in the name of Comrade Lenin, the world revolution and the international proletariat. But then the civil war came to an end, leaving in its wake the heroic collectivization, heroic first five-year plan, heroic construction of the first metropolitan in the world, heroic conquest of the arctic, heroic Stakhanovism movement, heroic three months on the ice floe from Pacific to Antarctic without food, heroic Soviet-woman the mother of ten winner of the parachute jumping tournament. Aaron yearned for another revolution.

He found it in Spain's international brigades. When the republic failed, he fled back to Russia, stopping at my grandfather's. He was trying to arrange the papers to get his fiancée across the border. One sunny morning he went to the post office to send her a telegram. Nobody saw him again.

"Now at least we know what's in the suitcase," said Levin. "You keep it, Joseph. Keep it."

"I will," said my grandfather. "But I won't send my son to Minsk, Levin. This is a setup, don't you see? And with my passport? Come on."

"You only have a 'wolf's' passport, that's true. You can't live in Moscow, or in any other city, but at least you're alive."

"Alive!" my grandmother interrupted. "You call this a life? Nobody would even register them! They tried Tver, they tried

Podolsk, they tried every damn pin on the map. No place, nobody would have them!"

"Don't you worry, Anna," said Liza. She seemed to be looking sideways, her gaze avoiding the others. "People are kind. They give us everything we need: food, shelter, a place to keep our equipment. Sometimes money too."

Many years later, I recalled Liza's words. In the 1960s, when nobody sitting around that table in that remote, dimly lit room was alive, I discovered why people had been kind to the Levins. After twelve years in the camps, denied residence and the right to work, the two of them once again found a way to hoodwink fate. For several years after the war, they walked from village to village, magnifying passport-size photographs of the dead. The pattern was always the same: suspicions when they arrived and grateful farewells when they left. In many places after the war, the names of the dead outnumbered the living, and the Levins never lacked for work. Levin learned that it was easier to look into the eyes of the dead on a photograph than into the eyes of their widows and mothers as they opened the door to ask what was it he wanted from them.

Levin proved to be very good at his new trade. The men on the tiny photographs he was given were stern, solemnly closed into themselves, with a generic, vacant expression. But when he enlarged and retouched them, they acquired a benevolent, soft, even mildly romantic look. Under Levin's skillful hands, these vague, slightly out-of-focus faces would come to peace with their destiny. Mounted on the wall or placed on a chest of drawers next to a small cluster of artificial flowers, they finally achieved immortality. At long last, safety was theirs. The Levins were doing so well that they even managed to put away some money, the investment in the elusive dream of their future freedom.

My grandfather was as good as his word. He kept his son from travelling to Minsk. It must have been the old man's sixth sense, his insider's knowledge of the manhunter's lore that saved my father's life. But it didn't save Levin's.

He was arrested again, charged this time with poisoning the wells in a city he'd never visited. He died in a labour camp the year before Stalin's death. What happened to his brother's suitcase? It somehow disappeared from our family orbit. I vaguely remember my grandfather wearing colourful turtlenecks and gaudy short-sleeved shirts that looked strange on this taciturn and sombre man.

After Levin's arrest, Auntie Liza went into hiding. A moving target, she rode the freights, slept in railway station latrines, shipping containers, or abandoned sheds. The blind chance that had destroyed her son and husband at the end let Liza off the hook. When I saw her again in much milder, "vegetarian" times, she was toothless, all skin and bones, her hair gone completely white; more than ever she seemed to belong to the weightless feathered tribe, the only one that could go where it pleased in her homeland.

I visited her in her six-square-metre "corner" in a communal apartment shared by eight families. There was almost no furniture in her room. She sat at the window, looking vacantly into the street. Since her husband's death, she had loads of time on her hands. She wasn't scribbling names on scraps of paper any longer.

God had forsaken this land – she now knew it.

In late May of 1964, Auntie Liza received a summons. As a victim of Stalin's "purges," she was now entitled to her own apartment, a small second-floor studio with a separate kitchenette and a bathroom. Coincidentally, she was supposed to view it on her sixty-fifth birthday. To our surprise, Aunt Liza refused to even look at the new place, never mind move in.

It was then that my brother, Sergey, and I came up with a plan. We bought a big bouquet of flowers, a biscuit cake, a box of marshmallows, and even a bottle of champagne, intending to invite all Liza's neighbours to her birthday party. But first, we wanted to talk her into getting into Sergey's new car for a thirty-minute drive to her new apartment. How exciting! The first housing projects in twenty years since the war! Fresh air, sunshine! Young mothers strolling with their prams!

"The second floor would be perfect, just perfect for you!" I kept saying. "The first is unsafe because of break-ins; the third, too high without an elevator, but the second? It's really the luck of the draw!"

"You'll have your own bathroom too!" my brother chimed in. "When was the last time you had your own tub with running water? Your own kitchen? Never, right?"

Aunt Liza raised her eyes to Sergey but said nothing. I started setting the table for the guests, who would be there when we returned.

Then I opened a box of chocolate and handed it over to Aunt Liza. "Have some," I said. "Before we go."

She was hesitant and looked away.

"Please take some," I repeated.

Aunt Liza looked at me, and her face suddenly brightened up.

"Do you remember?" she said. Her fingers took tentative aim at one accordion-pleated pink rosette. "Right after the war, you were eight or nine then, and you promised when you grew up to buy me a whole box of Bird's Milk."

"Come on, let's go, Aunt Liza," said my brother impatiently. "We'll take the marshmallows with us. You can eat as much as you want on the way there."

The new apartment smelled of paint and thinner. Newspapers were scattered on the floor, which was bordered by piles of plaster in the corners. We propped Aunt Liza on a stool, the only chair left by the construction workers in the middle of an empty room. In the kitchen, the pipes under the sink were sloppily connected. Water dripped onto the floor. While Sergey was looking for a bucket, I looked out the kitchen window. Construction debris littered the landscape, competing with tree stumps and mud puddles dotting the bare earth. But one bush of white lilac survived, overlooked by the bulldozers. It stood alone, intact, tall and in full bloom.

I yanked on the window: I needed some fresh air and I wanted to let the scent of lilac into the flat. "Aunt Liza! Look what I found!" I wanted her to see the bush and yanked on the window again. But it was painted shut. Sergey found a knife, poked here and there.

Just when the window seemed to yield, we heard a thud and a weak cry. In the living room, Aunt Liza lay on the floor next to the stool. Her hands clutched her chest, and she gasped in whistling gulps. There was no phone in the apartment. Sergey ran outside to look for a public phone. I sat on the floor next to Aunt Liza, helplessly watching her jerk her head from side to side. Beneath her face, beads of sweat collected on the floor. She was still alive when they carried her through the narrow door, twisting the stretcher awkwardly.

It was in the ambulance that God, who Liza believed had abandoned her forever, finally returned to her side, gently took her by the hand, and led her into the golden glow of spring. She floated free on the fragrance of lilacs above her longed-for city; over the young girls in school-uniform skirts playing hopscotch on the asphalt; over crowds still in winter coats queuing up for food in long, dark, zigzagging lines; over the street cars cutting quick arpeggios on their celestial cords, smudging every turn with sheaves of fire. By the time the ambulance stopped in front of the Corinthian columns of the Central Hospital, Aunt Liza had already joined her husband and son. She joined them in that radiant, shimmering land that alone had given her a shelter and a permanent home, a land of honey and Bird's Milk, and a land she would never need to escape.

Angel

1

I came here two years ago, shortly after my father's death. More than anytime before, I felt at loose ends in spite of the large inheritance I so suddenly came into. Turning into a rich man in the blink of an eye may present certain difficulties for someone who's been a "dishevelled loser," as my father habitually called me from the age of five, referring, no doubt, both to my frazzled hair, not a strand of which I possess now, and my inability to put to any good use the strange talents that I somehow managed to tease out of my indifferent and negligent fate. I think it was this little bouquet of quirks lurking in the fissures of my brain and disguising themselves as the early signs of *wunderkinderism* that prevented me later in life from mastering any worthwhile profession.

The ability to multiply five-digit numbers in my head is one example of my arcane and totally feckless gifts. It used to be a sure bait for the girls I fancied, if only for a few dashing moments of initial acquaintance, when – pencil in hand – they'd quickly sketch a neat equation on a scrap of paper, verify the results, and then turn their sharp-chinned, sun-lit faces toward me in complete disbelief. "I can also do roots. Give me any number." Puzzled, they'd walk around me, a curiosity under museum glass, pause for a moment, and then flit off like sated birds from a feeder to join their rope-skipping flock in the schoolyard.

My other gift was my photographic memory. I could keep

intact page after page of books I had read years earlier. As a teenager, I stammered, but my most ingenious classmates laid siege to this predicament, teasing the string of battle dates and names of the generals out of me at the exams they forced me to write for them. For a while, my lopsided usefulness did keep at bay their desire to punch me the moment my round form got into their field of vision.

Only by fluke, at the age of thirty, did I finally stumble on something that could bring me a semblance of an income: It turned out I could make up elaborate stories and fables at the drop of a hat. At one point, I secretly fancied myself a writer, even a poet, though I couldn't show a single written page for my whimsy. But people in the streets didn't care about my misapprehensions when I'd appear on a busy corner, cap for coins on the sidewalk, and, strumming three strings on a banjo, follow the meandering paths of my imagination. "One word, ladies and gentlemen, give me one word," I nudged the onlookers, for it was all I needed to start spreading the magic carpet of my fantasies under the busy and indifferent feet of the city. I preferred concrete words over abstract ones and women over men, because women were a much more generous and empathetic audience for a lost soul like me. I liked women's bodies and the way they moved; I liked their twitter, their quick shift of subjects, their wide-eyed compassion toward the hurting ones, and the girlish playfulness that illuminated with sudden innocence even the oldest and the most lived-in faces of their tribe.

Unfortunately, women didn't pay me back in the same

coin. Was it my natural shyness or my appearance that deterred them? Yes, I am a short and rather heavily built man with bulging eyes positioned wide apart on a head too massive for my smallish body. In spite of that, women always told me I had some charm, if only because they sensed I was ready to serve them. And – oh, my pathetic self-pity! – how many men with far less pleasing exteriors had I watched becoming happy husbands and fathers! I, on the other hand, was destined to live and die alone.

It was this final realization that elevated my fears of death to a degree of paranoia. I've heard that people who haven't used up the full measure of their lives have a hard time dying. Remorse must make the physical pain of passing into the Neverland unbearable. That's when it dawned on me that I, for one, hadn't even started living, asI couldn't, in full honesty, count as life the tediousness and the boredom of days that had filled up the almost sixty years of my existence. In a nutshell, I suddenly became afraid of the pain of dying! "There must be some way out of this fear," I said to myself during the long sleepless nights I was by then quite accustomed to. And I began to hope, in a very childish manner, that the love of one woman, which I'd never experienced yet, could deliver me from the fears of the final passing. Oh, the dreams of an old decrepit man! "Get back to reality," my father had been hammering into my head all his life, and then, finally, his call reached my ears in the form of a huge inheritance that I reluctantly, against all my instincts, had to deal with.

2

This shift in my life was as unexpected as it was immediate: suddenly, a man in whose existence nobody had shown the slightest interest became the longed-for target of an invisible, smiling, finger-crooking crowd.

I began to receive invitations for dinners, gala concerts, and charity events. I had never owned a suit or tie, so I had to rent a tuxedo with a satin vest and a black bow tie to show up at the functions organized by my father's retinue. The phone barked at me from the corner of my half-empty apartment, becoming my new worst enemy. Needless to say, I never considered getting a cell. The sight of sealed envelopes oppressed me. Like Satie, the composer, I was afraid to open my mail.

It was at that point that I decided to drop everything, and guided by mere chance rather than choice, I came here to Zipolite, a small Mexican village tucked away on the Pacific Coast. I was looking for some meaningful way of getting rid of my money, if that makes any sense, which...well, it did then to me: an orphanage, a hospital for sick children, or a school for the handicapped lurked in my imagination as a summary rescuing plan of sorts.

Zipolite consisted of only one street lined with dilapidated bungalows and stalls roofed with palm leaves where Indigenous people from the hills laid out their trinkets. This humble yet nonchalant life strangely suited my mood. As the daytime heat receded, the local beauties came strolling along the main drag mixing with stray dogs and barefoot toddlers; a fat American with a shiny skull, owner of two local hotels, watched the crowd out of his hammock on the balcony of his El Paraiso. At night, in the backyards, villagers burned their *basura*. Plastic bags, containers, and leftovers morphed into black pillars of stench that crawled over the beach, reaching out into the ocean. Old tires provided an atavistic entertainment for the local youth who burned them every night in bonfires dotting the beach line. Till dawn, the air was unbreathable, and I was coughing away through the nights, struggling with insomnia. Days were no better: sinking into a sweaty drowsiness, I asked myself why on Earth I came to this forsaken village.

One late afternoon, unusual noises outside jerked me out of my slumber. I went downstairs, past the hammocks bulging with sun tanning vacationers, past the vendors, to the ocean front. Part of the beach was sealed off with a red ribbon that stopped the agitated crowd. I couldn't understand what excited these people: my eyes could see nothing but the expanse of the ocean beyond the ribbon. A man in a white shirt shouted in Spanish into a loudspeaker. I noticed that everybody in the crowd was holding something in their outstretched hands. I went closer.

And then I saw her. She was on her haunches, on the other side of the ribbon separating the crowd from the smooth, hard sand of the surf. While the agitated, forward-pressing mass was facing the empty ocean, she alone was facing the crowd; there was movement all around her; she alone was still, except for her hair – a magnificent jet-black waterfall cascading all the way down to her thighs. With a strong thrust from the breeze, her hair suddenly transformed into a wild bird, then took off from her shoulders, spread its wings, soared, and landed again on her back; for the first time then I saw her face. It revealed an austere and proud beauty: the chiselled cheekbones, the perfect arch of her eyebrows, the aquiline nose gave her both an air of arrogance and a fragile aloofness. There was grace in her stillness, but also loneliness.

I thought, Only the daughter of an ancient Aztec priest could look like this. But there must have been mixed blood – the blood of Spaniards, Moors, and Jews – running in the veins of her ancestors as well. She was young, not more than thirty. She was watching the crowd through a camera she had improvised out of her index finger and a thumb.

"*Buenas tardes,*"I greeted her, and squatted trying to get inside her finger-framed world.

She scrutinized me silently through her camera. I smiled and mimicked her gesture with my fingers. She put her hand down.

"I don't really speak Spanish," I continued. "*Buenas tardes* and *adiós* are about the only words I know. Do you speak English, by any chance?"

"I certainly do, but you're in my way," she answered with a splendid confidence and got up to her feet. As she was rising, I noticed a small diamond pendulum nestling between her half-bare breasts. On fire from the setting sun, it caught my eye with sharp multicoloured sparks. Her wraparound skirt tightly hugged her narrow hips, concealing her legs but leaving her flat belly exposed.

With her elongated El Greco limbs and neck, she stood considerably taller than me.

"You speak with a British accent," I said. "Where did you

learn your English?"

She brushed her long hair aside and paused, examining me. "Studied at the London Institute of Art for five years," she dropped nonchalantly.

"You're an artist, then?"

She kept looking at me without saying a word.

I realized it was the expression of her strangely still, almond-shaped eyes that more than anything else gave her that air of aloofness. She looked at me through a thicket of dark lashes without squinting. If the ocean was capable of gazing at humans from its mysterious depths, it would be gazing out of these eyes. What softened the air of severity about her, though, was her skin and her mouth: The skin had an olive tinge, magically warm in the setting sun. Her mouth was moving, as if she were savouring the sight not with her eyes but with her sensual, bow-like lips.

Nodding to the crowd, I asked my new acquaintance what was going on.

"Releasing baby turtles into the ocean. They do it every year, at the sunset."

"Where do they get so many?"

"Hatch them in the village," she said indifferently.

"La causa noble de la liberación de las tortugas permite a los miembros orgullosos de la comunidad," barked a man through megaphone.

"What are they saying?"

She suddenly broke into laughter. "The noble cause of liberating the turtles will allow all the members of the community to go to hell, or something like that!" She flicked her massive curls back, still laughing. "Is it your first time in Mexico?"

"It is." For a second, I felt embarrassed at being a stranger in her country.

"Mexicans are like children. They like entertainment and will pay to be told how great they are. Out of two hundred turtles, one might survive."

"Do you know why they release these creatures at sunset?" I asked.

"No clue. I don't care much about turtles. I came to watch people."

"You must be a photographer, then? Although I've never seen anybody taking pictures with a camera like yours."

I smiled, but she didn't take me up on it.

"I'm a painter, not a photographer," she said seriously.

"Well, isn't it close?"

"Opposite mediums."

She was abrupt, and I didn't know how to keep up the conversation.

As soon as the sun sank into the ocean, the man in the white shirt cut the ribbon, and people rushed toward the water, their tiny charges in their palms. They placed the baby turtles on the wet sand bared by a receding wave. The tiny creatures froze stiff, shocked by their first contact with the elements. Finally, a wave washed some of them off into the ocean, but others, still paralyzed, had to be carried into the water. My eyes followed their first helpless movements: it seemed inconceivable that these tiny clots of life would survive their first night in the cold abyss.

The girl turned around and started walking away along the water's edge. The incoming wave licked the hem of her dress, and she raised her skirt over her knees. Her legs were perfectly shaped. I found myself following her.

"By the way, I'm Joseph Parson, from Canada. What's your name?"

"Angel." She dropped the word without turning her head. I caught up with her and tried to keep one step ahead, not wanting to lose the advantage.

"Angela?" I asked, not sure I heard it right, "That's a lovely name!"

"Angel," she said brusquely . "That's what my mother called me at birth. Nothing special."

"Well...maybe. But the owner of the name is very special. She's a very attractive and intelligent woman." I knew how awkward my compliments sounded and got embarrassed, becoming aware of my unprepossessing appearance, of my uncovered bald pate. (I'd forgotten my hat in the hotel.) I touched my chin: a three-day stubble only increased my shyness.

Angel stopped walking and looked straight into my face: "So you like me?"

"Very much so," I said with a raspy voice breaking with excitement.

"Call me Angela, then."

"Would you care to have a drink somewhere along the beach, Angela?"

"Sure," she said simply, as if expecting to be invited.

3

It was getting dark quickly, and the stars were already out. I looked up, but I couldn't recognize the familiar constellations. They seemed to be at the wrong angle. The moon, like an overturned beetle, was lying belly up. The tables of a restaurant and bar were placed near the water, their feet sinking in the sand. We took the one nearest to the tideline. A dark-skinned, Indigenous-looking waiter brought the menu, set down some glasses, and stabilized the shaky table. Then he put his arm around Angel and kissed her on each cheek the way Mexicans greet each other. I opened the menu, counting on Angel's help.

"Oh, Angela, sweetheart! Where have you been? We were looking for you everywhere!" said a voice from a table next to ours. The three or four men sitting there seemed pretty loaded. One of them made an attempt, with some theatrical flourish, to move from his table to ours, but he couldn't disengage his dangling Frankenstein frame from the chair, which was sinking deeper into the sand the more he struggled. His two pals were egging him on.

"C'mon, one more time, just lift your ass!"

"Stay put, Bob, don't you dare move!" shouted Angel in English, waving a "no" to the man. "Francisco." she turned to the waiter."Go, talk to him."

"*De acuerdo*,"said Francisco, parting his gelled hair with a quick movement of both hands.

I turned to Angel. "Everybody seems to know you here."

"Sure. I come here every summer. See the white house on the

bluff? That's my studio."

Angel pointed toward the ocean, across the bay, but I couldn't see anything in the darkness.

"By the way, these three are also from Canada. They sleep by day, crawl out of their burrows at night and get drunk like pigs."

"How do you know them?"

"The tall one, Bob, was my model."

"He looks like a complete waste. Is he always loaded like that?"

"He is a picturesque type, that's all I want. Look at his head, his wide, heavy jaw. Look how his face narrows toward his forehead, a rare bone arrangement. He told me he is a *mestizo,* half-Indigenous, half-Norwegian."

"We call them Métis. First Nations people mixed with Whites."

"That's like our descendants of Spanish and Indian then. He's fighting for the rights of his people, he said, and he's obsessed with diamonds. He even gave me one. "She touched the pendulum on her neck.

"That's a generous gift!" I grinned.

"He got his portrait in exchange, didn't he? He had nothing to pay with, and I'm expensive."

"Where is he from, you said?" I was a little baffled by all this.

"Somewhere from the North, some kind of a knife." Angel shook her hand in the air.

"Yellowknife," I said. "It's true, they did find lots of diamonds there recently. The Métis consider the land theirs and want some share in it together with the Dene; there's a dispute, you see. But the Dene don't recognize the Métis. They are not Indigenous enough for them, and for the Whites, they aren't really Whites. The Métis are falling between the cracks, neither here nor there."

Angel didn't respond focusing on the candle between us, the reflected light of which danced in her squinting eyes. A stray dog came up and rubbed against her chair. The scruffy creature was hunting by itself for leftovers on the beach. Angel made an abrupt movement to scare it off, then got up as if ready to leave. I could see she'd lost interest in me.

"So you're a painter," I said eager for her to stay. "I know there's a rich art tradition in Mexico. What style do you work in?"

She gave me a quick contemptuous look.

"I'm sorry. I don't know much about painting. I mean, is it abstractionism or surrealism, or perhaps – "

But Angel interrupted me. "I paint lungs and vaginas," she said calmly.

"I beg your pardon?"

"Not human lungs, though. The vaginas are human all right, but the lungs are from sheep. I take sheep lungs, I dry them out. You know what they look like when dry?" She was now truly animated. "Like small white balloons, sausage-shaped And then I attach them to the painted surfaces. I have one piece in the Museum of Contemporary Art in Mexico City. You've been there? Perhaps you noticed the painted blue sky with clouds over the entrance arch. They look like painted clouds, but in fact, it's sheep lungs."

I didn't know how to react, so I nodded and smiled, just in case.

The waiter brought the sangria I'd ordered for Angel. He'd

obviously heard our conversation.

"She is famous, sir," he said in his heavily accented English. "Everybody knows her here and even in Mexico City."

"Oh, shut up, Paco!" Angel snapped.

"Poco tímida, poco dispuesta. Is true, what I say. You go big museum, she is there, like Rivera." Francisco patted Angel on the shoulder.

"Hey, buddy!" shouted Bob. "Get your hands off her and bring us another round!"

Then he made yet another attempt to disengage himself from the chair.

Angel said something to the waiter in Spanish, and he went over to the table where Bob sat with his half-drunk pals.

"If you wish to see my work, you can come to my studio," Angel said casually.

Later, alone in my hotel room, I couldn't stop thinking about her, the way she tossed her hair, the way her long slim arms danced as she talked. She had this habit of turning her head away in the middle of the conversation as if gazing at something only she could see. But her eyes remained strangely still, both searching for something yet indifferent to what they found. Her eyes watched you, but kept hidden what they observed.

4

Angel's cottage was perched on top of the bluff overlooking the ocean, and I had to climb up the winding stairs cut into the solid rock to reach abundant bougainvillea camouflaging the entrance to her studio. The door was ajar when I stepped into an unusual space of movable partitions, positioned at different angles to each other.

Between them the fresh breeze from the ocean wandered freely. The partitions looked like sails and were perfect for exhibiting art. One wall of the studio was all glass, and through it, down below, I could see waves beating against the rocks, and above them, the horizon. I felt I was drifting through shimmering azure that was both the ocean and the sky.

At first, I didn't recognize Angel, her hair tied up in a bun at the back, exposing her long neck. But her dry, businesslike manner contrasted with her attire: when she stood against the light, her diaphanous Turkish *chalivari* exposed her legs to the thighs. She was wearing the same diamond pendulum as when I met her on the beach.

"Have a look at my work," she said, pointing to some elaborate frames leaning against the wall. "This was commissioned by the Museum of Modern Art in Mexico City. I need to make three more pieces."

I looked for paintings inside the frames, but found none. Instead, there were fabrics of different textures and colours, mostly in red hues, from scarlet velvet to pink silk. The material was collected in folds to form an ovoid shape in the centre of each frame. "*Retratos de familia,*" said the sign.

"Do you like it?"

I removed my sunglasses in order to see better, but they slipped out of my fingers. As I bent down to pick them up, blood rushed to my head, and I had to sit on my haunches for a minute, waiting for the fiery circles behind my eyelids to stop their clockwork prance. Angel silently watched me.

"Oh, yes, they're quite unusual," I finally said, getting up and catching my breath.

"Do you like them, though? Well, you don't have to. Come, what do you think of those?" She moved over to three identical objects perched on high stools. They looked like leather purses with metal buckles."Just look inside them." I opened one purse and instinctively shut it back. I'd just glanced inside the female genitalia meticulously reproduced in pink leather.

"I came up with this idea, and somehow, it caught on." Angel chuckled."I have a rich client who wants ten of those. I can't fathom what for."

I imagined this woman spending her days readjusting the wrinkles, adding a little bit here, taking away there. Embarrassed, I looked sideways, and my gaze fell on small statuettes on a low shelf in the corner. One of them was a Mexican god with the face of a jaguar and an elaborate headdress. Painted blood was dripping from both sides of his mouth. The other figure was a sitting man, one part of him flesh, the other skeleton.

"These are replicas," explained Angel. "The originals are in the Anthropological Museum in Mexico City."

"I hadn't realized before I went to that museum," I said, "to what degree the whole culture was based on premeditated slaughter. When I first saw all this art collected in one place, I was truly repulsed."

"Magnificent artisans, though," said Angel, turning the skeleton-man in her hands. "Yes, it is morbid, I agree. But life is morbid – it contains death. They didn't deny the reality, that's all. Aren't we all walking skeletons, after all? Just waiting for the external layer of the deception to fall off?" She produced her whimsical smile.

"I spent two days in this museum, and I now have a hard time blaming Cortez for his cruelty. There was a statuette of a man wearing human skin on top of his own. Then these games...I didn't realize that even their games were a ritualized murder. *Palata* or *peleta,* I'm not sure."

"*Pelota.*"

"All right, *pelota.* But you know what I'm talking about, don't you? If, by mistake, the ball ended up flying counter the sun's movement, the whole team would lose their heads. Then they would pile those heads on the central city square. Imagine Aztec children passing by decomposing heads every day."

"Death can be beautiful," said Angel, and she smiled again.

"Yes, but every time I'll find myself in the *zócalo* now, I'm going to think of those heads. See, I respect the culture, the tradition. I know these were their beliefs, but the scope of it we simply fail to – "

We were interrupted by a knock at the door. Francisco stood on the porch, staring at me. Obviously, he hadn't expected to see me.

"Sorry, sir," he said.

"I'm busy now, Paco," Angel said, and I could feel her irritation. "We're working, Joseph and I. He is going to sit for my portrait. You can come and clean up later. By the way, did you get me some solvent?"

Francisco took a bottle out of his pocket and placed it on the table.

"That's good. Thank you. So around four or five, then, not before."

"*Entiendo*," responded Francisco, softly closing the door behind him.

5

"I didn't realize, you wanted to paint my portrait," I said to Angel.

"Of course, I do. I'm always looking for new models. You can only do so many vaginas. Usually people don't say 'no' to me. Everybody wants to have their image immortalized, but the problem is I don't want to paint just anybody. I will only charge you half price. After my death, your portrait will be worth a fortune. You'll make money on me if you ever decide to sell it."

I was taken aback by her intention to sell me something I didn't ask to buy. But even more bizarre was the casual way she mentioned her own death, as if she were talking about a complete stranger. More than that, she seemed to be sure that this stranger was going to die before me. Perhaps anticipating death was as much part of her culture as ignoring it was part of mine.

"You have an interesting face. Quite asymmetrical. I like that. Can you sit for the next twenty minutes without moving at all?"

She positioned me in a chair, then stepped back to her easel, gazing at me intently.

"Tilt your head a little forward, please. That's too much. No, just the way it was before."

"I don't remember how it was before."

She walked over to me, took my head in both her hands, and angled it slightly forward, then stepped back to her easel.

"Now you've lifted it again."

"Did I? Should it be like this?"

"No. That's still too much. Don't bring your head so far back. Gives you an air of arrogance. Which is not in your nature."

I was bemused by her perceptiveness. It was only the second time she'd seen me.

"Sit naturally. Relax. And now take off your shirt."

I didn't move. Had I misunderstood her?

"Undress. Down to your waist." It was an order, not a request.

"I thought you were going to paint my portrait; mostly, my face."

She didn't respond and continued to paint.

When I awkwardly pulled my shirt up, her eyes glided over me, taking me all in. It was a quick evaluating look, both intense and indifferent at the same time. I was no more than an object in space, a form that reflected and absorbed light in a certain manner. Sweat rolled down my armpits. I became painfully aware of dark flabby patches of skin under my armpits; of my grey bushy breasts softened and enlarged by age. I was embarrassed and hunched instinctively, hiding my chest, but then there were my hands: old, knotty, and dark against my pale protruded belly. Time has plowed and plundered my body, and I couldn't hide its debris from the young woman so mercilessly and coldly scrutinizing it.

My forehead was soaking wet with sweaty tension. Angel
noticed it and handed me a piece of white cloth. Then, with a quick
automatic movement, as if unaware of what she was doing, she pulled
up her own blouse.

Taken by surprise, I made an involuntary sound.

Her breasts were perfectly shaped, though unexpectedly heavy
for her slender body. They were lighter olive than the rest of her skin.
But her nipples were dark, with large dark areolas. I forced myself to
look away. Angel, on the contrary, showed no sign of discomfort, as if
stripping in front of a stranger was an ordinary thing.

"Don't move," she said. "I need you to look outside yourself,
not inside. Focus on something that interests you. That's why I've
undressed."

She started painting again, moving from easel to palette,
adding some brush strokes and then stepping away from the canvas. I
couldn't but follow each of her movements: the way her breasts sagged
forward as she bent over and then lifted up as she reached for the upper
corner of the canvas, swaying as she turned.

6

The sight of her nakedness transported me to a hot and humid
afternoon of my childhood, half a century ago, my mother, still
young, firmly clasping my steaming hand as she pushed her way
through a crowd of mostly Black and Latino women surrounding
tables heaped with discount clothes in the basement of a second-hand

store in Toronto. I must have been nine or ten, and I remembered women's torsos brushing against my cheek, the sickening, foetid smell of unwashed flesh. And then – the crackling of static. I was almost blinded, both repulsed and drawn to what I saw: folds of flesh brimming over and under brassieres as women quickly removed their tops in front of my eyes, pulling over their half-naked bodies sweaters and blouses they'd snatched from the tables. I panicked and tried to run away, but my mother held firmly to my hand, afraid to lose me in the crowd. And then I saw a young mulatto girl, not older than myself, with the long angular body of a boy. She also took off her top, but to my surprise, there was nothing under it except for two round, well-formed spheres, lighter in colour than the rest of her body, two alert dark-eyed creatures living a separate life on her small frame. I stared at the girl, transfixed. I was overpowered by a strange sensation: it was the first awakening of desire, but mostly, it was a deep longing for something elusive that I knew even then, as I still knew in Angel's studio, would always be out of my reach.

"Talk to me," said Angel. "It helps my work."

"What do you want to talk about?" I cleared up my throat trying to regain my normal voice.

"You. When people talk about themselves, they're never bored or tired. They come to life, and that's exactly what I want in a portrait. Where are you from?"

"I was born in Toronto, but then we moved to Winnipeg." She didn't react. I was sure she'd never heard of the place.

"Are you a businessman?"

"Why? Do I look like one?"

"You can never tell with foreigners. Some of them look like beggars on the beach, but then you find out they're famous poets."

"If I tell you I'm a poet, will you make me look handsome?"

"You are handsome. Very much so."

I found it hard to believe her. Her measuring eyes moved from me to the canvas and back in rapid succession. She wasn't really interested in me – again I became acutely aware of that – other than as a pictorial object.

"Well, I'm not a businessman, but my father was. He owned a factory in China. Made a fortune manufacturing plastic bags."

I don't know why I told her about my father. Did I intuitively sense that some genetic connection with money and success would make me more attractive in her eyes?

"Boring, no?"

"What's boring?"

"Manufacturing bags."

"Not if it brings you lots of money!"

"You sound like an American."

She came up to me, touched my shoulders, and tilted my head. Her naked breasts lightly brushed against my forearm. I lost my train of thought."Have you ever been to China?" she asked."I've always wanted to go."

"Oh, a long time ago. I was twenty then. My father hoped I would enter the family business and decided I had to see his factory. I met with his employees, Chinese girls, over a hundred of them, aged sixteen to twenty-five. They lived in a dorm, seven girls per room. My father didn't want them to commute to work."

"Your father was an exploiter, then?"

"No, he paid his workers well. Twenty-five percent more than anywhere else in China. He was a good man, but I still didn't want to become a businessman."

She put her brushes down and began to smudge paint on the canvas with her finger. "Money makes life easier," she said. "Lots of money, I mean."

"I've never been rich myself. But when my father died, things changed…" I was getting uncomfortable with the subject. "Well, now it's your turn to tell me about you."

"What is it you want to know?" Angel held up the stem of a brush against her outstretched hand, measuring the proportions of my body; then she moved it to the canvas, comparing.

"Your friend, the waiter, said you're already a well-known artist. Yet you're so young."

"Who said that? Francisco? It's true, he admires me. But he knows nothing about art. He is a handyman; makes frames for my pictures. Very good with his hands, but he believes I'll go straight to hell for my pussy bags!"

Laughter overcame her, and she put her brush down.

"Oh, look what I did to myself!" She cupped her left breast into her hands and tried to remove the yellowish stain from around the nipple with her finger. The stain smudged. She came up to me, still holding her breast absently in her hand. I felt intimidated.

"Can you lift your head again? Don't tilt it. Just keep it steady. That's it. And stop worrying about your hands. I'm not working on them right now."

I held my breath, I was so tense. But she stepped back, releasing the yellow-daubed breast just as absently, and I felt somewhat relieved.

"It's true, I lucked out. Had several exhibitions in London as a student, and after that I got a green light at home. They love it when the foreign press talks about you."

"Your parents must have given you a good jump-start in life," I said.

"My parents?" She smirked and rubbed something on her canvas with a piece of cloth. "My father I didn't know. I was two when he left. My mother has remarried and mostly lives in Paris with her new husband and children."

Angel fell silent. She glanced at me at rarer intervals now, absorbed more with her creation than with the original. Finally, she declared the session over, turned the picture so it was facing the wall – without letting me look at it, as it wasn't finished yet – and cleaned her hands with the solvent. I couldn't tell if she was happy with her work or not.

I felt tired. I hadn't realized how difficult it was to sit without motion. All the time I was aware of her nakedness and my own decaying flesh, and that made me even more tense. I closed my eyes for a moment, but I was startled out of my torpor by a light touch on my cheek. I opened my eyes – Angel quickly and lithely sat on my lap. The weight of her body and the coolness of her stroking fingers on my face were so unexpected that I felt limp, almost paralyzed, but she pressed her naked breast against my cheek and forced her nipple into my mouth.

"Lick that stain off, would you?" she whispered, rising, drawing me with her, manoeuvring me to the sofa.

I finally gave myself up to her body. She exhausted me in what somehow seemed a vengeful yet delightful delirium, and then I lay there, listening to the waves lapping the rocks down there, below her house. I listened to the shrieks of the albatrosses; to the subdued shouts of dark-skinned boys selling coconuts; and then my mind moved further away, drifting over her ancient and arid land that lay in wait around us with its enigmatic pyramids and the dead cities, long abandoned by priests and gods, who had sated themselves on human blood; and somehow Angel herself was this ancient land strewn with cacti; she was the orange flames of the sunset and the endless sky. She was a high priest ready for the sacrifice, and the innocent girl being sacrificed. The blood of both, the executioner and the victim, ran in her veins.

I looked at her, curled in the crook of my arm, which had started to go to sleep under the weight of her head, and was struck by her innocent look. Her cheeks were flushed, mouth slightly open, and all the predatory vigour, all the insatiability that had stormed inside her only minutes ago was gone. The arrogance and the aloofness that she had put between herself and the world disappeared. Here was a young woman, almost a girl, in her most natural and beautiful state. Never before did I feel such rapture and yet such tenderness for any human being. Her clean forehead was like a prism that collected in its focus all my love, all my tenderness, all my old longings. She was everything I had never had: my lover, my daughter, my sister, my wife. The more I looked at her, in that deep repose, the less I could imagine having made love to her, having actually penetrated her seemed so crude now compared to the feelings brimming over my soul, feelings for which I had no name.

I had no doubt that Fate had entrusted Angel to my care. The world was a sleepwalker wandering around with eyes half-closed, and now I had to protect her against this world. I imagined myself to be her self-appointed knight in whose presence, finally, perhaps for the first time in her life, she would be able to remove her mask and breathe freely.

My daydreaming was disrupted by a sudden noise. In our bliss, we had completely forgotten about Francisco, who had half-opened the unlocked front door. Angel grabbed a sheet from the bed, wrapped herself up, and went to meet him. I waited and then, a little shaky on my legs, carried my overpouring heart down the winding stairs into a freshly painted, festive, and ever-so-gentle world.

7

What were the days that followed that magic afternoon like? I can't quite tell you. Patches of morning light drifted from the water to the palm trees to Angel's hair when she was combing it after a swim; the unhurried movement of her hand; the ocean and the breeze; the sand, hot at noon, slowly cooling after the sunset; the distillation of my perfect happiness, my bliss – that's all I remember. The nights fell on us suddenly, and the granular light of the stars, as if seen for the first time, filled me with fresh awe. They were my witnesses, and I thought that my love for Angel was as uncanny as the light of these stars, created for us and us alone.

Sometimes, returning to my hotel from the cottage of High Sails (that's what I came to call her little studio on the bluff), I asked myself whether I was daydreaming or simply losing my wits. How could a young, exquisitely beautiful and talented woman fall for an utterly banal old man like myself? But the moment she put her lovely arm around me or looked at me, all my doubts would evaporate, and I, covering the velvety inside of her arm with kisses all the way up to a slightly wet, acidy armpit, would be instantly thrown into euphoria and feel that somehow I deserved her love, deserved that happiness.

I wanted to be with her all the time, but felt a teenaged shyness in her presence. I was afraid to touch her, but she always took the initiative, relieving me of my fears. She made love to me passionately, with abandon – and that gave me confidence I never experienced before. I was wanted, even desired, in spite of my age and unassuming appearance. All of it was new to me, and I gradually began to see myself in a different light. To think of it, I wasn't that old. And weren't the wrinkles, after all, the external expression of accumulated wisdom? No wonder many women found older men attractive. As for the folds of skin hanging from under my chin, when I looked at myself in profile, in dim bathroom light, I could easily see the resemblance to some noble aging Roman senator, if not Julius Caesar himself. There were also delightful moments of what she called "domestic coziness." And they, more than intense passion, convinced me of her affection for me. I could see that she, too, needed me, perhaps even loved me.

My utter inability to draw amused her. Sitting next to me, she loved to guide my fingers, awkwardly squeezing the pencil, over the paper. I laughed in disbelief when all of a sudden, out of nothing, emerged a cat climbing a tree, a hunchbacked woman sitting sideways on a chair, a Mexican boy carving something with a knife. She started teaching me Spanish with a patience that I didn't expect. When I asked her once why my knowing her language was important to her, she said that it would make her feel closer to me. I was enthralled. I repeated the sounds of her tongue that I grew to love as mantra, as token of our union.

Every morning, I continued to sit for my portrait; then we would have a light snack and go down to the beach with two big towels and a basket of fruit. One day, I was sporting white linen pants and a loose, colourfully embroidered shirt that she bought me from the local artisans; she had a yellow, wide-skirted sundress and a straw hat with a wide brim that suited her dark complexion so well.

Having grown up inland, I didn't understand the ocean, but my Angel was an excellent and fearless swimmer. Nevertheless, every time her dark head disappeared in the surging green precipices, my heart sank. I felt it was I at the mercy of the waves, for she now became part of me.

"Ask the ocean to throw you the key and then enter," she shouted between her dives, playing with the waves and my fear.

The breakers were high, and I stood there helpless, watching her. She taught me to count waves: while the tallest, the seventh wave, was amassing its strength and then smashing into the beach, I had to run into the ocean as fast as I could, then swim out.

"That's the only way the ocean will let you in," she shouted, "on the seventh wave."

Often, we were the only ones who ventured into the stormy surf, the locals sitting on the beach watching us. What a joy it was after the frantic paddling to finally reach calmer waters beyond the raging surf, turn around and watch the ocean thrust, with its flagellating power, onto the beach. I would try to keep up with Angel's quick crawl and hug her in the water, but she would slip out and swim away.

8

One day she told me she had to leave the beach earlier. A reporter was waiting for her in the studio.

"What reporter?"

I tried not to sound alarmed. Her dealings with men, particularly strangers, whom I couldn't know, made me a little nervous. But I didn't want to acknowledge even to myself that these tinkling needles in my brain were the first signs of jealousy.

"A journalist from the local radio station," she said, pulling her sundress on top of a wet swimming suit "I completely forgot. He's going to run a preview of my September show."

She was in a visible rush now. I helped her stick the wet towels into the canvas bag.

"I'll carry it," I said. "I'm going to walk you to the cottage anyway."

"Oh, that's all right. I can carry it myself."She turned and looked at me. "You know what I'd like to do?"

"What?"

"Guess?" She smiled conspiratorially. "After this interview, I'd like to come to your hotel and stay overnight. I'll be wearing this special dress, and I'll pretend I don't know you and then..." She whispered something into my ear, then burst into laughter.

Lately, I'd noticed a playful side in her that wasn't there before – and I loved it. I lifted her in my arms, overwhelmed with joy. The prospect of spending an entire night with my darling immediately reconciled me to the impending separation. At the cottage of High Sails, I kissed her good bye and began to go down the hill back to my hotel. The sun was getting very hot, and I thought I should take a nap to replenish my energy before her arrival later that evening.

I almost made it to the hotel when I noticed I was missing my wristwatch. It must have slipped into the sand somehow, and I hadn't noticed. Annoyed at myself – now I had to go all the way back to the beach – I reluctantly turned around.

The terrain sloped to the ocean, and I saw Angel from afar. She was on the same spot we both had left ten minutes ago, lying in the arms of a man, her suntanned legs wrapped around his much darker torso. Not quite trusting my own eyes, I stopped, then slowly moved forward. I couldn't see the man's face, but I recognized him from the back: it was Francisco. I felt that the world, as I knew it, was vanishing, or rather, the world was still there, but I was no longer able to grasp its meaning. Everything around me became drained of vibrancy. The sky seemed monotonously blue, the sand dull yellow. I stood there, still seeing and yet not being able to see, a dull drone in my ears. Then I moved forward as if still hoping the mirage would disperse.

When Francisco got up, I noticed how muscular his legs were. I stared at his hairy calves and thighs that seemed to threaten me and be the focus of my pain. Francisco hopped twice, balancing on one foot while pulling a pant leg over the other. Then he sat down next to Angel, and she put her arm around him, reaching for her bag with the other hand. She took out some of the grapes we had brought to the beach, inserted one into her mouth, then took Francisco's head into her hands and pushed it into his mouth with her tongue – her favourite game – the way she'd done with me so many times. At the beginning the man was passive, but then they both broke into laughter. He pretended to move away from her but she found his mouth again and they kissed.

I turned around and went back to the hotel.

Without removing my shoes, I collapsed on my bed and covered my head with a sheet. I didn't have any thoughts or feelings. It was late afternoon, and the hotel was filled with sounds. People in the hallway were talking loudly in Spanish; somebody was taking a shower, and then there was the erratic noise of running feet, must be children. I lay there listening through the sheet, waiting for night to fall. I still hoped for one and one sound only: Angel's light, hesitant tapping at my door. What would I do then? Pretend I didn't know anything and forgive her? My heart turned painfully in my chest. No, I wouldn't humiliate myself with explanations. I would simply leave the room without a word. I'd get out of the country as soon as possible – and then, from a plane, I'd write her a brief letter. She'd regret what she'd done, but it would be too late.

I raised myself to look at the time, then remembered that I'd left my watch on the beach. I must have spent hours in bed, because now it was completely dark. No sounds were coming from the corridor. I realized in an instant that Angel was not going to come because she was spending the night with Francisco. Though I could imagine her making love to another man, my mind refused to believe it, as if it was somehow against the laws of nature and therefore couldn't actually be happening. That night, I was unable to get any sleep at all. One moment I wanted to inflict pain on her, so that she would know all the measure of my suffering; the next, I wanted to forgive her; for some strange reason, I even felt sorry for her. I was sweating profusely. Then I started coughing. Unable to contain my fits anymore, I finally got up and went out for some fresh air.

In the hallway, a short blond woman was leaning against the wall, one barefoot leg rubbing the other. The moment she saw me, she snuck her feet into the stiletto shoes standing beside her. She watched me struggle with my cough for a while, then unglued herself from the wall and began to twist her foot inside the shoe, rotating her hips in sync with her movements.

"Fucking sand!" she said, balancing on one foot and emptying her left shoe out."Do you know where the laundry is?" She spoke in a raspy voice with the deep drawl of a Southerner.

"Pardon? The laundry? Sorry, I don't."

"I mean, where do you do your washing?" She emptied her second shoe. "I don't know anybody in this place. Would you like to spend the evening together?"

I looked at her more carefully: bleached hair, a nondescript faded face, a rather plump figure. She looked grubby, second-hand, yet her body had a not unpleasant roundness.

"It must be very late now." I said hesitatingly."What time is it?"

"I know a very good restaurant not far from here," she said without responding to my question. "They're open till midnight. The owner says his great-grandfather invented Caesar salad a century ago at that place. They still serve it the old way. Come on!"

I lifted my eyebrows in disbelief, then said I wasn't hungry and left.

9

I don't remember how I survived till the next day, but by late afternoon I couldn't take it anymore, and I found myself at the door of Angel's studio.

"Come on in, Joe." She smiled at me as if nothing had happened.

"I didn't sleep last night," I said, half-averting my face."I was waiting for you. I know what happened. I know where you've been." I tried to sound as calm as possible.

"You mean the interview? I was too tired to come to your hotel after the interview. It dragged on and on."She turned around and walked into her studio.

"You don't need to lie to me, Angel," I said, following her. "I saw you with Francisco on the beach."

"So what?" She turned to me, her eyes squinting. "Can't I talk to another man? What would you like to drink? I have some freshly squeezed mango." She opened the fridge.

"No, thanks. But let's not get off the subject. Why didn't you tell me you had a lover all along? Instead of telling me that he made frames for you and so on. Why lie?"

"What I said was true." Angel calmly poured herself some juice. "He does make frames for me. He even helped me build this studio."

I noticed the mist gathering on the inside surface of her glass. I felt sudden indifference to everything, but my senses seemed to have lives of their own, noticing everything, infusing every trifle with an annoying significance.

"And that's why you slept with him?"

"Don't you dare insult me!"she exploded,slamming her glass onto the countertop.

Juice poured over the counter, glass smatterings bursting in all directions. I watched one piece rocking behind the leg of a chair, its amplitude of motion smaller and smaller. Her sudden rage took me by surprise, but I noticed that her eyes remained cold as usual.

"Yes, he's my lover, and you knew all the time about us and chose to accept it!"

I was appalled at how quickly she had abandoned all her pretense and even the smallest effort to spare me the truth. Had she invented some semi-plausible story, I would have grabbed onto it and lamely, tortuously believed her.

"I just want to know one thing. Why did you start an affair with me when all that time you had another lover?"

I felt a sudden urge to relieve myself. I ran to the toilet but stopped short in front of the image staring at me out of the mirror: bulging eyes surrounded by deep furrows, the helpless grimace of a weak, drooping mouth and the long, vertical lines crossing my cheeks all the way down to my neck. There was no way, simply no way, that I, Joseph Parson, fifty-seven years old, could legitimately defend the claims of this monkey in front of that young woman full of life and vigour. I came out of the bathroom. Angel was applying some lotion to her face, the way she often did before going to the beach, and when I saw that familiar gesture, the helpless ugly ape that had stared at me a minute ago from a bathroom mirror, and with whose behaviour I had nothing in common, suddenly dropped on its knees in front of her, grabbed her legs, wept uncontrollably.

"Forgive me," I said, sobbing, "Forgive me! I should've never...never..."

"Why are you so upset?" said Angel, squinting at me. "It's just sex."

"I thought that you and I...that you loved me a little too; you can't love me the way I love you, I know that, but I hoped that..." My vocal cords gave up, the sound of my voice thinning into a whisper.

"I like you fine! You're somehow different, and your stories are funny. Francisco is a bore compared to you. He's a waiter, a handyman; he does my errands, for God's sake! How can you be jealous of him? Calm down, *querido. No hay que ahogarse en un vaso de agua.* You don't have to drown in a glass of water!"

A hopeless despair overcame me. Now rage replaced self-pity and words came back to me, gushing out of my mouth:"So you sleep with everybody you find funny, don't you! Or who you can boss around and treat like your slave! That guy, whatever his name is, that drunk who gave you a diamond? You slept with him too, didn't you?"

"What business is that of yours? I'm a free woman." She took another glass from the dish rack, poured herself some juice, gulped it down, and wiped her mouth with the back of her hand."After all, we're not married. Who are you to tell me what to do?"

"You mean if you were my wife, it would make a difference?"

"Maybe! Then you could have as much of me as you want, and Francisco would be our handyman, our gardener. Looking after our house for cheap." She paused, smirking. "Making more frames for my cunts!"

For the first time in my life, I was about to hit a woman. But I restrained myself. I got up and quickly left, determined never to see her again.

10

The next day, I started planning my return to Canada. Looking back at recent events, I saw clearly that Angel wasn't at all the person I'd taken her to be. An imposter with philistine pretensions using art to lure men into bed; a nymphomaniac, manufacturing pussy bags – that's all she was! The more I thought about her, the more my own delusions became painfully obvious to me. I became convinced that she didn't have as much as a spark of artistic talent in her.

How, then, could she have drawn me into all this, making me sit for her for a whole month? Was I completely blind? I'd anticipated my sessions with her with such impatience! The mere sight of bougainvillea camouflaging the door that led into her world had sent my heart into reverential leaps. The tireless choir of tropical birds flitting high up in the trees below her studio was like an overture to my entering a paradise. Her sleepy whisper in the morning when the first rays of the sun set her ebon hair on fire, that innocent whisper in my half-alert ear made me believe she was a fragile flower in need of my protection, whereas in fact she was cynical and hard as stones and I was an old fool, doting over a predator who toyed with me, her prey, before destroying it.

The memories of nights made for our love now existed solely for my torment. Anger, shame, and the old, still unquenched desire for her inundated me at night. I was out of breath, I was suffocating. The sheets felt wet against my exhausted body. My tortured ear would shut out the drone of the fan only to yield to the cadenced rage of the ocean below,smashing itself against the sand strewn with dead crabs and empty shells. What was this ocean raging against? The limits imposed by its shores? How pointless, how futile. Yesterday, I spotted decomposing white flesh on the sand. I thought it was a dead dog, but it turned out to be a huge turtle without its shell, its pale sinewy tissue exposed to the sun. The ocean burped it out, then left it there to rot.

In the time that followed, I tried not to think of Angel.

But I soon discovered that it was impossible, and the harder

I tried, the less I succeeded. My resolve to return immediately to Canada faded into ennui. Slowly, my anger gave place to a dull pain that nestled inside my heart and that I couldn't either pull out or ignore. I couldn't hate her – hating her meant hating myself. But no matter what I did, I was hurting as if I'd lost something vital to my existence – a pair of limbs – yet was forced to drag my body through the desert of smiling strangers, pretending that I, just like them, was whole. I knew I couldn't grow new limbs any more than I could love somebody else in what remained of my life. I felt more and more isolated from the world, and I gradually sank into the realm of dreams that alone seemed to be bringing me some relief. At dawn, I would go into slumber and watch the misshapen fragments of my thoughts (ragged little Daliesque creatures) floating inside my brain. I'd try to pull one out and hold on to it before it dissipated. One rectangular shape took the form of a coffin – on closer inspection, my own. I couldn't clearly see my face inside it: my white sunken cheeks were camouflaged with some quivering shadows of leaves that the trees obligingly lent me. Nobody followed the procession. The coffin was drawn by a horse that knew where to go.

My death seemed to be exactly like each of my birthdays, a lonely and redundant affair. Self-pity overwhelmed me, and I cried in my sleep. Then I woke up, flipped aside the gauze hanging from the ceiling. I couldn't stand being enclosed in a coffin, a swaddled larva, a mummy, a corpse! I made an effort to get up, but my resolve quickly evaporated, and imperceptibly I drifted into another dream. This one shimmered with the glory and sweetness of happiness, as Angel, my beloved, had returned to me as a very young girl, and I was very young too, and we knew each other almost all of our lives. In my dream, she wasn't my mistress but my wife of many years. We were the same age; we grew up together, married, became old, and then came full circle and regained our youth. Around us, the water was lapping gently, our bed drifting away into the warm, milky abyss. Angel was both delighted and scared.

"Don't leave me," she said, "I've forgotten how to swim."

"Are you afraid, my sweet? Nothing is gentler than water. I will protect you. I will go anywhere you go."

I woke up and knew I wasn't alone anymore. Imagining I could preserve the aura of her presence, her smell and her warmth, I didn't shower for two days.

That dream was a turning point in my life. It made me postpone my return home, because now I had an urgent task. I had to secure her new glorious existence inside me. Not only should the malice of the outside world be unable to touch her, but she should be beyond the reach of my own anger, my own jealousy, lest they destroy her shining image. I kept listening to the new music that was enveloping my soul with such tenderness. In a strange fashion, we reversed our roles; now she became my guardian angel protecting me from slipping into darkness.

How that transformation happened, I don't know. I think it was akin to satori, the awakening of the heart, allowing you to see the true nature of the world. That sensation couldn't have been drawn from any events that had preceded it. Yet it was irreversible. It was then that I forgave her and forgave myself for wanting her all to myself and hating her if she didn't belong to me alone. That forgiveness gave new freedom to my spirit and strength to my body. The world around me was bathing in a warm light of mercy.

Now I didn't love my Angel for my own sake, but for her own, and with that, my torment ended.

11

Two weeks after these...I hesitate to call them "events,"as they were simply shifts in my consciousness, but two weeks later, I received a letter from Angel. Would I mind sitting for her, one last time? She wanted to finish my portrait. She said she had wronged me. She wanted to apologize, and give me my picture as a gift.

Compared to the fragile but strengthening joy I felt in my heart, the letter somehow felt redundant. Yet it burned my fingers. It belonged to the old world of sorrowful vales, while I was hovering in the pure ether. Should I abandon my new beloved, beautiful and full of mercy as my own forgiveness had made her, and meet the real Angel? The idea scared me, and I hesitated for three or four days before finally overcoming my fears.

The door of her studio, so painfully familiar, was wide open. I quietly walked in. I saw her standing in the depth of the hall. The morning light enveloped her in a halo. She stepped out of this glow and moved toward me. I hadn't seen her for almost a month and was shocked at how she'd changed: her dark complexion concealed neither her paleness nor the bluish circles under her eyes. She looked washed out, pallid; even the well-defined line of her chin seemed weaker. I noticed a shapeless housecoat, so uncharacteristic of her, with an apron stained with paint on top. Apart from these obvious changes, there was a more subtle and yet profound transformation: the dry fire that had raged inside her seemed to be extinguished.

"Sorry," she said."I was painting, didn't have time to change."

I looked at her again and asked if she was all right. She said she had been sick most of the time we hadn't seen each other, but now she had recovered. She offered me some coffee. I politely refused: I was in a rush and preferred to get down to our work right away, I told her. She didn't respond, but it was obvious she knew I had nothing planned. We didn't talk while she was painting. Only once were we interrupted, by an unusual whimpering sound coming from the back deck.

A pelican, Angel explained, with a broken wing, had landed on her deck that morning. She had tried to give it some fresh fish, but it wouldn't touch it. We went out to see the bird. It sat on the floor clumsily, like a duck, tucked in the corner against the glass pane. With its pouch resting on the wooden planks of the deck, it looked quite grotesque. It was all white with a little red rim around the eye that gazed at us with great suspicion. I tried to go closer. The pelican made a clumsy attempt to dash away from me.

"Better not touch it," said Angel. "I tried."

"What's going to happen to it?"

"Most likely, it will die. There's nothing we can do for it."

She went back into the studio. I followed her; she turned around and put her hands on my shoulders.

"I'm so glad you came back," she said, "it was all really

silly, I'm sorry..."

It had been a long time since I'd seen her face so close to mine: no dream or imagination could replace the sensation of holding her in my arms, feeling the warmth of her body.

"I love you," I said. "I never stopped loving you ..."

She gazed into my eyes, then passed her hand over my cheek. It smelled of paint.

"What answer will you give me then?" she asked me. "Have you decided?"

She brushed her lips against mine without kissing me, and, slightly bending her knees, she rested her head on my chest.

"Answer?"

"Remember? I asked if you'd marry me."

I felt weak in my legs. Of course I remembered, except that the proposition, which she'd made a month ago, had seemed like simple mockery.

"Angel, you don't have to do this to yourself. You don't love me. You can't love me. I know that. But it doesn't matter, I will always be there for you if you want. If there's anything you need, just tell me. You don't have to marry me in order to keep me around."

My hands started trembling uncontrollably. I wanted to leave. But she prevented me from moving.

"I missed you terribly," she whispered into my ear, and I wasn't even sure that I made out the words correctly. "Terribly," she said again. "I could barely cope."

"Weren't you with Francisco all this time?"

"I'll explain it to you later, you'll understand. I was a fool, forgive me – you do forgive me, don't you?"

"Yes," I said feebly.

"You're the best person I've ever met. They all want me for something: for my eccentric art, or because of the people I know, but none of them love me for me, the way you do. You're a true saint."

She started crying. I had never seen her tears before.

"I know we could be happy together. I'll be a good wife to you, you'll never regret it. Please, say yes."

I was shattered by her tears and wasn't able to say a word.

"If you love me, please say yes!"

The despair in her voice. She felt guilty after all, and didn't that mean that she loved me in some way? Wild hope surged in my heart.

"Yes," my lips whispered on their own.

"Are you still hesitating? Are you?" She dropped her arms and quickly stepped back. Her eyes were misty.

"No, oh no...I love you. I can't live without you, if that's what . . ." I drew her back to me.

"Good. I can't live without you either." She wiped the wetness from her eyes.

"Ah, Joe, *corazón,* I'm so tired. Can't even think of painting today." She was now smiling as if relieved of some terrible burden.

"Can't we finish your portrait tomorrow? There are so many things I want to do together with you: travel, buy art, entertain interesting people. We'll have a happy life, won't we?" She hid her head on my chest, a little girl again.

"Of course, whatever you want, my love ..."

On the way back to my hotel, I stopped in bewilderment. What was I doing? One thing was the sublime love dwelling in my soul; quite another was to marry a woman like Angel. I avoided looking in the direction of that spot on the beach where almost four weeks ago I saw her feeding grapes to Francisco. I knew and trusted my sweet innocent girl. But did I know and trust Angel? Again I felt that familiar weakness in my legs, that nagging void in my stomach.

Remorse aside, it was inconceivable that she'd truly want to marry me – that much I understood. What could I offer? Twice her age, too old to start a family, a foreigner unable to speak her language, knowing not a soul in her country. Could it be my money? She never showed any interest in it, but even if she did, all she had to do was ask. I turned around and retraced my steps to the cottage of High Sails. I stood there at the bottom of the stairs for a while, hesitating, listening to the wind.

I remembered her tears, the fright in her eyes. How pale she looked, my poor girl, how tired. Didn't I promise to protect her, when we were floating in the ocean of my dream together? And, further, did I want to live, could I truly live, without her? Now when she said, "I'm yours."

I turned around and went back to my hotel.

12

All my life I've been suffering from migraines that, contrary to what doctors might think, result from the terrible clutter my undiscriminating memory foists upon my mind: a volley of faces, gestures, scenes I strive to yet can't erase.

The only time my brain gives me respite and my memory stops collecting its usual crop of disparate impressions is a day or two preceding the onslaught of pain. When that happens, my sensations are numbed. I observe life as if through a fish bowl: the luminescent fan of a tail, the grotesque bulging stare of an underwater monster swooning by.

I only vaguely remember the kaleidoscope of Angel's friends presenting themselves to her apartment at Chimalistac, a quiet enclave for the well-to-do of Mexico City, in the days before the wedding: artists, critics, curators, and socialites. I never got to meet her parents; as usual, they were living in their separate capitals of Europe.

There was a cascade of multicoloured boxes filled with jewellery, Venetian and Mexican masks, Talavera pottery, canvases, brushes, shoes, French underwear, embroidered fabric ordered by Angel and now arriving to our door with a merry-go-round frenzy. I saw myself from the outside: a short bald man wiping sweat off his forehead and writing out checks, then retreating to the coolness of the patio to fill up the glasses of yet another batch of guests.

Strangely, the two images my memory was able to salvage from the murkiness of these prenuptial days had little to do with my marital bliss. One was a huge pyramid assembled of pots of red-and-green leafed poinsettia and posing as a Christmas tree near the Cathedral of Santo Domingo, where we were going to get married. The other, next to that tree, was a nativity crèche with two sheep, an ox, and a donkey grazing at the hay in a manger, surrounded by a crude plywood fence. What made these beasts surreal in this anthill city of twenty million is that they were alive. I had a strong desire to stroke the dusty grey curls of the sheep, but then remembered my tuxedo.

My bride's costume à la Frida Kahlo – the multi-layered stiff lace, the intricately embroidered birds of paradise – seemed equally exotic to me; it outshone everything else in the opulent theatre production that was my wedding.

Angel's black hair, arranged in triple braids on top of her head and crowned with red roses, her pale solemn face, our kneeling at the altar, our exchanging of the vows and rings, my throwing rice over my left shoulder to ward off the devil, who, I was told, would always hold his grip, given the slightest chance – all that became no more than an assemblage of indistinct memories. On stage, I was an uninspired and rather fearful first-timer nobody had prepared for his role. The last scene of the show ended with a copious meal. My sense of reality briefly returned to me with the departure of our last guest, a man who vaguely resembled Francisco.

As soon as he closed the door behind him, I went up to Angel, took her into my arms, and planted a long, breathless kiss on her mouth.

She struggled out of my embrace, pushed me away, and collapsed on the bed, the gauze of her dress flaring and burying her head. "Leave me alone or I'll scream my lungs out!" Her cry braced my brain with a cement hoop, and I descended into pain that lasted for the next three days, obliterating all sensations and memories.

13

Shortly after these events, we went to Canada to settle my inheritance. The morning after our disconcerting nuptial night, my beautiful bride had apologized for her behaviour. The whole "show" had just been too much. Since I'd felt much the same, I was mollified. But I was worried about the trip. What would she think about my almost bare apartment on the outskirts of a snowy provincial city? Of my run-of-the-mill friends, none of whom were artists? My fears came true. The energy, the sharp purposefulness that Angel had back home, evaporated; most of the time, she just looked bored. Only rarely would she pick up a pencil and sketch the bleak winter landscape that stared at her from behind the window pane: another cement apartment building, two or three cars buried in snow. The climate didn't agree with her. She felt cold and feverish, though I couldn't understand how one could feel both at the same time. And the food nauseated her; she found it bland and tasteless.

Of course I noticed the abrupt changes in her mood. She tried to regain the old passion she once, I thought, had for me, but these attempts were so artificial that they left us both greatly embarrassed. After one such bout, she went into a delirium, biting her own fists, beating her hands against the headboard – that wooden, hard, alien sound – and then collapsing with sobs onto the bed. It all horrified me: her violence to herself, her uncontrollable shivering, and, worst of all, the way her body would first stiffen and then become soft and listless. I wanted to comfort her, to hold her in my arms, but I was afraid to so much as touch her, lest that make her suffering even worse. We were back to the same scene as on the night after our wedding, and I cursed myself for my self-indulgence, for wanting to make love to her incessantly, for believing her when she'd abruptly stop sobbing and jump up shouting "Do it, go ahead, I can't get enough of you!" Then she'd collapse again, all soft and yielding, weeping like a little girl and asking me to forgive her. She'd whisper into my ear that she knew, she understood it all, oh how awful, how very unfair to me, the nicest person on Earth, but one day it would all be over, all resolved, for she'd hide in a remote monastery, with daily *Pater Noster,* just like in her Catholic childhood, and could I please bring her some water and kiss her when she needed to calm down. I'd soothe her burning face with a wet towel, and then she'd finally fall asleep, felled by fatigue.

It was clear to me that we had to leave Canada, the sooner the better, even if some of the business connected with the inheritance remained unsettled. On a plane back to Mexico, Angel became sick. We were travelling in business class (was there anything I would begrudge her?), and she didn't mind the skillful care of the flight attendants, but to my "ridiculous doting" she reacted with her usual irritation. I was afraid she'd go into uncontrollable fits again – when she said, her face turned to the window, "Stop fussing. I'm pregnant, and if the nausea didn't stop on the ground, you think it's going to at 15,000 metres?"

The news that I, at my age, would become a father threw me into ecstasy! I awkwardly, sheepishly, pulled myself to her side and kissed her hands. She pushed me away. I sat there trying to regain my breath. I didn't mind her dismissals now. I felt this child was

God's response to the vows of love and forgiveness that I'd made in the Zipolite hotel before she summoned me to go back to her.

Now the three of us – Angel, me, and the baby – would have a totally different life. I imagined myself appearing arm in arm with her at vernissages and cocktail parties: an older man, with a young beautiful wife bearing his child.

The truth is I didn't really know what it was like to have a baby around. All I knew was that the baby girl would make my world brilliantly and freshly new. Somehow, I was sure it would be a girl, if only because I had no use for a boy, who, by the mere token of our blood connection, would understand my inner workings, a mirror reflecting my fears, my uncertainties, my pitfalls. The girl, on the other hand, would make me feel real, the way I had never felt before; she would expand my shabby self to new dimensions, because he would be of my flesh, yet as different from me as a remote star.

The only thing I regretted is that my poor darling hadn't told me about her pregnancy earlier. Had I known, I would've seen the tormenting three weeks in Canada in a completely different light. But it wasn't too late. I'd make up for my previous failures. I'd do anything it took to make her life comfortable so that she could bring our child into the world without any strain or hardship. I wanted her to remain who she was, a talented and original artist. (I didn't doubt her talent for a moment now! More than that, I was surprised how I could have doubted it in the past.) Yes, we would have a cleaning lady, a cook (Angel wasn't that keen on cooking), a nanny, and a gardener. She wanted to collect art? I'd buy her art. She wanted to try out sculpture and was talking about going to Italy to buy Carrara

marble? Then yes, we would do that too. A hot wave of gratitude
was choking me. I got to my feet and hugging Angel gently – not to
overwhelm her again – and then I went to the end of the passenger
cabin, looking for a place where, unwatched, I could give vent to my
euphoria.

14

We bought a run-down villa 100 kilometres from Mexico City.
Angel avidly plunged herself into grand plans for renovations. She
redesigned the layout of each room and made drawings for intricate
parquet and wallpaper patterns, drapes, and even furniture. In that, as
in everything she touched, she never failed to surprise me. I expected
her tastes to be cold, sparse, minimalistic. Instead she was seeking
to reproduce a Venetian *palaccio* on a smaller scale. She wanted the
warm glitter of gilded surfaces, lush silks on the walls in our bedroom,
old armchairs, oriental carpets on the marble stairs. She had her mind's
eye on authentic Renaissance furniture she hoped to bring back from
our travels to Italy that summer. Angel was now four months pregnant,
and we decided not to postpone our trip in spite of the fact that the
villa wasn't finished. But before leaving, we wanted to spend a couple
of weeks at the cottage of High Sails, a place I both loved and hated.

How can I conjure up the days that followed? What can
do justice to these most horrible – and in hindsight – most idyllic
times I've ever had? The delicious tedium of marital bliss (at times
I still couldn't believe Angel was my wife); the sweet lassitude of
hot, lazy afternoons. Pregnancy mellowed and pacified her, and I

found her dependency on me deeply touching. It seemed that she'd finally reconciled with something that had been gnarling at her from inside. Our days rolled on from dawn to sunset like identical smooth pebbles; our laziness, our *dolce fare nienti* was complete, permeating the very core of our existence as if some benevolent universal life force was living and breathing for us.

We once spotted a cobweb gently swaying in the air currents between the two potted magnolias in the corner of our bedroom. But to get up with the purpose of ruining it seemed inconceivable, and so we both stayed put.

After the first three days, we quickly settled into a routine of few words and sparse gestures. I would get up very early and go for a walk along the beach, feeling the cool morning breeze on my face. When I got back, Angel was still in bed. I'd bring her breakfast and watch her as she poked lazily into the fruit salad that I'd chopped up for her. Her face, bloated from sleep and pregnancy, half-buried in her hair, darkly contrasted with a white lace nightgown. I found all the signs of her condition particularly touching, everything she herself was unhappy about: her deformed body, the dark spots on her cheeks, her swollen lips, and that enigmatic line that stretched along her belly from her navel all the way down to her pubis.

After breakfast, she would paint for two or three hours, moving around with somnambulist slowness. She wanted to be alone then, and every time, I had to think of a new place to go, of something to do away from the house. She never asked me where I'd gone, or what I'd been doing. I had already explored all the coastal villages and towns; wandered through the dusty streets of Puerto

Angel and watched people at Pochutla market. I loved bringing her trinkets from the local artisans: a crudely painted pot, an embroidered napkin, a pair of earrings. She laughed at my unsophisticated taste – and, indeed, I never saw her wearing anything I gave her.

One day, it had rained heavily during the night but let up in the morning, and I wanted to get on a bus early to get groceries at the market. By the time I came back, loaded with fish, cheeses and fruit, it was around 10:00 a.m. Angel was not at home, and I sat for a while on the deck, looking out at the ocean and wondering where she was. She must have gone for a quick dip. The bathing towel and swimsuit were missing from the drying rack in the bathroom, her nightgown and her house robe scattered over the bed. I felt uneasy about it; we'd agreed that she wouldn't go into the ocean alone. But I tried not to be alarmed and made breakfast for the two of us. Then I sat in a rocking chair struggling to read a book. Then I went out to the deck again and watched the ocean. Two hours passed, and I began to worry in earnest. I went down and walked all the way toward la Playa de l'Amour, the most remote beach separated from our strip by rocks. This was the only gay beach in the country, and affluent yuppies flocked there from Mexico City. I doubted that Angel would go there, but I couldn't spot her anywhere else.

The day was still cloudy, yet you could sense the presence of the hot sun behind the grey puffy veils. I looked at the ocean. Its surface had a menacing steel tinge, the breakers higher than usual. I had heard stories of imperceptible whirlpools or underwater currents that pulled even experienced swimmers out into the open sea.

By the time they'd realized the danger and shouted for help, it was usually too late; the powerful beat of the surf would muffle any plea for help. Angel loved swimming, and she loved risk. But would she venture alone into the stormy ocean in her condition? I tried to think of other alternatives – perhaps she'd gone to the local bar, or was visiting some friends I didn't know? Disturbingly, none of it made any sense.

I went back home, vaguely hoping to find her there. But the house was empty. There was the sound of a tap dripping. I went to tighten it and tripped over a painting leaning against the wall. It was my still-unfinished portrait that Angel, for some reason, had never wanted to show to me. I don't know what I expected, but what I saw stunned me.

Instead of a face, the figure on the canvas had a yellow oval, empty inside. In contrast to the oval, my hand (the right hand, to be exact) was painted with meticulous verisimilitude; my veins, dark, bluish ropes, branched under the dried skin in all directions. The left arm was replaced with some protruding form that ended in tree roots, growing through the floor all the way down to the earth, full of dead bodies crunched up like fetuses. I was fingering them with my root-like hand. This is how she sees me, I thought, a faceless monster, a deformity, sorting out corpses

For the next three days, police searched for traces of my Angel. On the third day, they found one of her sandals half buried in the sand five miles from our house. Her body, partially decomposed and fed on by sharks, turned up in a rocky bay three weeks later. I refused to look. It was identified by the wedding ring and by what was left of her swimsuit, which they showed me.

Angel's friends and fans organized both her funeral mass and her interment. In the church of Santo Domingo, I stood in a semi-dark corner, away from the crowd, nodding silently to the condolences of people passing by. I didn't know the liturgy and watched the priest moving around the closed casket, waving some incense. At one point, a tall dark-skinned man came up to me and said he was Angel's father. Words stuck in my throat, and I nodded to him too, without meeting his eyes. Then, closer to the exit, I noticed a kneeling figure. I recognized Francisco.

He looked older and somehow smaller than I remembered him. The intensity of his prayer surprised me – I didn't anticipate such religious fervour from this man. He felt my glance, turned around, then quickly withdrew his eyes; I thought I saw tears in them, but perhaps I only imagined them. Something akin to pity stirred in me: after all, he too had loved her. I wanted to talk to him, but then changed my mind. He, however, got off his knees and approached me. "I need to see you," he whispered into my ear. "I have something for you, something belonging to your wife."

After Angel's death, I couldn't see myself staying either in her studio on the bluffs or in her apartment in Mexico City, so I moved to our unfinished villa outside the city in complete seclusion and had no reason to come into town. I told him I lived there now and had no reason to come to town, and he replied that he would gladly visit me over the next couple of days. He asked for my address, and I gave it to him.

There was no furniture there yet, and when I finally got home, I dropped my few possessions right on the floor, away from the mounds of shavings and sawdust gathered in the corner. Some window panes were missing: there must have been break-ins while we were on the coast. A mattress and a blanket served me as a makeshift bed, and this is where I spent day after day in a motionless oblivion, feeling nothing, knowing nothing, coming to my senses only through the involuntary stirrings of my body, which gave me the immediate anguish of remembrance, and I whimpered with pain in my delirium. I lost count of days and became only vaguely aware that Francisco hadn't shown up as promised. But what was morning, what was night? My sleepless nights were the times of my greater lucidity and my increasing suffering, and so I hated them, their alien life, secreting unknown sounds that tormented me with some vague menace. Yet what was there to be afraid of? What kind of loss or pain was there left after Angel was gone? Once I heard two birds echoing each other: one, with a low forlorn whooping, another with the sharp shriek of a disturbed harlot. I'd never heard anything resembling these sounds, and my soul hung in the interval of anticipation between the shriek and the howl piercing the sticky walls of the night.

One morning, I woke to the ring of the doorbell, which I didn't recognize as such. Nobody had ever visited me or rung the bell. I had forgotten all about Francisco, who must have been ringing for quite a while before I opened the door.

He looked at me standing in the doorway, a barefoot, feeble old man wrapped in a blanket, my face crumpled from sleep. I couldn't tolerate light by then, and the rays of the sun that Francisco had inadvertently let in blinded me. I observed his tightly fitting black suit, shiny shoes, a silk handkerchief sticking out of his breast pocket. I apologized for my house and my appearance, then began to look for something for us to sit on. Francisco waited silently. I finally fetched two wooden stools, but he remained standing.

"I come to say how your wife die." He fixed his gaze on me. "I was there."

"My wife drowned in the sea," I said quickly, swallowing a lump of pain. "Please spare me your nonsense."

"She no drown alone. I give her to fishes."

"You're raving mad, Francisco. Grief must've made you lose your mind. Please leave. This is a bad time for me to deal with insanity."

"Was me who kill her," he said, without changing the tone of his voice. "She is a witch and put a curse on me."

I saw how pale he grew. His eyes had the glare of a maniac. I became fearful of him and stepped back.

"Wait, I'll call an ambulance – they'll help you."

"You'll do not that thing! Or you go to hell with her." He quickly stretched his hand toward me. A knife flashed in my eye.

"Your wife agree die. She wanted. I push her off the boat. Virgin Mary show me path, blessed be Her Name." He quickly crossed himself. "She come in my dream, she say, get a boat. The Virgin Herself stay on the bow and show that place." He crossed himself again. "Angel go to fishes quickly. A proof she a witch."

"Did you know she was pregnant with my baby?" I whispered, suddenly having a nightmarish vision of being in front of a murderer, not a raving lunatic.

"Talking of my bastard? Is my bastard, not your. His blood on my hands. She say to me I'm pregnant. I say, okay, then I marry you. She say no, you're poor, I marry the rich gringo." Still holding his knife in one hand, with the other he pulled two gold watches on long chains out of his breast pocket. He threw them on the stool. One watch slipped off with a clacking sound.

"Take your bloody gold. She buy for me with your bloody money. I don't need this of you shit."

I recognized one old watch that had belonged to my father. The other one was new.

"You better strangle your whore your hands, not leave dirty job for an honest man. She pay me your money for sex. Two hundred dollars a fuck. She tell me come to your house every morning. You go someplace walk, I must come. I'm no slave to a whore, I'm a free man!"

"You're a liar, filthy liar," I protested in a weak, unused voice. He cocked his head, then dug a letter out of his breast pocket.

"Read this!"

I recognized Angel's handwriting on a bethumbed, crumpled envelope.

"Can't see without my glasses, sorry." My dry throat suddenly made a wimpy, puny sound. Francisco gave me an odd look, then lowered his eyes and shook his head.

"Go find your glasses, gringo, I wait." I hopelessly looked around at the jumble of unsorted things, but was unable to move.

Finally Francisco calmly said, "I read to you."' *Mi pollo...*'" He stopped and looked at me. "You understand Spanish?"

I was dumbfounded.

"I translate," he said in a monotone voice. "*'Chicken, why you refuse make love to me yesterday? You say it hurt our baby. I say, no hurt if mother love his father's verga.'* You know *verga*?" Francisco pointed to his crotch.*"'If mother love father verga, baby love it too. Come tomorrow by ten, when old fart at the market. I love watch the sun shine on your butt! His body cold and wet like worms of death, your body dry and hot, like hot sand of desert. No shade in you, only light. I touch you – I'm on fire. I touch him – I die. I desire you like no other woman desire you. You never marry this slut of yours: you belong to me: your liver, your guts, every hair on your chest...*"

"Enough!" I shouted. "Enough! Get out of here!"

"As you want," said Francisco, stepping back and handing me the letter. "Before I go, I need five thousand dollars for my wedding. And another five, for the friars at St. Michelle. They pray for the soul of my innocent child that I killed."

"I have no money," I said dryly.

"Stop bullshitting, gringo," said Francisco, flipping the knife in his hand. "You a rich man. I need cash right now, and a check for the rest of it. After that, get the fuck out of my country."

I suddenly woke up. "I will call the police, you murderer!"

"I be careful with words, gringo, if I am you," said Francisco. "One more sound, you dead. I find you, don't matter none where."

He grabbed me and let me go only after I'd done what he told me to.

Already in the doorway, he turned around: "As I said, keep your mouth shut, and thank you for your gift, gringo."

I sat on the floor till the night sprawled over my head, all its terrifying magnificence and engulfed the crumpled piece of paper lying next to me.

Angel, my Angel! Why didn't you tell me? I would've set you free. I would've let you love the man you loved. I would've raised your child. Once in my dream, I promised to follow and protect you wherever you went. Will you ever forgive my betrayal? Will you ever forgive my sordid love that has taken away your life? Will you forgive my old dirty fingers for touching your beatific body? Now in death, your soul is pure again, the way it was when I first saw you: your hair like the wings of the soaring eagle, and your eyes sweet and calm like the sleeping water before it rose and took you away from me forever.

There are No flies on Machu Picchu

1

My wife died in her sleep a year ago. I rolled over, sleepless, to nuzzle her awake, so we could make love, but she was still, her eyes open, her mouth caught in a grimace."

On the first anniversary of her death, two books afforded me some solace: *The Book of the Dead* and *The Zohar: The Book of Splendor.* The Cabbalists can predict with unfailing precision, *The Zohar* tells me, the hour of our death encoded in a man's name. To face eternity with dignified resignation, we must know beforehand the exact moment of our passing.

But I, for one, deem such foreknowledge utterly useless. What good would it have been to her or me had we known? Besides, my wife was not Jewish.

I'm wrapped in impenetrable sheets of silence. Remorse, a black-winged bird, is pecking at my muteness. Since her death my eyes have become intolerant of light. I spend most of my days in the semi-darkness of drawn curtains...I haven't been making my bed for months now. If I drop something on the floor several days will pass before I pick it up. Instead of taking a shower I often find myself opening the medicine cabinet and sniffing Albertina's lavender soap, then walking out of the bathroom unwashed. I haven't touched an oven or a microwave, subsisting mostly on cold sandwiches. I might crumble some cheese on with a knife, but luckily I have no appetite to worry about. In this apartment time has come to a standstill;

perhaps her death abolished it altogether. Familiar objects stare at me with a subdued shriek. Their meaning eludes me: The cobalt pitcher on the countertop, the doily on her dressing table – why are they there? What for? I knew when she was alive, but I don't know now: The world around me is unfathomable. A person's belongings die with their owner; I'm surrounded by the shells of departed souls. In my sleepless nights these dead objects become my judges, but in the morning – victims at my mercy. If I ever find courage to dispose of her clothes, it will be in the early hours of the day.

I know Albertina will not come back; yet I'm waiting. I can't explain or help it. Numbness protected me like a shield in the first month after her death: I tried to escape my grief, as a wounded soldier escapes the battlefield under the anesthetic of shock. In the second month of mourning, however, I discovered that there was no place to hide from the truth suddenly revealed to me: my wife had abandoned me in an act of betrayal, perhaps revenge.

I sit here alone in our bedroom, my lips sealed. Yet I know I must speak, I must, because therein lies my salvation. Will she give me any signs? Will she hear me?

Through the crack between the burgundy velvet curtains, the sun sets aflame the slippers she left on a round rug next to our bed. Later, when the shadows lengthen, these two lonely boats acquire an almost sinister look, their tips growing sharper and meaner. But when the day burns out, under the artificial light of the antique floor lamp, they mellow into sadness. I have no willpower either to remove them or look away.

Three days ago I found her wedding ring. When I picked it up,

it left a distinct circle, its spectral double, on the polished surface
of her night table that hadn't been dusted for a year since her death:
I had instructed our cleaning lady not to touch anything in the
bedroom. But the ring disturbed me. In the quietness of the night,
when I could finally hide from the world under my sheets, I tried to
fit it onto the small finger of my left hand, but it wouldn't go beyond
the first knuckle. As it absorbed the warmth of my palm, it became
lighter and lighter till I couldn't feel its weight anymore. Tears
choked me: I felt both ashamed of myself and strangely relieved.
That piece of metal was all that was left of her. But then a sudden
thought undercut my breath and hit me right under my diaphragm: In
twenty-five years of our marriage not once had I seen her remove her
ring. Why did she do it on the eve of her death? Was it an act of final
renunciation of our union? Did she want no part of me in the nether
land she slipped into? Or was the opposite true? This gleaming,
glowing, imperishable part, that's what she wanted to leave for
my safekeeping. The thought calmed me for a moment. But then I
thrust the sheets off my head and sat up. A sentimental fool! What's
happening to your brains? She must have removed her wedding
ring for a trivial reason: her fingers were swollen, a sign of the heart
disease that none of us had detected in time. She never complained
about heart pains. According to the doctor who examined her dead
body, her heart attack was one of those cases when the only symptom
of the disease is death itself.

2

Strange to say, but I don't remember her face, the face I could observe so closely for so long. The only things that returns her to me are the photographs. Never before did I realize how many pictures lived side by side with us all these years. They never seemed to have reached my consciousness as I glanced at them in passing. On her dressing table, a five-year-old on a pony, her father standing by, reins in his hand; on a mantelpiece, a young girl against the whiteness of her grandparents' house in Provençe, in a light dress, her face cut in half by the shadow from a wide-rimmed straw hat. Whiteness, blinding light...On the piano, in a carved wooden frame, our honeymoon is blooming under the arches of the San Juan de los Reyes cloister in Toledo. There is some darker round shape on the left margin: Something small must have escaped the frame seconds before the camera clicked; it caught the shadow, but not the object that had projected it. What was it? A stray dog? A cat? And why didn't I ever notice it before? Another picture: Both of us touring some old cemetery – where was it, in Europe or North America? She is smiling, her head turned toward me, while I'm looking straight into the camera. Who took this one and when? I never noticed the sign to the left: "Beware of Gravestones and Monuments: *They May Fall Over and Cause Injury.*" Bizarre!

If I still haven't moved to another apartment, it is because I don't know what to do with all these photographs. Shall I buy more albums and tuck them away? What about the empty frames, then? I could put away the photographs together with the frames, but the empty spaces they'd leave behind? Those shallow dust-free patches? No, I can't escape.

When she died, her friends stopped talking to me, saying she died of grief over the state of our marriage. I insist that that was rubbish, total rubbish,I insist that my wife wanted to live. This is not a trite metaphor: her life *was* a meadow spun into existence by her agile fingers, a meadow she kept embroidering till her very last day.

She often used her patterns on whatever came handy – sheets, tablecloths, bed covers, pillow shams – before transferring them to their final canvas. We slept on a baby unicorn cozying up in the arms of an aristocratic lady in a pointed hat. Why did these medieval girls like to cuddle with that creature? Did they truly believe in its existence? And why was my wife so attracted to that motif? On our bed cover there is a unicorn in the Garden of Delight done in white silk, his front legs firmly pressing against what looks like a Tree of Life studded with red pomegranates. His hoofs and his horn are the same golden thread. I can see that protuberance at the foundation of his forehead where the silver thread subtly blends with the golden one. She ran out of her days, leaving the horn half-finished. Now the creature looks strange, half-horse, half-deer, half-done.

On the eve of her death we had guests. Two of her colleagues from the Louvre with their wives, two private collectors and a curator from de Cluny, who hoped to solicit my wife's help in attributing a piece of tapestry his museum had recently acquired. But the star of the party was an expert from St. Petersburg's Hermitage, his ill-fitting suit a strange mismatch with his impeccable French. He was looking for help from De Wit Manufacturers for restoration of the Life of the Virgin series.

"No, the revolutionaries did not confiscate the masterpiece," the expert explained to the guests."Prince Gregory Gagarin personally gave it to the Hermitage around 1887. As you know, we have excellent restoration workshops in the Hermitage. But this is a sixteenth century Flemish tapestry, and we believe the restoration has to be carried out in Flanders. Would you be able to help us?" He turned to my wife, and I noticed an involuntary twitch of his right leg.

"Which of the series, in your opinion, is particularly damaged?" asked Albertina.

"All four parts need substantial repairs, but I believe *The Assumption* has suffered most," replied the man. The effort to both control his tic and remain pleasantly sociable gave his face a tense, searching expression.

"Unfortunately, I know the work only through photographs," said Albertina with a smile. Her voice always climbed to a higher pitch when she was excited or wanted to charm somebody.

"When will you be able to come and see it? Unfortunately, it may take three months, sometimes more, to process the invitation and the visa. An inevitable red tape " The expert sounded as if he were apologizing for small warps in an otherwise perfectly functioning mechanism."But your stellar reputation is known in Hermitage. We're interested."

What an unpleasant fellow, I thought. He is on alert, as if expecting to be conned with a forgery.

But the prospect of receiving a commission from the

Hermitage must have thrilled Albertina. She was unusually talkative that night and drank quite a bit, quickly getting tipsy. She is – I mean, was – of a rather pale complexion, but on that last night of her life her cheeks caught fire. I complimented her on her looks and attempted to kiss her as we stood in the hallway, behind the stained-glass door separating us from our guests. She gently, with her usual irony, brushed me off. I returned to our company.

3

As soon as everybody was gone, Albertina went to bed, but I stayed up and helped the maid we'd hired for the party to tidy the mess. By the time I joined my wife, she was already fast asleep. I lay there for a while listening to her deep, rhythmic respiration. There were some vague sounds in the apartment, old oak parquet lightly cracking, as if settling for the night, happy to be freed from the burden of many feet. Finally the house became quiet.

It looks like she's secured a deal with the Hermitage, I thought. The baggy-pants man, in spite of his stern demeanor, was completely taken by her, I could tell. He was ridiculous though, with that tic of his, his ill-at-ease body, his cockerel-like cough. Well, we might get a trip to St. Petersburg out of him, and that actually might be fun, was my last thought before I slipped away into oblivion.

Close to dawn I woke up to relieve myself. Not counting on the effects of alcohol to last till morning – Albertina was sensitive to the slightest sound – I tried to slip out of bed quietly. I left the door of the bathroom ajar to avoid the screech of the hinges that

I knew needed oiling, and urinated with careful aim to avoid the water. I needed a cigarette, and without turning on the light I tiptoed out to the kitchen and found the pack in the drawer. The darkness outside the window was already liquid brown, diluting with a slow November dawn. I sat there naked on a kitchen stool feeling cold.

The dawn drizzle muted the sounds of tires. I listened for a while to their sad, persistent lisp. Without any reason, a certain melancholy overwhelmed me. Paris never slept but came to a point of stillness, gripped by an inexplicable paralysis just before daybreak. This was the time when every sound stood out: Heels striking the cobble on the empty streets, their click-clack resonating in my sleepy brain. A woman must have been returning from her lover. I had an instant desire to see the face of this stranger, but my body refused to move. I continued to smoke, listening. Her heels became louder now – she must have passed right by my window before the sound suddenly died. Had she turned the corner? Were we neighbours? I imagined a slight, faceless figure groping for her key, unlocking the entryway, then pressing the elevator button. She must've lived alone, I was certain of that. Now she was removing her coat, then walking over to the stove to start her coffee. She took off her dress, folded it on a chair, and stepped into the shower. Without her heels, she was small, probably petite.

Perhaps as short as Karen, but slimmer. Karen had a broad Indigenous frame, wide shoulders, flat feet. For some reason I always think of Karen being barefoot. I imagine her footprints on wet sand, on a beach, a continent distant. She smells of fish and seaweed, just like the first time I saw her on that remote beach, when she let the three men carrying the boat pass by, before stopping and looking at me. She didn't smile. As I came close to her, I saw small silver fish beating inside the net she carried. Her straight long hair was moist, the wet hem of her dress sticking to her full thighs.

Since early morning I had been wandering aimlessly among the dilapidated houses and junk cars on her reservation on Quillayute Island in Washington State. I had my tape recorder at the ready, hoping to catch the clicking sounds of Quillayute, a language unrelated to any other and one of the five in the world with no nasal sounds. She laughed at me and tossed her head when I spoke in Quillayute. "I'm Karen," she said. "That's what you call me, simply Karen." As for her Indian name, it was a secret not to be disclosed to strangers.

Later that afternoon, she said she would help me record her language, and then, as part of the deal, she seduced me on the moist pine needles near the desolate beach, and she finally whispered her true name into my ear: "Qahla." The ocean breathed heavily, scooping boulders and pulling them into the water and then burping them back up with a tremendous thunder. "What is it again?" I shouted."I can hardly hear you!" She whispered, "Qahla," moving away from me, playing with me, teasing me. I reached over to her, pulled her down, pressing the weight of my body on her again: "Now tell me your real name, your true name. I want to hear it."

"Qahla, My great-grandmother called me Qahla three days before her death. The sun setting in a blood bath, she saw it in a dream. Qahla means the sun."

For the next two weeks, intoxicated by the vastness of the

ocean and the astringent smell of the cedar-soaked air, Qahla kept teaching me the words of her own native tongue: *water, wood, fish, silence.* The ease with which the sounds of her strange language slipped off her obedient palate, in hindsight, could have been explained only by her ancestral collective memory rising to the surface of her blood with each breath.

An American, married to a Belgian woman and living in Paris, I could never get those sounds right; the oily softness of her consonants turned out to be my strongest aphrodisiac. I kept coming back to the West Coast for the next dose of it every summer. We made love on the beach and I compared the curves of her body with the musculature of the driftwood, and the cries of the albatrosses were her cries.

4

The dawn was grating against the kitchen's windowpanes, returning red to the tile on the floor, developing the negative of the chrome fridge and oven and cooking utensils hanging on metal hooks. I stubbed out my cigarette feeling the cold through my spine. In the bedroom the warm rancid air hit my nostrils: A smell of alcoholic breath mixed with something I couldn't define. We should open the windows in the morning, I thought, sneaking under the sheets and pressing my nakedness to my wife's side. I vaguely hoped to use Albertina's slim body for Karen's full forms, making love to both, finally overcoming – under the pretext of sleep – the silent veto that my wife had placed between us a long time ago. Then I recoiled.

214

The body lying next to mine was ice cold, already stiff with rigor mortis, or so it seemed to me at this first contact with death. I checked again and was horrified by my instant aversion to what used to be her. I had been away from the bed not more than ten minutes, and it could only have meant one thing: I must have spent a night – the whole night after her breathing had stopped – side by side with a cadaver without being aware of it.

I didn't go to her funeral. Afterward, the silent glances of her friends and relatives accused me of morbid insensitivity. But I couldn't come to terms with her death then any more than I can now. The betrayal. Not only had she shattered the world we'd built together, but she had also taken away the best part of me, the part that loved life, loved its texture, its smells and colours. It sounds strange, but her death also snatched away the women whom I lusted for – I had no desire to see them any longer. As if my dead wife took away my future.

Three months after her death, I decided to move from our bedroom onto the sofa in my library, If there are any changes at all, they creep on me through the back door of my dreams. One night I dreamt that I had no legs. Somebody, some kind of crank, had persuaded me that my legs were rotting and therefore of no use to me anymore. And besides, the smell of the spreading gangrene annoyed the administration of my university. They threatened to fire me. I resorted to a kitchen knife, and when it came to the bone, I used an axe. Having soldiered through the beastly pain, I stuffed my two legs into a black garbage bag. The horror of the dream was not as much in the pain or the absurdity of my limbless condition but rather in the colour: There was nothing dead about my amputated legs; they were pink, baby pink, I remember that vividly. So the bastard had cheated me – my legs were still quite usable – and therefore, I had to find him, chase him, cajole him, beg him, tell him I wanted my legs glued back to my body. But how to catch him with no legs to run after him? The only way out of the impasse was to wake up. And that seemed no easier than pulling myself out of a swamp by the hair. Then I began to scream. I kept screaming in my sleep, all the time aware that no sound was coming out of my mouth.

In hindsight, I know now that all my troubles with language started with that nightmare. It was that monstrous effort that produced nothing but a hollow, mute cry that ruined my voice, and with it, my ability to articulate my thoughts. But I also don't rule out that the occasional stumbling on a wrong word and the eclipse of the right one had come upon me earlier, shortly after Albertina's death, and the dream was no more than a catalyst for an earlier condition. My muteness was her form of revenge, the worst torture she could have inflicted on a man living through words and words alone.

Back to my dream now, or rather to the moment of awakening. The first thing I noticed was the dictionary of Mohawk that was lying on the floor next to my sofa. It was in this dictionary that I found a temporarily relief.

Entering the body of a new language has always both soothed and excited me. It is much like penetrating the body of a new lover, the uncharted territory that fills me with the thrill of anticipation. But this time the mechanics of an unknown grammar left me cold.

What's more, my memory was refusing to retain any new words. Not to be able to memorize a dozen new words after you've learned thirty languages or so, what can be more alarming? Albertina! Were you that night butcher who persuaded me to cut off my legs? No, no, you would've pitied me had you found out what happened to me after your death. You're not beyond care, are you, my pale swan? Even if you've abandoned me so cruelly, you still care for me, don't you? A gentle sigh of sympathy from beyond the grave,that's all I would want for comfort.

For some reason, you never appear to me in my dreams.

Instead you instigated this spectral telephone call, no doubt to torment me further, never allowing my guilt to subside. Drowsy after a sleepless night, I couldn't clue in right away; then I recognized the voice of our visitor from the Hermitage: Invitations and visas for both of us were ready, it informed me. Could we come at our earliest convenience, in the view of some new developments? The Hermitage had teamed up with the Metropolitan Museum in New York, which had invited the Life of the Virgin series as one of its showpieces in the forthcoming exhibition *Tapestry in the Renaissance: Art and Magnificence*. The restoration of the famous tapestry was now even more urgent, he continued, and the timeline was tight. Work of this scope couldn't be carried out in the Hermitage's own restoration facility. Name any price, we will accommodate.

I kept listening, mesmerized by Albertina's capacity to bear malice to me from beyond. "Albertina is dead. Dead!" I barked into the pause between his long-winded explanations. Then I hung up.

217

5

I wonder if any of my students have noticed that my speech has become laboured, or perhaps that's how I hear it inside my head, whereas for any listener my utterances remain perfectly coherent. Whatever the case may be, the problem is not of a neurological order. It is simply that by the middle of the sentence I lose interest in my own thoughts. Every time it happens I stop, quickly shift gears, and move in another direction with a straight face.

That is not to say that I have lost any of my professional acumen: I am enjoying my international reputation as one of the leading specialists on Native American languages, and I pride myself on my ability to galvanize my students with an unexpected joke or an anecdote. Let's face it, linguistics can be as dry and boring as performing a particle analysis of sawdust. The other day, for example, in my Language Acquisition Theory seminar, I said to my freshmen: "Conrad was known to have such a heavy accent in English as not to be understood even by his close friends. At what age should he have emigrated from Poland in order to have no accent at all? Or take another famous example, Andersen, the fairy-tale writer. He couldn't write one grammatically correct sentence in his own mother tongue till his twenties. At what age would it still not be too late...to...to... "

There was an awkward pause. I let the chalk slip out of my hands; picking it up afforded me some desperately needed time. "So, my dear colleagues – " (in the spirit of false camaraderie, I always call these kids "colleagues," boosting their new-fangled academic vanity) " – so, my dear colleagues,since there is ample evidence that the ability to spell well or badly, as the case may be, runs in families and depends on genes more than on education, how plausible it is that in the near future we will be able to single out one specific gene responsible, say, for spelling; another, for *plus-que-parfait* French, yet another for, say..."

I felt myself on slippery ground again and quickly changed course. "Instead of boring you with more theory, let me give you an amusing example that will illustrate my next point, namely: Linguistics is as precise as mathematics, and we can't simply rely on our intuition when we draw conclusions about...about...just about anything in our field. Do you know where the word *pumpernickel* comes from, for example? During one of his campaigns in Central Europe, Napoleon stopped at an inn and was served a loaf of coarse, dark, sour bread. But he was used to the white baguettes of Paris, of course, so he sneered, '*C'est pain pour Nicole*,' Nicole being his horse. *Pain-pour-Nicole*. Pum-per-nickel. Isn't it wonderful?"

I looked around. There was an expectant silence.

"Any comments on that?" I asked my students, not addressing anybody in particular. "No? Well, then! It's obvious to any linguist that the whole thing about Napoleon's horse is a hoax! A hoax made up by some drunk journalist and his buddy in an Irish pub. The word comes from colloquial German meaning *farting goblin*!"

Suppressed laughter ran through the aisles.

As usual, I left the my class triumphant.

6

And so during one of those seminars, a freshman, a girl with dark cropped hair, in a mini-skirt revealing the longest legs I've ever seen, asked me how I had mastered all the languages I knew.

"That's nothing, given that there are some four to six thousand languages in the world, is it?" The class stirred approvingly at my joke. "The answer is trivial," I continued after quietness was restored. "I choose simpler languages. And by the way, is there such a thing as a simple language, dear colleagues?" I paused, grabbing the opportunity to entertain as well as to educate my students. "If you believe there is, could you prove your point?" (Direct provocation, apart from my jokes, was part of my teaching arsenal.)

But the long-legged girl saw through my ruse and raised her hand. "All languages, even the languages of what used to be called 'primitive tribes,' are very high-tech. Take Bantu group of languages, for example. It has hundreds of prefixes and suffixes. French, with its underdeveloped morphology, pales in comparison! The only languages with simpler grammar would be artificial languages like Volopuk or Esperanto, the reason they never really functioned. Redundancy is a mandatory characteristic of any language if it is to fulfill its communicative function."

"Well done!" I said. "Indeed, no living language would be simple. That much we can be certain about. All languages are equally complex and have always been that way at any known stage of their development."

"Professor," persisted the girl. "You didn't answer my

question: How did you become a polyglot?"

A tenacious little thing, I thought."Well, it's simple. First, you must have a burning desire to communicate with people; with all sorts of people, all over the world. Second, I do not do languages in which the number of noun cases exceeds twenty-two. Here is a riddle then:Which languages will not get my attention?" Of the whole class I was now addressing that girl alone.

"Tabasaran, for one, the language of the South Dagestan," responded the brunette. "It uses forty-eight noun cases. Inuktitut uses sixty-three forms of present tense. But you were talking only about nouns, if I understood you correctly?"

After the seminar was over, I approached her in the corridor:

"I'm impressed by your erudition," I said. "Sorry, I don't know your name, though I suppose I should by now."

"Solange Moreau." She flashed her eyes at me and was gone.

7

I must say, without false modesty, that my fame, a natural outcome of my hard work, quickly grew far beyond the university auditoriums. I was now lobbying three governments, those of Canada, Russia, and Greenland, to introduce a completely new alphabet (of my own invention), so that the sixty-five thousand Inuit of these respective countries could understand each other's written texts. There is no sense, I pointed out in my numerous memos, no sense at all for the Greenland and Alaskan people to use the Latin alphabet while Siberian Inuit (or Yupik, to use a more specific term) were using

Cyrillic and the Canadian territory of Nunavut resorted to the Inuktitut syllabary, an invention of my perverted ancestor James Evans, a pastor, a missionary, and a seducer of little Ojibway girls; a man who believed that the rather primitive circles and squares he had doodled during long Arctic evenings would acquit his charges from burning in hell once they learned to read the New Testament. I, however, was proposing a much simpler and more sensible system of writing for all three peoples. I claimed that the lack of a common script would isolate the three nations even more than their artificial geographical borders. Solange Moreau was assisting me with the project. We worked well together, and it was only natural for me one day to invite her to my apartment. It's been my habit, my liberal habit, to meet my students at home, in an informal environment, to let them browse through my books, and, occasionally, even to join me and Albertina for supper. But this time Albertina was out, and I had to play host myself.

"Who is this?" asked Solange, her eyes gliding over the rows of books in my study to the portrait over my desk.

"Supposed to be me, or rather my younger version. No resemblance, you think?"

"Is that a watercolour?" She came up to my desk to have a closer look at the portrait. "No, it doesn't look like you at all."

"My wife's gift for our twentieth wedding anniversary. She wove it. Have I changed that much in the last five years?"

"Woven? I thought this stuff only exists in museums!"

"You're right. It is a dying art form. Though Paris has been the center of tapestry since the thirteenth century, and still is. My wife restores medieval tapestry, but she is also an artist in her own right. Please take a seat." I pointed to an armchair across the room.

"*C'est superb*," said Solange."I'd love to meet her one day. I prefer this rocking chair over here though." She moved to a rocking chair close to me. "You don't mind, do you?"

"No, not at all. What would you like, juice or wine?"

"Wine, of course. Red," said Solange, rocking, her crossed black-stockinged legs exposed halfway up her thighs. I turned my eyes away. Her unabashed confidence both annoyed and intrigued me.

"Tell me, Professor, don't you sometimes get confused?"

"I'm sure I do." I chuckled. "What exactly do you mean though?"

"I mean, the thirty or whatever languages you speak. Don't you mix up the morphemes, perhaps whole paradigms when you speak? I'm just curious."

"Ah, that! Sure, it happens. I don't know exactly how it works. I need to hear the language, to live with it for a month or two, before I can speak it."

"How do you remain sane, with so much to remember? I've been studying Sanskrit for a year now, and I still read it with difficulty."

"Well, dead languages are difficult to master. But Sanskrit is a good choice! Once you've got Sanskrit, you have all European languages up your sleeve, as you know. You're very capable, you'll get there. Have you heard of Cartesian linguistics?"

"Yes," said Solange quickly. "Well, sort of. Not really."

Clearly, she didn't want to lose her credentials with me.

"Don't be shy to acknowledge that you don't know something." I poured pinot noir into her glass. "That's the only way we can learn, by asking questions. Chomsky drew his ideas of deep and surface structure from Descartes, you may say. The deep structure is common to all languages, forming a universal grammar, Chomsky's term. The transformational rules convert deep to surface structure and may differ. Therefore, it is quite possible to learn another – "

"You intrigue me," she suddenly interrupted. "I find you fascinating."

She put her glass down, rose to her feet, and, looking straight into my eyes, walked up to me, her lips slightly apart.

"I want to know how your mind works," she said, putting her arms on my shoulders.

"I see the language as an organism," I said, tracing my finger over her face. "Language has organs, just like our body. The idea is not at all new. Darwin was the first to notice the parallel. Nature used a very small inventory – vertebrae, legs, breasts in mammals – to create a seemingly endless variety of species. So it is with languages. Universal grammar."

She brought her face close to mine.

"The distinctions between languages are superficial," I said."On a deeper level, there are more similarities than differences." I began unbuttoning her blouse.

8

I have always been a champion of moderation and balance. Excesses are simply not in my nature. Between annual field trips to the Pacific Coast and weekly trysts with Solange, I felt in top physical form. Solange was as diligent and efficient in bed as she was in her linguistics studies. By the time I'd show up in her *mansard* every Monday between 3:00 and 4:00 p.m., she, already naked under a silk kimono, would quickly put her cigarette out on the fish-shaped ashtray and slip under the cold sheets, soaking me in her smoky breath. This routine hasn't changed even since she got married to my colleague from the philosophy department and moved to a luxurious apartment in the 7th Arrondissement.

There was some disruption in our schedule only for the last month of her pregnancy and the first five weeks after she gave birth to twin boys, exactly what her husband had always wanted, she told me once after we had made love. Giving birth to twins was one way of saving time, she said, and I must admit, Solange was the most efficient time manager I'd ever met in my life. Before the newborns were two months old, we were already on our normal schedule, adjusting the time to between 10:00 and 11:00 a.m. to accommodate the nanny who took a two-seated pram to Jardin des Tuileries exactly for that hour. The only awkwardness of it all, as far as I was concerned, was the sugary smell of Solange's leaking breasts, which I found distasteful. Sometimes I would rush to leave her under the pretext of my pressing schedule, being vague about the whole thing, yet suggesting we should wait another month or two. Without looking at me, she would get up, light another cigarette, walk across the room to the window, and stare silently at the street below it. She wouldn't say a word, and before I knew I would be at her door again the next week, right on time.

I must say that my three-faced existence suited me perfectly. Solange's boyish body tantalized me, and the clinical feel of our affair put a piquant touch to my urban existence. As I was running past Le Musée d'Orsay with the metal legs of La Tour Eiffel flicking by, in an hour between lectures, I felt the accelerated rhythm of my heart beating in synch with the parched rhythm of the city.

As for Karen, I saw her only once a year during my summer field trips, with no communication in between. She was more than a continent away, and that suited me just fine. She seemed to be glad when I arrived, yet displayed no signs of regret when I had to leave. I never questioned her on her life between my visits. That she would have a lover or several lovers in my absence seemed most probable. Again, I didn't see any reason to ask.

And just as I couldn't imagine Solange ever having a moment free, so I couldn't imagine Karen ever being busy. I had no idea what she did for a living. An abundance of time washed around her flat face, her suntanned calves, like a tide around the narrow strip of sand we lay on watching the sunset. But her tide was an eternity. Her compact body seemed to know a secret that eluded me. She belonged to the surf, to the rocks, and the cedar woods the way I never did or could. She amused herself by lying naked on top of a massive tree trunk, an amputated torso with one end anchored in the sand, the other dangling in the water, coming to life with each incoming wave, washing over her nakedness. Lazily, I watched a seagull landing on the tip of a rock sticking out of the water and quickly, in a neat origami-like movement, folding its wings, then lingering a moment before soaring up again directly into the fiery cone the sun had sliced into the darkened surface of water, from the very horizon to our feet. And at that moment I never wanted to be anywhere else: Karen's stocky, earth-bound body, the gull rising into the sinking sun, were my languorous ecstasy, my illusionary, long-longed-for home, that I knew would disappear together with the last golden patches of light.

9

Did I have any guilt about my affairs? Not now, nor then. None of these were affairs of the heart. Yet they gave me a physical sensation of well-being; a kind of a sturdy solid core that made me feel invincible. I became generous and more patient with the outside world, which included my wife. I could now forgive her imperfections with much more grace. I realized her aloofness wasn't a weapon aimed against me; it was simply a form of childhood shyness she'd never been able to overcome.

She was eighteen when we got married, a girl with pale hair, transparent skin, and no goal in life except one: To be close to me any time of day or night. I couldn't understand how somebody so reserved, so unexpressive in her feelings, and in no apparent need of human company was at the same time so stubbornly, feverishly needy of my physical presence. Without me she seemed to be adrift, lost in a world toward which she seemingly held no interest. What was she doing during my absence? When I would come home, tired after the long day of lecturing, I'd find her sitting where I'd left her in the morning,her eyes following absent-mindedly some photos in a trashy lady's magazine. Couldn't she have at least tossed some potatoes in boiling water so that I had something to eat? I found it more and more difficult to suppress my frustration. Her response was to take up knitting.

True, I did choose my wife on the principle that she would be the complete opposite of my mother. I didn't need to be told how to live my life every goddamn day. I refused to accept tantrums as the most effective way of teasing compassion (if not love) out of me. And yes, at the beginning, I did find Albertina's shyness charming. She was quiet. She didn't talk much, as if her tongue were too relaxed to form words. And what an easy prey for my vanity! Her grey eyes lifted to my face in rapture, in an almost superstitious awe at my ability to pick up any language in three months. My colleagues were Gods from the Olympus she peeped at from behind my back. How totally trusting she was, how completely dependent on me! I was deluding myself then, deceiving her at the same time: For how could I think that this taciturn girl could satisfy all my ambitions, my vanities, my cravings for longer than a whiff?

I'm not a psychologist. I can't explain why things change. Perhaps, an ideal woman for any man is an elusive chameleon, a magician with new tricks up her sleeve every sunset. All I know is that soon I felt bored. And the more bored I was, the harder I tried to hide that boredom.

We still lived in Brussels then (my wife's native town), and my career at Université Libre was rocketing. I became one of the leading experts on Native American languages, having penned fifteen important articles and being on my second book. Greedy for new faces and places, I wanted the adventure, the excitement of new ideas. I don't want to pass myself off as a petty tyrant, but every time I came home I knew exactly what to expect: timid anticipation, helplessness, pale guilty fingers fluttering around the knitting needles undoing – the moment Albertina heard the sound of my key in the lock – the portion they had just accomplished. I could never understand why she insisted on knitting those damn sweaters or scarves for me when she could buy any number of them in the stores. (Please note, I never begrudged her any money or ever mentioned the fact that for years I was the only breadwinner). What was it for her in this compulsive knitting that had never resulted in one finished article of clothing? An old-fashioned way of demonstrating her wifely devotion? A hiding place afforded by the same mechanical routine? And was the undoing of her own work the expression of her secret fear of never being able to please me?

Our youth passed under the sign of coloured yarn balls in metal basins that moved with us from one apartment, city, or country to the next.

10

The turning point in our lives came when one morning I saw an ad in a local newspaper: "Restoration of Ancient Tapestry. Conservation and Hand Weaving. Demonstration of Traditional Techniques." De

Wit Royal Manufacturer of Tapestry, the oldest and most reputable
house in the country, invited new apprentices to a three-day
workshop.

We got on a train and in twenty-five minutes were in
Mechelen, a quiet medieval town of brown brick churches and
abbeys, huddled together over the river – what was its name? Doshle
or Dijle? it doesn't really matter – but the river was so slow, so
peaceful that we too felt cozy and appeased as if somebody had
wrapped us up in cool cotton wool. There are such places on earth
that for some unknown reason give you an intimation of happiness, if
not happiness itself. Was it the sounds of bells that made us dreamy,
almost somnambulist? The air was tender; there was that smell, that
peculiar aroma that I came to associate with joyful lightness. On
street corners matrons in white aprons were crocheting laces: it was
the beginning of tourist season.

The visit to De Wit was a stroke of luck. Albertina finally
found her true vocation. It was hiding in faded tableaux that
unknown hands had woven several hundred years before. She turned
out to have patience, precision, dexterity of fingers, good taste – all
that it took to become an excellent tapestry restorer. She could spend
hours over the imperceptible juncture where the feet of peasant girls
dressed like duchesses sank into the muted greens of the meadow.
Once it took her four months to mend a cloak depicting some duke in
a hunting procession.

After a brief trial period, Albertina became a full-time
apprentice at De Wit. I remember now, with great nostalgia, the
month of August when I accompanied her on her trips: as usual, she

was reluctant to go alone. We'd get off the train and walk into town. Albertina always held my hand before entering Tongero Abbey, De Wit's headquarters. Near the entrance I'd hug her goodbye, she'd hesitate, start on her way, then quickly turn around and dive into my arms again, a child reluctant to leave her parent. We'd say goodbye all over again; she'd press her cheek to mine for a moment and then be gone.

Idling away the four or five hours of her absence, I'd sit at a sidewalk café, my dictionary at hand, and try to focus on the sixty forms of Algonquin verbs. Sometimes, to kill the time, I would go to the Museum of Toys and stare at dolls, yellowish frills and laces, plump meaningless faces untouched by time. Why do we grown-ups cherish toys of bygone generations? An erupted nostalgia for our own childhood? I liked the green cabriolet dragged by a wooden horse, sporting shiny red wheels and a coachman in a faded uniform on top. And then there was a wooden circus arena, with seats arranged as an amphitheatre, red carpet running down the stairs and golden curtains with each pompom meticulously reproduced. Musicians in blue tunics played silently, one holding a saxophone, another a violin. In the middle of the arena cavorted a clown in one shoe, both hands busy, a parachute in one, a hat in the other, balanced forever on one naked toe. I came to the museum several times just to look at the carriage with its horse and the arena with a hapless clown.

In the afternoon Albertina would appear in the frame of the Tongero Abbey portal bathed in the luminescent golden aura of the vespertine sun. Her light hair against the emerald of the Abbey's manicured lawn seemed to be enveloped into a halo that moved together with her. The quiet radiance fluttered around her blouse, reaching to the hem of her dress, then her shoes. I was in love with her again, the way I had been before I married her, and I loved that sensation of love most; perhaps more than I loved Albertina herself. In hindsight, I know that my truest happiness was in the anticipation of her appearance, when the heavy door would finally let her out and I and I...well, somehow her actual physical presence could never live up to the ecstasy of the foretaste. I would look at her trying to hold on to that magic, that I knew would soon fade, betray me, leaving me alone as the golden aura would go dull the moment we started talking. I sincerely wanted to know what she had learnt. But her words were as vague as her smiles, no match to my excitement. "I'm tired," she'd say putting her head on my shoulder when we got into the train. And then she'd be gone, sleeping or pretending to sleep. Did she not know how I had been missing her all that time and how I wanted to talk to her? Perhaps she couldn't believe that I could be truly interested in weft and warp – or was her reticence a way of guarding her newly discovered world against me? I felt disappointed. The rhythmic click-clack of the wheels punctuated my loneliness. My tenderness, my desire for her would evaporate: I felt the weight of her head on my shoulder, now a burden paralyzing my muscles.

It was in those rides back home that we began to spiral away from each other into our illusionary worlds: I continued to perfect my knowledge of languages no longer in use; she continued to mend tapestry, painting life the way it had never been.

For Albertina's thirtieth birthday I brought her from Italy a small sixteenth century tapestry. Cost me a fortune, half of my mother's inheritance, to be precise. She raised her brow. I said, "You're going to be a real expert, one of a kind. It is important for you to have an authentic work in front of your eyes at all times." She agreed, turned the piece around, examined the reverse side of it, waved her hand in the air, and stepped out of the house to get some groceries.

"What does that mean?" I asked her later in bed. "Didn't you like that piece?"

"I did," she said, without any expression in her face. "But..."

"But what?"

"I don't know. It must be so expensive..."

"My dear, the price is not the point. It's your birthday, and besides, you know why I bought it? Why you have to have an authentic Van Aelst at home?"

"Why?"

"So that you could look at it and learn from it!"

"But I can't. It's so beautiful that I...that I...I can't!"

I kept buying her books on medieval history. I didn't want her to be an ordinary seamstress with agile fingers. I wanted her to know the history of her craft, to have a perspective on things, the context. In other words, I wanted her to become one of a kind, a world-class restorer. But I don't think she ever opened any of the books. Curiosity was not in her nature.

Yet with time, and somehow in disdain of my efforts, Albertina became what I urged her to be, an expert on medieval weaving, a master of restoration in high demand. By that time we had moved to Paris. I was teaching at the Sorbonne and her name – my name!

– was now known in international circles. Private art collectors and curators of the leading museums were seeking her out.

11

They say money and fame spoil people. Maybe so. But in my case I witnessed something different. It was a sudden elopement – though who was the eloper? – not a gradual change of character. One day I looked around and didn't find the shy, angularly awkward girl who was my wife. Instead a sophisticate looked at me with a confident and dispassionate eye. It gives me shivers now to remember her glance the first time I paid attention to it. Apart from indifference it expressed something else: undisguised mockery; this woman was entertaining herself at my expense. I watched her closely at the *vernissages* and cocktail parties where we had become a binary fixture. She was indisputably the most elegantly dressed woman in any crowd, and perhaps the most beautiful. I also watched men watching her, the quick mutual exchange of glances, each glance a price tag. I can't pinpoint the moment when I became a worn-out shoe in her eyes, but that I did, I couldn't doubt. I had become her satellite. My wife was now free from me, I knew it in my guts. She didn't belong to me anymore. I had become her past, not her future. Her every gesture: the way she turned her head, the way she smiled, the way she leaned back in her chair, confirmed that it was so. When I finally realized it, rage and jealousy exploded inside me with an unforeseen force. What made things even worse is that the less available I imagined her to be, the more I desired her.

Albertina had forged a strategy – if I can call it that, for I don't think it was anything conscious on her part – a strategy of dealing *avec la situation domestique*, as she called it. She didn't actually rebuff my advances but condescended to them as to a certain childish weakness, the most debilitating punishment a woman can inflict on a man.

She also acquired new gestures that enraged me: at our evening meals she'd sit with her eyes half-closed, the back of her palm pressing flatly to her temple, as if my words gave her a severe headache. If I asked her a question, she'd squeeze her fingers till they cracked, and only then answer me. I was ready to strangle her.

When Albertina got pregnant, I welcomed it not because I cared for a baby but because I genuinely hoped that her pregnancy would return her to me. I did my best to comfort her when she had a miscarriage. But she must have felt that I wasn't truly able to share her grief – after all, the baby was her idea, not mine. My efforts at empathy must have seemed artificial to her. I then let her grieve alone. She retreated deeper into herself. When I as much as touched her, in a brotherly gesture of comfort, she grimaced. After the unfortunate outcome of her pregnancy she must have begun to perceive my body as a menace. When she moved to another bed, I was very understanding: she had to recuperate. Eventually, she did get better and did return to our bedroom, though not to me.

I don't want to put blame for my infidelities on this peculiar marital arrangement we ended up with. I started to have affairs long before her miscarriage. Did she suspect anything? I believe not, but even if she did, I couldn't imagine her being upset about it.

Sometimes I felt she pitied me, but perhaps I was just making that up. Mostly, I think, she was indifferent. Lying next to her, in our habitual state of chastity, it was me who felt sorry for her solitude: it would be good for her to find distractions similar to mine, I thought. Not that it was an idea I could entertain for long before losing sleep.

What I found so peculiar is that the further we moved away from each other, the better housewife and cook she became. She now loved to entertain. We were an exemplary couple, very much en vogue; it was an honour to be invited to our house. Albertina made sure that our home suited all my needs; it was quiet, cozy, tastefully furnished, with interesting *objetsd'art* and occasional bric-a-brac (a nod to her taste); a velvet or satin cushion here and there and numerous ikebanain unusually shaped vases, her latest hobby. I travelled less now and invariably looked forward to coming home in the evening. We seemed to have made a full circle. I knew she would be waiting for me, just as she did in our youth. But this time I could expect a glass of good wine, a table set for two with my favourite dishes: artichoke salad, bouillabaisse, foie gras chaud à la crème de lentilles. During one of my absences Albertina got a cat, a formidable blue-eyed Balinese called Dante. I objected to the name, but since the cat came with it, I held my peace.

Yes, we finally did mellow and, without rocking the boat any further, glided peacefully into our middle age. The years preceding her death were especially pleasant: to be able to perform every routine without frictions, with your eyes closed, so to speak, was a reward for living side by side for twenty-five years any sensible couple may hope for.

12

It must have been late April – the chestnut trees holding up all their candles to the deepened blueness of the sky – when my status quo, my fragile happiness, was shattered in the most trivial fashion, by insignificant banter one lazy Sunday morning.

Albertina was recovering from a flu. Her protracted dry cough made me feel uncomfortable, as if I were responsible for it and could have done something about it but didn't. I'd take her out for breakfast to a small brasserie in our neighbourhood, I thought. The weather was splendid, air delicately fragrant with blossoming bushes whose presence you can feel in Paris in spring even on the busiest streets. We took the one free table left outside. While we were waiting for our order, I was watching people buying newspapers at a stand across the street. As usual, I tried to second-guess their characters, their professions: this potbelly will open the auction page first; and the shaved head wants the sports section only; the middle-aged damsel will read, who knows what she'll read, well, let's make her gobble up the gossip column first, then look at the fashion pages. Across the street a teenaged white girl was dragging a dark-skinned baby along; an old woman in a hat strewn with artificial flowers limped along the sidewalk. Two young men and a girl came up to our table. I recognized my students. When I asked them to join us, they were in the middle of some heated debate, something about the state of modern marriage. "Being married to the same person half a century is an absurdity, don't you think, Madame?" the young girl addressed my wife, casting a quick glance at one of the boys sitting next to her.

Albertina turned her face to the young girl. "I'm no judge," she said smiling softly. "My marriage is not very conventional. I've – " she paused for a moment " – I've never really been married, and so I don't know what it's like." The girl started to giggle the way girls often do when they are embarrassed. Then she joked about her parents, who had become the happiest couple as lovers since their divorce after a twenty-year marriage.

"I'd love a beer instead of coffee," said the girl, looking at her young man. Everybody felt awkward. Yet I could see Albertina was not at all apologetic. She had purposefully humiliated me in front of these kids, my own students.

When we came back home I locked myself in my study to finish the article I was working at, but there was no way I could focus. Never been married! Do twenty-five years with me count for nothing? Or had I misunderstood her? Did she really mean that she'd rather be married to somebody else? Did she have a lover all these years and had now finally spilled the beans? Old jealousies stirred in me: my own emotions took me by surprise, but by the end of the day I felt poisoned the way I felt many years ago at cocktail parties, suspecting a lover in every man she smiled at. Perhaps my suspicions were nothing, I tried to persuade myself; but even so, I didn't know what to do with them, ask her directly or continue to live in torture waiting for some evidence of the disaster to explode our lives? But suppose I'm imagining things, I thought, suppose she has always been faithful...while I have had lovers. But this is not the point at all; my lovers are not the point; what matters is that I was kind to her, I loved her, I helped her to become who she is, I supported her as long as she...no, that's not it again; the real question, the painfully nagging question is what have I done to make her so unhappy? Can she have been that disillusioned with me all these years? What if she was right? Our relationship had never really been a marriage. A kind of daycare arrangement in its early stages and now...what is it now?

A wave of fury choked me. Aha! She's going to play the martyr! A victim of my depravity, a silent sufferer! I was locked in a vicious circle rattling around the same old emotions: astonishment, resentment at her ingratitude, self-pity, then guilt, then jealousy, then rage, and somewhere, at the very bottom, the same old sensation of the pettiness of life bordering on vaudeville.

In June of that year I went to the Pacific Coast intending to stay there a whole month instead of my usual two weeks.

13

It was during that trip to the Quillayute that I made yet another sudden discovery: Karen had a six-year-old son. Where had she been hiding him during my previous visits? I never found that out. The first time I saw the boy, he was sitting on the edge of a chair rocking back and forth, his hands tightly pressed between his legs. Greasy, unevenly cut strands of dark hair covered half his face. When I entered the room, his mother told him to stop rocking and stand up; he reluctantly obeyed and lingered there, his head down, shoulders slumping forward, his hands still on his crotch. I don't think I've ever seen such an off-putting child in my life. Without saying a word, Karen removed his hands from his genitalia. The boy then reached for his eyes rubbing them relentlessly. He must have Down's syndrome, I thought. The boy raised his face, and I saw dark inflamed circles around his half-closed lids. Then I knew he was blind.

"What's your name?" I lightly touched his shoulder. The boy shuddered and clung to his mother.

"Jeremy is shy," said Karen. "He doesn't talk much."

"Nice name, Jeremy. Glad to meet you, young man." I held out my hand for him to shake, forgetting he couldn't see it.

"Give me five. I've got something for you."

I slipped my watch off my wrist and put it into his small palm. His fingers quickly closed around it.

"Listen: tick, tick, tock. Somebody must be hiding inside my clock. Who do you think it is?"

"A coyote," whispered Jeremy. "No, a squillel. He clacks nuts."

(He still can't manage his alveolar retroflex, I thought.)

"I've never seen a coyote," I said. "Where do they live?"

"In the woods," said Jeremy, cocking his head. His face had an unfocused, fuzzy expression, typical of the blind.

"And how did a squirrel get inside this watch?"

The boy didn't answer.

"Will you show me the woods where squirrels live, then? Your mother will come with us."

I had never dealt with children before, never mind blind ones, and I was groping in the dark here no less than the sightless boy. He took an uncertain step forward, searching for my hand, then wrapped his arms around my left leg and pushed me falteringly toward the door. I let him initiate the movement, pretending he was guiding me.

"Is it scary in the woods?" I made a frightened face, forgetting again that Jeremy couldn't see. Moving like Siamese twins – him pushing me from behind yet holding on to my pants, me pretending not to know my bearings – we finally reached a small grove a short distance from Karen's cabin. The early evening light made an arcade of the rainforest, an Oregon grape and salal setting for Quillayute elves, devil's club for the trolls among the mossy logs of windfall.

"Take me to gluba-tlee," said Jeremy once we had entered the grove.

"He calls it *gluba*, that tree over there," Karen pointed to a cedar, no different, I thought, from any other. "He can't say *r*."

At the tree Jeremy stood still, for the first time letting go of my pants. Then his hands began to work up the trunk till they found a crack in the bark. He adjusted his lips to the crack and produced a long piercing whistle. Then he turned his face, with the semblance of a smile, roughly in my direction as if waiting for my approval.

"Well done, Jeremy! Now show me how you did it." I wanted him to know I was excited.

Hard as I tried, no whistle came out of my mouth when I applied it to "gluba," but as a compensation I started making all sorts of funny noises. I became a rooster, a duck, a frog, and Jeremy imitated me with amazing accuracy. For a moment we both went wild, Jeremy jumping awkwardly around and emitting sharp brief shrieks of delight.

"Leave the man alone, Jeremy, this is stupid!" shouted Karen from a distance. I had never heard such displeasure in her voice.

Our game was interrupted when a mosquito bit Jeremy on his neck and the boy immediately gave out a terrified scream. I noticed how little resistance he had to pain. Unable to predict the direction it might come from, he felt totally defenseless.

"It's always like that," said Karen, not addressing anybody in particular. "Either he sits like a bag of potatoes doing nothing, or screams like mad."

I rubbed the bitten spot on Jeremy's neck and scooped him into my arms.

"Don't cry! You're a strong big man, Jeremy! The mosquito was tiny. We've rubbed him right out! He'll never get you again."

But the boy kept sobbing, his head buried in my armpit. Luckily, the mosquito had been a loner with no retinue to follow it.

"Do you want to hear a mosquito story?"

"Aha," said Jeremy, sniffling.

"There is a city called Machu Picchu. It is so high up the mountains, you can't see one mosquito flying around."

"Not one?"

"Nope. It's too cold for them and too high."

"Any flies?"

"Nope."

"Have you been?"

"Yes. I climbed many steps right up to the very top. It is so high you can touch the sky."

"That's why thel a' no flies?"

"Too high for them and too cold."

I told Jeremy how the city was built and then abandoned, how strong the houses still were: a knife blade wouldn't go between the stones. But what impressed him most was that there is a city in the world with no flies or mosquitoes.

"Will you take me?"

"You have to grow up first," I said.

"I glow up fast," said Jeremy.

"Time to go home," declared Karen "Back inside."

The sun was retreating into the ocean, splashing the sand, our clothes, and the unseeing face of a little boy with its last glory.

"I don't want to," said Jeremy, grabbing onto my shirt.

"I'm coming with you. Let's go, big man!" I stood the boy on his feet. He hugged my left leg, and in that fashion, glued together, we slowly moved forward.

14

The boy's hand remained firmly locked in mine all the time he was having his dinner. His mother plopped some spaghetti with tomato sauce on his plate and left. I heard a TV click in her bedroom. With only one hand at his disposal, Jeremy quickly made a mess out of his meal. He scooped up a forkful of spaghetti: red-slimed white worms slipped off the fork and sprawled all over the table; some fell on the floor. I kept scooping them off the worn coral arborite back onto his plate, wondering how he would manage eating spaghetti without anybody's help. I had no doubt by now that he was receiving little assistance at home. Karen seemed to be watching *Survivor.* At one point, I tried to go to the washroom, but Jeremy quickly got down on all fours and crawled after me, a method of locomotion he apparently resorted to when he needed to get to a familiar destination as fast as possible. After dinner he curled up in my arms and instantaneously fell asleep. I listened to his light snoring. The boy was tired. I kept my face away from his hair, which was giving off the sickening smell of grease. I remember Karen had told me he was afraid of water and scissors.

The next morning Jeremy wanted to take me to his gluba tree again, but it was pouring rain.

"The gluba tree is taking a shower," I said. "We have to take a bath too."

Karen was still luxuriating in the bed we had so usefully occupied.

I thought it was rather a brilliant tactic of mine, until I realized I had to get into the tub with the boy if I ever hoped to get him washed. And so I did. Soon we were taking turns soaping each other's arms, chests, and backs. He finally let me wash his hair and trim his nails.

"Tomorrow we'll cut your hair, and you'll be a big brave man, you promise?"

"Plomise," said Jeremy and sighed. Then he made a little strange sound, turning his head away from me. Somehow he sensed that his mother had entered the bathroom, and he clearly wanted me all for himself. Karen, wearing her sunburst-patterned shift against the early chill, evinced no objection. She seated herself on the toilet with only a grumbled "Morning." I turned away.

As I was rubbing his scrawny body with a towel, Jeremy's fingers detected a small scar on my forearm, and I had to come up with some explanation: pirates had abducted me when I was just a kid. I then jumped into the ocean and outswam the sharks, so strong and fast was I, but the pirates shot arrows from the deck of their schooner, and then one arrow scratched my shoulder and my arm before I finally reached the shore. Hence, the scar.

"When I glow up, I'll fight pilots too," said Jeremy.

"Say *r*. Pirates."

"Pilots. I'll fight all the pilots in the wolld!"

"Pilots are good. You don't want to fight them. You want to fight pirates. Say *pirates*."

"Pilots."

"All right. Do you want to hear a story about a good pilot, then?"

I was combing his wet hair, holding him up with my other arm.

Karen had started frying bacon in the kitchen. I noticed that we had splashed a small lake of bathwater onto the floor.

"Step over here," I said."I'll clean it up, or your mummy will be angry." I started mopping the floor with my towel and the shag mat. It had the image of a leaping orca woven into its ocean blue. Jeremy, his wet little body wrapped in his own towel, waited patiently, but I saw him shiver.

"Let's get dressed first, we'll finish this later," I said.

"Tell me about pilots," said Jeremy, awkwardly stepping from one foot to the other.

"All right. When I was a pilot on a plane, the engine broke, and I had to parachute down. And then I saw a star, and it fell right out of the sky. It swished right past me, that close! Scratched my neck a little and my arm."

"Let me touch it," Jeremy explored the scar on my forearm once again. He was in awe. The contradictions between the two versions of the scar's origin didn't bother him in the least.

"When I glow up, I will be a pilot and we'll fly togetha?"

"We will, Jeremy, we will."

15

After three weeks, almost at the end of my stay, Jeremy asked me if I had children. I said I had none.

He sighed deeply. "Will you be my Dad, then?"

I fell silent. Karen had told me earlier that Jeremy never had any father. She could think of at least two or three plausible candidates for the role, she said, but in her mind obviously that added up to none. I looked at the boy. He was patiently waiting for my answer.

"Yes, of course. Only I live so far away."

"Can I come and live with you, then? I know how to dless myself."

"I would take you with me," I lied, "but it's so dusty and noisy in my city, you won't like it there."

"No, I'll like it. I like it wheh you a'."

"Jeremy, my friend, I go to work every day. You would be very bored alone."

Jeremy thought for a moment. "Then I'll wait fo' you. You'll be my Dad when you come back. You'll come back soon, light?"

"I'll come back, I promise."

"And then we'll go to Machu Picchu?"

"Yes, when you glow up!"

16

As I watched the wing of my plane diving in and out of the clouds, I felt some deep layers shifting inside me. I kept thinking about the scrawny blind little boy with a misfitting name and realized that nobody in the whole world needed or loved me as much as he did. Nobody knew or touched my face the way he did: his transparent fingers traced every cranny and wrinkle, ran along my forehead, my cheeks, hesitating at a dimple on my chin, then paused to press gently on my eyelids, eager to understand how I saw the world forbidden forever to his own eyes. Not only did he know my moods, but he also had an uncanny ability to intuit what I would feel or want the next moment, and knowing that, he tried to please me, to make me happy. Blind, himself in need of protection, unbeknownst to himself he kept at bay the dangerous whirlpools that lay dormant inside me; uncannily, he returned me to the true source of my existence, to that tenderness and warmth I had buried under the musty layers of mechanically lived life.

Never before had I made up stories for anybody. And nobody

had ever listened to me with such trusting naivete, turning me into the hero of my own awkward inventions. How was I to live up to that fake glory? That I didn't know. All I knew was that there was an invisible thread connecting us: Jeremy was holding one end of it on a tiny far-away island, throwing the other end to me, here in Europe. His little figure, hunched in the uncertain posture of the blind, would grow in front of me in the middle of my lectures. He sat at our table sharing supper with me and Albertina. With an invisible hand, I helped him with his meals. We walked together through the Jardin du Luxembourg and I was naming things we passed, for that was the only way I could make him "see" what I saw. I found myself often laughing as I talked to him. The rest of my days somehow faded: the university, Solange, telephone calls, my endless obligations, my domestic life, our guests were nothing but an annoying interruption of my inner monologue addressed to Jeremy. "I will come, and we'll go to Machu Picchu together," my lips whispered. "I just have to find the way."

I started researching blindness. Congenitally unsighted children remain unsociable and even mute if their parents do not put extraordinary efforts into their mental development. Clearly, Jeremy was a very gifted child, given the circumstances of his birth and the meager attention he had been getting since. How had he learned to talk at all? To find his gluba tree? To whistle into it? To imitate the wind, the sound of a tide? These were all small miracles. When I attempted a duck's quack or a grasshopper's chirrup, he immediately outdid me, sounds being his natural realm. Perhaps he could become a musician? My imagination took a wild flight.

One of the first things I did when I came back to Paris was to buy Jeremy a set of percussion instruments in a specialized toy shop. (He liked to bang on his mother's kitchen pots and pans.) I imagined his fingers touching the smooth cool surfaces of the cymbal and something melted in my chest.

Soon my office turned into a storage room where I kept all Jeremy's toys before sending them out to the United States. Once I couldn't make it to the post office on time and showed up at Solange's doorstep loaded with parcels. I could furnish no explanation for them – except that these were presents for her twins. She accepted the gift with some incredulity: Never before had I shown any interest in her children, nor had we ever fallen into the habit of exchanging gifts. If my move was a signal a new turn in our relationship, she wasn't willing to accept it, that was obvious. I dispersed the awkward moment with a joke. An hour later, running down the stairs from her apartment, I was vaguely aware it wasn't simply my hands feeling light, now emptied of Jeremy's presents. It was something else I was letting go of. As I opened the door to the buzz of the street, I knew that my relationship with Solange had died there and then, of natural causes, as they say. My heart jolted with an unexpected sensation of freedom.

17

But it was two other events – my wife's death and Karen's sudden disappearance from the reservation – that radically changed the course of my life. Both happened about the same time, in November.

The first overshadowing the second, I couldn't foresee all the repercussions of Karen's sudden disappearance on my future. Did she simply shut the door of her home and leave, or did she meet with some violent death? Both scenarios were plausible. As I mentioned before, it had never entered my mind to question Karen's faithfulness to me during my long absences from her life: I knew there could be no such thing. Loyalty was not in her character. She came and went as she pleased, receiving with languid passion the simple physical pleasures that I or any other man could bestow on her body. Like nature itself, she was at once abundant, generous, greedy, and indifferent. Some said she was lured by a man from another reservation; others insisted a body resembling hers was washed to the shores forty miles away from her island. When I heard that rumour, it struck me that her Indian name was Qahla, prompted by a dream of the sun setting in a bath of blood. But that could have been just my imagination tormented by the death of my wife. Except for Karen and Jeremy, I knew nobody in her village, and hard as I tried, I couldn't find out what had really happened to her. I certainly couldn't ask the boy.

Something else that I can't omit for the sake of truthfulness had fallen on me around the same time. If before, as I mentioned, I would forget some words only rarely, now the simplest notions began to drop out of my speech at an embarrassing rate, and I could no longer compensate for my handicap in a discreet manner.

All of which prompted me to act. I would adopt Jeremy and bring him to France. I would teach him Braille and music. That would free me from Albertina's death and my own guilt. The boy was to be my redemption, my fragile trail back to convalescence and to life.

As soon as I started carefully planning my actions, the desert of loneliness I found myself in after Albertina's death began to shrink. First a letter to the Native Committee of Lalyuit with a generous financial offer (they'd take the bait); then the paperwork for the government. I'm an American citizen, and I anticipated no hurdles there. Then my trip to the West Coast. But first I had to let Jeremy, who couldn't read, know that I was coming to pick him up. I recorded and sent him a tape with three sentences: "Jeremy, my little boy, remember Machu Pichu? Your Daddy is on his way. Get ready."

Stepping out of the post office into the sunshine, I felt great relief. Finally, I had made a transition from contemplation to action. What should have followed my resolve was an immediate trip to Machu Picchu. Hadn't I promised my boy? And shouldn't I finally, at long last, be as good as my word? Yes, we'd go right away. I'd carry my blind son on my shoulders through mists and fogs all the way up, four hundred stone steps up,to the harsh magnificence of the Great Abandoned City. No, he won't see it with his eyes, but he will know it as he knows the full abundance of my love. The only obstacle in my way was the shoulder pads. I needed some good ones, both soft and sturdy, to carry him to the very top.

I returned to the post office. "I've just sent a little parcel to the United States, remember? But I forgot to ask you something. Do you by any chance carry good shoulder pads?" The woman at the counter gave me a strange look and said if my shoulders were sore, I'd be better off shopping at a pharmacy. Unhappy with this dismissal,

I walked two blocks down the street, looking for a shop offering medical equipment. Finally, I came to what looked like a hospital. People inside were walking in all directions with those characteristic implements hooked around their necks. These must be doctors, I thought. I stopped one of the wired people and asked him for shoulder pads. "Do you have acute shoulder pain?" the man inquired. "No," I said, "I don't have pain right now. But I surely will later. And besides, I want Jeremy to feel as comfortable as possible during our Machu Picchu ascent."

"Who's Jeremy?"

"A blind boy I'm going to carry on my shoulders. He is going to be my son, but right now he is abandoned by his mother on the Indian reservation on the Pacific Coast. I'm going to carry him four hundred steps up, which is not a joke even for a seeing person, to say nothing of a man carrying the burden of his love. Jeremy may sway and destabilize me, you see. Then we could both fall. Of course, we are going to practise walking on the beaches of his island. Plenty of sand there. All I need for now are the shoulder pads." The man said they might be able to find some, but first he had to admit me to the hospital in order to give me a good examination before such a challenging trip.

18

In the small hours of morning, my heart began another attempt to escape. I counted its wild thuds in my throat: one, two, three, four. Frightened little rat, always panicky! I won't abandon you, we'll flee together, I promise. The perverse angel from the nursing station gave me a chase as usual: "Help me, help! This client is making a run for it again!" My ear cringes at this verbal abuse: *clients*! They think their euphemisms can cure us of death. Clients can never be needy; they can't suffer or die; they pay their dough and bug off. But patients? Bad things happen to patients! Not to worry, Jeremy my boy, they can't keep me here forever. Sooner or later your Daddy will find his way to you! There are no obstacles to love.

I said to my undergraduate seminar in comparative linguistics, "The road to hell is paved with euphemisms. As human beings, you should avoid this peril." Then one nymphet, resembling Solange, rose to her feet. "Professor, I was thinking of lumping them all together under the cover of a dictionary to prevent the contamination of our society." "*C'estremarquable*!" I said, eyeing her naked midriff and her crotch in tight jeans. The pant leg on her left knee was sliced open according to the fashion of the time. To keep everybody from panic at the sight of that open wound, I addressed my audience: "Linguistics is a serious discipline. Words can fall through cracks and pauses of hesitation. They can fall through holes in your pants. To avoid this danger, I urge you to follow dress codes in my seminars! No goddamn jeans with holes!"

The class roared with laughter. They thought it was a joke, and only a few students looked puzzled. Those, no doubt, understood that I was dead serious. Anyhow, I have always had an excellent rapport with my students.

But let's not get off the track here. I know I'm sick, pathetically so. All the same, they have no right to keep me here.

"We're trying to help you, to find a cure." There is no cure for me: Albertina has taken my cure to her grave. Most of my languages are gone. But my internal speech is still there. Therefore, I must escape before it too gets consumed by some enigmatic monster sitting right there, right there in my temple! Who is he? And how did he manage to get in there, in the absence of a stroke or a brain injury? Oh! the ruins of my former splendour!

So the nurse caught me again, and I was unable to avoid yet another of the doctor's rounds. This time the intern (where do they get such pumpkins?) did her best to engage me in conversation. What is your name? Where are we right now? If today is Monday, what day was yesterday? There was no yesterday. I live for tomorrow, young lady. As for where we are now, let me assure you we're in purgatory, if not in hell.

And in any case, dear lady, what do we have in common, you and me, that might compel me to open to you my quivering heart? Do you deserve my trust? Oh yes, you have very pretty eyes, the rarest hue of green. (The superlative degrees of adjectives are intact, please note.) I'd say leaning toward yellowish, with a dark rim around the pupil. (Derivational morphemes, namely, diminutive suffixes, have not suffered so far, which is extraordinary because suffixes are the first to suffer, hence their name.) But that doesn't mean that I didn't pick up on the immediate resemblance between your eyes and that of the sister of the Roman hero Albanesi, who saw her brother triumphantly carrying the cloak she herself had woven. Needless to say, she flew into a rage and her brother, equally offended by what he considered her betrayal of the Roman cause, killed her with the same sword with which he had won his victory. Cimarosa (pronounced as *ch*) describes this scene beautifully in Gli Orazi ed i Curiazi, the only opera still performed out of the sixty-one he penned. Which tells us that time is a severe if not an impartial judge. Albanesi, by the way, is not a derivative of *albino,* nor of *Albertina,* the name of my late wife, who, as a matter of fact, was an albino. Almost, but not quite. The superficial *sozvuchie* (which translates from Turkish or Russian as *concord* or better still *sonority)* between the name and the lack of pigment in the hair is completely coincidental – or *coexisdental* might be a better word, for their co-existence in one person is a fact of sheer coincidence. Some nod toward Proust is in evidence in her name, though you, young lady, are not the one to pick up on that. And again I emphasize: she wasn't a true albino, for her eyelashes were quite dark, whereas in undisguised albinos they would've been completely discoloured. Do albinos become grey as they age, is that your next question? The great experiment of living was cut short for my wife, and we failed to establish the fact. What happens to near-albinos after death I have no way of knowing, though in her case she might have reached the state of full albinosity, pronounced the way it is spelled. Why, you may be wondering. The reason is simple: the only way of returning to one's original design is through decay. By the way, have you noticed how nicely *albinosity* rhymes with *luminosity*? Very appropriate in my wife's case: carnality had never touched her thoughts in the last ten years of our long-suffering marriage; my wife was indeed a luminous being, a source of light and delight in my life, and now, after her death, there is nothing but darkness.

19

Now, what about his writing? Excuse me, gentlemen and ladies, as
one petty crook from Odessa used to say: How dare you talk like
that in my presence? I'm not deaf, nor autistic, nor a child. To write?
In which of the thirty languages at my disposal do you want me to
communicate my thoughts? No, sweetheart. Spare me the trouble. You
are so unbearably, embarrassingly monolingual, through no fault of
your own, no doubt. Working-class background, parents' unawareness.
Show me your hands, don't be shy, sweetie. See, I'm right, your face
is pretty, but your short sausage-shaped fingers with bulging nails tell
their own story: low pedigree, generations of peasants tilling dry earth.
May I touch your palm? Some ladies have very rough skin inside
their hands, though they didn't do any physical work even once in
their whole lives. Don't stretch your hands in supplication toward me,
darling...we ain't doin' no writin' nor talkin' today.

20

Could you please pass me a glass of water? This internal thinking
will make anybody thirsty. Just push this mess off the table. That's it.
Done! Never mind the broken glass. They have plenty of those. You
still don't understand what I'm trying to tell you? This is strange. You
see a towel wrapped around my throat? That would have been the sign
that I'm unable to talk on account of my sore throat. But today there is
no towel; therefore, listen carefully.

Obviously, you, my Yellow-Eyed Rabbit (may I fondly call

you that?), are trying to figure out how to communicate with me in the absence of any material traces of my thoughts. No sounds produced, no waves transmitted. But let me tell you that phonology, ephemeral as it is, is a crude matter compared to the subtlety of human feelings. Can you believe me if I say I love you, love those ugly little fingers of yours? But the sublime by definition has no form. Which makes communication even more difficult. My preferred method of interlocution, O, the Yellow-Eyed, would be telepathy, soul to soul, heart to heart, and body to body. Not that I would want you to share my bed, God forbid. But I'd like to share one secret with you. I have a request to make! Shh! This is only between you and me. First let me lay out some rules. Rule number one: never judge a man by his pronouncements. Judge a man by his silence alone. Rule number two: do not judge a man by his Broca or Wernicke areas, for both can fail him. The question arises: By what shall you judge a man? I have no answer. All I can tell you is this: describe aphasics as you would describe God: we know what God is not, but we don't really know what He is. My other suggestion: always take your supervisor's observation with a grain of salt. When he tells you I'm a Broca case, he is out to lunch. Broca victims mingle up morphology in the most peculiar way, whereas mine remains intact any time of day or night. The Wernike people string long sentences together with unperturbed syntax, but they have no clue as to what they are talking about. Not my case either. There is always a purpose to my deviations. Take Gli Orazi ed i Curiazi. The reason I mention the opera is because most scholars agree that the libretto was concocted to provide an origin for the Roman legal practice of allowing appeals to the people in criminal cases. Why do we need appeals, you might ask? Appeals are the only link to divine mercy available to mortals. Not that this dispensation always works. I'm appealing to you, for example, but you don't seem to hear. I'm appealing to Albertina, but she is not coming back. So let's leave that for now in favour of better examples. When I was still *enforme* (vocably speaking) I kept my linguistic muscles flexed through a simple routine: I'd pick a random phrase and try to translate it into all the languages I know. For example, "The chimpanzee is the only animal that can recognize itself in a mirror." I'd do that in Urdu, Turkish, and even try Inuktitut except that the Inuit have never seen any monkeys on their snowy plains. But I liked the challenge nevertheless: good exercise for my brain. After Albertina's death I lost so much weight that, unlike the chimps, I couldn't recognize myself in the mirror. Not for a moment, however, did I consider myself a monkey (pay attention, my emphatic inversions are still intact). No, I'm a human being who has lost his capacity to speak, but not to feel or reason. A man with a purpose in life. My purpose is to restore weight to words, to prevent them from fluttering over the surface of my brain. I repeat: words should be heavy like stones that crocodiles swallow when they need to sink to the very bottom of the river. Heavy words, words of authority, words of trust. Did you know that words are stored each in its proper drawer? Verbal nouns live in a different drawer from non-verbal? How clever! A stroke victim may lose a proposal, as in "I tabled a proposal yesterday," but he will never lose a table, as in"There is an apple on the table!"

Half of my drawers are called Albertina and another half

Jeremy. I am going to will both drawers to you, my sweetheart, in case I forget how to write. You're the one who has to sort them out. After you have finished, please take the cheapest tape recorder (any dictaphone will do) and record one paragraph, just one. Do you hear that onomatopoeic rain drumming on the leaves of a tall alder outside that window? Have you noticed how every leaf nods when the rain bullet reaches it? It nods and then cringes with pain; nods and cringes. But when it starts pouring in earnest, leaves accept the pain and fall silent.

This is what you have to say to my son: "Jeremy, Your Daddy is coming. I've got shoulder pads for our ascent. On Machu Picchu there are no flies..."

Christmas Eve Tango

1

Though I'm almost thirty, I'm still shy with women. I'm not particularly good looking, you see. My lanky frame does not put its height to any good use. I stoop and walk in long, uneven strides, with a slight jerk at the end of each step, an unconscious attempt to make the difference in my shoulders' height less conspicuous. My adolescent bones couldn't cope with rapid growth, you see, and I developed scoliosis, overlooked by my absent-minded mother.

In my whole life, I never managed to figure out what to do with my arms. They often dangle alongside my body without any purpose. But there's nothing wrong with my face. You can't say anything against my face. My eyes, for example. You'd always want to look at them again. Out of curiosity. It's their colour, mostly: washed out blue, almost white but with a dark rim around the pupil, unusual for a man. Redheads and albinos have such eyes, but I have a mass of dark hair on my head, and a shy little smile that doesn't expose my teeth. Lately, I've been trying to grow a small goatee.

Even though my features are not irregular, they must harbour some warp, some intangible swerve. Women find it disturbing. They like a straight line. And where can I get that line with my constant self-doubts, empty pockets, and holes in my socks?

One girl – nice legs, otherwise nothing special – burst into tears at that very moment when normal women are supposed to melt into blissful fatigue. Anyhow, this girl sobbed into my ear: "I don't

really know what you want! You hate me because you hate yourself!"
Where did you get all this pop psychology crap, I wanted to ask her.
And why would I hate her? I didn't care one way or another. What
I mean is that women expect a man to know "what he wants, and
where he's going," as they say in sitcoms. But how can I know what
I want? Every minute I'm pulled in opposite directions. To go for one
thing means to deny myself another. And if I deny myself that other
wish, I'm only half fulfilled, while the other half of my confused,
contradictory self remains forever needy and orphaned!

For some men, all it takes is to narrow their eyes and say
nothing; stand and sway lightly on their heels, hands in their pockets.
That's it. Deep down, every woman wants to give herself up, to
surrender completely, body and soul: "Just take me, lift all the
responsibility off my shoulders, and I'll be yours." Scary business.

What spoils the game for me is that I always give away
my eagerness. Too much yearning in my eyes, too much *I'd give
anything to have you*. True, I sometimes manage to put a stern mask
of indifference on my face, and then there's no way out of it, except
rubbing my mask against theirs – a dance many of them are so good at.

?

Talking of dance.

One Sunday night, when I had nothing much to do and nobody
to call, I decided to satisfy my curiosity and take a tango lesson.
On windy December nights in Montréal, the world is aloof and
unyielding. Rare passers-by in the street, brooding lonely ghosts.

They'll cross over to the other side of the road before you get close. But tango! Who knows who I might meet there? It was the middle of the month, and no studios accepted drop-ins. I had to pay cash for the rest of the course, seven or eight classes, so I took my grandfather's old chronometer that was collecting cobwebs in the corner of my room into the antiquarian marine shop. The two hundred bucks I got solved the problem.

"Walk like you breathe, *tranquillo, tranquillo*," commanded Alfredo, a dark Argentinean in black velvety pants and a massive golden chain showing through the open collar of his loose silk shirt. "It's easy," he said. Easy? Never, never could I learn to walk like him.

Thrusting back his gelled pitch-black hair, he walked with the confidence of a commando and the regal sleekness of a cat. He firmly, but gently, probed the floor with the tip of his arching foot, caressing it ever so lightly, and then thrust his hips forward, while his torso was still slightly tilted back.

"*Tranquillo!* Look. One leg over other leg, you hold it. Like you want to pee really bad, but you hold it. *Entiendes?*"

There were twice as many women in the class as men, and I had to dance with each of them to be fair to all. In tango jargon, women are called "followers" and men "leaders." Most of the followers were plain-looking, rather tired middle-aged ladies who had summed up youthful buoyancy for the occasion; only two women were in their twenties, and of those two one was pregnant. Like me, these women were struggling with their steps. Awkward and gravity-bound, they sheepishly trod the floor, as if stepping into a capsizing boat. They jolted in the most unexpected places or came to a sudden halt, abandoning the music completely.

But I had an even harder time with the whole thing than these women. While "followers" at least could focus on their steps, I had to choreograph those steps for them, all the time paying close attention to the music. I had to watch out for other couples and navigate the floor, always counter-clockwise. Leading turned out to be tricky, and I sweated profusely. Besides, how do you silently communicate to a woman what you intend to do next?

"With your whole body, not just your arm," explained Alfredo. "Hold her light, but firm, Chasen!" That's how he pronounced my name. "Where your hand, where your body? The arm on her back, the body went out for lunch. They together, your body and arm, no?"

"They should be," I conceded.

"Put your hand over there," he said, pressing my listless hand against my partner's back. "Strong, but easy, don't push her. She feel your power through your chest. From the waist up, you one creature. Make senses, no? Make senses." He answered for me, as was his habit.

"Move closer to her, no fear. She's a woman, you're a man, no? Walk like an expensive cat! That's better now. Ladies, leave your head home, ladies! I don't want your head. I want your body! This is tango! In Buenos Aires, we dance close embrace, you better used to nice close embrace! You like him, he likes you! Men, ankles together, ladies, knees together. Not beautiful knees apart, ladies! Don't look at your feet. Close your eyes, ladies, feel the man. You don't feel him, he don't lead. No lead, no dance. Don't boss your man on the floor! It's not your husband! And we go now. One, two, three, four, five, six, seven, eight! Now, the music!"

3

My only saving grace was my sense of rhythm. I had come to love tango music, and gradually it entered my blood stream. It took me five months of steady practice to learn to walk. And then it came to me. It happened to me, it entered my core: Together with the music, I cried for the world, I wept, I melted with sorrow. Tango both humbled and raised me out of the ashes, all in a single note, sighed out by a *bandoneoni*. Sometimes, fear would overcome me again, and I'd become uncertain of my steps. Then I would breathe the air of movement and hope, right through my core, through the centre – no, not through the lungs, through the diaphragm, as Alfredo used to say. And the greatness of tango filled my heart, loosened my legs.

I walked to the sad and solemn sounds of "La Cumparsita." I was that soul in the masquerade, a soul waiting at a wharf in an alien port while the foreign ships, ablaze with garlands of light, came and sailed away, and left me waiting.

> *La comparsa de miseries*
> *sin fin desfila*
> *en torno de aquel ser enfermo*
> *que pronto ha de morir de pena.*[1]

I now felt the addiction of tango. It was like life itself: repetitive, yet always new, full of unforeseen trickery, archness, and

---

[1] *A masquerade of miseries/ marches endlessly around me./ Soon/I too will die of pain."* (Translated by the author.)

drama; it teased me with rich promises that were immediately taken away, and it bestowed upon me sudden, unexpected blessings. Like life, it had a powerful undercurrent, an all-penetrating pulse that could drown you if you were not attuned to it. You had to dissolve yourself in tango, in music, and let the music carry you to the place of your greatest fear and sadness, and take you out of it and bring you back, while you had to take its dark throbbing into your very veins, and look into the abyss it was leading you to. You were naked in tango, you couldn't hide, no more than one can hide from life. You had to trust tango as a newborn baby trusts his existence. You had to be exuberant, cruel but gentle, while the music was still playing.

You had to draw the knife at the sight of treachery but then pause and tuck it away and turn around and forgive that woman.

And sometimes, in moments of confusion, you had to stop moving and absorb the stillness; for there was a pause in the trajectory of the flight.

I discovered that there were women who knew the steps and danced well; but then there were others whose knowledge of the technique was deeply buried inside them: They could stop and do nothing at all or take the risk and accompany you on a perilous journey because they trusted you. They had an uncanny knowledge of how you were in the world and how you breathed; they intuited your next step and moved together with you effortlessly, with a certain languished passivity, as if they had no will of their own; they did not devour your freedom; they just followed you along the undulations of the music. These women were the very best dancers and most in demand.

A long time ago, I passed the point of no return. To pay for more and more classes, I sold antique jewellery my mother left me. I moved into an even smaller flat further east, and supported myself doing odd jobs during the day while continuing to dance at night.

Yet, at the beginning, tango didn't make my life easier. The contrast between the times spent in the studio and the drawn-out hours I wasted in the room I could never call home made my solitude even more unbearable.

I remember one occasion especially, when I stepped into the night after practising tango and saw the stars over my head dry and shiny, freshly washed. I couldn't bear the immensity of the sky, so I looked down. The city, sullen and empty, lay deflated under my echoing footsteps. On a night like that, it stops sprawling upward; instead, it topples over on its back like a hibernating beast, horizontal, forcing its infinity on my ant-like crawl. I inspected the cracks in the pavement, vaguely hoping to find a key to their intricate pattern, which I sensed would be less inscrutable than the enigmatic blueprint of the starry void above me. But the meaning of both eluded me.

I remembered the pain of a year before. That after I'd lost my last job and I'd been looking for a new one ever since, but nothing had panned out. People in the old job humiliated me. And I wouldn't have it. I might starve, but I won't tolerate the slightest sign of disrespect. Ever since then, I'd got into the habit of roaming the streets. I think I was vaguely looking for a miracle in the low-lying winter-frozen spaces of the city: a chance encounter, perhaps, a freak opportunity that would never stroll into the four walls of my drab attic.

What I met through my nocturnal wanderings was the wind. Indiscriminately, using the props afforded to it by every season, it piled up spectral slabs of chaos on the sidewalk. In autumn it sated on leaves – dispersing, then spinning them into ephemeral castles. In summer, it clogged the passageways between houses with mobile hordes of dust and crumpled balls of paper; it leafed through the fat weekend *Le Devoir* editions page after page, exposing stale news to the indifferent legs of passers-by.

In winter, when there was no snow, and the unswept leaves, dark and oblong, like ancient Egyptian boats, got frozen solid into the ground, the wind's credibility hung solely on aimless phantoms like myself. It fingered my spine under my shabby loose coat, vertebra after vertebra, all the way down to the tailbone, till it found an exit through the hole in my pocket.

Just like the wind, I kept up an appearance of movement under the monotonous absence of change. In order to stretch my dwindling budget, I moved from one crummy room to another, all the time staying put, so to speak. All these rooms were carbon copies of each other: all on the top floor, right under the roof. They all had wallpaper of an indefinable colour coming off at the junction with the ceiling, and most had showers that didn't work. Since I was often late with my rent, I kept my mouth shut about the shower and didn't wash for days.

I wish the wind would stop. Its aimless wanderings disturb me. Sometimes, I fantasize about my city. I imagine that, in the past, it was all soft and pliable: wax-like gyrating staircases climbing along the faces of the houses; the houses themselves soft, framed with trees, lithe like lianas. Then, I imagine, the wind came along and stiffened all form, so that nothing was left from the initial design. Skeletal branches knock against the window panes along the dark façades.

I even imagine that the cracks in the crooked sidewalks are also the wind's work; that the wind slanted the pavement toward the middle of the road and swept the few pedestrians away. Now people walk in the middle of the road, forcing the infrequent cars to swerve into the oncoming lane to pass them.

I too gingerly step into the middle of the road. I give nothing of myself to the city. And the city closes itself to me, begrudging me every speck of itself, till one day I finally venture to a real Saturday milonga. And that changes my life.

4

At first, to avoid embarrassment, I decided to ask only the beginners to dance, leaving some possibility of an escape in case I completely screwed it up. But I was mistaken in my strategy: Though good dancers were seeking out partners of equal skills, there were many other forces at play that I couldn't quite grasp at the time, and which I still don't understand. There would be a girl – a young, smooth, insipid creature, hardly able to make two coherent steps – in the arms of an experienced, even excellent dancer, usually an older man. Perhaps, I, too, in the inversion of roles, could ask a good dancer without feeling I was going to crack.

At my first party, I felt elated. I liked the muted ambiance: the flicker of candles on each table; the smell of perfume on the women's heated skin mixed with cigarette smoke reaching the floor from the stairwell where people puffed between *tandos,* two or three dances forming one theme. The fact that I could always go to the bar, have a glass of beer or whisky, and watch others dance in case I suddenly got cold feet suited me just fine. I liked the way men quickly sprayed breath freshener into their mouths before inviting a woman onto the dance floor and then put the spray into their breast pocket with the same quick, clandestine gesture. I liked the provocativeness of the women's outfits: their black shimmering skirts with slits at the side that bared their fishnet-stockinged thighs; their see-through tops held in place by the flimsiest promise of an imperceptible strap. I liked the way women closed their eyes while dancing, as if in complete abandon. Sensations overwhelmed me. The most powerful of all was the heat, coming from my partners' bodies after I danced two or three tangos in a row. Some women felt like balls of fire, all burning and melting inside, my only protection a layer of clothes – the silk, the velvet, the chiffon. Underneath the fabric, I could feel the clasp of their bras.

I instinctively avoided placing my hand on women's naked backs (I noticed that other men did the same) and moved it to the area safely protected by fabric. But once, inadvertently, my hand slipped up my partner's bare shoulder blades. They were cold and sticky with sweat, and I was struck by the unpleasantness of the sensation.

If my right hand, always resting on my partner's back, had

some level of defence (no matter how light and transparent the fabric usually felt), then the left was completely exposed, and I semi-consciously hoped for the exchange of some silent messages, some mysterious current travelling from her fingers to mine...but nothing was communicated to me, and I was left disappointed.

Dancing the tango, I discovered how different women's hands felt: some very soft, others dry and rough as men's. What kind of lives might women with such hands have had?

Then there was the sensation of their breasts. In calesita, women leaned over me at sharp angles, their bodies linked to mine at the chest. It was a never-ebbing excitement to feel the weight of a woman's body so publicly placed on top of mine. Some women's breasts felt small and firm, some were big and soft, and I learnt to transport the tactile sensors from my fingers to my torso. Not an unpleasant experience, misplaced as it might seem.

5

Two women in particular attracted my attention.

One, in claret-coloured tight pants and a tunic, with a pale face and emaciated, almost breastless body, had a languid, careless way of moving. She danced obliviously, as if divorced from her own self. Her long ash-blond braid, too, seemed to have a life of its own, only remotely echoing the turns and twists of its owner. I was mesmerized by these double unsynchronized rondos, the way this ankle-reaching snake lightly swept against the floor when the woman suddenly went into a deep lunge. When I finally plucked up my courage to approach her, fish-like unsmiling eyes transfixed me. I thought what an excellent dancer she was, in her strange, inflexible, rake-like way. Yes, in my mind, I thought of her as a rake, and was both repulsed by and attracted to her. She was staring right through me. What would it feel like to hold her in my arms? The more I desired her, the less I was capable of inviting her.

And then there was another girl, almost as tall as me, with wide hips and chocolate skin that brought the azure waves of the Caribbean to lap at my feet. I started walking toward her, but she was quickly intercepted by another man. And then I watched the oily smoothness of her dance, and I imagined her in my arms. Sometimes she was a goddess, and sometimes a mysterious creature out of the depths of the ocean, a mollusc in search of its form. And I was the shell that could absorb her and give her this form, had she only trusted me with her exquisitely slow undulations.

The music stopped. At that moment the yellow band holding the Carib girl's voluminous hair back slipped off her head, and she bent over to pick it up with a careless gesture. She was now an ordinary girl, perhaps accessible. Desire burned inside me.

"Aimeriez-vous dancer?" a high, somewhat childish voice asked, breaking into my reverie.

"Bien sûr," I replied to the owner of this voice, who, to my surprise, turned out to be a short, middle-aged woman.

Must be in her late forties, early fifties, I thought. Much shorter than me (a disadvantage in dancing), but it was the first time that a woman had invited me for a dance, and I felt flattered.

"My name is Pauline," she said, switching to English when she

274

heard my laboured accent.

"I'm Jason."

I was trying to catch the beat of the music before making the first step.

"Have you been dancing for a long time?"

"Oh no, I'm a beginner."

"That's all right. It takes a while, but you'll learn, you'll see."

I was slightly annoyed, first, at her patronizing kindness, but more by the fact that she needed to talk to me at all while we danced. It prevented me from concentrating on my steps. Her bleached blond ringlets were at the level of my chin. I didn't see much of her face or her body, but she felt cozy and feminine in my arms, with those neat unhurried steps of hers. As if she were crocheting something with her small feet. I noticed her wasp-like waist neatly emphasized by a tight black belt that set off her generous hips. I also liked the feel of her fuchsia dress. It was soft, old fashioned, with loose translucent sleeves falling all the way to her shoulders when she raised her well-shaped arms. A row of small pearly buttons rose to an upright collar that left only a small wedge of flesh at the top of her neck exposed. There was something touching about her being so traditional. As I was leading her into forward *ochos*, I caught a glimpse of her knee: it was smooth and round, a gently outlined slope that seemed to be completely boneless. Pauline's whole body didn't have one sharp line. Her shoulders and her chest were cozily plump, and fitted perfectly in my arms, in spite of the fact that she was so much shorter than me. I soon discovered that Pauline was one of those rare, superlative dancers who wasn't flashy on the floor but could intuit your slightest move.

6

While dancing with her, I became aware of a peculiar fragrance. It wasn't the smell of perfume – I don't think she was wearing any – but rather that of her skin. It reminded me of something remote, long forgotten, and I couldn't figure out what it was. Then, in a flash, in cadence with the music, an old country house in England came back to me.

In the year of my mother's death, my aunt took me there to spend a summer with her. I was ten years old, and we were slicing up juicy green apples from our garden and spreading them over towels on the floor of our little shack at the back of the property. I thought then that they looked like small round moons, those apples, but later, when the air cooled and the real moon and the stars came out, we had a sudden visitor: A hedgehog came trotting along with the heavy tread of a trooper. He rolled onto the apples, hooking with his needles as many he could. Then he disappeared. Pauline's skin smelled like those slightly withered apples, twenty years ago, in the August of my mother's death.

While dancing, Pauline didn't fuss around on the floor, nor did she press me into constant movement. I could stop and relax to the point of not thinking about my steps anymore. Most of that evening we danced together, and I felt no need to change partners. But when I got home after midnight, I felt completely spent. Taking off my shirt, I saw a damp spot on my upper sleeve left by Pauline's armpit. The smell of apples haunted me.

7

I was soon spending my days in anticipation of the weekends.
My head was filled with scraps of music and vague yearnings
for Pauline, whom I now danced with regularly. One night
was particularly disturbing: I dreamt about making love to her
incessantly. When I saw her the next Saturday at the dance studio, I
felt embarrassed and invited other women to dance instead. When I
finally danced with her, I avoided looking into her eyes.

Between dances, Pauline and I hardly talked to each other. I
knew nothing about her life. My arms knew her body, but otherwise
we remained complete strangers. I liked this anonymous intimacy of
the tango. I found the physical proximity to a woman who was old
enough to be my mother exhilarating. It intrigued me, and raised me
up in my own eyes. I felt like an iceberg, the whole of which nobody,
not even me, could see.

At a special milonga the night before Christmas Eve, we
danced far beyond midnight, till the candles were extinguished and
the chairs put up on the tables. We came out into the street and were
confronted by a ferocious gust of wind.

"Where do you live?" Pauline asked.

"Ten blocks away from here, on Park Avenue," I said, lying. I
didn't want her to know that I had no car and had walked across half
the city to get to the milonga.

"I'm driving in that direction. I can give you a ride."

"Well, I could walk...but sure, if it's not out of your way."

Climbing into her white car, I noticed a pair of crutches on the front seat next to her. She must have read a silent question in my eyes.

"I fell down and broke my *cheville*...how do you say that? My ankle. That was a couple of months ago, and now it's much better."

I recalled then, through the unconscious memory of my arm, that in *ocho* Pauline would lose her balance for a split second and lean more heavily than needed on my arm. She did have that imperceptible limp.

"It must hurt when you dance?" I asked.

"It hurts some, but not too bad. Another three weeks, the doctor said, and it'll be completely healed."

What a devotion to the tango, I thought, and what endurance! A hard little nut in spite of her delicate looks.

"Could you stop right at that corner, near this building, please? I live over there." I pointed to a nondescript façade that I thought could pose for my apartment.

"It was wonderful dancing with you tonight," she said taking off her seatbelt and hugging me goodbye. She pressed her body to mine, and I held her for a minute, postponing the inevitability of having to get out of the car. I wanted to continue what we had started on the dance floor, though I wasn't sure what that might be. Perhaps, making love. So I kept holding her.

"I know it's late, but I wish I could dance one last time with you. Today is Christmas Eve. We should celebrate." I was whispering in her ear, taking in the sweat mixed with apple fragrance again. "What if we go to... I mean, would you mind if...I have some good CDs, but my sound system is not working... I mean, it's in the shop... In the meantime, could we not, perhaps, dance at your place?"

She gently freed herself from my arms and paused. Then she turned off the engine. We were now sitting in the car in darkness. There was no sound, except the wind gnarling at the car's flanks.

"I suppose we could," Pauline said finally without looking at me. "But it's late now and I'm tired." She paused again. "I need to go to work in the morning."

"Pauline," I said, almost losing my voice, "you're the most beautiful woman I've ever met. Dancing with you is like... it's really very powerful! I can't imagine waiting till next Saturday."

"Oh, please..." She chuckled, then patted me on the cheek: "You don't need to flatter me, you know. I'm an old woman."

"What does age have to do with it?" I said with some vehemence. "You have experience. You have that special beauty of maturity... And you're a wonderful dancer!"

"Oh that – perhaps!"

"You're not old, you're beautiful!" I caressed her hand. Pauline laughed faintly but didn't remove her hand.

"You're right. I'm not that old, just old enough to be your mother."

I let go her hand, moving away from her. She gave me a long sideways glance.

"Oh, okay," she said with averted eyes. "I guess we could stop at my place. For a very brief while."

"Yes, for a brief while," I replied. I reached for her chin, turned her face toward me, and kissed her. Her lips felt soft. She didn't resist. While she was driving, I put my hand on her knee.

We were now in Westmount, and she finally parked the car

in the driveway of an old Edwardian house. While she fumbled for the keys in her purse, I stared at the stained glass in the porch door. Not shitty. She has a good life, this woman. I wiped my feet on the doormat, a straw elephant dangling a WELCOME sign from his trunk.

Inside, I smelled a suffocating mixture of dried flowers, baked pies, and the familiar fermenting apples. It was warm, even stifling, as if the house was seldom aired. The hallway was full of antique low tables, chiffoniers, baskets. A bouquet of tulips splayed out of an elephant-shaped vase served as a lamp. Each tulip was made of coloured glass, with a bulb inside. I noticed that there were no Christmas decorations of any sort.

"Would you like some tea?" she asked. "I don't drink wine so late at night. Wake up with a headache in the morning."

"Tea is fine," I said, somewhat disappointed.

I followed her to the kitchen. There, I found myself in an elephant kingdom run amok. Gaudy beasts with trunks lifted like trumpets winked from the tea towels, curtains, and tablecloths. There was a tiny elephant sitting on top of each canister; there were elephant mugs and pots and cups on the shelves. The tea cozy was an elephant, and so were the backs of the chairs around the table. Two of the four chairs were occupied by huge stuffed beasts with erect trunks, all four pillar-like legs up in the air. One beast was pink, the other blue. The blue one was staring at me, the pink one at Pauline.

"It'll take a couple of minutes before the kettle boils. What kind of tea would you like?" she asked, leaning against a cushion where two crocheted beasts intertwined their trunks like the copulating snakes on the caduceus.

Under the bright kitchen light, Pauline looked much older than in the semi-darkness of the dance studio. She was obviously tired. Her smudged makeup revealed all the trappings of age: the swelling under the eyes, the deep wrinkles around her nose, the sagging skin of her cheekbones. Perhaps aware of the effect that her face had on me, she turned off the overhead light and lit two candles. Two sharp shadows reached the middle of her cheeks with their narrow tongues, then licked her nose, her lips, cutting her face into swiftly moving triangles.

"Your elephant collection is quite remarkable," I said, avoiding looking at her. "I've never seen anything like it."

"Not mine," she said. "My ex-husband's. We travelled a lot. We lived in India for several years, and there he took up carving. Elephants were easy to make, and we brought back quite a few. Friends assumed we collected them. For each birthday party or anniversary, somebody would bring us an elephant. And then I guess we fell into this trap and started looking out for them in different countries. Some are made of real ebony, some copper, there are even a couple of gold ones... More than six hundred in this house. Would you like one?"

She got up and reached into a small shelf where a family of black elephants was walking trunk to tail along a crocheted meadow toward the frosted window. She removed the smallest baby elephant, last in the file, and handed it over to me.

"Thank you," I mumbled, slipping the silly little thing into my pocket.

"For luck," said Pauline, pouring tea into two elephant cups.

She handed one to me.

"Have you ever had your palm read?" Pauline asked, sipping from her cup. "This is one thing I'm really good at. If I look at your hand, I can tell everything about your character, your past, and your future. Give me your hand."

She held my hand in both of hers; her clasp was cozy and warm.

"Oh, what a big palm! Nice shape too! You've had a hard life. "She gently unfolded my index finger. "It's because you're a dreamer and an artist. You're very impressionable, very soft inside."

"How do you know?" I asked, smiling and drawing her closer to me.

"The palm tells it all. See, between the valleys of Venus and Mars there is a little mound, and then there is a line, separating those two valleys. Yours is very deep. Only artists have it."

"Can you foretell the future as well?"

"Yes, there is lots of travelling ahead."

"Travelling and a big fortune, right?" I said, laughing. "They always say that. Do you really believe in this?"

"Big fortune, hmm... that I don't know. But travelling, that's for sure. Look!" She showed me some more lines on my palm.

"Where should I go? Is that also written on my palm? How about going to Buenos Aires together?" I now took her hand into mine and pretended I was studying it. "Let's see if your hand says you agree to travel with me. This line, right?"

"It's not that simple," she said, laughing. "You have to look for a pattern, not just one line."

"All I want to see is if you're going on a trip to Buenos Aires with me," I said half-jokingly. "That's all I care about."

"Oh, don't be silly!" She puffed up her cheeks and, with a little smack of her lips, let the air out coquettishly. She was suddenly acting like a little girl.

"No really, I'm dead serious! If I have to travel, why don't you come with me? Everybody goes to Buenos Aires: Alfredo, Jorge. The whole gang. Sebastian has a place people can stay at. I think he's turned his own house into a hostel for tango people. And he doesn't charge that much."

She looked at me with a mixture of surprise and incredulity.

"Are you serious?" She hesitated a moment. "We hardly know each other."

"So that'll be our chance!"

"You're a dreamer, I was right about that!" She was laughing now in an easy, light-hearted way. She didn't take me seriously, I could see that.

"Look, it's not impossible," I said, persisting. "We just have to plan ahead. You said you work? I mean, can you take a leave?"

"Sure, I work. My next vacation isn't till September."

"So we'll go in September. It's nice there in September, not too hot; the tourist season will be over. It would be wonderful, I promise!"

I saw that part of her wanted to be persuaded. I moved closer to her and took her in my arms. I couldn't restrain myself and started kissing her neck, her hands. My breath was short.

"We'll walk down those streets in Buenos Aires, the same

barrios where our tango started."

I said "our" as if we already had some mutual history, as if
"our" life was just a continuation of what started generations ago in
the Southside docks and brothels of Buenos Aires and all I had to do
now was to resuscitate this life together with her.

I put my hand on the smooth knee showing through the slit
of her skirt. I had wanted to touch this knee for a long time. Words
poured out of me, uncontrollably, rapidly.

"I want to hold you in my arms forever. I want to carry you
– to protect you... I don't care what people would say... I've always
been looking for a woman like you."

"Oh, stop it. It is just tango, that's all there is!"

"Why don't you believe me?" I desperately wanted to make
love to her.

"I believe you, all right, I believe you!" She suddenly started to
sob.

"What's the matter? Why are you crying?"

"I'm sorry, this is silly. I'm really sorry."

"Did I hurt you?"

"No, Jason. It has nothing to do with you. It's been a year
today since my husband left me. Anniversaries are hard."

"How could he have left such a wonderful woman? Especially
at Christmas?"

What I said was stupid, of course, and I meant it as a joke, but
my hands were working up her black-stockinged leg, words were
popping out of me, and I didn't care what I was saying anymore.

Pauline quickly removed my hand from her knee and pulled

the two parts of her skirt together. When she burst into tears I was completely confused. I never know how to deal with female tears. To me they're a punch below the belt, a plea for help that hardly leaves me any room to manoeuvre, urging me to act without telling me what I'm supposed to do. They make me feel guilty. But what am I to blame for? That her husband left her? That the world is such a fucked-up place? I didn't create it; it's not my responsibility.

"Were you married a long time?" I couldn't think of anything else to say.

"Almost twenty years. They were happy years. We never quarrelled, not once." There was a pressing, raw sincerity in her voice.

"Okey. But all that's in the past. Forget about it." I scooped her into my arms and started to undo the upper buttons of her blouse.

"Don't," she said dryly. "Don't."

"Why not? Please..." My voice became coarse, a stranger's voice.

"Don't, I'm telling you."

But it was too late. While my left hand was travelling down her back in the attempt to undo her bra, my right hand dipped under the bra's wire. Oh, the delicious sensation of soft female flesh! One more second... and I pulled my hand away in disgust. Instead of the breast, I had run into a flat surface, hard as a board.

"What's that?" I asked, not trusting my own hand anymore.

"It's what's left after the surgery," she said calmly.

A mixture of horror and cold curiosity suddenly took hold of me.

"Show me."

"No."

"Let me touch it, then."

"No. Please don't. My husband left me because... "

"Because of that?"

"Yes. Several months after the surgery. He couldn't...couldn't cope with this. Don't touch me there. Please don't."

I unclenched her fingers grasping her blouse. Yes, I had to see it for myself. Removing her top, I gently ran my finger over her former breasts, first the left one, then the right. Strangely, it wasn't as horrible as I expected. There merely were no breasts anymore, just a flat surface, much like the chest of a man. There was even a residual layer of fat, between bone and skin. How cleverly she had camouflaged it while dancing with me, I thought.

I felt a sudden overwhelming sense of fatigue, as if something had changed in the air. Perhaps the wind had abated. It was eerily quiet. Pauline slipped the top back on, leaving the padded bra where it had fallen on the floor.

"It's late," I said. "Time for me to go."

"Yes, of course. Shall I give you a ride?"

"No, thanks. I need to walk a little. It'll be good for me to walk."

"I understand. I know you live far away...though you said you live nearby. Sure you don't need a ride?"

How did she know? But I felt too tired to go into any explanation. After all, I'd danced well past midnight. It'd been a very long day, and frankly I didn't care.

"Merry Christmas to you," I said.

"Merry Christmas," she responded. Then she closed the door behind me.

I took in my first gulp of fresh air. Then wiped my feet against the straw elephant holding out to me his "WELCOME" trunk. That was weird. I wasn't coming. I was going. But then everything felt weird at that hour of the wolf on Christmas Eve. Tango seemed repulsive to me now. And I couldn't fathom what on Earth had moved me to squander my last money on it. Tango was a deceit, a chimera. Women were a chimera. So was life.

I walked out into the street gasping for the crisp, frosty air that felt like a special gift for my oxygen-starved lungs. The delicious fragrant chill caressed my skin. Oh, the joy of escape, of moving again wherever one pleased in brisk carefree steps!

It didn't bother me in the slightest that I had to cross half the city to get to my place. Something had indeed changed around me. A strange quietness clad the city, as if a voice had been cut short mid-phrase. Yes, the wind had stopped. The wind that had been whistling down the streets for months, that wind had dropped its daggers and left the city. Gone, as suddenly as it had arrived, replaced by white spectral mourners that had alighted on the ground in complete silence: whirling around broodingly; powdering houses with snow; frosting trees, shrubs, porches and the sharp peaks of the fences; cushioning sidewalks; and sweeping over the minute untidy indecencies that the wind had revealed.

Within half an hour, the city was fully dressed in its new attire. It lay there in solemn purity, white and sinless. It seemed to become lighter with each thrust of snow, as if ready to ascend. I, too, felt I could rise to the skies; all I had to do was to get rid of the ballast that kept me earthbound.

Slipping frozen hands into my pockets, I felt something smooth and solid. Pauline's baby elephant. It still retained the warmth of the house I'd just left, much warmer than my hand. I held it for a minute. Then threw it into a freshly blown mound of snow. Softly it sank down into the white shroud, legs and trunk up, making no more than a dent. I stood and watched it quickly disappear under the abundant whiteness falling from the night sky.

Rapture

1

"You know I love you."

"Yes. You've told me. Many times."

"Remember, you're..."

"I'm what?"

"Let me finish. You're not alone in this city. I'm only a phone call away. That's what I mean."

Ralph raised his finger, then thrust his hands forward, his shiny cufflinks catching the light of a candle, and quickly pulled his plate forth and then back again, rearranging the perfectly arranged cutlery.

"I'm off to London next week, but as I said, no matter where I am, you can always call me. If something happens, I always have your back."

"But...what can actually happen?"

"I'm not saying anything will. But if you need anything, in the evenings, I'm always in my hotel, working. Time difference between London and Vancouver...let's see...about eight hours, not so bad. If you call me in the morning, your morning, that'll work fine for me."

"But.... I really don't need anything."

"Yes, you do! Of course you do! If you want, I'll talk to D&M. They may need a secretary."

"That's kind of you, Ralph, but I'm...I'm not good at this kind of thing."

"What do you mean, not good? You can do anything...anything

you apply yourself to. See my point?"

"I don't understand technical stuff, Ralph and besides...it's really not for me, the secretarial job."

"You don't need to be a techy for this kind of work. You know how to type. You can schedule meetings, right? You're nice with people...when you want to be. Even with me, sometimes," he chuckled, "when you're in the right mood, I mean, khee, khee."

Hands interlaced on his round tummy, he stuck out two thumbs that he speedily rotated around each other, a gesture accompanying that characteristic mixture of a chuckle and a cough. "You need some steady income, khee, khee, khee, that's the thing."

"Thanks for telling me!"

"Oh, don't be angry with me, Maya. I'm just trying to help. When you have salary, then you can start looking around for a better job, that's all I'm saying. One thing leads to another. When you lost your CBC position, did you inquire if there was another one, in another department, even part time?"

"It would've been pointless. I didn't have enough seniority; that's why they laid me off. Along with hundreds of others."

"But have you tried?"

"Tried what? To humiliate myself? I know someone from the newsroom – they rehired him as a free lancer. The same amount of work as before but for a fraction of his previous salary. That's not for me. Thanks."

"But in the future, he might move on to something better. See, that was your strategic mistake. You had two young kids then. You should've asked. Never give up, never! Well, there's no point in going back to it now. You were a radio journalist, a producer. Couldn't you have switched over to newspapers or something? Also no? Okay. But what happened with your teaching? You had a steady load of work in two colleges. Why did you give it up? You never told me."

"Oh, never mind."

"Well, go back to them. Ask them if there's an opening."

"They've probably hired somebody."

"See? You're assuming things. But life might surprise you. As I said, don't ever surrender. Good wine, eh? You want to know how I earned my first buck? Buying for two dollars and selling for four, not a bad business for a twelve-year-old kid, eh? I was quite a haggler... khee, khee."

"I'm sure."

"Look, I'm not suggesting you sell lemonade. But you can sell bolsters, for example."

"Sell what?"

"Yoga mattresses, bolsters, whatever you use for your classes. What do they pay you per hour?"

"Depending on the studio. Twenty dollars an hour, usually."

"That's what I mean. You can't make a living that way. *You* have to hire people, not let them hire you. You start your own business, and once you have your own studio, you can organize a little store on the side. That's an additional income. Somebody comes in for a class – they forgot their own mat. No problem! They can buy it from you."

"Ralph!"

"Yes?"

"Do you hear what I'm saying? I'm saying, I don't want to

manage a studio...look, business is simply not my thing! If I can't do what I really like, at least I can teach yoga for now."

"Wait! How do you know you're not good at it, unless you try? You know what your problem is?"

"I'm sure I have more than one."

"Your low self-esteem. That's the first thing we have to fix: every morning, when you get up, you stand in front of the mirror and you say, 'I am capable of anything. I'm beautiful and I'm smart. I'm beautiful and I'm smart.' You say that ten times. Okay?"

"Only ten? Sure!"

"If I help you to rent some space not exactly downtown, but close enough, say for ten to fifteen students, how much would the rent be? How many employees would you need, and how much could you afford to pay them? Make a business plan and show it to me."

"I'm going to scream."

"Please, don't be mad at me, Maya. It was only a suggestion."

The restaurant, on the top of the forty-four-storey Empire Landmark Hotel, the tallest building in Vancouver, was slowly revolving. In the twilight of the dying day, the lights on the mountains of the North Shore, separated from Vancouver by a dark streak of Burrard Inlet, were slowly shifting. A cape, with Stanley Park jutting out into the ocean, was also retreating, the dark mass of its cedars and firs going backward, while the downtown core, ablaze with twinkling lights, was sailing toward us.

"You are not coming back to Montreal, are you?" Ralph asked, pouring me a glass of Sauvignon.

"Obviously not. Why?"

"Our agency has been looking for a Russian instructor lately, I hear. We're collaborating on a number of projects with Russians astronauts. You could teach Russian, couldn't you?"

"A pity," I said brusquely, putting my glass down. "Why are you telling me about it now?"

"Oh, it just came up. Their instructor is going on a maternity leave, I was told." He paused. "Well, it would be a temporary position anyway, not what you need. You don't like this wine? You liked it last time, I remember."

"Don't feel like drinking right now. I need to get back home soon."

"I'll give you a ride, don't worry. Tomorrow is Sunday. You don't teach, do you?"

"No, not on Sunday."

"I'd like to see you tomorrow," he said quietly. For the first time, I noticed dark areas around his eyes. Then he paused for a moment and gave me that bold, penetrating look that excluded any objections. "We can go for a walk in Stanley Park. I've only been there once. I'll be busy working in the morning, but I can free my afternoon...for you."

I didn't reply. Ralph poured himself another glass of wine and sat back, his fingers drumming lightly on the table.

"Tell me something: did you leave Montreal because of me?"

"No. But you were a big part of my decision, if you really need to know."

His outstretched fingers froze, spread out in the air. "Ah! You wanted to get away from me so badly that you jumped over to the other side of the continent, with no job, no connections, just go, as far away from terrible Ralph as possible?"

"Well, at least I tried. Obviously, not very successfully."

"You're a straight shooter, aren't you?"

"What can I tell you? You asked me a direct question, I'm giving you a direct answer."

An ugly little creature stirred in my chest, inflating it with anger. The little monster wanted to punish Ralph for his dogged kindness; for the cushy job at the space agency that could have given me – even if temporarily – some relief, but had gone to somebody else (never mind that I had left the city before it came about); for Ralph's sloping shoulders that went up and down when he giggled; for his small, pale, well-kept hands; for his neat, child-size feet in expensive brown leather shoes.

I looked out the window. The city was putting itself on display with an arrogant indifference, as if I were an accidental visitor here, in no way related to its picture-perfect mountains, beaches, and bays, all gradually extinguished by the encroaching darkness that was softening its daytime harshness of glass and steel. High-rises, their silhouettes standing out against the indigo sky, were now all ablaze with lights. Down below, in the city's deep caverns, the fireflies of cars were scurrying about.

"Am I really so repulsive to you, Maya?" Ralph said, fingering his yellow striped tie. His blue eyes gazed at me with childish helplessness.

"You're a good person, Ralph. I know you really care for me, and I appreciate it...but I just can't...I can't share your feelings."

"And if I were free, would that have changed things, in any way?"

"You know the answer. We've been through this so many times. Why torture us both? I can be a friend to you, and I am. I respect your knowledge, your abilities, but for the rest, I just don't have it in me, what it takes..."

"What it takes what? I'm not asking you for anything. I'm not asking you for sex."

"Oh, you're asking for more than that! But I can only give you what I have. What I don't have, I can't...and there is nothing, nothing in the world I can do about it! Don't you understand?"

"Yes, you made it very clear."

"If so, why do you keep...?"

"It's called cognitive dissonance."

A fast talker and mover, bristling with vivacity, and fussy energy, he suddenly froze, as if some internal mechanism had broken and come to a stand still. For a moment, he stared at a plate of hors d'oeuvre. Then he quickly wiped his mouth with a starched napkin, tossed it on the table, and, pushing his chair back, abruptly got up.

"I'll be back," he said brusquely.

"I'm sorry! I didn't mean to."

"Nothing to be sorry about," he said, without looking at me. "It's not your fault."

Relieved to be alone, I pulled a book out of my purse. It was a compendium of poets from different countries at the turn of the twentieth century. In a preface, a memoirist reminisced about Brusov, the founder of Symbolism in Russia, and the extraordinary circle of young poets surrounding him. "The Maître demanded an ardent way of living from us, young poets," the memoirist wrote. "Every day, in fact, each waking moment, we had to search for the transcendent, for rapture. We had to partake of some surreal light that would transform our souls, lead us to revelation. Hunters for illusive images, drugged without drugs, we turned ourselves into somnambulists who..."

"What are you reading, may I ask?" I heard Ralph's voice behind me. He was leaning over my shoulder, peeping into the page.

I was quick to shut the book. "Nothing special, really."

"Oh, c'mon, Maya. You're always so secretive about your reading. I'm not a complete idiot. I read books too, you know. "

"Of course you do. I just don't think this is your cup of tea."

"Well, try me!"

"If you insist. This we'll skip...and this too. Well, maybe this. Rubén Darío. A Nicaraguan poet."

"And you're interested in him why?"

Again, I felt tightness in my chest, an urge to rebel. "Why? For no good reason, I suppose. I'm going to write a book about him, that's why. I'm going to write a book about the poet you know nothing – well, many people here – know nothing about. A seminal figure, the founder of *modernismo*. What's wrong with that? You don't think I can do it?"

Ralph looked at his watch. "I didn't say you couldn't. But one has to prioritize things. Steady income first, and then hobbies, the artsy things. Anyway, what's going on here? Where's the main course? We've been waiting for fifteen minutes already." He snapped his fingers, trying to attract the attention of the waiter, then impatiently moved things around on the table. "Why don't you read to me while we're waiting."

"But it's in Spanish. I mean I can...but it will be a rough, literal translation. Well, I can try: 'Queen Mab rose in her chariot, cut out of a single pearl, and waved her veil, barely tangible, as if it were woven of breathing dreams – sweet dreams – and life through that veil appeared to be immersed in rosy light. I covered with her veil all four of them: emaciated, desperate, yet daring. And their sorrows abandoned them and hope nestled in their chests, and in their heads took root a merry sun and a crafty imp of pride that indulged poor artists in their moments of despair. And since then, in the attics of poor misfits, azure dreams are reigning, and the day to come seems radiant; their laughter chases away their sorrows, and the wild farandole is whirling in front of white Apollo in a shape of a gaudy canvass, ramshackle violin, and a faded manuscript.'"

"Hmm. What's it all about, anyway? Artists building castles in the air? That's what makes them happy, eh? I'm just a simple man. I could never understand these things. Will you teach me?" He leaned over the table, bringing his ingratiating grin close to my face.

"Teach you? You know so much more than I do! What can I teach you?"

"What you've just read. You know why I love you? Why I can never be angry with you? Because you live in the world that I don't understand; but when I'm with you, it feels like I'm getting to some place different...another moment and something will open up in me." He sighed. "I may be just fooling myself. Like your poor artists. Feeding on an illusion. When did he live, your Rubén Darío?

"Died a hundred years ago."

"Long time ago."

"Do you know what my name means in Sanskrit? It means an 'illusion.'"

"Well, Maya, you're not my illusion. You're my obsession."

The main course finally arrived. Ralph moved his tie out of the way, and pounced on his steak – he was obviously hungry. I looked at his strong, healthy teeth, his neatly trimmed, greying goatee; his bald patch with silver in the rim of his hair, dark and curly in the past. His was not an unattractive face. From time to time, he would lift his bright blue eyes at me: they expressed his unquenchable ebullience, satisfaction with food, wine, and the world around him. But I knew how quick-tempered he was; how forceful and bossy when displeased if what he thought was his due was not instantly delivered; how impatient with those who failed to get things his quick and astute mind had already grasped. He was a talented physicist turned top manager in charge of a huge budget and hundreds of people. He did not spare himself and was used to long hours of work, demanding the same from others. He successfully channelled his prodigious energy toward reaching his goals, accomplishing complicated projects and bending other people's will to his ends.

"Do you hear anything from Kolya in Moscow?" Ralph asked.

"No.

"Hmm...And your older son?"

"Mathew? He rarely calls. Busy with his student's life, I guess."

"Doesn't call his mom?"

"He dislikes Waterloo."

"So? Shouldn't be so hard to make a phone call. Waterloo has the best undergraduate math program in Canada. He must appreciate what you did for him. By the way, Aaron calls us every second day from Harvard. If he hadn't called, he would've gotten hell from his mom, and he knows that. Khee, khee, khee."

"I taught my children to be independent. Maybe too independent. How is Malka doing, by the way?" I was feeling more and more lonely as the evening progressed.

"Malka? Oh, fine, fine!" Ralph cut up his beefsteak in neat squares, sending one piece after the next into his mouth and watering them down with wine. "Hmm, nice steak, very nice. Cooked just right! Want to try a piece...No? How's your fish? Did I tell you Malka graduated with straight A's? I'm sending her to Europe for two months. My graduation present."

"She goes alone?"

"Oh, no! Her mother would never let her. Three of them go, Esther, with both kids. And then I'll join them for a couple of weeks, after my conference in London."

I wondered how he was planning on my phone calls.

"We're going to spend a week in Greece, then in Italy, and end up in Israel. I'll have to return to work though, but Esther will stay in Israel for another month with the kids, visiting relatives."

Why is he telling me all this? Am I his sister? His wife's friend? Ah, letting me know he is going to be free for a whole month, that's why.

"This time, I felt it was time to arrange a holiday for the whole family. Esther complains that I practically live in Montreal now. But what can I do? I can't move my space agency to Toronto, can I?"

"You're still going back and forth to Toronto every weekend?"

"Comes up to a little more than a weekend. I leave Montreal on Thursday. That's Thursday, Friday, Saturday and Sunday – almost four days I'm with my family. But it doesn't seem to be enough lately. In a way, I can see my wife's point. I've been commuting back and forth for how long now? Almost eight years."

"It's hard," I said, keeping a neutral tone.

"Well, I've optimized the process. I don't pack. Everything I need is duplicated in both homes. I travel with a briefcase."

"Couldn't you move your family to Montreal?"

"A difficult proposition. Esther has all her friends in Toronto. Then there's the synagogue...we've both been members for decades. Esther is the head of an educational program. I's on several boards. Kids had their bar mitzvahs there. I was saying the Kaddish for my father there when he died. He had his Jahrzeit just before I came out to Vancouver."

"What's the Kaddish?"

"A prayer for the departed. I went to that synagogue to pray every morning for a whole year. When I was in Montreal, I went to Beth Zion. Just finished recently. Feel better for it."

"A whole year? How did you manage, with your schedule?"

"You do what you have to do...I loved my father, you see. Was very close to him. Missing him terribly. But when you pray, you're not alone. You're part of the minyen. It becomes your support group. And it helped me to cope...to cope with my grief, you see." Ralph looked away, his eyes misting over.

"I didn't know you believed in the afterlife. Being a scientist, I mean."

"Theoretically, you can't prove the existence of God. But you can't disprove it either. Newton was a believer, and so was Pascal."

Ralph finally finished chewing, and rolled his tongue inside his mouth checking it for bits of meat stuck between his teeth.

"You want some dessert? Coffee? No? I'll tell you what...Why don't we go to my room? I have a present for you."

"You shouldn't be buying me presents, really."

"What do you mean, I shouldn't? It's your birthday."

"In a week's time, not today."

"Well, I won't see you in a week. C'mon. It's not that late yet."

2

Ralph took off his navy blue jacket with shiny buttons on the sleeves and hung it on the back of an armchair. I caught a glimpse of his suspenders and looked away.

The standing lamp responded to the pressure of his foot, illuminating a nondescript abstract picture on the wall and throwing concentric patterns on the grey carpet. A box sitting on top of a coffee table contained my birthday present. I pulled out a clunky vase of ornamental crystal.

"Looks nice, don't you think? I love glass! May I kiss the birthday girl?"

I stuck my cheek out for a kiss.

"That's all I'm getting today? Put it down, the vase. Let's sit down for a moment." He pointed to a sofa and, sitting next to me took, my hand in his.

I reached for a lipstick in my purse, the only pretext I could find to free my hand.

"You don't need any lipstick, darling. If I wanted to kiss you, you think the lipstick would stop me? Put it away, will you?"

I hesitated, but then obeyed.

"Now tell me, what's going on, Maya? Why are you in such a terrible mood today? Did I do or say something wrong? We had a nice meal. Your birthday is coming. What can I do to make you happy? Shall I put on some music? Let's see, there must be a radio somewhere."

"No music! Please!"

"You don't like music?"

"I hate music, any kind of music, just so you know. And I'm not in a bad mood. Actually, I'm in an excellent mood! It's funny, come to think of it. Really funny!" I couldn't control my laughter.

"What's so funny, all of a sudden?"

"It's hilarious! I just imagined you leaning over your drawing board, sleeves rolled up, sweating."

"Nobody uses drawing boards these days, Maya."

"Or whatever! No, it's really funny. Such a difficult project! A hard nut to crack! Ralph is sweating! But he's a problem-solver. Will he ever give up? Oh no! Never! The rocket should be launched! He's thrashing around, trying this and that – no go! Phrrr-brrr-pff-pff! Fumes everywhere, tram-tara-ram! Boom-boom! One technical problem after the next. It's totally stuck! But Ralph is stubborn. He'll get if off the ground, even if it kills him."

"What're you talking about?"

"You and me."

"And you find it funny?"

"Isn't it though?"

Ralph shook his head from side to side loosening his tie as if it might strangle him. He walked over to the window, his arms crossed over his chest.

I came to him and touched his shoulder. "I'm sorry if I hurt you, Ralph, I didn't mean to. Really."

"Yes, you did,"he said without turning around."Of course you did. But I deserved it."

"No, it's just...you're right, I'm not in my best mood. We've known each other for how long? Two years, more? And you still have the perseverance, the stamina...all this energy you're spending on me. But why? Why? I'm an ordinary woman. I don't know what on Earth you see in me! Why did you even start talking to me, there, on a train? A good-looking woman, all alone, so you decided to try your luck?"

"Enough, Maya. Enough! I'm not a skirt chaser! I don't pick up good-looking women on trains, as you very well know. But if you really want to know what happened to me on that train when I saw you for the first time...well...I'll tell you. You were sitting alone, next to a window. I don't know how to put it, but there was such an aura of resignation about you, like you'd given it all up. I asked something, you responded. Automatically, without paying any attention to me. But then, you raised your eyes. I'll never

forget that moment. There was a silent plea for help in your eyes.
I fell in love with you there and then. I know you well enough by
now. Even if you need me, you'll never show it; always keeping
your stiff upper lip, too proud to admit any weakness. You can be
stubborn; you get angry with me and say nasty things, then regret
it and take your words back. It can be confusing sometimes. I don't
know what you really want. No, not true. I do know. But look, no
matter what you say, I still see that vulnerable little girl in you,
the way I saw you for the first time. And I want to protect you. To
love you the best I can. It is a hopeless endeavour, that too, I know.
And I'm lost, lost, the way I've never been in my life, don't you
understand?"

3

Where exactly did these crumbling steps in Trastevere lead? I
couldn't remember now. Up and up, past the tangle of climbing
roses, ivy, and wisteria lacing the ancient walls on both sides. Five
steps ahead of me, without looking back, Al was ascending in big
strides, carrying with ease his tall, lithe, long-limbed frame. Al.
I liked his name; It was a pictograph, a code to be deciphered, a
magic box full of secret meanings, or different masks one could
wear. Albrecht, as his Swiss father called him; or Alistair, according
to his Irish mother; or Albert for some stiff and indifferent people;
but for me, Aleshenka, an appellation of a gentle caress to which
he responded with a delay, and a little chuckle. No, my Aleshenka
didn't need to look back: I would follow him. Always, for the rest of

my life. I didn't want to distract him: let music, that great enigmatic power, which was consuming him, let this power alone rule his life, as love for him would rule mine.

We came to Rome at the invitation of orchestra Della Accademia Nazionale di Santa Cecilia, the most prestigious music institution in Rome. Al Zollenger, a performer, composer, and conductor of international repute, was to conduct his own symphony in Basilica di Santa Cecilia. The work required a full orchestra and a huge choir. Sitting through the dress rehearsal, I compared it in scope to Mahler's Third, and thought how magnificent this discordant musical edifice was, if I could only understand, feel, and absorb it!

But contemporary classical music didn't speak to my soul the way Bach or Hayden could. And listening to the frantic cadences that rose and fell and rose, replaced by serene passages and then carried away by the new turbulence of the woodwinds and the screeching of the violins, I didn't know what would be best. Should I confess to Al that this kind of music was beyond my grasp, or should I add my voice to the choir of his admirers, his coterie that followed him wherever he went? But that conundrum didn't diminish my awe in front of the artist who could create – out of nothing – an edifice, a cathedral, of such complexity and scale.

In his tailed tuxedo, his white bow tie and white shirt contrasting sharply with his shiny, charcoal-black hair, this man fitted to perfection my ideal of a musical genius, a conductor, the slightest twitch of whose baton was obeyed by a whole orchestra. Except, as it turned out, Aleshenka didn't use a baton. It was a matter of conductor's choice, he explained. The orchestra could decipher with equal ease the dance of his hands. When he was quite young, he said, he was lucky to be present at one of Stravinsky's last performances. By that time, Stravinsky was so frail that he could neither stand nor conduct; he simply moved his baton in a haphazard manner. But the musicians did not humiliate the great man: they kept the tempo themselves, pretending they followed his lead.

But on another occasion, when we had watched Fellini's *Orchestra Rehearsal,* Al was surprised at the gaffe the Italian film director had made. "Why didn't Fellini consult a professional musician? His actor doesn't know the first thing about conducting. Faking it all along!"

"Show me how you do it! A couple of movements...tell me what they mean!"

Al smiled, then took me by the wrist and guided my hand in this direction and that, explaining how he communicates with an orchestra. I listened eagerly to the sound of his voice, letting the meanings of his words slip by...What stayed in my memory was the sensation of his touch: his hand over my wrist, his eyes becoming sleepy, the way they always did when he looked at me. Every time I remembered this, I blushed.

At that memorable concert in the Basilica di Santa Cecilia, I was wearing a flowing mauve dress with a single string of purple amethyst on my neck that suited my complexion, my light chestnut hair. I knew I couldn't compete with the stylish Italian *beau monde* – that would have taken practice and money. But Al loved me the way I was: unpractised, and without money. He'd given me many proofs of his attachment in his undemonstrative, gently aloof way. It was there, in the Basilica, that he introduced me as his fiancée.

During the performance I sat in the front row, to the left of the conductor's podium. From that angle, Al's profile resembled Liszt's on the portrait I saw as a child in my piano teacher's studio. Al's was a sensitive, handsome, and intelligent face, sculpted by ardent labours of art. He had a high, open forehead and aquiline nose; dark melancholic eyes of a velvety shine that often gazed, slightly squinting, above the heads of his interlocutors, as if what was visible to him was concealed from everybody else. His chivalric, old-fashioned manners enchanted women. And why, of all his female admirers, he had chosen me, a single mother of two boys, long past my prime (even though younger than him by twelve years), born and raised in a different culture, a musical dilettante – why did he fall for me?

I tried to chase those thoughts away. At least my musical ignorance didn't seem to bother him. When I told him that, yes, I liked his symphony, especially the second, more lyrical part, with the slow graceful andante that reminded me of the Willis dance in *Giselle,* he assured me that I knew enough. Could it be, I asked, that he, Al, had also been inspired by that passage, or was it just a coincidence?

He smiled, obviously entertained by such a suggestion: You know that ballet well enough to remember the score?

Some of it, I said. That old-fashioned ballet was my favourite of the classical romantic repertoire. His andante in the second part was a bit like the dance of the Willis, ephemeral young virgins who die on the eve of their weddings, betrayed by their unfaithful fiancés.

Turning into ghosts after their deaths, the Willis lure wayfarers into the woods and force them to dance to exhaustion and ultimate death.

That conversation took place in an empty Basilica after the audience and the musicians had already left. Al drew me closer and, bending over me, planted a kiss on my closed eyelids. "My clever girl, you do know some things, don't you?"

I was moved by his words, by that closeness under the marble watch of angels. Back in our hotel, I confided in him in a childish whisper: slightly, burring my words, that I didn't consider myself clever at all. Unlike him, I still didn't know what my real vocation might be. Being a successful radio journalist and producer in the past, now a popular instructor at the university college, well... none of it grabbed me. What I really wanted to do was devote my life to art, a goal so far elusive. I did write poetry, I whispered, heaving a choking sigh, but I didn't think it was any good. I tried my hand at prose, but doubts often eroded my efforts. Did I really have what it took: perseverance and an ability to say something new, when everything had been already said? Distraught, I rubbed my nose against his neck looking for consolation.

But that's not what he gave me. Instead, I remembered clearly, when I mentioned that I didn't think I had anything new to say, Aleshenka detached himself from me and, casting a sidelong glance, said emphatically, separating the words: "Don't write if you can help it. Unless it's a question of life and death, do not write!"

I heaved a little sob to show him how real and how painful my predicament was, but deep down I was grateful for his frankness. He confirmed what I had intuitively known all along: The torture of hunting for the elusive light was not worth it, if you could live by the reflected light of the beloved. Love was more precious, more essential, than the eternal yearning for the ephemeral. Love was life; the rest, a chimera. By removing my tiresome burden, he was liberating me, giving me permission finally to live. Just live.

His words, as true as they may have been harsh, pointed to a new direction in life – and I was ready to take it.

4

When we left Rome and travelled south, all the way down to Bari on Adriatic coast, where Al was to give another concert, there, again, he introduced me as his fiancée.

After the concert, his Italian colleague, another conductor, invited a select few, a crowd of about twenty, to his country house (he referred to as his "villa"). There they ate, drank, and talked in a chaotic, jolly, affable Italian way under the golden rain of laburnum dripping off the pergola, with shrieking peacocks walking between their feet. I marvelled at the oranges you could pluck from a tree growing in front of the composer's house, and at a platter of enormous green olives sizzling in oil. Holding the platter, the Italian conductor – what was his name? – tarried near me, eyeing me frankly and flickering at me that knowing smile that made me uneasy at the time, though I later remembered it with vain joy. The next morning, we went to look at the *trulli*, for which Apulia was famous. The composer insisted on accompanying us. Walking at my side, he smiled at me, complimenting my faulty Italian, while Al walked ten steps ahead, as was his custom. The congregation of these small, primitive, round dwellings with conical roofs sitting on top of dry stone walls made me think of Snow White's dwarfs out for a stroll. It was there, at the sight of the *trulli*, that the sense of unreality took hold of me with a renewed force. Was I dreaming all this time, with my eyes open? Had fate simply inserted me, as an extra, into some fairy tale, while the real protagonists were waiting in the wings?

But that strange feeling of uncertainty disappeared once we were on our own again. Moving north to Switzerland, our next destination, we stopped over in the small hill town of Panicale, in Umbria, at the foot of Mount Petrarvells. Spaces inside medieval walls, surrounding the ancient fortress, had been repurposed for a hotel. I tried to hide my parochial awe at the sight of Italian avant-garde interior design, that insisted on its contrast with ancient beams and stones.

In his white cotton pants and jacket, Al looked younger than his age. He was now relaxed, and his soulful, sad eyes smiled at me benevolently. We walked past the walls of the fortress to a small square with a medieval fountain. He picked up a metal rod and, with boyish nonchalance, tried to tease sounds out of every object on his path: the metal fence serving as a xylophone producing rough, uneven *wo-o-o-s*; the trunk of an oak exuding a dull hollow moan; and the stone refusing to co-operate.

We left the town and walked past the vineyards down towards toward Lake Trasimeno, a glimpse of which we had caught out our window. Al wanted to see the lake, where, in times of antiquity,

Hannibal's army had beaten the Romans.

Pines and juniper covered the slopes, and when we descended into the valley, the fresh breeze died out and waves of hot air, perfumed with the smell of pine needles, caressed my face. The pinks and the yellows of the oleander blooms and the dusty silver of olive trees enchanted me. I felt I was now in communion with this timeless world. My Aleshenka was at my side, and in his presence I felt peace and contentment, as if he'd handed me some magic shield protecting me from apprehensions and vague forebodings nestled deep inside.

Beauty, in all its forms, beauty in nature and art, had always disturbed me somewhat, as it sharpened the contrast between its divine harmony and my own imperfections. But now, because of him, the impenetrable boundaries between myself and the world were melting away; the sharp corners were being smoothed out, the questioning, the discontent appeased. I accepted the world, and the world accepted me. All of it, I felt, because of Al's love...

The trail sloped gently downward. When we crossed a little brook, Al reached for a reed, cleaned it off, and blew into it, producing a coarse, dull sound. "Pan must have sounded better than that when he played his flute," he said. "They say he wanted to compete with Apollo himself. You know that flute was my first instrument? Violin the second?"

"Pan? What Pan are you talking about?

"Wasn't there only one? Have a look! There, hiding behind the trees! See? That lovely creature with horns and hoofs."

"How do you know Pan lives here?"

"What's the name of this town, darling?"

"I see. And what exactly is he doing in our woods, you'd say?"

"In his woods, you mean. He is doing what you and I are doing: fooling around, without a thought in our heads; chasing nymphs and making love to them ..." Al drew me close and, leaning over, planted a kiss on my cheek.

"Alesha's kiss. Can we do Pan's?"

"That wasn't good enough? You want me to ravish you? To tear you to pieces? But I can't compete with the hoofed one, my dear. Between Dionysus and Apollo, I'm afraid I made my choice a long time ago!"

He let me go and suddenly took off scampering down the hill. When I finally caught up to him, he was sitting on a boulder, gazing at the remote lake partly veiled by milky haze.

I sat down on the warm soil next to him and wrapped my arm around his waist. "What are you thinking about, Aleshenka?"

"Nothing in particular. Just wondering where Claude Debussy got the idea for his *L'Aprés-Midi d'un Faune.* Maybe he, too, visited this place."

5

"Why don't we plan on spending six months a year in a hilltop town like that, Maya? I could take a sabbatical next semester. I'll compose and you...you'll find something to do, won't you?"

I wanted to tell him that I couldn't think of anything better than being with him in a hill town in Italy, but since I was teaching in two colleges, to get away for a whole semester was hardly possible.

"My darling, I don't want you to waste your talents on these part-time, low-paying jobs. They are simply exploiting you. You know that! I want us to be together! You come to San Diego. We'll get married. Then we'll travel. And then, if you want to teach, if you say you must, we'll find something. But who knows, perhaps you'll want something else? "

"Like what?"

"Like looking after your old, decrepit, exhausted, good-for-nothing Aleshenka. How is that for a life goal? By the way, have I officially proposed to you? I can't remember."

"You can't remember?"

Al suddenly dropped to one knee. "Well, here it is. I'd love to push daisies with you. What would you say to that, my Maya?"

"To do what?"

"Just say yes or no!"

"Of course no! I don't want to push daisies! I want to make love...here, in the woods!"

Al got up off his knees, brushing twigs off his pants. "First you shatter my heart with your refusal, then you want to make love to me? Fine, I'll marry your mother instead. We were getting along fine when we played Mozart with four hands."

"Okay, okay! Try me again before marrying my mother! Propose. But come up with something better, this time."

"Let's see. Hmm. Can you milk a kicking cow?"

"Oh, my God! Will I ever get a normal, sweet, asking for a hand and heart, or whatever one is supposed to ask for?"

"That's the way they proposed in Sligo, where my mother's family is from. A peasant girl is supposed to be hard working. If she can't milk a kicking cow, then she is no good." He fell silent, then said after a pause, "Yeats was born in Sligo, did you know that?"

Al was taken with the idea of buying a house somewhere in Umbria or Toskana, and so the next couple of days they spent driving around and looking at properties. And then, as planned, we flew to Switzerland. He wanted to introduce me to his Swiss relatives and especially to his daughter, who worked for the United Nations in Geneva.

His relatives turned out to be ordinary farmers, living on a farm, kind and simple people who welcomed me with an open heart.

But it was Al's daughter with whom I made an immediate connection, a rare occasion between a grown-up woman and her would-be stepmother. Understanding was at half-word and half-look.

6

I received a prenuptial gift from my fiancé. In the memory of our Italian trip, he gave me a signed score of his symphony that he had conducted at Santa Cecilia. His future mother-in-law received the manuscript of Mozart's early minuets, a copy of the original.

My relocation to the States required paper work, but Al urged me to come to San Diego, his city, without delay. Our wedding would be simple, without much ado: he was in the middle of a new composition, and interruption was not welcome.

I'd visited him in San Diego before. His house in La Jolla, in a Spanish colonial revival, with a red tile roof, was sheltered by tall eucalyptus and jacaranda covered in spring with purple blooms. A round tower attached to one side of the house, with a separate entrance, served him as a studio.

The living room was Spartan, with only a few pieces of furniture: an antique chest of drawers and chairs with carved Gothic backs around an old oak table. The only bright spot was a Persian carpet that covered a portion of the tile floor. In its austere simplicity, the room reminded me of Vermeer's Dutch interiors. There was something abstract, lacking all signs of domestic coziness about this space. But the very abstractness of it, I thought, suited the abstract art of music and its devotee: a benevolent but distant genius whose sanctuary it was.

I never asked to see his studio, yet I wondered what kind of musical instruments he kept there, as there were none in the house.

He had a violin, a flute and a Steinway in the studio, all of which he seldom used, he explained, as he composed in his head, with a pencil and a piece of paper in front of him. He could hear each instrument separately, and all of them together, the way they would sound in an orchestra. That ability seemed to me nothing short of miraculous.

7

When we finally sat down to make a list of guests for our wedding,

Al suddenly remembered that he was running late for a department meeting at his university. He apologized, changed, and soon was gone.

I looked at his scribbles at the top of the sheet, at the abandoned pencil that still held the warmth of his fingers. The house suddenly felt alien to me – I didn't want to be there alone. I paused, then stepped outside.

The palm trees, along the perimeter of the inner courtyard, responded with a dry whisper to the wind, fingering intermittently their narrow leaves. Several eucalyptuses growing on the property gave out an unfamiliar medicinal smell. I touched a white flowery centre of bougainvillea, surrounded by waxy scarlet petals, to make sure that the flowers were alive, real, and not cut out of paper. The sun was approaching the zenith, and soon the heat drove me back into the house.

Sulking is not good, I told myself. Do something useful: make borscht, for example. When Aleshenka came back, he'd appreciate your efforts.

Darkness fell, but I was still alone. When the heat finally eased, I opened the window to let in the fresh breeze from the ocean. And then I heard the faint sounds of a violin, coming from his tower. He must have gone straight to his studio, not checking with me first. I sat in the darkness, without turning on the lights, listening, waiting. At around nine in the evening, he finally returned to the house. I rose to turn on the lights. "No, no, leave it like that, please," he said. "I'm tired."

Without touching my borscht, in the darkness, he went to his bedroom and closed the door behind him. For some time, I sat in the dark, afraid to move. By the time I finally entered the bedroom, he was already asleep.

The pencil and paper on which we had started to compile the wedding guest list sat on the table for another day, then disappeared.

Hot monotonous days dragged on like molasses. Al always returned late from work, too tired to talk. One evening, when he came back late, I decided to cheer him up with some music. Out of his small collection (I was surprised at how small it was), I chose a CD with Beethoven sonatas. He looked at me with utmost horror – so I immediately turned it off.

Next morning, having nothing to do, I thought I would go to the beach and swim. The surf was calm and low, fringed with white foam. Excited to see the ocean, to taste it, to feel its power, I stepped into water. That was my element, the water. The glittering infinity embraced me; I felt great exhilaration in my body, similar to what I felt in Al's now melancholic presence. Here, I didn't have to restrain myself, to scale it down, the way it was with Al. I gave myself to the waves with abandon, and when they filled my mouth and nostrils with bitter salt, that, too, felt good, that was life, that was my lone happiness.

I swam in powerful, exaggerated strokes, as if Al were there and could see what a good swimmer I was; what a good body I had. Feeling the elasticity and the strength of my muscles, I kept charging forward. When I finally looked back, the figures on the beach looked puny.

I quickly turned around and tried to swim back with smaller

strokes to save my energy. But the harder I tried, the less progress I made. I was now loosing strength, yet didn't want to admit what I already knew: the ocean kept me captive. It didn't let me move forward an inch.

"Lucky I saw you," said the lifeguard who pulled me out of the water into his boat. "You got into a riptide current. People die here."

"Why such recklessness when we have a swimming pool here?" was Al's only reaction. The way he said it made my heart sink.

My visit to the zoo I decided not to mention at all. It would have sounded childish, even silly. The last time I had visited the zoo was when my children were small. But now, when I didn't know what to do with myself, the famous San Diego Zoo was as good a place as any to kill time.

And who knew? Maybe I'd never come back to San Diego. Once that idea bobbed up to the surface of my consciousness, I began to feel sorry for myself.

My only interest at the zoo was the primates, those caricatures of humans. Everything that we humans did in secret – picking our noses, scratching, fornicating – they did in the open, and that's what made them look both obscene and funny.

The monkey enclosure was empty, except for two long-haired chimps, the mother, and the baby. The mother climbed on a boulder, several inches away from the wall. There, facing it, she froze in total stillness, furry arms hanging listlessly along her body. This strange behaviour reminded me of the way children, in my childhood, had been punished for the smallest infraction by immobility at the wall they had to face for an hour or two.

Some chance, some mysterious force that governed my life must have brought me to the zoo, to this chimp enclosure, to show me that I, too, was now confronting a wall. I, too, had reached a dead end. If that was the case, I'd leave San Diego. I wouldn't humiliate myself.

Just as I had that thought, the mother chimp slowly, with a human clumsiness, got off the boulder and let her baby take her place. Now the baby stood in the same position, on its hind legs, resigned to the wall he was facing. I have to leave San Diego as soon as possible, it's a wall! - I thought panicking.

I took a deep breath and closed my eyes, and when I opened them again, it suddenly dawned on me: The only place providing some relief from the scorching heat was the shade cast by the wall. Mother was cooling herself down, then letting her baby do the same.

How this gesture of mother's love translated into hope for me, I didn't know, but I suddenly felt that not all was lost! All I needed was to have an open, candid conversation with Al. I'd be empathetic. I'd ask him what worried him, why he seemed so unhappy when only recently we'd both been so confident in our future together. If he had any concerns at all, he'd be relieved to find out how patient and understanding I was. I didn't want to rush him into anything. It actually made sense to wait a little longer. We weren't young; we both left behind failed marriages, and we'd lived so many years apart, our habits had formed. Once he was reassured, he'd relax, and the bliss we'd enjoyed in Panicale would alight on us in San Diego.

8

Now that I'd made the decision, I cheered up. After returning from the zoo, I walked around the house humming merry tunes; I smiled, just to show Al how lighthearted I could be, in spite of our mysterious, but no doubt temporary, difficulties. No doom and gloom here. I'd make good use of my time. I'd take charge of the kitchen, cook nice meals, give him a sense of real home when he got back from work. I even danced a little around the stove while cooking, all the while waiting for the right moment when we could talk.

Yet that moment never came.

During the day, Al was at the university, and, after work, he would lock himself in his studio. My lonely dinners, with me being the only consumer of my own elaborate concoctions, were followed by equally lonely nights. Al would fall asleep complaining of fatigue while I would lie next to him staring at defused shafts of light that moved across the ceiling. I didn't know what the source of this light might be, but it illuminated Al's face, pale and solemn in its sleep; it fell on his dense and long eyelashes, unusual in any man, the more so in a man in his fifties.

And so it was: in spite of my patient waiting, the key to a shut door was never offered. I decided to look for it myself.

Patiently, I retraced our steps in time, hoping to pinpoint the moment when this estrangement crept in. What had I done or said, that he suddenly turned away from me? Coming from different cultures, we had no common frame of reference. Could that be the reason? But it didn't seem to bother him in the past. Why now? And didn't love conquer all?

That phone call from a woman who'd been after him for a long time, he told me – could that be a reason? Every time he went to Ohio to visit his sister, that woman, brash, crude, illiterate (that's the way he described her), would insist on meeting him at the airport; insist on carrying his suitcase. She owned a laundromat, and her son was in prison. She'd turned herself into a real nuisance, he said.

No, that wasn't it.

Then what was? Did I say something that offended him? Some stupid remark that he'd taken personally? I couldn't think of anything, except, at his friends' house, during that dinner party, with Richard and his wife, Gail. Cutting asparagus, Richard, a musicologist, asked me what I thought of a performance two weeks before. It had been an open air concert with two full orchestras on two makeshift stages next to each other, performing two different pieces simultaneously, with two conductors, one being Al, another a guest conductor from Japan.

No, I said, I didn't like it at all."The truth is I can't imagine anybody liking it either, if they're being honest. "In that exemplary house, among those genteel people, her words sounded savage: nobody there talked like that. I paused, realizing I'd gone too far. "Well, maybe as a musical experiment, it has some value."

Richard replied, "I wouldn't be so hard on Al, who organized the concert. It's an experiment, as you rightly noticed, and without experimentation, modern classical music would stop evolving. To achieve something great, you need to expand your consciousness, you need to get outside of your comfort zone. We' re all creatures of habit, aren't we? We need to simply be shaken out of it! Too often we use cliché to express ourselves, as I'm sure you'll agree..."

"Are you familiar with John Cage's *4'33"*? That, too, seemed strange, even unthinkable, at the time. Now it's accepted as his most important work. Never heard of him? Let me explain. Four minutes and thirty-three seconds. It's not a random number. There's significance to it, but we won't get into that now. Anyway, all this time, musicians are on stage. They don't play any music, mind you, but they're there, with their instruments. You're watching them as you usually do during the concert, but now you listen not to them but with them. And this tiny bit of semantics opens up the whole new world: not 'to' but 'with.'"

"Sorry, I'm not getting it. Listen to what, if there's no music?"

"You're listening to the symphony of life, and that, the symphony of life, becomes your most visceral, most primal, and, ultimately, most cherished experience. You pay attention to sounds that in the past your brain would automatically have shut out; but now, through this active listening to silence. Well, it's not real silence, is it? I mean, once you activated the process of listening without assigning arbitrarily any hierarchy to sounds, it becomes transformative. In simple terms, Cage forced you to jettison your expectations and to recondition your brain. You hear some coughing in the audience, people usually try to suppress it, but now they're awakened, and freed. They're wondering what's going on, and naturally cough more. Then you become aware of the traffic, cars honking; that too has its own beauty. Then you hear the chairs being pushed back when musicians finish and get up to take a bow – you embrace it all! Cage liberated you from your cage, so to speak. He finally allowed you to live! You went from an ivory tower to the symphony of life. You see?"

I should have nodded in agreement, but instead I said, "But why do I need to buy tickets to a concert hall to listen to traffic noise when I can simply stand on any street corner for that?"

Did Al hear me? And thought me a conventional snob, a philistine? He was standing away from us, near the glass wall facing the garden. Rows of flowerpots flanked the staircase that came right up to the glass wall and, studded with similar flowers in similar pots, continued inside the living room. It united indoor and outdoor spaces into one, creating an illusion of the endless garden, and I thought it would be nice to suggest a similar idea to Al for his house, once I moved in.

9

He'd already switched the key from major to minor and back again several times, till it became ambiguous right through to the final bars. Freakish, frantic. Shostakovich had done it before him. In *String Quartet No.12*. Quoting the great Russian, quoting somebody else? Nothing wrong with that. But too many of his recent compositions were either revamping his earlier ones or borrowing from others; that was the problem. He'd run out of fresh ideas, and he knew it. They – that collective "they" of international connoisseurs and nosy critiques – so far, they hadn't sniffed it out. But sooner or later, they would. Look! The king is naked. Look, he's all dried out! He's finished!

Finished at fifty-seven.

Maya understands little of what I'm doing, so she admires me. Those rapturous eyes...The imposter is going to deliver a glamorous world on a golden plate. I should disabuse her from her illusions. But how? I tried to play it down, tried to withdraw, to use some irony... Yet she's implacable. Made an effigy out of me, cranked it up on a pedestal and now keeps propping it up with both hands. Walking on her toes not to disturb me. Thinking I don't hear! I, who can hear every wisp of sound! What tension, what anguish it gives me!

Not to mention the lights, that's another one, sitting in the dark, like a nun displaying penitence. Am I begrudging her the electricity?

And then her moods: from low to high, in a split second! Is she bipolar and I haven't noticed? That dress she put on the other day, the one she was wearing in Santa Cecilia. A "subtle" hint of our happier times in Italy. Dancing, prancing in front of me...What a tacky, brackish spectacle that was! I won't deny it; we had some happy moments in Panicale. Because I did well in Rome and then in Bari, that's why, and yes, she looked lovely, everybody noticed, and I was touched...Thank God, there was little of her "high-brow talk" there. Poor thing – she somehow feels compelled to do it when she tries to impress me, "to live up to me," as she once put it.

But in the Panicale groves, she let go of her pretensions. And she looked pretty. I thought I was in love...But here? She doesn't belong here, that much is clear. Is it my fault? Hers? Nobody's.

But you said you loved her, didn't you? You thought you loved her there, in the groves of Panicale. And if you did, what happened to your love? What happens to all our loves? If I were God, I would've answered that question. Yes, that's it: where is God? I lost the sense of His presence, and then...then God abandoned me. I can't compose any more – He left me.

She came late into my life. But had we both been younger, had we met when I was at the height of my abilities, would things have been different? Who can now tell?

This section in the first movement that I've been working on for weeks, it's a throwaway. In the past, I could compose a symphony in a month.

Compose? It always felt like it had been there already, waiting for me...I was but a conduit, a channel through which God's energy, the energy of the universe, was flowing into me. All I had to do was submit myself. Listen humbly, patiently, and then write it down as soon as possible while it was still there, often without any corrections...The fever, the ardour of those fourteen-hour workdays, the exuberance when I could go without food, and sleep, my enemy, seemed a waste of time...

But did I forget what would happen after? The despondency, the overwhelming sadness that was the price I paid for my triumphs. Bach, Mozart, Telemann, they wouldn't waste a moment; they would get down to their next piece and the next, and the next.

But not me, no. I would lick my paw, feeling totally spent, empty, void. In the perilous days that followed, I yearned for a woman's body. Her softness against my chest. Her sleepy sweet voice, the way they talk in bed, pretending to be little girls before falling asleep.

Yes, I wanted a wife then, and I took a wife, future mother of

Fiona. Ultimately, it didn't work between the two musicians, both young and full of ambitions. But now, in my "sunset years," do I really need a wife? I don't know anymore...

What I need is some simple, ordinary woman who would be there for me; a silent, unquestioning presence when I am finished with a day of composing; a woman who could look after my house and free me from chores, which devour so much of my time right now.

But if I were to go ahead with Maya, and uproot her, I'd have to take care of her, and I can't afford that! I can't afford losing time. I still have so many irons in the fire. I will compose and conduct and perform and surrender to music again, the way I've always done in the past, humbly, and ecstatically, akin to surrendering to a woman, a simple, strong, earth-bound, sensual woman, with an audacious body that will ease me out of my shell, free me from my ego, just like music has always freed me.

And Maya? Admit it: she's not that woman. She has a nice body, but somehow her ways leave me cold. Why? I don't know why. What difference does it make? It's not like I have someone I have to report to? You're a coward! A cad! You don't even have the guts to be honest with her. But I don't want to hurt her, and I'll do all I can not to! How do you break the news to a woman in love? I mean I do like her...I will seek help. I will seek God...I will seek faith.

He buried his head in his hands, trying to subdue a sob that suddenly escaped his throat.

It was already close to midnight when he finally returned from his studio to his dark and mute house.

10

The psychologist that Al insisted we see, a big, burly, black man with an engaging smile, extended his arms as if he wanted to embrace them: "You guys love each other! Look at you!"

Al's problem was, according to the psychologist, his fear of commitment. "You have to overcome your fears, my friend – I hope to be invited to your wedding! In the meantime, you, Maya, you'll have to give your fiancé a bit of time. Are you ready for that?"

I couldn't but smile back at this jovial, bear-like man, and promised to make the best use of his advice.

When later in the evening I told Al that I'd already bought a return ticket home, he was visibly upset. At the airport, he looked disoriented, dazed. Our love would prevail, he said; just had to find the path that he'd temporarily lost. Before I said the last goodbye, he pressed a letter into my hand.

I landed in Toronto to see a sick friend, and a day later, I got on a train heading to Montreal. Sitting next to the window, I looked apathetically at the wintry landscape running backward. While on the plane, I couldn't pluck up my courage to read Al's letter, but now, finally, I opened it.

In it was a check for five thousand American dollars and a note: "I hope the time of deep introspection we both need will show us a path to happiness and contentment. With much love, Albrecht."

I put the note back into the envelope. The check slipped onto the floor. I didn't notice it. When, a moment later, I lifted my eyes, a short man in a spiffy suit was standing in front of me, handing the check to me.

"You're scattering your fortune around, miss," he said, smiling. He introduced himself as Ralph Gartenberg and asked permission to take an empty seat next to me. He talked fast, spluttering with laughter at his own jokes. It seemed utterly strange that anybody could find anything funny about this world. When we got off the train, he offered me help with my suitcase. It turned out we were almost neighbours: he lived at Côte Saint-Luc, two blocks from me.

That spring – to my surprise – I received a letter from Al's daughter. Fiona reminisced about the good times and conversations we had in Geneva. She expressed her sincere regrets that my marriage to her father had fallen through, and added that her father had recently married a woman from Iowa, a friend of his sister. Fiona expressed great concern about her father: she thought that the couple was poorly matched, and that her father was not happy. She wished me well and invited me to visit her in Geneva if I ever happened to be in Europe.

11

When, almost two years after these events, I moved from Montreal to Vancouver, Ralph seemed to have disappeared from my horizon. But one day, I picked up the phone and heard his voice. He was calling from Vancouver. "Space agency people will now have to come over here to talk to me. I moved all my meetings to Vancouver, khee-khee!" he said, with a familiar self-satisfied chuckle.

When, after dinner in a rotating restaurant, we both went back to his room, Ralph said: "You like your present? I wanted to get you some roses to put into the vase, but I came here right from the airport. Tomorrow, when we go for a walk, I'll get you some good ones. Do you think flower shops are open on Sunday?"

"I'm actually not sure about tomorrow. Not sure, about the walk in Stanley Park..."

"Fine. You don't have to if it makes you so unhappy. Just don't be angry at me, Maya."

"I'm not angry. I feel sorry for you."

"Sorry? Well, don't! It makes things worse. Maybe I'm a bit drunk, on two glasses of wine, but just so you know...if you really insist talking about it again...I hate myself for what I'm doing to you and to my wife. I'm an idiot, all fucked up! I never told you, well maybe, I did...but Esther is very unhappy. She's sensed that I've changed. In a way, she's like you: vulnerable, unsure of herself and...proud. But she needs me. I'm her fortress. No decision is made without me. My father taught me to be a mensch; to protect my family, and I always have.

"But with you, I don't know what's happened to me. All I know is that I love you the way I've never loved another woman in my life. When I'm in Toronto, I miss you terribly. I count the days till at last I'm in Montreal and can call you, hear your voice...I came to Vancouver to see you. I had no other reason. You understand? No other reason whatsoever!"

He paused. I sat at the edge of the sofa, motionless.

"But listen, if you say now that you never want to see me again, if you really say that – I'll disappear. I promise. Just say it.

Don't say you pity me. Don't say I'm a good man. Don't say you're grateful for my help. Say what you really feel: that I'm a nuisance; that you want to be rid of me. Say all I'm doing is hurting you. Say it. Say it and I'll never bother you again!"

He turned away from me, his voice breaking. "I'm wrecked. I'm not myself any more. But I'll keep my word."

Holding back tears, I whispered, "I never meant you or your family any harm. You know that."

"Yes, and I respect that. And, yes, I'll keep my word. But if you want me to have any kind of peace in the future, promise me one thing: you're alone in this city, but if you're in trouble or you need anything at all, you'll let me know. I'll find the way. You promise?"

"Yes."

"Oh, Maya, my darling, my sweet baby! Sit next for me for a moment. Like that...You have such smooth hands...wonderful skin... Hug me. Let me kiss you. Our first and last."

I felt his quick, stiff tongue stubbornly searching in my mouth, and for a moment, I lost my breath.

"Take it off. Take off your bra. You don't need any of that. There. Oh, you smell so nicely."

"I'm cold. What on Earth are you doing?"

"Cold? It's stifling hot in here."

He quickly ripped the blankets off the side of the bed, pulled me over, and covered me with a sheet.

"Better now? Let me touch your face, just your face...Your neck, there, there...your breast is so smooth."

"Ah, it hurts! My breast is hurting."

"Hurting? I hardly touched it. I'll be gentle."

"The light, turn it off. It's in my eyes."

"No. I want to see you. Want to see your body. Let me kiss your nipple."

"That hurts!"

"Look, I'm not doing anything. Your nipple is erect; you're excited."

"No-o!! My nipple is scared!"

"What do you mean, scared? Nipples don't get scared. There, I'll calm her down, you poor little thing, so sensitive. Now what? Are you having your period, that you're so jumpy?"

"No, in ten days from now, but it already hurts."

"Your ears aren't hurting though, are they? Give me this little snail, so perfectly shaped. You're my sensitive princess on a pea. That's why I love you! Now, your armpit. Your tummy. Your belly button. Oh, my sweet girl, my darling...I want to do all kinds of things to you. And I will."

"Like what?"

"You'll see. Where's your lipstick? You had lipstick somewhere."

"My lipstick? What for?"

"Just tell me where you put it."

He rolled over to the edge of the bed, reached for my purse sitting on a night table, and got the lipstick out. Then he drew scarlet circles around each nipple.

"Now we'll know where it hurts, so we don't touch it. We're just going to drink milk out of these pink buttons. Imagine that I'm your baby!"

"For God's sake! You're crazy!"

"Oh, that tastes good. Now I got you," he whispered, drawing horizontal lines across my belly, my inner thighs, then crisscrossing them with vertical lines.

"Oh stop it! What on Earth...you're making a terrible mess."

"Don't worry, they'll wash the sheets, it's their job."

"It's like I'm bleeding all over myself!"

"No. You're not bleeding now, you told me. You're being jailed; locked behind red bars. That's where I'll keep you. You're mine now, mine! Open your legs."

"N-o-o!"

"Oh, yes! You're going to do what I say. This last time. You're so tight inside. There! You're going to have a real man now, my princess."

"But you're hurting me!"

"If it hurts you, it hurts me too, don't you know? It hurts us both. We're now one. You just fell out of practice, darling. But we'll take care of it. With such a body you need a man. You're going to have a man every goddamn night now. Me!"

"Oh, stop talking...this garbage...stop it!"

"I'm always talking when.... when I make love...whether you want it or not, you're going to have a real man now. And then you'll be happy! I'll finally make you happy, you'll see. You'll love it. You've got to love it! There, there!"

"It hurts, I'm telling you!"

"That's all right. You can take it from Ralph. Not going to be long. Once, just for once. Do you have any cream or something?"

"What? What are you saying, for God's sake?"

"You never thought it would come to that, did you, my innocent girl! Then lipstick will do. Bear with me. You just have to take it. See, it's better now. That's a good girl! It doesn't hurt now, does it? Oh, that was beautiful...You feel so good. I love you! Love you, love you...oh my God, Maya!

"Don't move away from me, my sweet girl. I'm not done for the night! I was dreaming of it, do you know for how long? Do you know? Let me rest for ten minutes, and I'll have you again. Oh, my God, what have I done to you...?"

He was mumbling, his voice drifting away, away into the haze of sleep.

His feet jerked convulsively as he fell asleep. That's how it ended: in a dance of death.

I separated myself from the sweat of his limp body by rolling up the edge of the blanket and placing it between our two bodies. He was lying on his side, the light from the lamp illuminating his uncovered shoulder. There was a tuft of half-grey curly hair on his upper shoulder, a shoulder that, stripped of his executive jacket, looked small and unprotected, like that of a child. I lay there lead-heavy, listening to his breathing turn into snoring, with a thin whistle at the edge of each exhalation.

Sirens sounded. This city was never quiet. A police car, an ambulance? Someone was having a heart attack. A stroke. Somebody was dying. They'd take him in and start filling out the papers. But it would be too late. That person would die. They'd all die like I was dying right then.

No. You will not die. You will get up, wash this goop off and go. Just go. Taxis are always in front, waiting. Just get up, that's all you need to do.

But I couldn't. Couldn't move my pinky, never mind washing my body. But you could wash at home; for now, you just needed to get up. Slowly, quietly, one leg off the bed at a time. Bra? No need. Into my purse. Panties and hose? Not that cold. You'd manage. This disgusting taste in my mouth. My lips were all parched. That musty smell. Something unpleasant. Because I was there, in that awful place, that was why. As soon as I got home, I'd forget all about it. Forever. It never happened. Never!

But it did happen, didn't it? That's why I was dying...I was dying, but he stopped twitching, thank God. He wouldn't wake up now. I pulled the corner of the sheet to wipe the red off and disappear.

But he'd be upset when he woke up. He loved me. I had to be fair to him. I didn't hate him. He deserved my pity. Oh, I was falling asleep. Another ambulance. And another...driving right into the hotel. Somebody was dying. They were all dying right here, behind the walls.

"What's going on here? What's that sound?" Ralph sat up in bed, instantly alert, as if it hadn't been him snoring a second ago. "Are you all right?" He reached for me.

"Couldn't be better," I replied without looking at him.

"A fire alarm. Get up, Maya. Dress, quick! It's serious. There's a fire in the hotel. We have to leave right away. Get up, get up, Maya."

All composed, he dressed in a minute, his briefcase in hand, ready to flee.

"We're not using the elevator. Going all the way down the stairs. But don't panic. It's only the fifteenth floor. And I'm with you. Please don't panic, we'll be all right."

Suddenly I felt a rush of angry, vindictive energy. Bossing me around as if I were his spoiled, helpless wife! Little did he know me! I wasn't her! Ha, ha! Let her be on a short leash of his nauseating care, not me!

"Who's panicking?" I shouted, running down the stairs, skipping steps for the sheer fun of it."What's there to panic about? It's fun! Don't you see how much fun I'm having?"

I didn't give a damn about fire, about anything at all! Let that hotel, together with this world, go up in flames. I was alive! Boom, boom, alive!

"Wait! Not so fast! You're scared. Don't panic! It'll be fine!"

A perplexed crowd, with faces crumpled from sleep, some still in their pyjamas, congregated at the hotel entrance. Nobody talked or asked questions. It was drizzling. A small greyish day was about to hatch.

We never found out what happened. Not wanting to scare off their clientele, the hotel administration assured the crowd that if was safe to go back. Nothing happened in the Empire Landmark Hotel on that particular day. Nothing at all.

"In your case, I think it's better to see your family doctor," said a young female doctor in the walk-in clinic.

"I don't have one," I lied.

"Is this your first pregnancy?"

"I have two grown-up children."

"Well, that'll make it easier. Still, I'm sure you're aware that a pregnancy at forty-six can be a bit risky to the baby and the mother. You have to give yourself plenty of rest."

"There isn't going to be a baby. Do you need me to sign any forms?"

12

In twenty years, Vancouver had changed beyond recognition. The cost of land drove retail away to the remote suburbs, with malls, gas stations, and bookstalls replaced by expensive condos.

My rash wish for the Empire Landmark Hotel to disappear off the face of the earth was granted. The hotel didn't go up in flames. Instead, workers surgically removed each floor, starting with the rotating restaurant on the forty-fourth, all the way down to the fifteenth and to its very foundation. The hotel was located in a densely populated area, and a strong jet of water was poured over its cement and steel ruins throughout the demolition.

I had to travel to Montreal for a book launch. My sixth book had just come out. To my relief, the European flavour of the city remained intact. Solid, old grey stone houses with gables, garrets, ornate balconies, and staircases winding along facades that gave a sense of permanence, of an established life, of an unbroken tradition. I stayed with a friend in Côte Saint-Luc, the same area where I used to live so many years ago.

One afternoon, at a vegetable stand, I noticed an emaciated old man, his shaggy beard and unkempt hair flying in the wind. Leaning heavily on his cane, he was stooping over a cardboard box full of watermelons. A small line of customers watched patiently while he awkwardly, with one hand, turned over the watermelons, trying to find one that he could lift with one hand. His left arm hung listlessly from his sagging shoulder, obviously of little use to its owner. He kept trampling around, tinkering around, in his worn-out sandals that showed dirty, uncut nails.

"These ones are too big for me to handle," he said to the vendor. "Do you have anything smaller?" The voice of the old man sounded vaguely familiar, but I couldn't place it. I went closer. A smell of an old, unwashed body enveloped me. The man's watery eyes encircled by puffy bags gave me a cursory, tired glance.

"Ralph?" I said, still hoping I was mistaken, yet knowing with certainty that this crooked form belonged to no other than Ralph Gartenberg. "You don't recognize me, do you? It's Maya."

"Maya?" He looked me over again. "Is that you? Ah. How we all have changed. You were much slimmer then, if I recall. Yes, we all change."

"What are you doing here?"

"Buying a watermelon, as you can see."

"I mean, do you live in Montreal now?"

"Yes, in Côte Saint-Luc. Where I've always lived."

"Your family ultimately moved to Montreal?"

"No, they stayed put. I moved."

I watched him as he finally found a smaller-size watermelon, paid for it, managed to slip it into the canvass bag, and then tried, with his right hand, to mount the bag over his right shoulder.

"Let me help you, Ralph."

"No need," he brusquely replied. After several attempts, he succeeded, and then, slowly dragging his left foot, limped off.

I followed him unwilling to let him go. "We haven't seen each other for what? Twenty years or more? Your children...and mine too, they're all adults now...How are yours doing, by the way?"

"My children are not in touch with me, so I can't answer your question."

"Oh? I'm so sorry to hear that."

"So am I. Goodbye, Maya."

"No, wait, wait. Can I do something for you? Help you in any way?"

He stopped, shifted his bag on his shoulder, and then, for the first time, our eyes met. "No. You can't help me, Maya." He paused. "So far, I'm managing on my own."

"Oh, I see...Eh-eh...I suppose you've retired now. But your health seems to have deteriorated." I carefully stated the obvious. "Somebody must be helping you then. I hope Esther is in good health?"

"You remember my wife's name? Hmm. Didn't I tell you a minute ago that Esther doesn't live in Montreal? She divorced me many years ago."

"Esther...divorced? How can that be?"

"Anything is possible in this world, as you can see."

"Forgive me for asking, but why? What was the reason?"

"You really need to know? The law of entropy. She found out about you."

"But...I didn't...Since that fire in the hotel, we haven't been in touch!"

"That's correct. But after you left, I couldn't really, well...I wasn't coping very well, especially during the first year. Esther was my closest friend, the mother of my children. I couldn't cheat on her any longer. So I told her."

"But it's been years! There was nothing between us...Besides, people forgive each other, reconcile."

"Oh, yes. She forgave me. And we reconciled. But she said... well..she said I should be free to love whoever I wanted. Goodbye, Maya. I really need to go now."

He limped away, dragging his left foot, raising his right shoulder to prevent the bag from slipping off.

It was June and the poplars were shedding their summer snow, their fluffy cottony tufts. The transparent balls were rolling over the pavement, getting stuck in every indentation in the asphalt, clogging the gutters. Playfully, as if engaged in some game, they spooled under the wheels of cars; whirling in a wild farandole in front of white Apollo, in the shape of a ramshackle violin, and a faded manuscript.

Ralph stopped for a moment, hit a poplar snowball with his cane, and then continued on his way.

Salmon King

1

Autumn moves almost imperceptibly along the trails of the Sunshine Coast. The sky turns sombre, the water in the lakes darkens, and the slow-witted firs shake their beards of lichen and shrug their shoulders, as if to say, "What is this to us? We'll stand here just as we have always stood, be it autumn or spring or winter and their various downpours." Only the lean trunks of occasional aspens, incidental guests in the low-lying areas living solitary lives beside the gloomy evergreens, will quiver and shed their small heart-shaped yellow leaves and then disappear, dissolving among their shaggy hosts until spring.

On one of those still-warm autumn days, I turned by mistake off the main highway onto a dirt road and got lost. The road came to an end at an estate surrounded by a dense hedge of pliant yew. I stepped out of the car. Silence. Nobody anywhere. I walked through an archway entwined with faded yet still fragrant honeysuckle. In the middle of a green lawn stood a dwarf Japanese maple, its leaves turned red, its slender musician's fingers trembling in the breeze. A flowerbed by the main entrance was bursting with small, pale violet stars of aster, and heavy light blue blossoms of hydrangea hung down to the ground. On the building's facade was a small sign that read Rest Home for People with Impaired Vision. It was an establishment for the blind, most likely, but the proscriptions of militant public optimism had evidently banished the word blind from use there. But whatever the estate's purpose, it was now empty.

Behind its main building began a stand of ponderosa pines. A soft light radiated from their long needles gathered in tight, elegant, low-growing clusters, and their yellowish-brown bark gave off a vanilla-like scent. High over my head, an eagle soared beneath the clouds. Its thin, plaintive screech seemed to live in the sky all by itself, independently of the powerful bird. I recalled seeing two eagles the previous spring clutching each other in the air with their talons. Unable to release their fatal grip and spread their wings in time, they fell into the ocean like a stone.

Somewhere in the distance, I heard what sounded like a waterfall. A trail rose steeply through the pines, then turned to the right and ten minutes later, brought me to a broad mountain stream. Its icy, crystal-clear water rushed down, in places exposing its pebbly, multicoloured bottom. Moving through the water were crimson flashes. I went closer. The stream was seething with fish of a bright purple-red colour. It seemed that the elements of fire and water had been combined into one. Swimming torches, igniting the rushing water, were stubbornly moving in schools against the current.

My first degree being in biology, I knew about that astounding phenomenon of nature, and now I was an accidental witness of Pacific salmon returning to spawn in the same mountain stream where they had been born. Overtaking each other, the big fiery fish can leap out of the water by as much as two metres as they soar over rapids, logs, and other obstacles on their way to . . .their death. By a cruel dictate of nature, the instinct in salmon species for procreation and death has become a single thing. Only once in their lives may wild salmon spawn. After that they die.

Every stage of that cycle is a mystery.

Salmon are born in shallow mountain streams from which they begin their long path to the ocean, swimming many hundreds of kilometres down with the current. And then their first metamorphosis takes place, the adaptation of their organisms to salt water. But how does that happen? Scientists have determined that the hormonal changes needed for the passage from fresh to salt water are stimulated by the lengthening of the day, and indeed the migration of salmon smolt from rivers to the sea does occur in the spring.

During the several years of their life in the ocean, salmon eat their fill, gain weight, and grow up to a metre in length. During that time, their silvery light-blue scales are not much different in colour from those of other fish. But then the time comes for them to set out on the return path to their source. Again their hormones are activated, this time ensuring a reverse adaptation from salt to fresh water. And then a most striking change also takes place. Over the long weeks of contending with the current, rapids, and waterfalls, the salmon's scales will turn from silvery blue to bright red, the same colour as their roe. In sockeye salmon, the fish's head even turns green, and the upper jaw of the males grows longer and produces a downward hook called a kype, and teeth emerge, giving the fish a hideous grinning expression. But why are teeth needed? After all, it's known that during the long, arduous weeks of return to their birth places and spawning and death, the salmon eat nothing. All their strength is spent on the struggle for the life of their descendants.

And how among hundreds of mountain rivers and streams do

salmon find the ones where they were born? And why do they try to go only there and not to another mountain river or stream? Is it like someone who has lived a long time in a foreign land who wants to return to his native place to die? Metaphysics has no place in the arsenal of scientific investigation, and so far there has been no answer to that question. But the secret of how they find their native rivers has, it seems, been discovered. Ichthyologists believe the fish use Earth's magnetic pole to orient themselves in the ocean, and they find the river where they were born by its taste and chemical composition, information that was stored in their memories in infancy.

At last the goal is attained. After travelling hundreds of kilometres against the current and over obstacles and climbing as much as two kilometres above sea level, female salmon hollow out a depression in shallow water with their fins and deposit their eggs. The males fertilize the eggs, and the females then cover them up with sand. By that time, all the life forces of the salmon of both sexes have been exhausted. Making no provision for their restoration, nature immediately releases the mechanism of death: a programmed collapse of the fishes' internal organs.

Eagles then swoop down on the free banquet. Snatching the injured, tattered red carcasses from the water presents no difficulty, even if a large, healthy fish in the previously migrating mass might have been able to resist. I didn't know eagles could swim. Gripping the fish with its powerful talons, the eagle swam butterfly style, first lifting its wings out of the water, then immersing them again. It was the first time I had seen a bald eagle up close. Its beak was bright yellow, the plumage of his body was a dark chocolate-brown, and its head, neck, and tail were white, the white head of course giving it its figurative name.

Jumping from rock to rock, I ran down along the stream, hoping to see the battle's end, but the current was so strong that the raider and its victim were soon carried out of view.

2

A hundred metres or so downhill around a bend, the stream was wider and calmer, turning into a small river. Looking like crimson ribbons with green tips, the fish there were moving more calmly in the same dense schools, shoulder to shoulder so to speak, and ascending cement steps secured to the river bottom. Such ladders are installed to help the salmon bypass dams and other steep obstacles. People assist them in a more decisive way too. In some places, the fish are scooped out of the water and taken upstream by truck to their spawning grounds.

Downstream just below the ladder, I saw an old man of about eighty. He was standing by the water making odd movements. He bowed repeatedly, raised his hands to the sky, and then sat down in a strangely awkward way. He was so absorbed in those activities that he didn't notice me, or at least pretended he didn't. I stopped and began to watch.

He was barefoot and terribly thin. His legs, with their aged veins, extended from under his faded cut-offs like crooked poles. All his hair had migrated from his bare head to his face, covering it with grey tufts from his chin to his eyes. Next to him, on the sand, lay a faded baseball cap with the words *Save the World* on the front. A shabby leather jerkin hung loosely over a gaudy turtleneck sweater that not only had been out of fashion for some fifty years but was completely out of keeping with its owner's wild appearance. Then I looked closer. What I had taken for a turtleneck were tattoos. Their multicoloured designs covered his aged body from his neck to his wrists.

Over his tattooed chest hung chains with amulets of some kind. The biggest one, shaped like a wheel with woven string inside and feathers outside, I assumed to be a dream catcher like the ones found among Indigenous peoples from Canada to Mexico. Ending his strange ritual or dance, the old man stepped to the side, turning with an obvious hobble, picked up his baseball cap, pulled it down over his head, and lowered himself down onto the shingle. Resting his rough, gnarled hands on his knees, he turned his face toward the river.

"Hello, there!" I called out. "I'm lost. I made a wrong turn, which got me to the river! So many fish! I've read about it but never saw it myself.

"What's that?" the old man replied, turning toward me and cupping his palm around his ear. "Speak louder! I can't hear you over the water!"

"A lot of fish, I said!"

"A salmon run is why," he growled and turned back to look at the water.

He clearly had no wish to talk to me. But I wasn't going to leave.

"An amazing spectacle!" I shouted, trying to be heard over the stream. "But tell me, you were doing exercises. What were they? Tai chi or maybe kung fu?"

The old man measured me with a glance but didn't reply. Then, moving sideways like a crab, he got up, extended his arms toward the river in a gesture of respect, made several bows to it, and then lowered himself back down on the shingle.

"It wasn't your tai chi, but a sacred salmon dance," he said at last.

"I didn't understand. What kind of dance?"

"You eat salmon, right? Who's going to thank it?"

"Thank whom? The fish?"

"What did you think? It swims to us every year and offers itself for sustenance. I can grab it here with my bare hands and it won't resist."

I could hardly keep from giggling. "You think it comes here for us on purpose?"

"What do you think? The fish understand everything. We bipedal dim wits don't want to know about anything but our gadgets, but the salmon is a wise creature."

The old man looked at me with a sly squint that completely mystified me. Was he having me on, or was he serious? Or maybe he was just pretending to be simpleminded. Out there, far from the city, there are lots of eccentrics.

"After you eat it, the salmon, you should return its bones to the river. That's how it is!"

The old man pressed his clenched fists against his chest, and then, opening them, thrust them away from himself as if he were tossing something into the water. "If you leave out even one bone, the salmon will take offence and not come back. Our First Nation brothers knew that and followed the law."

Then I thought, *Even though he's draped with amulets, there's something about him that isn't like an Indigenous person.* Local Squamish and Sechelt people have fleshy, olive faces with broad cheekbones and dark, wide-set eyes. The old man had light-coloured eyes, a narrow face, rather small features, and a duck-like nose. Indigenous people, as a rule, are beardless and rarely bald, but here everything was the other way around.

"Well, since you've come to us, why don't you take a seat?" the old man said, suddenly relenting and indicating a place on the shingle, as if the riverbank and the river with its fish were his own property. "My name's Stan. Since you're interested, I'll share a legend with you. What's your name?"

"Marina."

The old man grinned. "Well, you don't say! What are you, a mooring or a harbour, then? I have a boat not far from here in a 'marina.' When spring comes, I'll go north or to the Fraser River for three months of fishing."

"Isn't there anything to fish here?"

"Well, these fish belong to the Salish. If you take them, it's like stealing. And there are too many people on the Sunshine Coast anyway. Developers and others have come. But there in the north, is a different story. But where are you from? Your accent says that you aren't from here."

"I'm from Russia."

"You're kidding! From what city?

"Moscow."

"Speak louder, I can't hear.

"From Moscow!"

"Really? From Moscow itself? Well, how is it there in Moscow? Russia is at war. What are people saying? Are they against it?"

"They aren't saying anything."

"Hmm. In the States, we protested during the Vietnam war, we planted bombs, but in your country they're what—afraid?"

"Sure...You can go to jail for saying anything against war. But I left there a long time ago. I live in Vancouver now."

"Aah. I know only one word in Russian: 'NYET! NYET!'" the old man shouted with a toothless chuckle.

"I need to find the ferry, but there aren't any signs—to keep me from getting lost again."

"The ferry's only twenty minutes from here. You turned left when you should have gone straight for another three kilometres and then turned."

"Maybe I can still make it."

The old man looked at the sun weakly shining through the clouds and shook his head. "You won't. The ferry will cast off in fifteen minutes. The next one will be in two hours."

Since I had time to kill, I sat down on the shingle near him. He pulled a little metal box out of the pocket of his cut-offs, took from it a pinch of grass, got out of another pocket some rolling papers, rolled a joint, lit it, and took a drag. The sickeningly sweet smell of marijuana floated in my direction.

"Here," Stan said, extending the joint to me after he had taken another drag.

"Thank you, I don't smoke."

"A mistake! The juices flow more merrily through your veins from this grass. You want to dance! You say that the salmon dance is a strange one. But I'll tell you, I lived for a while with the Salish at the very tip of Vancouver Island. That's their land, their domain. Worked with them in a cannery. I rented a room from a pal and his old lady. She still remembered their language and could speak it and knew spells but talked in English with us, of course. We would come home from work, his lady would put on a pot of fish soup and tell us stories. How the Salish believe that there's a salmon nation in the world. A mighty nation, with chiefs and elders, who all live in longhouses on a distant island. One time, the salmon nation heard that the Salish were dying of hunger without salmon. The nation decided to turn into fish and place itself at the mercy of people. And so it went until after a while the salmon nation changed its mind about going up the mountain rivers, and people had nothing to eat. What could they do? The Salish decided to find the salmon nation and just say to them, 'Save our children from hunger, return in the autumn to our rivers.' Well, they fitted out a kayak, gathered as many gifts as they could put in it, including various kinds of medicinal herbs, but they still didn't know where to go. Then the sun told them, 'There, at the end of the ocean is an island where the salmon nation lives in longhouses.' Good. The Salish sailed to that island. They saw a village, the houses, and totem poles. The salmon tribe received their guests well and, as was their custom, arranged a feast for them. And during the feast, the chief of the salmon tribe, their king, ordered four of his brothers to go into the ocean. As the brothers were entering the water, they immediately turned into fish.

The chief caught the fish and fed them to his guests. The guests ate their fill and, as was their way, threw the fish bones back into the ocean. And immediately the brothers turned into people again. Well, they did and didn't, since they emerged from the water as cripples: one had part of his cheek missing, and another his arms. Somebody among the guests hadn't thrown all his bones back into the ocean, you see, but had hidden them. But when he returned those bones to the ocean, the salmon-men were completely whole again. So it went! What do you think?"

I was silent. Stan looked at me expectantly. Something in his face unsettled me. His eyes were too close together, giving him an expression of owl-like perplexity.

I couldn't help myself. "A beautiful legend. But sheer paganism!"

Stan grinned."Paganism? But weren't the ancient Greeks pagans too? All those satyrs and dryads. How is that any different?"

"I'm sorry, but you... do you actually believe that legend?"

"I don't believe in legends, or in paganism, or in any of that stuff. Religion, like any ideology, has one purpose—to take away people's freedom. To deprive them of a choice. But I'm free."

And he again took a drag and let loose a sickeningly sweet stream of smoke in my direction. He had completely confused me.

"Then why were you...making those movements before? Why were you dancing?"

"Maybe I was a salmon king in a former life, who knows? And the time will then come for me to return to my people, when they won't turn me away from the gate but let me enter my home." And he grinned again and again blew more smoke from the stinking hand-rolled cigarette.

That completely befuddled me. Was the old man joking or serious? He was in any case enjoying my confusion.

"Niels Bohr had a horseshoe nailed to his door. 'Can you, a physicist, really believe in horseshoes?' they asked him. And he answered, 'No, I don't. But whether I believe in it or not, it could still bring me luck.'"

I didn't understand anything! How could Stan know about Niels Bohr?

"What, did I confuse you? I'm not what you thought I was? Yes, I'm a physicist by education. I was born in Seattle. Only I gave up physics. It wasn't for me. And that was during the Vietnam era and obligatory military service. Who wants to die for no known reason? I slipped away to Canada with a pal. The Canadians accepted draft dodgers with open arms. They were all against the war too. A Canadian border officer even called a taxi for me and gave me some money so I could get to the nearest town."

"Have you never had an urge to go back?"

"When Carter announced a pardon for draft dodgers, yes, I could have gone back. And I thought about it."

"But you stayed? You must have fallen in love with a Canadian girl, right?"

The old man grinned again. "Exactly. I did fall in love. With the Canadian North. It grabbed me with its cold claws and wouldn't let me go. And turned me into an...aborigine! Haha! And now I wander. Three months in a boat, and in the fall and winter here in a bus."

"You travel around by bus?" I asked, not understanding.

"Nah! A have a school bus. You know, a yellow one. They retired it, and I bought it cheap. I re-equipped it with a stove and a refrigerator, and I live in it commune-style with no rent—for nothing. Haha!"

"But how much do you have to pay to park it?"

Stan shook his head. "Nothing! A pal of mine here owns a five-hectare forest. He and I have an understanding. I'm young, haha! but he's already an old man and feeble, even though he's ten years younger than I am! I chop firewood for him, fix whatever needs fixing, and for that he gives me the land . . . under my bus. 'Stan, park your jalopy on my parcel, only far away from my house so that egg yolk will be out of my sight. Or repaint it green,' he says. Done deal!, I parked it down below his house behind a cliff next to a brook, thank goodness!"

The old man sighed and shook his head.

"And so I'll live there until spring, and then I'll go to the Fraser River. I have a brother there in the river. I haven't seen my bro in a long time. Around three years. If he's still alive."

"Your brother?"

"Yes! He's a sturgeon, the king of fish. The oldest fresh-water fish in the world. It's said that they used to catch sturgeon six metres long weighing half a ton, but now they've mostly disappeared because of the dam. I caught my brother three years ago and released him. He was close to two hundred kilos, for certain."

"But how did you catch him?"

".I didn't pull him up to the surface, you see, but only looked at him. Since fish, especially ocean fish, can't be returned if they come from a great depth. The difference in pressure will kill them."

"How did the sturgeon get to be so big?"

"By not scurrying about. They lie on the bottom gathering wisdom and can live for a hundred years. But now they're toxic. We've dumped poisons in the rivers, and they collect them from the bottom. But I only fish for salmon and then only as much as I can eat, and leave the rest for bears."

"Are you saying there could be bears here too?"

"Whenever a salmon run begins, bears come down from the mountains to catch the fish. When it starts to get dark, expect visitors."

I involuntarily glanced around. The sun was still quite high. On both sides of the river were stands of spruce. They were especially thick along the riverbank. I had read somewhere that fish skeletons left by feasting bears serve as excellent fertilizer for spruce growing along the riverbanks. The trees strengthen the soil with their roots and help maintain the cool river temperatures that salmon need for spawning.

The old man finished smoking, stood up, stretched, and then limped over to the water and started groping in it. He moved his hands here and there and then pulled a large fish from the water.

"See, it's quite shallow here. Big ones like this get stuck and can't go any farther. But I'll just tickle its belly, and it will immediately jump up and leap onto the ladder by itself. Here, you try it!" He held out a huge, trembling salmon with its awful grimace.

"Oh no, thank you!"

"Scared? But it won't bite. I'll just tickle his belly like this, and immediately all the anguish will pass. You'll feel at peace. You people in the cities are searching for the meaning of life, and here it is, the meaning!" He threw the fish back into the water closer to the ladder, and it merged with the school. "The fish here are still free. Despite the ladder, they really don't depend on anybody. Not like the ones from the hatcheries—a hopeless case!"

"What's the difference?" I asked in surprise.

"The hatchery fry can't find their way to the ocean by themselves, that's what. A lost generation!" The old man grinned.

The sky was starting to frown. A light rain had begun to fall, and it immediately got colder. I looked at my watch.

"Go how I told you. About three kilometres, and then a turn. Make sure you don't miss it."

I was sorry to leave that mountain stream and its salmon nation. I didn't want to part with that strange, mysterious old man either. Looking for a pretext to delay, I said,"It was good to meet you. I learned a lot of interesting things from you. But I wanted to ask: That talisman around your neck, is it a dream catcher? I've seen them in souvenir shops, but yours is more interesting."

"What have shops got to do with it!" the old man said in obvious dismay. "A woman shaman gave it to me. It's a soul catcher. When I was young, I worked as a lumberjack near Whitehorse. I fell from a big Douglas fir, and I couldn't stand for a month. Both my hip bones were dislocated. I was close to the other world, but Niimi returned my soul to me with this wheel. Because my soul's time had not yet come, you see. She said, 'Don't part with this talisman, but when your time does come, return it to the salmon king. He himself will swim to you, only you'll have to recognize him among the other fish—look carefully for a sign. Then he will accept you back into your home.'"

The old man sighed and fell silent. "I'll never forget her, Niimi," he said after a pause.

"Go now, go," he said without looking in my direction. "Or else you'll miss the next ferry."

After I left, I turned around to look back at him. Stan was still gazing at the mountain stream. It was as if I no longer existed, was no longer in his orbit. But there was the same unceasing, eternal sound of the mountain stream and the bright crimson flashes of fish straining toward birth and death.

Translated by J. Rosengrant

Parting

"What kind is it?" Inga asked the enormously tall library patron as she handed him two Stephen Kings and a John le Carré.

"An African grey," he said, smoothing the breast of the large parrot on his shoulder.

"Can it talk?"

"Say 'thank you,' Pepa. 'Thank you for the books.'"

"Kiki, kiki," the parrot replied.

It was after that encounter that Inga at last decided to retire. And then, my goodness, she would finally be free to live her life the way she wanted! Instead of going to work at the library everyday as she'd been doing for the past twenty-five years, she too could get a parrot, say. The giant reader considered its intelligence superior to a dog's and even near that of a four-year-old child. Wonderful! Inga would teach hers to talk, first some words, then whole sentences.

And after she and Arkasha (she already knew its name) had got used to each other, she would take up bonsai – cultivating dwarf pines or oaks in glazed ceramic pots. Then, and why not, she would enroll in a belly-dancing class. She wasn't the right age, of course, but it would still be good for her health. High cholesterol, blood pressure – she definitely needed to lose weight. And then, and again why not, she could suddenly wave aloha to Hawaii! Only who would look after Arkasha? First the trip to Hawaii, then belly dancing, and then Arkasha and a bonsai, in that order. Yes, except that she forgot the most important thing. Painting! For the last year, she'd completely neglected it. And people had been saying for a long time that she had talent. One expert had complimented her birds and insects in particular – she had a series of them – and compared them to Louise Bourgeois's spiders, even if Inga had only seen Bourgeois in reproductions and hadn't liked her scary geometry at all. And the French-American woman's last name was strange too. Was it her real one, or did she make it up? No, Inga's acrylics were warm and lovely: gentle butterflies, domestic worker ants, tremulous dragonflies, affectionate titmice, wagtails, and finches. Lively, sweet people bought them...She'd long wanted to switch from acrylic to oils. Leisure would be needed for that, since the technique was laborious and the paint took a long time to dry. "So," she firmly resolved, "I'll work through the winter and spring, and next summer I'll retire. I'll do it for sure."

And then, after she had planned it all so well: bonsai, wagtails, belly dance, a speaking parrot, and even Hawaii, that's when it happened.

It began with her mother asking her the same thing on the phone four or five times. That had put Inga on her guard, but she didn't really give it much thought, and stepping over the debris of repetitions as over things that had been accidentally dropped in her path, she went on with her life. During the day she handed out and sorted books, and in the evening she got together with her girlfriends, people as lonely as she was, or she watched TV serials, while every Sunday she did her washing and cleaning and cooking, and occasionally, if she had time, some painting. And only when a couple of weeks later her mother started to complain that people had been stealing everything: her glasses, her keys, and now her gold wedding ring. "Just think!" she said, "the ring with the little diamond that belonged to my grandmother, who was shot by the Germans during the war – the soldiers didn't touch it, and it's clear why. Diamonds wouldn't mean anything to that rabble, but gold, well, that's something else!" It was only then that Inga gasped as if someone had just struck her in the solar plexus. But she didn't panic that time either. She quickly covered over in her mind the indent that was beginning to look like a precipice, put on her sandals, and set off for the drugstore as she meant to do, to get some vitamin B3, which was supposed to be good for the arthritis that was starting to bother her.

However, when her mother called her one morning at work to tell her that the entire human race consisted of gangsters out to poison her, the sheet of paper Inga had just taken from the printer started to dance in her hands. She thought in terror of the cruel duplicity of fate that instead of her beloved, intelligent, wise mother was trying to pass off...*that.*

To get a grip on herself that evening after work, Inga took down from the shelf one of her mother's books. Considered to be one of the best translators of English and Italian poetry into Russian, her mother had continued to translate even after becoming the editor-in-chief of a large Moscow publisher.

Interspersed in the little volume of Cavalcanti canzones Inga was holding with her mother's preface, translations, and commentary were reproductions of works by Giotto, a contemporary of the poet. Looking at the pictures, Inga remembered her and her mother's last visit to Italy fifteen years before. In Padua, they "dashed" into the Scrovegni Chapel: Visitors were allotted only fifteen minutes to see the Giotto frescoes. They were taken past throngs of saints with golden haloes and narrow, Chinese slits for eyes, and Inga's mother, straining to be heard above the constant hum of the dehumidifier, said that Giotto had departed from the dominant Byzantine style with the invention of a unique optical illusion – an early example of Renaissance perspective. Her mother stopped in front of the fresco depicting Judas's kiss, and Inga kept staring at it, trying to see what it was that had struck her mother. Judas had a crude Neanderthal-like face with a low brow and projecting jaw. He was rudely thrusting his jaw towards Jesus's face for the treacherous kiss that would serve as the signal for his teacher's arrest. But Jesus was looking at Judas with a tranquil firmness, without moving his face away from him.

"Did he really betray him for money?" Inga wondered when they were back outside.

"Was it the usual greed? But he was his disciple, he loved him, right? Or maybe envy of his teacher's fame?"

Her mother squinted in the sunshine and inhaled the gentle, caressing air with evident pleasure.

"How lovely! Can you smell it? Either acacia or blossoming oleander. Just wonderful!"

Inga's mother could take exquisite pleasure in the smallest things: sunny weather, a new little scarf, or a glass of good wine. Unlike her mother, Inga never could yield to trivial things, could never let herself go over trifles. It was as if there were a tightly wound coil inside her released only when she was painting her wagtails.

But her mother was free. Instantly changing registers, she could turn from a delighted girl into a scholarly adept able to discourse on "celestial topics," as Inga called them. Her mother's intellect was acute; her erudition and memory never stopped surprising her daughter. There was no one like her mother, and Inga had been convinced of that since her childhood.

"Greed, you say?" her mother picked up the conversation begun outside the Scrovegni. "But I, for example, don't think it could have been anything so insignificant. I have no doubt that Judas loved his teacher. But if he hadn't betrayed Jesus Christ, there would have been no crucifixion, and mankind would not have been saved. According to one theory, at least. A kind of everlasting plan fulfilled through poor Juda. Christ knew, after all, that one of his disciples would betray him, but he couldn't oppose the will of God. Which is why he's so composed in Giotto's rendering. Actually, Borges refuted that idea in his "Three Versions of Judas," as you know. Or is there no call for him at your library?"

"Mama, when would I have time to read? A shoeless cobbler..."

"Oh, well, that's why I'm telling you. So Borges, or the character of his little sketch, thinks that Judas wouldn't have had to single out Jesus with a kiss. Everybody already knew who Christ was. He had openly preached, healed the sick, and performed miracles. No, the reason was a more subtle one. By the way, did you notice how

Judas was dressed? In a bright-yellow, golden robe that was almost the same colour as Christ's halo; that is, Giotto had depicted him as a reflection of divine energy as it was interpreted by theologians and painters after them. Christ shares his spirit with the traitor, with his betrayer."

Inga's mother tossed back her dark chestnut hair with its grey streaks, raising her face to catch the warm breeze. They stood still for a moment, unsure of where to go next. Two young men glanced at them and then continued to look at her mother. Inga was used to the fact that it was her mother who attracted the attention of men, even though she was shorter than Inga was and twenty-five years older. There was something about her that was lacking in her daughter: an abundant joie de vivre that was apparent in every gesture, in her smile, in the turn of her head, and most of all in her lively, laughing, light grey eyes.

"To me," Inga said, "it seems that Giotto just wanted to put Judas in the centre of the composition, and that's why he chose the bright-yellow toga...so he would stand out."

"Well, he could have clothed him in red, the colour of blood, and you wouldn't have failed to notice that either. But instead we have noble gold. That is, the heavenly, the exalted, and the earthbound have at a certain point come into contact with the mean and base. And at that point, the opposition of their natures disappears. Read "Three Versions of Judas" yourself; it's all there. How is it in Borges? Judas is one of the twelve apostles. He's been singled out, acknowledged, and it follows that he's entitled not to have his motives interpreted in such a primitive way. He's a mirror image of Christ. Christ chose a base death by crucifixion. Judas chose death by eternal dishonour. It's as if he considered himself unworthy of goodness. His treachery was an extreme form of asceticism and abnegation."

"How could that be? It turns everything on its head," Inga muttered, starting to lose the thread and growing distracted. The University of Padua was nearby. Crowds of students were hurrying among its columns.

In the rarefied atmosphere of speculative constructions, Inga's mother was in her element, but Inga could keep pace in thought neither with her nor, all the more, Borges, and she quickly lost interest in the abstract discussion.

They found a little café with an ivy entwined courtyard, and Inga, who was fond of sweets, ordered tiramisu while her mother sipped a cappuccino through a plastic straw. Taking hold of the back of her chair, tipping her beautiful head back, and youthfully crossing her legs, exposing her plump, nylon-clad knees without any of the boniness of age, she examined the other customers with interest.

"Look, they're the same faces we saw in Giotto. The young woman over there at the corner table – don't look! – with her broad peasant face like his Madonnas. You close your eyes, and it's as if seven centuries had never passed."

Inga's mother took a notebook from her purse and jotted something in it. For as long as Inga could remember, her mother had always been writing things down: an unexpected thought that had just occurred to her, or a word that she'd been looking for. It didn't matter where she was. She wrote things down in the subway, while driving, while having supper with her family, even in the presence of guests. But this time, when she took out her notebook, her eyes, undimmed by age, impishly lit up under the thin arches of her raised eyebrows. "You know, Giotto had a lovely sense of humour. Once, as he was walking down the street, there was a herd of swine coming the other way. He wasn't alone, of course, but accompanied by friends, since in those days people rarely went out alone. The streets were muddy, so it was not at all unusual for the swine to splatter Giotto with mud as they went by. But he didn't take offense. He was eternally in their debt, he said, for there was no telling how many of their bristles had gone into making his brushes."

Inga closed the copy of Calvalcanti. It was already around midnight, and she needed to get up early the next morning. She took a sleeping draft, which would leave a bitter taste in her mouth the whole following day, but still couldn't sleep. The horror of what lay before them drove sleep away. Staring into the darkness, she kept remembering her mother the way she had known her all the long years: amiable, with deft, clever hands and quick and ironic mind.

Inga's father died when she was four. Her mother raised her, with her grandmother sometimes coming to Moscow from Leningrad. Then Inga got married and left with her husband and children for Toronto. Her mother didn't want to give up her beloved work, and so for a time she remained behind in Russia. It was never said in so many words, but it was understood that the separation was temporary, that sooner or later mother and daughter would be reunited some other place on the globe. A few months after their arrival in Canada, Inga's husband fell in love with a clerk at a Russian store and left her. Fearing further unpleasantness (they all knew each other in the Russian community), Inga left with her children for Vancouver. As a single parent she needed help, and it was then that her mother finally decided to join them. And just as it had been in Inga's own childhood, so it was now: Home was wherever her mother was. The magical gift of turning a strange place into a warm, cozy home delighted Inga, since it was a gift that she had never possessed.

And there was in Inga's mother, besides her strong will and clear, sharp mind, something that drew people to her, making her the centre of any situation: apart from her physical beauty, it was her inner resolve that inspired the certainty that that diminutive, grey-eyed woman with a quick smile that lit up her whole face could find a way out of any situation, and that everything around her would somehow work out, and work out, moreover, in the best possible way. Her mother was an unerringly accurate judge of people and could anticipate what they would do, and Inga, as indecisive as her father supposedly was, had, like all their relatives and acquaintances, grown used to relying on her mother's advice and judgment.

Diffident by nature herself, Inga was amazed by her mother's fearlessness. She'd been afraid neither of the KGB generals who kept a close watch on her publishing house nor of the minister of internal affairs of Georgia, a protégé of the Stalin's henchman Beria, who, after noticing her on a beach at Pitsunda on the Black Sea coast of Abkhazia when she was still a young woman, pursued her for a long time. He would come to Moscow and arrange to meet her in fancy restaurants. To put an end to the business, Inga's mother, without a word to anyone, packed a small bag and vanished from Moscow for two months. Where she had gone, not even her husband knew.

Sober pragmatism was combined in Inga's mother with an inner zeal and an excess of empathy. Unhesitatingly, like a sailor to a gun port, she rushed to the aid of any sufferer. She commiserated, she phoned, she hurried across the city, she cajoled, she nagged... And knowing the irrepressibility of her own nature, she sometimes masked her inner fervour with irony or with an intentional aloofness and even brusqueness.

Inga was the epicentre on which the vectors of her mother's love converged. The magnetic field of that maternal love was so powerful that for a long time Inga could not decide just who and what she really was. However, with years Inga happily made herself at home in that citadel, with its secure defence against every tempest. And just as it would be impossible to live without air, so it now seemed impossible to Inga to live without the abiding gift of that passionate, energetic, maternal interest in her, without their mutual concern and sympathy.

How and why could that powerful and, it seemed, inexhaustible spring have begun to dry up? How could it have happened that the hand the already greying Inga had got so used to feeling in her own over the long decades was now inexorably slipping away? How and why had her mother suddenly left her? To prevent the catastrophe, to return everything to its previous place – that's what Inga had to do now. She had to be resourceful, to find the way. Her mother would have done everything possible and impossible for her daughter. Now it was Inga's turn.

She shivered and gasped for air, as if suddenly there wasn't enough oxygen in the room. The earrings, the bracelets piled up on the top of the chest of drawers in her bedroom, she first had to put them in order. To sort them out, to put each in its proper place, in their tiny cell. Her mother loved order and that's what Inga would do now. Restore order first here, then in their lives.

Once, in September, as she was coming home from work later than usual, and a hard, cold, relentless rain was falling and it was so dark all around that she could barely see anything at all, Inga let her tears stream under the cover of the darkness and rain and then began to wail like a simple Russian village woman, and all the more since no one else could hear her in her car. "I won't survive this catastrophe, please, take it away, make it disappear, I won't be able to handle it, I haven't got the strength, I won't get through it, please stop it!" she pleaded to God, in whom she'd never believed. And suddenly, off to the side of the road and high up in the air in that pitch-dark wetness, a fiery cross appeared that seemed to hang in the sky all by itself. Only afterward did Inga realize that she'd been driving past a Catholic church, its steeple topped by an iron cross with lights along its edges. But at the time the cross appearing out of nowhere, hanging in air on its own, it seemed, struck her as a frightening portent, as the pointing finger of God: This is your cross, and you'll have to carry it to your Golgotha.

Inga brought her mother groceries, cooked and left meals for her, and did the cleaning. And she drove her to look at the puppies too, a new pastime in which her mother took squealing and ignoble delight. As they neared the dog park, her mother would stick her head out the car window and, ignoring the pet owners, start yelling, "Here boy, here boy, come to me, silly, let me kiss your little mug! And that other stupid one, I don't like you, get out of here! Go away! It's written all over your face that you're a dummy!"

They'd been in Canada for twenty-five years, but when they went to restaurants, Inga's mother would now, without a trace of doubt, address the servers in Russian, since her English had largely evaporated, along with a good portion of her other three working languages. Her whole professional life had formerly been directed to bringing, in all its fullness and clarity, the thought of one person to the consciousness of another, but now she was completely indifferent to the fact that she wasn't understood. "They're just pretending!" she would exclaim. "I'm explaining it all very clearly to them!"

And sometimes her mother would ramble on without stopping about pantyhose or a banana she'd eaten that morning while Inga, in keeping with a recently acquired habit, would just absently nod, avoiding the eye contact with her mother. But once, she caught, out of the corner of her eye, her mother tearing the chicken apart with her hands and then licking her fingers. As if scalded, Inga winced inside and started coughing, hiding her face in her plate.

Her mother immediately reacted. "What's wrong? What's the matter with you?"

"I got a bone stuck in my throat," she lied.

"Why are you eating bones? Here, take my chicken. Take it and eat it, I'm telling you!" And she pushed her plate toward her daughter.

After that supper in the restaurant, Inga returned home exhausted, with her head ringing like a bell. And now, as she recalled the moment, she broke into a sweat, just as she had then. She threw off the covers and sat on the bed in her nightie. Pressing her hands between her knees, she suddenly started to rock from side to side. That metronomic movement calmed her. The collapse of logical connections in her mother's mind partly resembled a return to childhood, or removing articles of clothing: first her memory, then civilized habits. And how unreliably flimsy was that clothing, how easily it fell away!

Inga sat without moving, listening to the swish of tires on the street outside her window. A siren howled and then the sound faded, dissolving into the night. It was stuffy in the room. The moon gazed through the open blinds with bright, indifferent face. And Inga, hardly moving her bloodless lips, began to explain to that silent interlocutor that it was out of pity, out of love for her, that her mother had contrived the long, gradual crossing into non-being.

So Inga would have time to get used to her absence.

A year passed before Inga finally took her mother to see a geriatric psychiatrist, and the doctor, a tall, tanned, handsome man with an ingratiating smile, leaned back in his chair, stretched out his long legs in their patent leather ankle boots, drew a circle on a piece of paper, and asked her mother to put numbers inside it with arrows showing, say, a quarter after six.

"If you want, you can check it against the one on the wall," he said with a friendly glance at the clock behind her.

Inga's mother turned the paper one way or another, randomly wrote in several numbers and then suddenly burst out laughing. It was evidently amusing to her that the doctor had given her such a trivial assignment. What did he really take her for? Could it be that she appealed to him in a womanly way and he was flirting with her?

"If you think about it, who needs a watch these days?" she exclaimed, slapping her palm on the desk and merrily pushing the pencil and paper away. "Young people will soon completely forget what a clock face is. They have only, what is it, well – " she started to mumble in Russian " – those watches that light up with numbers."

"You mean digital watches?" Inga prompted. "Or cell phones?"

"Exactly right!" the doctor animatedly replied. "Clock faces will soon fall out of use. Which is a pity, isn't? I, for example, am used to my watch. It tells me the month and the year too. Now it's August. Can you name the months in reverse order? August, July, and so on?"

"Do it in Russian, Mama, and I'll translate," Inga said.

"Why? I can tell him in English," she exclaimed, not realizing that she was answering in Russian. Inga looked down and translated. "The point is, sir, I can't stand August! The heat and midges or something very nasty. There never were any before. It's an awful time of the year, don't you think?"

"Very good," the doctor said without reacting to the inappropriateness of the tirade. "Can you try to name five words that begin with F?"

"It's unlikely she would be able to in English, but I hope she could in Russian," Inga quietly observed, turning toward the doctor so her mother wouldn't hear.

"That doesn't matter, whatever is easier for Mrs. Ol-Ol-khovsky. You'll translate for me."

"*Fifa*! They called me a *fifa* at the university because I wore a hat with a veil!" Inga's mother said, using an old slang term for a tart and breaking into loud laughter with a coquettish gesture.

Inga hesitated, unsure of how to respond. "*Fifa* is an old expression, doctor. Perhaps she could recall something else? Mama, can you remember any other words that begin with F?"

"I already told him!" her mother said indignantly. "Enough already!"

Inga blushed, embarrassed by her mother's abrupt, completely unmotivated change of mood. The doctor noticed it and, as it seemed to Inga, said in an unbefitting, falsely hearty tone, "Well, excellent, Mrs. Ol-olkhovsky! Very good, indeed!" and then turned to his computer and rapidly typed something on the keyboard.

At that point Inga took a folded sheet of paper from her purse, and quietly pushed it across the desk to the doctor. Written on it were two words: *dementia* and *Alzheimer's* with a question mark following each word. Distracted from his computer, the doctor glanced at the paper out of the corner of his eye and then quickly drew a circle around the word *Alzheimer's*.

"Sometimes it's hard to differentiate, but the picture here is clear enough. An early stage," he added, looking up at Inga.

"How many in all?" she asked in a lowered voice.

"Stages? Usually seven, but that doesn't mean – "

"I understand, I understand, and how long does each one last?"

"Again, that depends on the individual. The first, from three to five years; the second, it's hard to say. In all, that is, from the initial diagnosis to...In a word, perhaps as much as ten years. But I repeat, it's hard to predict anything."

The doctor turned back to his computer screen.

"When did you first notice that your mother's memory was failing?"

"Over a year ago."

"That's usually how it goes. Even two years may pass between the first symptoms and a visit to us. And in general the process of memory loss can begin even earlier, sometimes as much as a decade."

"He's going on about memory as if there were nothing more to it?" Inga thought in vexation. "My mother is no more! Her personality is going, that's what it is. "

"You know," she said in a low voice while leaning over the desk toward the doctor, "my mother was very smart, very...well... she knew a lot...I mean...she was an erudite, with a photographic memory. That is, not was, but is. She has a doctorate and is a gifted poet, and I just don't understand how such a thing could...Naturally, nobody's immune, but with her intellect, I expected whatever you like, only not this. No, that isn't what I meant, forgive me, I know it's silly, but all the same I just cannot...Perhaps there's some medication?" Inga could no longer control the muscles in her face, which was about to contort in an indecent tearful grimace.

"I completely understand," the doctor hastened to reassure her. "I'll prescribe some vitamins for her. And some tablets. They'll halt the process temporarily. And improve her memory."

"Is there anything besides the vitamins that might help?"

"It can be beneficial to go out every day, to take a walk."

A walk? Did he say a walk? It was then that Inga realized that her mother was doomed.

She felt faint, as she often would in the recent months. Why didn't she let herself go, didn't reveal the extent of her despair? The doctor was in no way at fault, of course not, yet she couldn't control a wave of animosity rising inside her. Those razor-sharp creases in his pants. Who ironed them for him every morning? His wife? A housemaid? He was too successful, too polished to be able to grasp the horror that had befallen them. For him, as she saw it, her mother was just another file with a disease history among hundreds of other files, whereas their situation was unique, not as a disease, no, but because her mother wasn't like anyone else...She was drowning, and the only one who could have thrown her a lifeline was her mother, but her mother was herself departing into unknown depths and not even aware of it. A knock on the door interrupted her thoughts. A young blond woman of unprepossessing appearance came in.

"Sorry I'm late. There's construction everywhere and the roads were closed."

"Come in, come in. We're just about finished here."

The doctor indicated a chair with a tilt of his head.

"This is Neshka Boleznova. She's interning with us. You won't mind? By the way, she's a former neighbour of yours – from Bulgaria."

He handed Neshka some papers and, lowering his voice, quickly added, "Take a look. High IQ patients can sometimes use their intellectual capacities to compensate for other deficits."

"What kind of name is that, Boleznova?!" Inga wondered with distaste as she examined the intern's shoes: lettuce-green ballet slippers with little multicoloured seashells on the tips.

"Maybe you could prescribe some tablets for me too, doctor?" Inga asked, masking her despair with a playful tone. "Something strange has been happening with my own memory."

The doctor stared intently at her, and then slowly said, "Those tablets won't help you."

"No? But why not? I'm not so young myself. Sometimes a word will be on the tip of my tongue, but I can't think of it!"

"Those tablets will only help with Alzheimer memory loss," the doctor repeated in the same flat tone.

"But what's the difference?" Inga said, refusing to yield.

"The difference is that you're aware of what's happening to you, while Alzheimer patients aren't. But keep in mind that memory is often worse under stress, as is typically the case with people who look after the sick. You're close to your mother, are you not? In such situations, there's often a transference, an identification with the person who's dear to us. We may subconsciously mimic or project his illness onto ourselves." Here, he confidingly leaned toward Inga. "You need to take a break at every opportunity. And find your mother a home for...people with that disease. If you need documentation, I can help."

"What? Already?"

"You unquestionably need to plan ahead. She won't be able to live very much longer by herself. A crisis typical of the disease will eventually occur, and you need to be ready for it."

Outside, it was sweltering. There hadn't been any rain all summer. Everything seemed to gleam in a blinding yet muted way. You wanted to hide from it, but there was no escape: the diffuse sunlight followed, surrounding and exhausting you.

"Why are you so upset?" Inga's mother wondered as they got in the car. She'd unerringly caught Inga's mood, just as always.

"They gave us a bad diagnosis, Mama."

"What diagnosis is that? That I'm crazy? Who cares what he said! Don't believe doctors. They're only good for filling out forms."

"No, she still doesn't understand," Inga thought in despair. "She doesn't understand any of it, just as he said..." Inga had no close friends, although she did have acquaintances. "You and your mama were close, right? Think how lucky you were, since that doesn't happen every day," one of them said. "So be grateful for what you had and accept what's happening now as your due." Inga knew she was fortunate and was grateful, but she couldn't accept "now" as her "due." And she was gripped by another fear: that she would remember her mother the way she was now, with the image of her decline eclipsing that of the woman who'd once been gifted with talent, rare spiritual qualities, and striking beauty.

Another acquaintance said, "But your mother isn't suffering physically, so be thankful for that. Would cancer have been better?" Anything would be better than losing your reason in plain view of everyone. Of all the possible sentences, that's the most terrifying, Inga thought. And who said she doesn't suffer? Staggering through a murky forest of dwindling consciousness, mother would recoil in horror from the inexorably approaching darkness. But sometimes she would still stumble on sunlit patches, on untouched glades of light. In one of these lucid moments, she asked Inga: "Take me to the ocean. Help me. I can't do it myself. Wading into the sea without returning. You just keep going, keep moving forward without a backward glance."

The hardest thing for Inga was her mother's phone monologues. She spoke excitedly, vehemently, as if under siege. The trivial actions of her neighbours seemed like deliberate crimes. While her indignant voice went around and around, Inga, putting the phone down on the kitchen table, would wash the dishes, put everything away, and sweep the floor. Coming to the end of a sentence, her mother would invariably return to its beginning, and it was astonishing that despite its loss of content, her speech retained its precise grammatical structure. Like learning a foreign language, only in reverse, Inga thought. When the lexical stock is limited, you get by with general phrases, you step around and adjacent to your own thought, simplifying and distorting it. Or else it's like when you're flying and you look out the window and see only the general outlines of the city you're approaching, but then as the plane is landing, you can make out buildings and little toy-like cars speeding along the highways. Whereas with her mother it was the opposite: the higher she climbed, the denser the fog that obscured the details of the landscape and left in her field of view a limited assortment of demonstrative pronouns: "So it's that, that thing, this...what's it called? That, you know." Inga was dismayed by the illogic of her mother's speech that in Inga's youth had intimidated her with its meticulousness, its irrefutable arguments, and the richness of its phrasing. Something about that dismay, even revulsion was instinctive, as if Inga were afraid of infection.

Her mother took care of herself the way she always had. She plucked the little hairs on her chin, touched up her eyebrows with a dark pencil, and trimmed her own fingernails. But the more she "maintained her form," the more Inga recoiled from it. The pamphlets said that Alzheimer's patients have a special need for affection, but that very affectionateness, that simple physical contact, was something Inga avoided. The loss of memory had brought with it a loss of personality, and without personality, there is no life. To hug a shell in which death made its nest meant to yield to death yourself.

But she reproached herself for that. After all, is the essence of life in logical thought, in intellectual activity? Plants and animals don't discuss things. Her mother still experienced taste, smells, colour, hot and cold, delicious and not delicious, pain and not pain. Even though life had narrowed the eye of the needle, it was still life, or wasn't it? Her mother still played the piano and had recently finished a biography of the poet Joseph Brodsky, even if she couldn't recount a single word of it. Life or not life?

And for the umpteenth time, Inga sworn to be gentler, kinder, more patient.

Her mother now gave off the heavy, ineradicable odour of old age. And despite Inga's promises to herself, she would try to shorten her visits.

But when the mother was hospitalized with double pneumonia, Inga pleaded with all her heart to some invisible being to let it pass, and let her mother to survive.

To get to the hospital, Inga needed to drive across the city. At first in front the windshield flashed residential blocks with one-and two-storey wooden houses behind cypress, yew, Japanese holly, and boxwood hedges. The crowns of mighty chestnuts, maples, and elms met overhead in continuous arches, with the long, slender, rain-laden seedpods of broad-leafed catalpa sometimes lightly sketched between. But from time to time there'd be gaps in that luxurious foliage, since many residential blocks were slated for destruction. It seemed in fact that a war was going in them, that they were under siege and bombs were randomly falling first on stately Victorian mansions, then on the gingerbread roofs of Tudor cottages. Inga had changed cities many times in her life, but a city bent on subtracting itself street by street from her space without her moving from her spot had never happened to her before.

The houses fated to be bulldozed could be identified at a

distance by orange plastic netting stretched over rectangular wooden frames. The builders used the netting to screen the trees from the new construction sites. It was said that a million new residents would soon be moving to the city. Orange rectangles were added daily. As Inga drove past, on the left and right flashed ditches and pits surrounded by piles of dark-brown dirt and gravel, and then rippling orange netting again. According to the papers, in one year alone some 1,500 residential buildings had been razed, although Inga thought the figure underestimated the true number. It was known that Chinese millionaires were buying up the land and that the greedy city authorities were doing nothing to preserve the local architectural styles. The lots were subdivided, and where once there had stood a spacious home with a garden, three houses without gardens sprang up, the original lawn paved with asphalt. Since quality played no part, they built with lightning speed. The rapidly erected little boxes were designed to be razed again in ten years. Often, what was built was larger and uglier than what had been torn down. Large numbers of newly built homes remained empty, their new owners in China. Those crematoria and mausoleums, as Inga nicknamed them, would be quickly resold at a profit.

As she proceeded east, the residential blocks gave way to a commercial zone. There, the denuded land was packed with mirror-black cubes and truncated tetrahedrons housing computer firms, insurance companies, real estate offices, and the like. The lots between the structures were filled with rows of new and used cars for sale, their windshields competing to catch the soccer ball of the August sun. To lure buyers, little flags of various colours were stuck along the perimeters of the lots, and sometimes waving in the air above was a tethered figure made of what looked like large inflated sausages. From the air pumped into the creature, it came to life like Frankenstein and waved its lopped-off sausage arms, and there was something indecent about the way it would suddenly double over from a gust of wind as if it had been punched in the stomach.

Inga's mother did survive but was very weak, and when she regained consciousness, she was unsure of where she was. The nurses had been secretly dealing drugs the night before, she said. Please take me home.

Once, after feeding and calming her mother, Inga stepped out into the hospital hallway for a breather and noticed a young man in a wheelchair by the nurses' station. He devoured her with his eyes as if he were passing his hands over her body. Either he was attracted by the festive summer dress that clung to her plump but still pleasing figure and so paid no attention to her face, or else in the hospital's absence of real fish, her crayfish had been enough for him, but he looked at her the way no man had looked at her in twenty years. She blushed and lowered her eyes. And in lowering them, she realized that the young man had stumps for legs. They'd been amputated above the knee.

The way home lay due west, and in the haze the setting sun blindingly shimmered along the upper edge of the windshield. Holding on to the steering wheel with her left hand, Inga rummaged in the glove compartment for her sunglasses, but they were no help. The diffused light breaking through the thickening milky-grey haze beat against her eyes and temples. There were no clouds to be seen, but the now yellow-grey haze had become so thick that she had to turn on her headlights, which produced strangely indistinct shadows. In a corner of the windshield, and seemingly just outside it, glimmered something round and bright: the blood-red disk of the sun. Amazingly, she could look directly at it without squinting. She had never seen anything like it. It wasn't a solar eclipse but something else, something unaccountably disturbing.

Slowing down, Inga continued west. Mixed with her usual post-hospital fatigue, there was now a feeling of vague regret. Although about what was not at first clear. She remembered the gaze of the legless young man, and realized what it was: She'd shrunk from it and averted her eyes, conveying, perhaps, that she was frightened by his deformity. People don't want to burden themselves and instinctively look away, since that's easier to do, and she, too, had lost heart and acted like everyone else instead of mastering that impulse and finding the courage to return his gaze. But how to do that? How should one look at the mutilated? By pretending they're no different than anyone else? But that would be a sham, a deliberate lie. With a person who has lost his legs, a catastrophe has occurred, the everyday details of which healthy people cannot even imagine. To look with sympathy, with compassion? Would that not be humiliating for the person who's deformed?

But isn't there a shared humanity that unites us over and above our physical conditions, over and above injuries and amputated legs? Yes, without legs it does unite us, whereas without memory it may not...Without memory, there's no being...

Inga began to think about her mother again and a dangerous

new symptom that had appeared even before she was hospitalized. Her mother had under various pretexts been refusing to eat. Inga had started putting food in different containers in her mother's refrigerator, but her mother was still unable to remember what to eat for breakfast and what for dinner, nor did it occur to her to open the containers and look. Inga couldn't conceal her fright and started to explain, started to scold her mother the way one would a small child who hasn't been paying attention. Her mother got angry and insisted that forgetting was normal at her age, and that other people were even worse. She didn't like to be reminded of her infirmity – one needed to act as if nothing was wrong. The need to dissemble only added to the burden. Inga's nerves had long been a mess. The legless man was young, only a bit over thirty, probably. He had a sort of egg-shaped head that may have looked that way because it was shaved. His face, however, was full, without creases or the pallor of people who'd spent much of their time in hospitals. It looked like his misfortune was fresh, and he still hadn't gotten used to it, still hadn't lost the habits of a healthy person, which is very likely why he had looked at her so greedily.

That night, for some reason, Inga dreamed about the legless man, although his features were blurred, with other features she had not recalled for years beginning to show through them as in an old film. An invisible director had shifted something, had altered the dream's decor, and now she was at a girlfriend's dacha outside Moscow, both fifteen then, in the month of May. She dreamt of a meadow, every bit of it, down the last blade of grass, lit up by the sun and fragrant with the warm, bitter smell of wormwood, cornflowers, and chamomile; and in the dream she was again permeated with the affectionateness and openness to the world that are experienced only in very early youth.

An air of deep, gentle blueness seemed to stream with bliss, and the day was enhanced and given voice by the presence in the dacha next door of a youth with the wide-set eyes of a quiet, deer-like dreaminess. He was tall and slender, and when he leaned over her, his straight, rust-coloured hair fell across his forehead. He pushed it back with his hand, and for some reason the gesture seemed special and was remembered...Inga's head spun from the nearness of his calmly pensive, light green eyes. From happiness and timidity, she began to laugh: a grasshopper had jumped onto the hem of her calico dress, and that seemed funny to both of them. The grass tickled her bare heels, which was a source of mirth too. But the main thing was that the deer-like youth liked her, and it filled her whole being with intoxicating joy.

In front ran two hounds, temporarily entrusted to them by an aging ballerina, another neighbour (since the dachas were for the artistic elite), and Inga and Seryozha (as he was called) pretended to be English aristocrats hunting hares. And then, gripping the dogs tight by their collars, Seryozha asked, "Would you like me to call out a hare?" and suddenly started to bay like a hound (Inga hadn't at all expected that he could make such loud, harsh sounds). From the woods nearby, a white hare jumped out, and the tip of its tail was black, as if it had been dipped in ink – that she saw clearly and remembered. The hare stood erect on its hind legs and then instantly disappeared beyond the edge of the woods. They kept walking among tall grasses, the hounds running ahead of them. Seryozha touched her hand and she suddenly became weak and swooned and not to fall sat on a warm, sun-drenched grass. Seryozha sat next to her, then gently took her head in his both hands and brought his green, deer-like eyes so close to hers that their foreheads touched.

"*Se agapo*," he whispered.

"What is it?"

"You'll see."

He called the dogs up and was gone. She closed her eyes in some kind of exhaustion, and when she opened them, he stood in front of her, a bouquet of wild flowers in his hands.

Inga and Seryozha met again in Moscow the following winter. Fluffy, freshly fallen snow lined the tree branches, doubling their size. The buildings looked like gingerbread. The tableau was calm and soothingly festive. Without touching each other, they glided along the sparkling black ice formed over the sidewalks, as if trying to prolong the bliss of that summer day, but they were sixteen, no longer kids, and the childish skating seemed awkward and contrived. A handful of fluffy snow fell off a branch down Inga's collar. Seryozha silently watched as she took off and shook out her fur coat, and she remembered how detachedly he watched without offering to help, remembered because it was then that she, stamping her feet and shivering from the cold, understood that their festive happiness had ended. Why it had, she no longer remembered, and perhaps she didn't even know then.

That summer day, the happiest of her life, remained the only one, never to be repeated.

Seryozha, with the deer-like eyes, became a famous writer, and Inga became a dyed blond putting on weight and suffering from arthritis and varicose veins. The years lived through since were as grey as mice, and none stood out from the rest. Her life had for the most part consisted of overcoming hardships: two divorces and between them a desert of loneliness, dull years of work in the same library, a daughter and son from different marriages who had no time for her, and now her mother's illness.

Inga started to feel sorry for herself. She ate a thick slice of chocolate cake with white frosting, which is what she always ate when she was tired or upset. Then it was time to go to the hospital. She put some plums in a bag for her mother and thought she would treat the cripple to some too as a way of doing something nice for him. Or perhaps it would be better to take him a book? But she had no idea whether he even liked to read. Her son, about the same age, read nothing and only thought about computers. Plums are good for the digestion...But how to offer them? "Hello, I got them for my mother and have some left over?" No, that wouldn't work. She would have to come up with something but didn't want to think about it just then and decided to rely instead on the circumstances.

She saw the legless man from behind as he was going down the hallway, energetically turning the wheels of his chair. Then he turned around and came back toward her just as fast. Apparently, the motion amused him.

"I've got some extra plums." Inga said with a tentative smile as the young man was abreast of her. "Would you like them?"

He stopped and indifferently ran his eyes over her as if he'd never seen her before. She felt the strap of her camisole slipping off her shoulder, which embarrassed her even more, but she didn't try to straighten it.

"What would I want plums for?"

"I brought some for my mom, but she doesn't eat much. Well, maybe your relatives don't come very often, so why don't you take them? Plums are good for the stom..."

Inga cut herself off mid-word: none of it felt right. The young man was wearing a tee-shirt that exposed his tattoo-covered biceps: two clenched fists on one arm and a three-eyed owl on the other. The front of the tee shirt read, *Zombies eat brains. You're safe!*

"Why don't you go get me some beer, lady? Maybe the cafeteria has it. Though probably not. You say relatives. I haven't got any."

"Nobody at all?"

"Well, there are two sons: one in seventh grade and the other in fifth. Only they don't visit. They're scared of seeing their legless dad. Or maybe their mother won't let them come..."

"Excuse me, it's obviously none of my business, but doesn't your wife visit?"

"No, we split."

Inga looked at his stubs and immediately averted her eyes, just as she had the first day. But he noticed her glance.

"No, it was before that. When I was healthy. I was a soccer coach at a school and coached my own kids too. I wanted them to be stars and everything was going really well for them. Someone from an elite program in the US came and said he would take both of them, since they were talented kids."

He was silent for a moment.

"So I'd just bought a house and was making a real effort for my wife. And while I was doing all that, she left me for some Greek guy. And even got custody of the children after this happened." He looked down at his stumps.

"That all sounds so terrible!"

"What's terrible about it?" he asked defiantly. "It's life!"

"Even so, you mustn't lose hope! The children will grow up and understand and come back to their father. I'm waiting too. I'm alone and waiting for my son. I'm trying not to lose hope, since everything changes."

"It does? Well, what else is new? But what does that have to do with me? I don't care. I made an effort for my kids. And for her. And what did I get for it? A smack in the head."

He turned abruptly and quickly wheeled himself away without taking the plums.

Inga continued to her mother's room. Her mother was muttering something, and Inga drew the curtain that separated her mother from the patient in the room's other bed, sat down beside her mother, and then couldn't stand it anymore and burst into sobs.

Her mother stopped mumbling and reached out her hand to her. "What's the matter, my girl? Is it because of me?"

Inga smelled the hospital air, a mixture of disinfectant and camphor. "I'm sorry, it's just that my nerves are shot. But you're better, and that's the main thing and all I need."

"What's upsetting you, then? That I keep repeating things all the time? That I forget words? But how old am I, after all? Well, yes, I'm finding it harder to think clearly, I say stupid things sometimes, but I'm still alive! And I love you as much as I ever did. Don't cry now, my little one. When I'm truly dead and gone, then you can cry. But for now you really must not! You must not be upset about me. I've lived a very long life. And it wasn't designed for that."

"What wasn't, Mom?"

"My body wasn't designed for such a long life. It happened by accident. But so far we are still alive! And will continue to be for a while longer! You remember how it is in that poem?

"Which poem, Mama?"

"Why, in the one, what's it called?"

"Whose?"

"I translated a lot of him. He drank and died young. During a reading tour in America. From Wales..."

"Do you mean Dylan Thomas?"

"Yes, yes, that's the one...He has.... a poem about the sovereignty of death. It's the famous...wait a second, I'll remember: 'And death shall have no dominion...' It goes, 'Under the windings of the sea,/they lying long shall not die windingly'...And before that, 'Dead men naked they shall be...' And something like, 'When their bones are picked clean and the clean bones gone,/They shall have stars at elbow and foot;/ Though they go mad they shall be sane,/ Though they sink through the sea they shall rise again.' That's all I can remember. It means that those who are losing their reason will recover it. Those who have drowned will be raised up. Death shall have no dominion...Go home, my child. And don't come tomorrow. Take care of yourself. You've been through enough as it is."

It was already starting to get dark when Inga left the hospital. There was a burning smell in the air, and the yellow-grey haze now covered the whole city as if it had sunk to the bottom of the ocean. You couldn't see more than five metres in any direction. On the radio, they said that forest fires had surrounded the city in a tight ring and that over 200,000 acres of forest had already burned. She finally got home and unlocked her front door.

Her porch railings were coated with a fine layer of ash. There was ash on the window ledges and the tree branches too. She turned to look behind. In the ash covering the porch, she had left a narrow trail of footprints.

Cassandra

Part I

"You crowned your city with towers. They are dust. You brought ruin upon your own land."

- Euripides, The Trojan women

"I see the house dripping with blood."

- Aeschylus, Agamemnon

1

W hen I came to Moscow in 2011, one of the first things I did was to make my way to Arbat Street so I could visit Sasha. Her full name – Alexandra – we'd abandoned years before, stepping down the teacher-student ladder, she on top, I on the bottom, to the even ground of cautious friendship. By that time, Sasha was the only remaining inhabitant of the old stucco edifice, with its mouldings around the windows and cornices of flying cherubs holding soot-covered grapes and wreaths. After the revolution, the floor occupied by a family of a doctor, his wife, and his children was turned into a communal apartment for thirty or forty champions of that very revolution, all crammed into tiny rooms along the narrow, semi-dark corridor, with several generations of family per room, and only one kitchen and one bathroom with one toilet for them all, everyone converging on a single, shared cold-water tap in a dark corner of the corridor and a telephone attached to the wall under a naked bulb. But now the building stood almost empty, its inhabitants resettled in Devil's Horns, as they called Domodedovo, Novogereevo, and other residential backwaters.

For example, two alcoholics, Peter and his daughter Zina, were evacuated to Orekhovo-Borisovo. And then there was Ivan the drunk, his current wife Olga, and his former wife Tonya – all three of them ended up in a two-bedroom apartment in Medvedkovo, an immense upgrade according to both women, who'd for years shared one room with Ivan, the tiny space divided down the middle by a rickety wardrobe and the shadows it cast in either direction. Policeman Vova, with his three cats, got a studio closer to downtown, but then, he knew whose palm to grease.

As for Max and his wife, Elena, the two "stinking intelligentsia," as their neighbours labelled them – he a painter, she a piano teacher – nobody knows where they went, nobody except Alexandra, the heroine of our story. But they were the first to move out as their neighbours looked with suspicion at their piles of boxes filled with books and art works wrapped in newspapers and crisscrossed with ropes, waiting in the yard for a friend with a truck. Apart from a stool for the piano, the two didn't seem to own any furniture. Opinions about Max tended to vary: some called him a warlock, a necromancer who dealt in black magic; others suspected him of being a clandestine priest, with his massive beard and unruly mop of reddish-grey hair that had never known scissors. No one liked Elena either. She was shy, small, and thin like a girl, and the neighbours not only saw her smiling – and why the hell is that? - they also saw her giving alms to beggars. But the main thing was that with all this monkey business unfolding right under Elena's nose, she was warned many times, and what did she do? Nothing. At least three women tried intermittently to corner her in the corridor, at the sink with its permanently dripping tap: Peter's alcoholic daughter Zina and both of Ivan's wives. But either Elena was dumb, or she was a saint. Whichever it was, she was annoying and a little crazy. Their attempts to boycott Alexandra lead to nothing either: Alexandra simply ignored them.

But then the perestroika interrupted the resettlement plans, and Alexandra was simply forgotten. She didn't push for more comfortable, spacious living conditions out there "in the bushes" but continued to live the way she always had: among her numerous books, many of them by the obscure poets she translated from several languages; without hot water or showers (replaced by weekly trips to a bathhouse) but with the communal kitchen now all her own. Out her window, right across the closed courtyard formed by the yellow two-storey stucco buildings standing shoulder to shoulder, she could see the famous Gruerman's maternity hospital, where everybody who'd meant anything in the history of Russia for the last century and a half let out their first scream. And that's where, thirty-five years ago, Alexandra had given birth to her only child, Annie, now married to a Harvard professor and living in Cambridge, Massachusetts.

2

When I came to see Sasha, she wasn't alone. Vera Petrovna, a scrawny, grumpy eighty-five-year-old perched at the corner of the table, was sipping tea through a sugar cube squeezed between her teeth, the two front ones in golden crowns. Where had she acquired this peasant habit anyway? To my knowledge, Vera had never lived in a village but spent most of her life in fancy places like Albania, North Korea, Sudan, Ethiopia, and, further north, up the African continent, in Egypt.

I could never understand what connected Alexandra and Vera, two women so different in character, interests, lifestyles, and age. Vera was more than twenty years older than Alexandra. They'd met a long time ago: before being dispatched to India, Vera needed to learn some English, and Sasha tutored her. Both of them now lived alone, Vera a widow of many years, Sasha never married.

As far as I could tell, the only male presence in Sasha's world was her grandfather Mark, watching over her from a faded sepia photo above her desk. Having left this world before Sasha had the good luck of entering it, the two never met. A polyglot, Mark Luntz had invented alphabets for the Indigenous peoples of Siberia. Because he knew fifteen languages, he spent most of his life afraid he'd be accused of spying. And his fears eventually came true. In 1937, he was executed. Defying the laws of the country, Sasha's mother formed her daughter's patronymic from Mark's name: Markovna. Alexandra also carried her grandfather's last name: Luntz. In her early youth, Sasha shared her room with her mother and later – after her mother's death – with Annie, her daughter. But then Annie grew up and left for the United States, and Sasha found herself alone in this world. Alone and poor.

Vera, on the other hand, never had any concerns about money. Apart from a prestigious apartment in Stalin's high-rise, her late husband had left her a car and a *dacha*, both now overgrown with moss and weeds: Vera didn't like the country, and she never drove. As a civil engineer, she'd spent most of her life building dams, tunnels, and bridges in friendly countries. When the Albanian leader hit on a brilliant idea of digging 700,000 bunkers in his land, engineers from Russia rushed to help, Vera among them. But the brightest jewel in the crown of her illustrious past, the jewel that kept casting its heroic glow on her present, was the Aswan High Dam in Egypt, one of the largest and grandest structures in the world financed and built by the Soviets. Standing on a makeshift podium under the relentless Egyptian sun, Vera greeted with loud applause the first gush of water that came cascading down after the sluice gates opened for the first time. Standing next to her was her husband, the wide-chested eagle of Soviet aviation. He personally trained Egyptian pilots to fly Soviet jets into Israel during the Six-Day War of 1967. Before their foray into the enemy's territory, he ordered his charges to paint over the Russian insignia on the jets' wings. Happy flying, Egyptian aces! Easy landing! But it wasn't so happy, as the Israelis captured three thousand soldiers and pilots, taking them prisoner.

Later, Vera's husband recognized his Egyptian friend Tariq in a photograph of an endless row of prisoners squatting on the scorched sands of the Sinai Desert, their hands tied behind their backs, Israeli soldiers standing next to each one with a flask of water, letting them suckle like helpless children. When he saw that, he had a minor heart attack and was dispatched back to Moscow. But Vera stayed to fulfill the party's trust and finish the Aswan Dam. She loved

Egypt. She loved the heat, no comparison to the misery of Moscow winters. In Cairo's noisy bazaars, she bought a rug, a hookah for her husband, a piece of papyrus, and an alabaster bust of Nefertiti. Egypt is an ancient civilization! The pyramids, the sphinx! She told her wide-eyed girlfriends about them back in Moscow. Egyptians were cultured people, they didn't cut off your right hand if you stole something, not like in Saudi Arabia, for example. Decades later, Vera would still drop her experiences into a conversation: "In our Egypt... that's how it was done in our Egypt."

The only thing that blighted her nostalgia for Egypt was her accidental visit to an Egyptian crocodile museum. She would've never set foot in such a place of her own volition. Never! But one cloudless afternoon, as she was waiting for a boat to Armant, the forces of nature cracked open the hot dome of Egyptian skies and plummeted the desolate banks of the Nile with a deluge of Biblical proportions. Rain in a desert! As rare as it was brutal! Through thick braids of lashing water, Vera discerned her salvation, a lonely hut. She ran toward it, gave the door a hard yank, and entered. In the shadowy entrance, she wrung out her soaked clothing, wiped her face dry, and blew her nose into a wet handkerchief, then lifted her eyes. Hundreds of brownish-grey crocodiles were giving her an almost singular bestial snarl from inside the dusty glass showcases. Some were three metres long, some newborn babies. Dust of millennia, silence of death! The Roman Empire had fallen, Persia had fallen, the French and the Americans had had their revolution, the Russian czars were gone, Napoleon, Hitler, Lenin, all gone, but here they were, these mummified gods of Egypt, grinning at eternity and Pygmalion human affairs from inside their glass tombs. What an abomination! Before she gave into her nausea, Vera ran back into the raging storm.

Now, in her old age, severe arthritis had bent her shrivelled body at ninety degrees to the ground. Not that it prevented her from getting on a subway car every morning at 6 a.m. in order "to do the real work" before her idiotic colleagues arrived. She didn't leave her small, airless office until 9 p.m., long after the shadows had thickened along the boulevards and the sorrowful faces of her fellow Moscovites had mellowed in the spectral light of the street lamps. Never hiding her disdain for computers, Vera used pencils and paper for her sketches and calculations, and then she let the young loafers transfer her designs onto their silly gadgets.

Everybody over sixty-five had been made to retire a long time ago, but not Vera. Why? Nobody knew.

3

My visit to Sasha interrupted what must have been an old argument between the two women. Vera condemned everything that fell into her ever-shrinking radius of observable life. "What's happened to our country? Girls on the subway sitting like men, legs apart, and look what they're wearing! In a public space? It's basically underwear!" Obviously, she could bottle up her inner furies for only so long. "And they all gang up in the streets, I've seen this with my own eyes, I swear, girls on horseback trotting along the sidewalk, right near Red Square. I mean, who's ever seen such a thing? Tell me!" She spat her words out as if afraid to get infected by the plague they surely carried.

But these were annoying trifles, the pulpy fringes of a much deeper wound that ate steadily away at her soul. Vera deplored and resented the disintegration of the Soviet Union. It wasn't just her personal tragedy but, in her mind, a disaster of global proportions.

"Take my word for it! This will end in disaster! Total disaster! The world isn't trying to stop *them,* and one day, the world will regret it!"

To which Sasha dismissively objected, as if swatting a mosquito: "Who *them?* And what was so great under the Soviets, for God's sake? Arrests, prisons, gulags?"

"Gulags? If you're an honest citizen, you don't have to worry about things like that."

"Vera Petrovna, have you forgotten? You were looking after little Annie when.. ."

"Oh stop! If you broke the law, you had to be punished. Surely you can see that. And today? Look around! Corruption, bribery! They'd sell their own mother for a dime, these thugs."

Sasha only shook her head. "I'm sorry Emma," she said to me, "I didn't mean to get you involved in this." But then, as if a spring had uncoiled inside her, she turned to her antagonist again: "Wait a minute! Are you saying there was no corruption before?"

"If you worked honestly, the state respected you. It rewarded you."

"Oh, come on, Vera Petrovna! I can give dozens of examples, things I saw myself." Sasha got up from the table and reached for a cigarette, then opened the window to let the smoke out, the evening of the city rumbling in on the breeze.

"Spare me your stories, Sasha! They only ever happened to you." Vera's hands shook as she tried to catch the hairpins falling out of the flat grey bun on her head. To calm down, she poured some tea from the cup into a saucer, peasant style, slopping a little on the tablecloth, her hands shaking slightly. She blew on the saucer to cool it down, then took a sip.

"I can tell you one thing," Vera said, wiping her lips with the back of her hand. "You shouldn't have quit your job at the university. I'll be eighty-six next month, and still working, by the way."

"You know I didn't quit, or did you forget that too? I was fired. And in any case, that happened almost thirty years ago. I'm retired now."

"What do you mean, fired? You never told me that!"

"Just joking!" Sasha shook her head in disbelief. She took a deep puff and blew the smoke out, then closed the window and returned to the table.

Vera threw a sharp glance at her friend, pursed her lips, and scrambled up to her feet. "I have to go now. By the time I get to the subway, it'll be ten o'clock. I have get up early tomorrow so I can get to work."

"I'll call you a taxi, don't worry."

Vera looked around in confusion, then let out a deep sign. Ultimately, she decided not to object.

4

With Vera's departure, the tension left the room, and I stayed on. I took a deep breath and, for the first time, looked around. While the world beyond these walls had changed unrecognizably, here, in this room, the arrow of time had lodged itself deep into the cork of our youth. Furniture, pictures on the wall, little knick-knacks that had belonged to Sasha's mother, now long gone, the very smells – everything was familiar. Like an archaeological dig, the room contained different layers of life, objects never discarded or replaced with newer ones more in keeping with the times. It was a cozy and inhabited old world, both rich and, somehow, shabby. Unwashed, old-fashioned lace curtains covered a small window, just an embrasure in the thick stone wall. Pale wallpaper, with faded patterns, was peeling around the edges of the ceiling. The same little shaggy rug lay in front of Sasha's narrow bed, which was covered with a brown and beige Afghan knitted by her mother. The old ornate cupboard still screeched every time Sasha opened its carved doors, massive as the gates to a cathedral, to extract, on the occasion of guests, like today, some old-fashioned china. Books in familiar bindings piled on top of each other pell-mell, spilling off the shelves that covered walls from floor to ceiling. Sasha had cast wide the net of her interests: philosophy, history, linguistics, poetry, architecture, folklore, mythology. Here and there, vases with dried flowers collected dust. They'd lost their individual colours a long time ago, taking on a uniformly earthly hue. What was missing, I noticed, was the piano. Sold to patch up un-patchable holes in Sasha's meagre budget, I assumed. But a swirling music stool, memorable to me, had survived, now multi-tasking in different parts of the rooms, as Sasha moved it around. What mitigated the small size of the room were the high ceilings, typical of old, pre-revolutionary buildings.

Now that Vera was gone, I pulled out of my bag an expensive Wayne Gretzky Brandy. "Let's have a drink!"

Sasha examined the bottle. "You dragged this all the way? You shouldn't have, really. We now have all kinds of brandies, Armenian, Fanagorian, you name it. I can't drink anymore, Emma. Well, maybe just a bit."

I remembered that, in the past, she didn't drink beer or wine, but, on occasion, she did like a sip of cognac.

"To our friendship! How long we've known each other? Thirty-five years? More?"

"To the success of our hopeless endeavour," Sasha chuckled, raising her glass.

"Oh?"

"Korzhavin came up with that, not me. Back in the seventies, I think. Before they kicked him out of the country. A fine, fine poet, and pretty funny too."

We clinked our glasses.

"Remember this thing with Salinger?"

"Salinger?" Sasha paused. "Oh, that! I doubt it was of any use to you in Canada though."

"That's not the point! True, my degree proved useless. In Canada, I had to do all kinds of things, nothing to do with journalism. I even was an officer once. But I'll always remember what you did for me then, Sasha."

"An officer?"

"Not the military, no. I officiated...at Pee-pee-sec."

"At what, sorry?"

"Don't laugh. It's an abbreviation: post-secondary-education or something. We were supposed to award accreditation to private schools. Like a dog-training school. Or a nail school, among others."

"Emma, you can't be serious!"

"I am. Totally. Each time they needed their accreditation, they had to submit the report and pay a thousand bucks to pee-pee--sec. I was a goalie, you might say. Had to read a report and reject it at least twice. Otherwise, how would we have made any money? It was a kind of a shell game: 'This sentence is wrong,' or 'Please resubmit.' We kept moving the shells, demanding they pick the right one. So they never really knew what we wanted. But the fun part was visiting these schools. I was an inspector general! Ha! 'Everything looks great on paper,' I'd say, 'but let's see what we have down here in reality.' I remember going to one place, their report in hand. A nail school or something. The usual stuff: 'Show me the list of your students to start with. How many, all in all? How many? What? Three!' The so-called director's daughter and her two sisters – those were the students. So that's one example of my officer's duties. Then, I remember, I had to inspect the ESL schools. Half of the population of my city was born outside of Canada, so we have scores of private ESL schools in town. I would look at their curriculum. Magicians at work here, and what work! Perfect mastery of English in one month!"

"Looks like you weren't the only one playing a shell game, eh?" Sasha laughed, and the dimples on her cheeks formed exactly the way I remembered from when we were young: several on her right cheek, but only one on her left. "But that stuff sometimes work, like with Salinger."

"It did! I'll never forget that. Never." I felt my head start swimming in the alcohol. "To the shells, then! To the hustlers!"

We clanked our glasses, emptied them, and poured another drink.

5

Alexandra and I had met in the vestibule of the Moscow State university in 1971. Our age difference – about ten years – was less important than our difference in status. She was teaching English Discourse Analyses, Theory of Translation, and American Literature. The fact that she was not just a translator of difficult poetic texts from English and Spanish but also a poet in her own right, she kept under wraps, separate from her university work. I think we felt some affinity for each other, a kind of an intuitive interest that eluded words. I was in awe of her intelligence, her erudition, her wit, her talents. I myself am rather plain-looking, but her exotic looks struck me the first time I saw her. There was something regal about her thin, ascetic face, with its fine bone structure, even though the bones of her cheeks converged too sharply in a small triangle at her chin. Slim, narrow in her hips and shoulders, with long limbs, she moved with a slow grace that concealed her intense energy. Alexandra was born with one leg slightly shorter than the other, and she compensated with a thicker sole on her left shoe. Her limp, however, was almost imperceptible, unless she got agitated or was in a rush. Somehow, her angular elegance reminded me of the Modigliani portrait of young Akhmatova, one of her favourite poets. Her somewhat exotic looks must have come from her father, who was Georgian, she later told me. It was from him, I thought, that she'd inherited her explosive temper, which she usually kept at bay, but it did sometimes burst through her composed demeanour. Looking at her, you could feel the breath and the drama of the snowy peaks of the Caucasus, not the monotonous flatness of mid-Russian dales. It must have also been her father's blood that gave her skin an attractive, slightly olive tinge and the waterfall of jet-black curls cascading down her back. Yet, except for her striking eyes, velvety dark and wistful, framed by the longest eyelashes I've seen, you couldn't call her conventionally beautiful. A slight asymmetry added strangeness to her face. Later in life, she'd cut down her magnificent mane to short grey stubble. And when I came to visit her this time, her face in profile reminded me a boy grown old.

I'd been Sasha's student, and by far, not the best one. Her seminars were difficult. Every time I handed in an ill-prepared assignment, I felt like I'd betrayed not just the discourse analysis, but her personally. All I'd get then would be a quick, sardonic glance, and for the rest of the seminar, I felt like I'd been marked by an invisible brand. Yet, in spite of that, my teacher seemed to like me, and she singled me out from the rest. Why? I don't know. But the day came when the barriers between us fell.

6

It was an early spring, my fifth and last year at the university. Only several final oral exams – state exams, they were called – separated me from my graduation and a master's degree. I'd already defended my thesis. Diamat (dialectical Marxism), histmat (historical materialism), scientific atheism, empirio-criticism (nicknamed, empirio-cretenism) – all this I swallowed without chewing, and now, a month before the birth of my first child, I considered the final exams a sheer formality. Ploshkina, a faculty dean, a middle-aged, heavily set woman, with a sour face, was presiding over the examination committee. The moment I approached her table, the baby inside me kicked so hard that my belly shifted from side to side, or so it felt. I knew (did my baby know it too?) that pregnancies were looked on with suspicion at best, if not with scorn. Here were two women, one middle-aged, prematurely faded, with a sullen expression on her puffy face, yet endowed with power and authority. And there was me, pretty with the prettiness of blossoming youth, but naive, idealistic, and powerless in every respect but one: I was right in the midst of what was called my "feminine journey," while Ploshkina was at the very end of hers, if she'd ever embarked on one at all. And there was yet another thing, an implied belief of the State that by getting pregnant a woman unwittingly acknowledged her allegiance to a secret, private life – namely, to a life of sex – which the State would have gladly annulled altogether, if it could. In fairness, with time, attitudes toward sex and love evolved. In the 20s and 30s, the State would simply turn a blind eye; after all, it needed a growing population to build the bright communist future. At the same time, in the eyes of the State, love was more suspicious and certainly more dangerous than sex, for nothing could distract a 'builder of communism' from the business of building more than love. And somewhere on the margins of this ideology was the church, a sidekick of the state, that wouldn't allow women in the dirty condition of pregnancy inside its sacred walls.

No matter how you looked at it, pregnancy and the final exams at the university mixed as badly as water and oil. No wonder I was suddenly gripped with the fear that my loose dress wasn't loose enough to hide my baby's antics from the dean's stern eyes. I took a deep breath and picked the examination ticket, the first in the pile: "History of the Communist Press of the Democratic Republic of Congo." All colour left my face. Congo? Conrad's *Heart of Darkness?* But Conrad had nothing to do with the communist press, if there was such a thing there. Its evolution? I drew a blank.

"Well?" Said Ploshkina, after some waiting.

"Sorry," I shook my head. "Sorry."

Ploshkina lifted her leaden eyes to my face. "Patrice Lumumba?" She threw a rope to the drowning.

Patrice Lumumba was somewhere on Lenin Avenue, that was all I knew. Exclusively for African students, the rich and the privileged. The building's entrance was forbidden to anybody else. Oleg's girlfriend, from second year, had had an affair with an African lover before Oleg, so she filled us in on stories of orgies and hard partying at Lumumba. *The* Moscow girls would sleep with the black guys from Lumumba for a bottle of shampoo, a pair of jeans, a folding umbrella, a box of tampons, anything that we, Moscovites, couldn't have but that they could, from special shops for foreigners or anywhere else in the wide world beyond our borders, locked to us but not to them, the sons of kings and rulers, the owners of immeasurable herds of sheep grazing on their immeasurable planes.

Such were the stories.

"You don't know who Patrice Lumumba was?" Ploshkina asked in disbelief.

"No," I said, swallowing hard.

"The future Soviet journalist doesn't know who Patrice Lumumba was?" Clearly, she'd sniffed blood. "You came here to do what, exactly? To take a state exam, or to give birth? This is a university for you, not a maternity ward!"

The baby kicked hard again. Not having a voice yet, it already had an opinion. I put my hand on my tummy to calm her down, and then I made one last attempt to save my miserable life. "Please," I heard myself saying. "Please. Look at my transcript, page four. I got excellent marks on my thesis. It wasn't about the press in Congo. It was about the British press, but still. The textual analysis of editorials...the comparison...you see? There, on page four...the comparison of *The Daily Worker* with *The Morning Star*."

"Wait a minute! Who gave you that idea? Why, instead of studying foreign literature, were you doing an analysis of the communist press? You shouldn't have been admitted to the state exams in the first place with that."

"But, but...it must be a mistake. That's what they assigned to me. I didn't have a choice. It took me years of work."

"Did you not hear what I just said? It's not valid. I can't give you access to the state exams. Next please."

With my mouth open in trembling shock, I somehow found my way back to the door.

7

Not relying on my legs for support, I leaned against the wall in the corridor. Breathe in. Breathe out. Yes, I'd always wanted to write a thesis on American or British Literature. And yes, they forced this crap on me instead. When did they change their minds and why? But who cared anymore? Breathe in. Breathe out. It wouldn't have helped me to know. Five years of study tossed into the trash! Bachelor degrees didn't exist in the Soviet Union. Either you earned a master's after five years of study, or you earned nothing. And there was nothing I could do anymore.

It was at this point that Alexandra saw me. She was hurrying along the corridor, her bulky, worn-out briefcase under her arm. The sight of me seemed to make her stop. Nodding, she listened to my muddled explanations, eyes fixed on the tips of her shoes. Then she drew back her massive hair, and for the first time raised her gaze to mine. "Come. Come with me."

We left the university, and I followed her down Machovoy Street, with the Kremlin's toothy walls grinning at us from across Manezhnaya Square. It was early spring, the few trees still bare, but you could tell they were already swelling with new live, their skeletal silhouettes enlivened by greenish fluff. The sporadic wind caressed the cheeks with moist freshness. Between grey puffy clouds, pools of tender blue deepened the sky, as if opening windows onto eternity.

In spite of her slight limp, Alexandra walked faster than me. We were in the very heart of Moscow, a city turned into a palimpsest with Stalin's ostentatious new alphabet superimposed over the precious old script. The eighteenth century classical mansions largely obscured by his empire of marble looked meek. We passed the spectacular Pashkov Palace sprawled on a hill, now blotted out by a rectangular mass housing Lenin's library. I paused in front of the forest of square black columns supporting the massive sarcophagus-like portico. Slowing her pace, Alexandra seemed to notice that I was out of breath. "We're almost there," she said. "Pass the Pentagon, and Arbat starts."

The huge general staff building, nicknamed the Pentagon because of its shape, was being erected on an enormous construction site that had wiped out three blocks of eighteenth century mansions. We skirted the site, descended into an underground passage, then came out in front of Praga, another eighteenth century mansion of yellow stucco. With its rotunda, an elegant dome, and a balustrade on the roof, Praga always made me think of a ship that had landed on dry land in the midst of a huge city of forlorn ants running in circles around its flanks.

"Are you hungry?" Alexandra asked. "Not much food at my place right now, but I can get some salads for us later in Praga."

Praga was famous as the only place with a deli selling salads, salami, and cutlets, all sheer luxury for Moscovites. Packed with people like herring in a barrel, the deli occupied only a small space on the first floor, and the busy herring had no access to the rest of the building, with its opulent restaurant of the legendary past. Tolstoy gave a reading of his novel *Resurrection* in that restaurant. It described a circle of friends gathered for dinner there: Chekhov, Bunin, Tchaikovsky, Shalyapin, the crème de la crème of that bygone era. With the restaurant taken over by KGB and apparatchiks dining there for free, no mere mortal was permitted inside.

Leaving Praga behind, we walked passed a row of drab two-storey houses with narrow, hesitantly drawn windows, yellow plaster falling off like dead lichen. They hunkered down, these buildings, neglect conceals their old pedigree, the fact that in their youth, two centuries before, they looked cozy and pleasant. Small, stuffy rooms on the second floor were now occupied by offices with most obscure names and purposes, so typical of the Soviet era.

We slipped under a low arch cut through one of these meek houses and found ourselves inside the inner courtyard with the Gruerman Hospital at one end and Alexandra's building on the other.

8

I stopped to catch my breath again halfway up the narrow, poorly lit staircase. Finally, we stumbled up to a padded black leatherette door at the top landing with ten or more doorbells to one side, the names of the tenants under each button. Alexandra opened the door with her own key. The fetid air hit my nostrils: boiled cabbage and cats' urine mixed with the smell of unwashed humanity, the signature smell of a tightly packed multi-generational existence. Various possessions had apparently migrated from the crammed rooms into the corridor: old mattresses and yellowed newspapers, chairs missing a leg or two, a rusty tricycle, a leaky washbin – everything that had outlived its usefulness, neither repaired nor thrown away, and I could smell it all. We slipped past trying to avoid the neighbours' eyes and ears. A young woman in an apron and with paper curls in her hair, glued to a phone in the corridor, looked at us suspiciously, and turned away to carry on flirting into the cup of her hand with somebody on the other end. Alexandra shut the door to her room, first making sure there was nobody behind it, then freed a small space on her desk, sweeping aside a clutter of books and papers. From the top of a carved cupboard, she removed a stack of paper.

"They want literature?" she said, brushing off a patina of dust. "Here."

"Literary Analysis of the *Catcher in the Rye* in the Context of American Bourgeois Culture of Alienation," the title page read.

"You can copy it as is. Need any paper?"

She pulled a piano stool from under the desk. Noticing my discomfort as I perched my heavy bulk on the seat, she removed some dresses and underwear thrown over the old armchair next to her narrow bed and carried it over to her desk. Then, turning back to the bed, she grabbed a couple of cushions with cross-stitched shepherdesses and piled them on top the armchair's sagging seat. "I'll be back when you finish," she said. And then she was gone.

And so I found myself face to face with my brazen act of plagiarism.

The long hours of sitting there and copying my teacher's thesis exhausted me. I made several attempts to get to a washroom, a tiny cell down the hall, with a single toilet. To avoid suspicious glances, I waited for the line up of tenants to dissipate.

The spring day was shrivelling. The sky took on an ultramarine tinge, the way it always does in spring before giving itself up to the full darkness. Stray cats descended from attics and hideouts into the courtyard and raised their horrifying mating shrieks, an accompaniment to the advent of spring in the city. I looked out of the window. The hum of daytime activity in the yard, the clattering of wooden crates, and the rattling and jingling of bottles – it was all dying out. I noticed a roll of cotton wool commonly placed between two window panes to block the cold winter draft. Its surface was covered with a thin layer of soot accumulated over the long winter. On top lay a dead fly. I don't remember a word of what I have copied. But I remember that black fly lying on top of its fluffy white coffin, its legs up.

It was totally dark when my teacher returned. I stood up from the desk and stretched my stiff body. I was thirsty.

"I'm a little worried now," I said. "About the whole thing. What if they find out?"

"Ten years later? Small chance."

"Where can I get some water?" I asked, surprised how hoarse my voice sounded. "I didn't feel like going to the kitchen with your neighbours around."

"Oh, I forgot to tell you Emma! I always keep some drinking water at home. Here."

From a hot plate, Alexandra lifted an old copper kettle with greenish oxidized smudges, and poured some water into a tee cup. My lips were parched. Me and my baby, we drank greedily.

"That idiot used to bring his cats to piss into my kettle at night. I never leave it in the kitchen anymore."

"Who? Your neighbour?"

"Yes, Dubov. A policeman. Two doors down from me, to the right. His idea of fun. Especially, after he's had a few drinks. Anyhow, in a week, you'll submit your new thesis. In the meantime, I'll talk to Ploshkina, the dean. You're my best, most talented student, I'll tell her."

"Not true," I said pouring myself a second cup of water.

Alexandra chuckled."You could've dashed this thing off with your pinky."

"Not like this, no."

"I mean, if studying were your priority."

"You know I got married in my first year."

"Sure! An excellent excuse. Chasing pink lizards."

She laughed, a quirky, whimsical sound she would often surprise me with as we got to know each other better. In the years to come, we never mentioned the secret we now shared. But we became close friends, the age difference shrinking to irrelevance.

9

Our friendship would blossom outside the formal setting of the university, away from the confines of our busy city life. I discovered with delight that just like me, Alexandra loved nature and the freedom of movement. She loved ambling through meadows and forests. I was flattered when she invited me to accompany her to Arkhangelskoye, one of the magnificent summer palaces surrounding Moscow. As we wandered between the marble statutes overlooking the grand staircase that cascaded down to the formal garden, Alexandra told me about the history of the place. It surprised me in how much detail she knew the biographies of the founders and the occupants of the palatial estate, all those Yusupovs and Galitzins, in their day the richest and most powerful aristocratic families of Russia. The Yusupovs were so enormously rich, she said, laughing, that if the tsar had lost his throne, they could've easily bought it out for him. The owners of the place were later thrown "to the dump of history," as Russian historians called it. For the more fortunate players, this historical dump was located in Paris; for others, on the killing grounds and in the mass graves. Yet the sheer opulence of the place somehow oppressed me, and I felt lost amid the busy geometry of ornamental hedges and bushes. When next time Alexandra suggested going to Abramtsevo, I couldn't be happier.

Abramtsevo! Since my early adolescence, I'd loved this enchanted and mysterious corner of Earth! Travelling only four kilometres from the meek cottage (the "*dacha*") of my grandparents, I spent many a summer there on the banks of the shy river Vorya that rolled its melancholic waters through shady spruce forests, occasionally emerging into the meadows only to hide its face again behind the braids of weeping willows, here and there washing them in the river's dark, unhurried waters. At the *dacha*, it was the same river,

the same air and sky, and yet Abramtzevo seemed to belong to a
different realm altogether. The firs and spruces and birches around
our *dacha* had been cut down long ago, yielding ground to several
pioneer camps, encircling and holding the *dacha* in their blaring
grip. The trumpets that woke up the pioneers tore the air to shreds
first thing in the morning and then again later as it trooped them to a
flag hoisting, and it would sound off again, for breakfast or lunch or
dinner, and then again at bed time, and once a week, a long, jarring
tune gathered the herd in front of showers. The dirt road splashed
its wet clay from under the skidding wheels of a bus full of sullen
and silent women overloaded with net bags full of groceries. The
bus would stop to pick up more women with tints and cans they'd
just filled with kerosene, sold inside a half-ruined church, one of the
many casualties of the 1930s, crows flying in and out of its black
orifice, once a dome.

But that road didn't reach Abramtsevo.

In Abramtsevo, a feeling of sublime tranquility and
contentment enveloped me: the rustle of tree crowns, the purling
of water in the streams, and not a soul on the overgrown paths.
Nobody on the little hunchbacked bridge, with its missing planks,
arching over the Vorya. No children playing near an ornate hut on
what looked like chicken legs, its appearance so magical it could've
come from a Russian fairy tale. On a knoll stood an old house with
a mezzanine, its doors locked, windows darkened. In the clearing
out front, uncut grass rose tall. From the house radiated several
overgrown linden alleys. Somebody must have lived here long time
ago, but whom?

Strangely, I always felt that I wasn't alone in Abramtsevo, the aura of some invisible and mysterious presence keeping me company. What was this sensation? I couldn't tell. In early summers, I'd spend days in Abramtsevo's woods. Further away from the manor house, I'd find a sunny meadow, and intoxicated by the smell of the sappy grasses and lulled by the buzz of the insects, I'd lie on the ground and doze off. Sometimes, I'd be awakened by a tiny green caterpillar inching up the inside of my naked arm.

Once, feeling weary after a day of wandering around, I found a grove of birches. I listened to the soothing and somehow enigmatic rustle of tree crowns high above my head. I watched from under my half closed eyelids as the dappled light played hide-and-seek on the slim white trunks. When I woke up, I found a small bouquet of forgets-me-not inserted into my sleeping palm. Nobody around.

I was sixteen then.

But now a lot of time had passed since then, and in a sense, a lot of time had passed even since that day at Alexandra's apartment, and there were three of us in Abramtsevo: Alexandra, me, and my two-year-old daughter, Rita. We came on a small pond, and found some shade to spread our blanket in. Rita was sleeping in her pram, and we kept quiet, watching the dragonflies hover over the yellow water lilies, every now and then brushing against one another with their celluloid wings. Alexandra's dark-blue sleeveless dress, with its flaring skirt, covered her feet. It was a tight fit to her slender figure, with the white narrow belt girdling her waist. She slung her lush dark curls over her right shoulder, and the exposed part of her neck and forearm looked unprotected and somehow vulnerable in their urban pallor.

"Shall I read you my latest translations of Verlaine?"she asked. And then, in her low, measured voice she recited first in French, then in Russian: "*Un vaste et tendre /Apaisement/ Sembledescender/Du firmament / Que l'astre irise/C'est l'heure exquise...*"

Her voice trailed away, and we sat in silence. Alexandra picked up a blade of grass and chewed on it. I watched her squint as she gazed fixedly at something in the grass. Near her feet was a red ant hauling a twig three times its size. It tried this way and that, and after huge efforts, somehow, it finally managed, bit by bit, to shift its burden in a direction only it knew. Why was it doing this? Couldn't it spend all that energy on a smaller twig? What kind of a hole did it hope to patch in his communal home with such a log? Who would meet its heroic efforts with applause? Suddenly, another ant appeared, and the two of them quickly coordinated their efforts, carrying the monstrous twig where they needed to go.

"See, they didn't argue at all," remarked Alexandra. "Just set out to work together. Ants know what they need to do to get their house in order, but we Russians don't. What kind of poetry do you like? Do you want to hear more?"

"You choose," I said timidly.

She went on to recite some Spanish and French poets I'd never heard of, then Mandelshtam, Tsvetaeva, and her favourite, Akhmatova. The amount of poetry Alexandra could retrieve from her prodigious memory stunned me. She recited almost without expression, putting no emphasis on separate words as professional actors usually do, but her chesty, low voice drew me in, the words' separate meanings dissolving in the incantation. My head spun. And somehow, in my imagination, the sound of her voice fused with the white clouds sailing over our heads, and their reflection in the water; with the whisper of foliage behind our backs, with a meadow, a little way off, gleaming with cornflowers and daisies. How to distill, how to describe the essence of happiness and bliss I felt on that particular day? My little daughter sleeping peacefully at my side, dapples of sunlight quivering on her pristine forehead; the woods, Alexandra's quiet voice, the poets that she resurrected and whose presence I palpably felt. The lyricism, the pensive and soulful beauty of the middle Russian landscape. This was my homeland. I belonged to it and no other. Only seven years later, fate would lead me down a very different path, but that knowledge, for better or worse, was still hidden from me on that blissful day.

Before our visit to Abramtsevo, I often wondered what it was that Alexandra, a poet, a scholar, saw in me, an ordinary girl, with no particular interests or talents. Afraid she might lose interest in me, I talked incessantly, trying hard – perhaps subconsciously – to sound engaging and interesting. But here, in Abramtsevo, a silence came over me instead, completely unforced. Alexandra was a full vessel that didn't need to be filled with my prattle. And for the first time, I realized that what she needed was a listener. I'd never expressed my admiration for her directly, yet I knew she felt and valued it, more than my attempts to impress her with my scant knowledge. Once I understood this, our relationship became smooth and easy. And listening to her, I understood, at least partly, my vague impressions of Abramtsevo.

I'll demur from the old idea that people leave some indelible spiritual traces in the places they've inhabited. If that were so, we'd have to conclude that some part of us – call it soul – doesn't die. Can it be true? I don't have the answer, and I certainly didn't think about it then, in the early afternoon of my life. But when Alexandra told me Abramtzevo was a real nineteenth century "cultural nest," when she told me that Tyutchev and Turgenev and Tolstoy all came here to visit, to walk the same trails, I knew why I was under the spell of something like...I'll call them orphaned memories, things neither seen nor experienced. Gogol, the eccentric genius who went mad and ultimately starved himself to death at the age of forty-two – incomparable Gogol lived here! He read *Dead Souls* to a choice circle of writers, right here, only four kilometres away from where I was spending every summer of my childhood!

Alexandra pointed in the direction of a hill behind us. "In the shabby manner house we can't see from here."

Yes, nothing was left but overgrown trails, a boarded up manor, and a small, silent church at the foot of the birch grove. But how did Alexandra know all this? From books?

"Max brought me here once," she explained. "He's a distant relation to Vasnetsov, the famous painter, it turned out. The hut on chicken legs, that's Vasnetzov's design. There was a great artists' colony here in 1880s. You've heard of Mamontov?"

"Vaguely," I said, embarrassed by my lack of erudition.

Savva Mamontov, the Russian Carnegie, was a railway magnate and one of the richest and most successful merchants of pre-revolutionary Russia, Alexandra told me. A flamboyant man of artistic temperament, a sculptor, an opera singer, an actor, and a stage director turned famous philanthropist and powerful patron of arts. Here, in Abramtsevo, Mamontov created the first private opera, with Rimsky-Korsakov, Shalyapin, Stanislavski, and Diaghilev among his close friends, visiting or living here. Yes, the whole colony of famous artists lived and worked here – till the revolution of 1917.

"Max loves this place," she added, then my teacher turned to me, her eyes smiling. "Why don't you call me Sasha?"

10

While Sasha was telling me all this, the innocent-looking puffs of clouds squeezed some drops of rain on our heads, then poured down on us a generous summer shower. Far away, a flash of lightening pierced the sky, and then, after the heavenly warriors had gathered all their strength, a thunder bolt struck. We quickly picked up our things and rushed to the hut on chicken legs, the only shelter in sight. We got inside just as the rain came pummelling down in a redoubled onslaught, plucking the gabled roof and the outspread wings of a bat carved on the pediment of the gable. As we crouched inside, another thunder bolt sent my daughter Rita into fits of screaming. I wrapped her in a dry sheet and cradled in my arms. But that didn't help.

"You know who lived in this hut before?" I asked as we perched on a bench attached to a wall of old thick logs that promised some protection. "Baba-Yaga! A forest witch! When little girls cried, she baked them in...well, she did bad things to them. But the good girls all got presents."

Rita paused from her screaming, her open mouth matching her round eyes."Baba bad?"

"Yes, bad, but if you don't cry, she's good." The rain intensified, lashing the hut in sheets that splashed us through the apertures that held no window panes. And Rita kept screaming. "Listen, Rita, want to hear a fairy tale?" Sasha asked, the impatience clear in her tone. "Or is she too young? Will she understand?"

"We can try. She's a clever little thing. Understands much more than she can say. Rita? Rita! Listen, darling, Aunt Sasha is going to tell you a fairy tale!"

"Once upon a time," Sasha began, "there lived a girl named Vasilissa the Beautiful. Her step-mother said to Vasilissa, 'Go to Baba Yaga, into the woods, and get me a flame for my candles.' So Vasilissa goes into the woods, and she sees a hut on chicken legs. Just like this one. And on the fence, she sees human skulls with lights shining in their eye sockets. Scary!" Alexandra paused for a moment shaking wet hair out of her face... "Well, we can skip that part. She doesn't know what a skull is, eh? Anyway, so Vasilissa comes up to the hut and says, 'Hut on chicken legs, face me and turn your back to the forest.' You always have to say these magic words, Rita. And sure enough, the hut turns around. Vasilissa enters and sees...whom does she see? Baba-Yaga."

The sound of light snoring came from the bundle in my arms: our toddler was fast asleep. As is often the case with young children, the shift from screaming to slumber was instant.

"I think the rain is letting of again," I said. "But I always wondered, where did this idea of a hut on chicken legs come from?"

"Most likely a contamination."

"A what?"

"Substitution of one concept for another. The initial *kurit* – 'to envelope with smoke' – was gradually replaced by the similar sounding *kura,* a 'chicken.' Though one has nothing to do with the other, of course."

"But how do we know it?"

"Well, ethnographers and anthropologists don't know everything, but some things they're certain of. Apparently, the ancient Slaves placed the ashes of their dead in the huts they built deep in the woods. These are the pagan, pre-Christian Rus we're talking about. Fumigation to ward off the evil spirits – that was part of the burial rituals, as far as we can judge. Funny thing about the dead: they always have that yearning, to come back to the world of the living, don't they? But the two realms don't mix. So you had to stave them off with smoke. "She paused. "I wonder if...well, you know, in Orthodox churches, the priest blesses his flock by fumigating them with incense. I'm pretty sure the origins of that are in paganism. Purification, scaring off the Satan."

Sasha never ceased to surprise me. Linguistics, American literature, poetry translated from three languages, history, and now this.

But she only chuckled. "And why not? What's in my way? You can ride a bike, or go by bus, or train, or you can fly – all to reach the same destination. Ethnography and Russian folklore are fascinating subjects."

"And where's the destination?"

"It's where you end up when you finally discover that everything is interconnected; you reach this place where you see a unified picture of the world."

"Okay. I'll give you that. But how do Baba Yaga and the chicken hut fit into this unified picture?"

"Baba Yaga? A spirit of the dead, turned a forest witch, a scare of little children? One theory is that, with time, the purposes and meanings of religious rituals were lost. What was left trickled down to us in the form of fairy tales, even children's counting rhymes. Baba Yaga must've replaced a demon that the Slaves believed belonged to the realm of the dead and guarded their houses, later to be turned into an innocent chicken hut in the imagination of folklore. The skulls sitting on Baba Yaga's fence are her attributes, the markers of the other realm she's guarding. Nice leftovers, so to speak. That carved bat on one side of the roof and the owl on the other are reminders of the same."

"Yes, but isn't Baba-Yaga good in some fairy tales?"

"She has to be both. Like in *Faust*, remember? She's part of that force that always wills the evil and always produces the good. On a much more modest pagan scale though. She's just a forest she-demon, with limited liabilities. But in her small way, she represents the same principle: that light and darkness are inseparable. Baba Yaga stands between two worlds, the dead and living, right there on the border."

We were quiet for a while, listening to the sound of rain on the roof, a measured sniffle of a child sleeping in my lap. Sasha was the first to break the silence.

"You know, there are many things in these stories that stir the imagination. Baba Yaga has to test a hero, what's called a 'cultural hero' in folklore studies. This is her role. And the hero's role is to go through various ordeals and trials in order to achieve his goals: a princess, or some ultimate knowledge or immortality or happiness for the rest of humanity, whatever that might be. For that, he often has to cross the border and descend into the Underworld."

"Wow. That's fascinating!"

"Yes, but these aren't my ideas. Read Propp, read Carl Jung – it's all there! Ulysses goes into the Underworld, and Vasilissa the Beautiful, in her small fairy-tale way, does the same. She isn't a Prometheus, but she still gets a flame. And she's also tested by an ordeal, serving Baba-Yaga, she did all the old hag's chores, which probably wasn't too pleasant!"

"And what does she get at the end?"

"The usual, a prince or even a king, I don't remember exactly which. But most important, she gets freedom."

"Freedom?"

"Yes, freedom from fear. You see, in every fairy tale about Baba Yaga the hero has to utter an invocation: 'Turn to me with your facade, and with your back, to the woods.' Meaning, I've arrived. I'm here. And I'm prepared to face you head on. I'll cross the border. I'll descend into Underworld and re-emerge victorious. In other words, I'm not afraid. With Baba Yaga, with all baba yagas of the world, there's only one choice, be brave or perish."

"Oh! You know what? I think Rita peed all over me in her

sleep. My dress is all wet. I was thinking, 'How come the rain suddenly got so warm?' Let me see if I have anything dry left in my bag to change her into."

11

Now, almost forty years later, and remembering our past, I felt a certain sadness, a certain nostalgia that accompanies such memories. Our paths forked. I lived in Canada, she'd stayed in Russia, in the same room, surrounded by the same objects of her youth. Amazing changes had taken place outside that room. Many things, of which I was unaware, had happened in her life as well. When I left for Canada, Sasha was still teaching at the university. Was she really fired, or did she simply make a joke about it to get rid of Vera and her nagging?

"Fired? Yes, but that came much later," Sasha said. "Are you really interested? Well, I made a lot of faux pas. I never knew, didn't have any sense, when it was the right time or place to do or say something. Like in that Soviet joke about the two Jewish brothers. Remember?"

"Hmm, no, not really."

"It's an old joke, long in the tooth, as they say. Well, there are the two Rabinovich brothers. The elder somehow managed to emigrate to the United States, but the youngest got stuck. He's lying low, afraid to breathe lest the KGB finds out about his brother. Suddenly, they summon him to Lubyanka, and the KGB guy says, 'Comrade Rabinovich, we've heard you have a brother in the United

States?' And Rabinovich goes, 'Oh, I don't even know where he lives. Never corresponded with him, nothing.' 'That's a serious mistake,' says the KBG guy. 'What's more important in life than family ties? Here's a pen and a piece of paper. Please, write a letter to your brother. Yes, right now. Tell him, we in that KGB are very concerned about orphaned babies. Trying to raise some dough for them. Ask your bother to help us a bit, will you?' Rabinovich says, 'But I don't know his address.' And the KGB guy says, 'Oh, leave that to us. We'll make sure he gets the letter.' Rabinovich scratches his head and finally writes: 'Dear Brother Aron: I've finally found the right time and place to contact you.'" Sasha looked at my unsmiling face. "You don't get it?"

"Well...it's not very funny."

"No, it isn't. But that's what happened to me. I finally found *the right time and place* to do a totally wrong thing!"

"Like what?"

"Accost the head of our department, Petr Tsarev. A cantankerousness old man! He had gout, I think, and was in pain most of the time. Anyhow, he always looked grim. I could never catch him in his office: too busy. Remember that promenade? From the major university building on Lenin Hills to the subway? Always empty somehow? So it's drizzling, and he's shuffling along, leaning on his cane. I catch up to him, and I go, 'Petr Sergeevich, I'd like to show you my latest article. I think you might be interested.' I'm pulling it out of my briefcase, and as luck would have it, pages fly all over the sidewalk, mixing with the wet leaves. He doesn't wait, keeps hobbling along, and I'm trying to rescue the sheets and run after him. He finally stops and goes, 'Look, my workday is over and I'm going home. You're trying to show me something that has nothing to do with me. Send it to our editorial board.' In other words, not my monkeys, not my circus, as they say. Get lost.

"That's when my pipes burst. I said, 'I've been working really hard. I produce at least seven serious articles every year, and I've been teaching for ten years.' And he goes. 'So?' 'But all these years, my official title has been lab technician, even though I've never worked in a lab for a day in my life. I'm teaching American literature and the theory of translation, as you know, but I'm paid the lowest salary.' And he goes, 'But you teach, don't you? You have access to students? And you like your job? I hear students like you too?' 'Yes, I've never had any complaints.' 'You have a child, I hear?' 'One daughter.' 'No husband?' 'No.' Then he crooks his finger, like that, leans over, and whispers in my ear, 'With your *fifth line* be grateful I'm still keeping you at all. You and your daughter could be panhandling in the streets.' And off he goes.

"*Fifth line?* I would've never guessed. I thought your father was from the Caucasus?"

"Yes, a Georgian, but he left before I was born. I was raised by my mother. She never talked about him. All I know he was a beach photographer somewhere in Suhumy while she was on vacation. She came back home pregnant. So, of course, I chose her last name and her ethnicity: Jewish."

"Did Tsarev finally fire you?"

"No. But when push came to shove, he saw no reason to stand up for me. Or maybe he couldn't have anyway. I don't know."

12

How well I remember the classical facade of the main university entrance, the original one, built by Catherine the Great right across from Red Square, the entrance left over from the tsarist times and miraculously persevering into the Soviet era almost intact. We Soviet students took that inheritance for granted, although if anyone would've appreciated their antiquity, it would've been Alexandra, on the fateful day that almost led to her firing.

I also remember the worn stairs leading to the second floor, each like a drooping eyelid, their marble edges polished and thinned by thousands of feet running and walking up and down them for the last three centuries.

Every spring, under the vaulted ceilings of the university, the entrance exams were held. After examining the applicants for the school of journalism, Alexandra was assigned to law school, where oral exam in English was also one of the requirements. The police officer barricading the entrance mistrustfully examined her ID. The vestibule was unexpectedly empty, except for security patrolling the floors. By the time she made it through several checkpoints, the examination team had already assembled in a large room with a long table covered with a dark green cloth. She recognized Igor Turinsky, her colleague from the Languages and Humanities Department. Three other men she'd never seen before. A handsome man of unerringly clean looks, Turinsky was partial to expensive ties and navy suits. A sharp crease on his trousers echoed the part in his shiny hair.

"Walking between the raindrops, that's what he was good at," Sasha told me. "And the other three suits. One was the party secretary, another the head of the Trade Union, and the third, God knows who he was."

The trio laid out the rules. Rule number one: Nobody leaves the room while the exams are in progress. "You get thirsty, flag our comrades," said one stern suit. "They'll bring you a cup of tea from the cafeteria."

Rule number two: Don't go to the washroom alone. "Ask one of our comrades to accompany you."

Finally, Loshadny (the party secretary, as it turned out) slipped a sheet of paper onto Alexandra's lap. "If you're in doubt, consult your compass."

The sheet was divided into two parts. On the left, the names of the applicants; opposite each name, grades, from five, the highest, to two, the lowest. Three was a barely passable mark, and four might get you in, depending.

13

That some Goldstein had no business being in the law school of Moscow State University and had been graded a two wasn't something Alexandra needed an explanation for. That Sarkasyan had four across from his name was equally clear. Armenians were granted a small piece of the pie as an ethnic minority, by far not the best one, but still tolerable, by Russian standards. But why Smolich – a typical Belarusian of a harmless ethnicity, generally speaking, considered third best after Russians and Ukrainians (at the time) – why did he have the fat swan of a two across from his name, a failure; that was much harder to fathom. Mysterious and impenetrable were the architectonics of the state's secrets. Who knew? Maybe his Belorussian grandmother happened to have lived on a territory occupied by Germans during World War II, which was all of Belarus? The indelible ideological contamination had been dragged into perpetuity by every generation of Smoliches ever since.

Or why, for example, was it that Ivanov, with a purebred Russian surname, was allowed to ride into future on a white horse through the grand University entrance, while Sidorov, with a similar garden variety Russian name, had to vegetate in life's backyard overgrown by weeds? Peasant labourer's blood must have been flowing through Ivanov's veins, while in Sidorov's, only mummified crocodiles would know what was floating there, as Sasha might have said, mimicking Vera. Maybe Sidorov's uncle lurked in the back wings with the wolf's ticket after he'd been released from the camps. Or maybe Ivanov had already served in the Red Army, while Sidorov hadn't served anywhere; or Ivanov had just arrived from the provinces, where he was, say, a policeman, the most advantageous occupation for law school applicants, while Ivanov had sat on his ass in Moscow all his short life, never aspiring to be a policeman, then suddenly deciding to become a lawyer.

The law school of the Moscow State University was a KGB franchise disguising itself under the university logo. It mainly recruited among peasantry and working class, preferably connected with policing and later aspiring to enter the KGB. But Sidorov was too thick to get it. As a result, he was knocking with a straight face on the wrong doors, where Alexandra had been posted to guard.

14

Motes of dust danced through the beams of light and swirled over the stacks of examination tickets, the clean sheets of paper on one side of the long table. A profound sense of boredom took hold of Alexandra. She looked out the window. Below, she could see the caryatids, so close to their cornice with their intricately braided hair. Further on, the Kremlin walls scratched the pale Moscow skies with their swallowtail edges. The policeman in the centre of Manezh Square, metres away from the Kremlin, whistled away a solitary jaywalker.

Fluent conversation skills, reading comprehension, grammar accuracy, and the ability to translate from English into Russian and back – these were the requirements of the entrance exams. Alexandra could rely on herself for rounding off the sharp corners, even ignoring small discrepancies. To shape a passable grade instead of a failure was not that difficult. But what to do with bigger and unmatchable gaps should they occur? In the beginning, things ran smoothly. The applicants talked about their parents, their favourite hobbies and their hopes for the future. They read and translated Steinbeck, Dreiser, and Twain.

That Loshadny, the party secretary, his name meaning "horse." No, he was more like a carp, the way he opened his mouth when he talked. As if the sounds lived beyond his lips and he needed to catch them by opening his mouth as wide as possible. Every time he did, Alexandra had to avert her eyes.

Carp called the shots, controlling the flow of applicants to the examination tables. Initially, Alexandra examined students with Igor, as a team. Then they were told to work independently – the stream of applicants was hefty.

To make sure fiction more or less matched the reality, from time to time, Alexandra peeped into her lap. And so far, it did, in general outlines. She didn't notice when Alyona Lebedeva sailed toward her desk. Alyona-Alyonushka! Sublime golden glow! From what fairy tale did you step into our misconceived world? The angelic purity of your demeanour! The innocence of your dimpled cheeks! A polka-dot dress with a modest ruffle running around your svelte virgin neck, a long golden braid snaking down one shoulder.

Alyona raked her languid gaze over the trivial world around her: examiners, desks, piles of paper. A decanter full of water in the middle of the table. Then she puckered her clean, slightly convex forehead and...froze. A butterfly of a smile took off from her blooming mouth. She waited. After a small delay, the examiners half-smiled back. Only then did Alyona approached the examination desk. Her long delicate fingers twanged the air, then her index and thumb came together and pulled one exam ticket out of the pile.

"Number seven. For sure, a lucky one!" Alyona sang, then released another butterfly from the luminescent depths of her hyacinths eyes.

"Ah, I'm a little scared," Number Seven sighed, pulling her

shoulders up coquettishly, a young nymph before stepping into a cool brook.

"Don't be nervous," said Alexandra in Russian. "I'm sure you'll do fine."

"You think?" Alyona demurely lowered the marvel of her eyelashes.

Alexandra switched to English, signalling the end of the informal part and the beginning of that silly formality that she – her tone implied – would love to skip for both their sakes. "Please tell us about yourself. Where did you study? What are you hobbies?"

The standard warm-up questions. Alyona shrugged her shoulders. Alexandra hesitated.

"All right," she said in English. "Let's see. How old are you?"

"Seventeen," replied Alyona in Russian.

"Good. You understood the question. Now try to answer in English."

"I dislike numbers!" said Alyona defiantly. "Why don't you ask me something else!"

"Well, these are the simplest questions. What marks did you get in high school, then?"

"Always good!" replied Alyona in Russian, looking straight into her examiner's eyes.

She's just mocking me, Alexandra suddenly realized. That's exactly what she's doing. What makes her feel so invincible? The awareness of her own beauty? Maybe she's right. Must beauty be always virtuous, as the ancient Greeks believed? And should ignorance of a foreign tongue be taken for a lack of virtue? English didn't exist when Greeks devised their theories. Does it matter that she doesn't know a word of it?

"Well, maybe you'll find translating easier. What's in your ticket? *An American Tragedy* by Theodore Dreiser? Let's give it a try. The very first paragraph, please."

Vengeful fire lit up Alyona's eyes. She decisively pushed the piece of paper away. "I'm not doing it. Period."

"You won't even try?" Alexandra squinted her eyes, waiting, "Well, it's too bad, then," she said wearily, her face a mask. Before reaching for her pen, she glanced at her knees, just in case: A fat, self-assured five, the highest mark, unequivocally positioned across from Alyona's last name.

The girl knew she was failing the exam, and her pretty eyes suddenly swelled with tears. She changed her tone instantaneously. "Please understand. I can't fail this. I absolutely must make it to law school this year. All my life, all my future – everything depends on it!"

Disappointing, the way she chose to humiliate herself, Alexandra thought coldly. But maybe that, too, was an act? What did she want with law school anyway? She should try the theatre school, with her ability to act. Alexandra would have no misgivings in ignoring the orders spread over her knees, she knew that.

"You've just graduated from high school," Alexandra said indifferently. "Nothing wrong with working for a year. You'll gain some experience, learn some English, and try again next year."

"You don't understand," said Alyona, with a quick change of register, now in full control of herself. "I've already been working. If

I fail, my career will be ruined."

"Career?"

"They promised a promotion if I get into law school."

"I thought you just finished high school?"

"Yes. But I've also been freelancing."

"For whom?"

"I can't say."

"I see...And...and how long have you been doing that?"

"For two years."

"So...since sixteen?"

"I'll be nineteen next month."

"You work for free, or they pay you?

Alyona ignored that question. "Please don't fail me. You'll ruin my life."

"I'm sure you'll have better luck next year,"Alexandra heard herself saying, as she hurriedly signed "Failure" next to Alyona's name.

15

Carp returned from one of his smoke breaks minutes after Alyona Lebedeva had left the room. He went straight to Sasha's table."What's just happened, my dear?" he said, lapping at the air with his tongue. "The moment I leave the room, there seems to be a problem. What have you done to the poor girl? She's crying her soul out in the corridor!"

"She failed her exam, so she's upset," said Alexandra

impassively.

"She failed or was failed?"

"She doesn't know a word of English. There's nothing I could do."

"You're a teacher, aren't you? You must be familiar with the principles of pedagogy. Did you manage to create a friendly atmosphere to bring out the best in our potential student?"

"I did my best, but...well...she knows nothing."

"All our knowledge is partial and, well, relative. Do you know everything? Does anybody?"

For the next two hours, he sat beside Sasha and monitored her every word and gesture.

Finally, with only one name left on the list, the day was drawing to a close. Sasha was hungry, and yawned furtively from fatigue and the lack of fresh air. Carp seemed to be tired too, taking smoking breaks more often.

It was during one of his smoke breaks that a man, not tall in stature, but slim and muscular, walked into the examination room. Older, he looked very different from the rest of the applicant crop. White turtleneck underneath a suede brown jacket, fitted like skin to his athletic body, and beige trousers, a casual, foreign chic. Sasha glanced at him, and for a split second, their gazes met. She was the first to lower her eyes, but he kept his evaluating glance steadily focused.

He approached her table, nonchalantly removed the first ticket off the top of the stack, and walked back to his seat. Under his weight, his chair didn't make so much as a squeak. Unlike the other applicants, he didn't show any signs of nervousness. Nor did he make any notes. Instead, he crossed his arms on his chest, leaned back, stretched his legs, and fixed his eyes on Alexandra, first one her face, then at her crossed legs, curtained by the green cloth at half-calf.

She instinctively recrossed her legs, hiding the one that was shorter. What an unpleasant type, she thought. When his turn came to approach her table, the air didn't seem to offer any resistance against his body. This economy of means with which he carried himself, where did it come from? Sasha didn't like any of it. She mistrusted the freedom of his movements.

"Which question would you like to answer first?"

"It's up to you, doesn't really matter," the man said casually in impeccable English, without a trace of a Russian accent.

Alexandra looked at him silently, masking her surprise. "And you name is...Sergey Dashinsky. Where did you learn your English, Sergey?"

"Well, it's a long story," he responded with casual arrogance." But let's say I travelled a lot."

She suddenly wanted to be rid of him. Obviously, the man knew English better than anybody in the room, Igor and herself including, but look how cocky, how full of himself he was! What if she took him down a notch? Instead of the five he was surely expecting, she could give him a four. Then we'll see how you talk, Mister Narcissus, Sasha thought gleefully. But he looked at her with a direct, evaluating eye, and again she felt unease.

"Well," she said, trying to win some time, "tell me about your travelling then." Just in case, she furtively consulted her knees. Across from Dashinsky's name was the number two, a failure. "Please continue," she said, her throat tightening. Was fate cooperating with her, or mocking her again? "What countries have you visited?"

"You want them in a chronological order?"

"Doesn't matter," she said, trying to hide her confusion.

"Let's see. The United States, Canada, England, France, Switzerland, Sweden, Australia, New Zealand. In this order, I think."

None of it made any sense. With this travelling record, he must be well entrenched, "their man" from head to toe. Who else was able to go around the globe, unless approved, and acting on their direct order? But then why are they failing him?

"I'm just curious," Alexandra said. "I mean, travelling to all these places? A remarkable record!"

"I was a ballet dancer in the Bolshoi, one of the leads. We toured a lot. Plus, I lived in Britain in my early childhood. My father was an attaché. "Dashinsky dropped this casually, as if his father had been selling doughnuts on a street corner.

Ah, but at least that explained his English, his smug confidence. The elite, the chosen, with all the comforts and riches at their knees: *dachas* with Jacuzzis, cars, gourmet food, the best clothing, free vacations anywhere in the world. But wait, the question remained: Why were they failing him?

"What an interesting profession!" she said, camouflaging her growing anxiety.

"No complaints. So far, so good, but I am thirty-three. I need to move on."

"So you decided on law school. Good choice!"

"See, I need to know our laws. To defend people, including myself, if need be."

Did she hear him right? She pretended she didn't, quickly switching to another topic. To defend people...hmm. Her attitude toward the man sitting in front of her was rapidly changing.

The door opened, and Carp returned from his smoke break.

"Why don't you translate half a page from Russian into English?" Sasha said, adopting a formal tone.

Carp came behind her desk, wrapping his arm around the back of her chair. "A tricky case," he whispered, leaning in close to her ear. "Be careful with this one."

"He knows the subject,"she whispered back.

"You heard me." Carp detached himself from her and walked over to Igor.

"You are going to fail me, right?" the dancer asked primarily with his eyes, moving his lips only slightly.

She responded the same way, only barely shaking her head as she lowered her eyes. "I'll try my best not to."

"I'll understand," Sergey said in English, shrugging his shoulders as if none of it concerned him anyway.

At that moment, Carp returned to her table. "I can see you need some help, young lady. Let's have a go at this applicant, together. One brain is good, but two are always better, right? Did you check his... what do you call it...his reading comprehension?"

Carp pulled a sheet out of the pile and handed it over to the dancer. It was an excerpt from *The Old Man and the Sea*. The dancer glanced at the text, then rapidly read and translated the indicated paragraphs. Silence followed.

"I myself am not a specialist," said Carp,"but Alexandra Markovna tells me there are serious inaccuracies...in your translation. You're free to go. We'll notify you of the result." Then, turning to a trade union guy, he said,"Andrey Petrovich, anybody else left in the corridor?"

Andrey Petrovich jumped to his feet and went to check. "Nobody's left. He was the last one."

"The door!" Carp ordered to the union guy. "Don't let anybody in. Alexandra Markovna, you seemed to have been impressed by this young man. Pulling wool over women's eyes is his specialty! Do you understand whom you're playing favourites with?"

"I'm...I'm not playing anything, Vladimir Ivanovich!"

"Vladimir Stepanovich!"

"Sorry, I meant Vladimir Stepanovich. This applicant, his English is very good. He toured the world with the Bolshoi."

"That's the whole point. The party trusted him to represent our great country. And how did he thank us? How? Used his trips abroad for personal enrichment. Smuggled in cigarettes, sold jeans on the black market. But we counted on his consciousness and for a while looked the other way. And how did he show his gratitude, your Romeo-Don Juan? By trying to defect. Betraying our trust even further. And you? What exactly are you trying to do? Sneak a criminal and a traitor into our university? It's eight o'clock already. Write 'Failure' down here, and put your signature there." Carp's index finger stabbed a line on the form. "Then we'll call it a day."

If she gave him "Satisfactory," Sasha's mind calculated rapidly, they'd change it to "Failure." Then they'd forge her signature. End of story. There was nothing she could do. Nothing.

"Well?" said Carp.

"I see no ground for failure," she heard herself saying, throwing her own logic to the dogs.

Not that she was fighting for justice. Or questioning the aftermath. She'd gotten used to compromising with her conscience a long time ago. Most likely, she'd never lay her eyes on this Bolshoi dancer again. What made her say "no" was an upsurge of anger. She couldn't stand the sight of Carp anymore, he and his ilk, their well-tailored suits, their matching ties, their white shirts and the sleek hair plastered to their sculls, their sleazy smiles, the way they looked at her...

"I can't," she said.

"It's very simple," said Carp, lapping up some air, his voice changing abruptly from cajoling to threatening. "You're not leaving this room until you sign. Is that clear? If you don't care about your job, why should we?" He leaned over her, putting his arm around her shoulder, and whispered in her ear: "You don't understand. I'm not letting this petty criminal in. Whether you sign it or not. But I prefer you to sign. We're going to stay in this room until you do."

She picked up a pen, paused, then, barely pressing the tip into the paper, signed her name opposite the number two.

1

Part II

It was close to midnight, but we kept talking. After the brandy, we moved on to tea, as no Russian can do without it at any stage of eating or drinking. Sasha liked the maple syrup and sweets I brought from Canada. I felt cozy, in a familiar place, and I didn't want to leave. But I was hungry.

"Do you have anything to nibble on?"

"You mean food? I'll have a look. "Sasha went over to her tiny fridge, wedged between her bed and a dresser. She produced a dried-up piece of cheese and put it on a stale slice of bread. I chuckled to myself. Things never change! Strangely, if gave me some soothing satisfaction.

"What happened to the Bolshoi dancer, Sasha? Do you know?"

"Well, for some time I was toying with the idea of finding him. I knew his name, after all. But then, what would I say to him? I ended up avoiding certain streets, afraid to bump into him by accident. I never talked about it to anybody, Emma, but I'll tell you: it gnawed at me for years. Why did I suddenly give in? It wasn't rational. As if somebody acted instead of me."

"What choice did you have? We were all forced to compromise, one way or another. We were all afraid."

"Fear, that's the point. But why are you fine one second and afraid the next? I've thought about that a lot over years. There comes a point when suddenly you're overwhelmed with a sense of total helplessness, the futility of it all, you know? Annie was at home alone. I mean, with Max, remember him? Max and his wife, my neighbours back then? By the time I got home it would've been night, and what would they do with my baby? Put her to bed in their room? No space to spit. Sit in mine and wait indefinitely till I return? Carp would've kept me there the whole night if he wanted. I knew his type. And I think what happened was that there comes a moment, quite suddenly, like a switch is flicked off, when you just stop caring. It's like you're swept up by a wave of indifference and apathy. Normally in a situation like that, all you want is to break free and come up for air. Breathe again to any cost. That's exactly what they count on. Intimidate us, exhaust us, and sooner or later, we'll break. But for that one moment, for that one moment of weakness, you pay the bill for years and years to come."

Visibly upset, she got up and walked to her bookshelves, limping heavily, and lit another cigarette.

"Sasha, but it all happened decades ago. We don't need to talk about it if it still upsets you."

"The problem is you have to live with it, that's the problem, "Sasha repeated, ignoring my words. "Do you know what Gorbanevskaya said? After they'd all been arrested in the Red Square in 1968?"

"Garbonevskaya?"

"Yes, the poet. When they protested against our invasion into Czechoslovakia? I met her, once. We talked. She visited Moscow in the nineties, after perestroyka. She said, 'I have never been a hero. It was a matter of honour, that's all. I did it to be able to look in the mirror the next morning.' And in 1968, she was young, just gave birth to a baby. Sentenced to three years of psychiatric prison and then exile. They were all young. Seven of them, plus her three-month-old baby in a pram. You know how long the whole protest lasted? Guess."

"No idea. Half an hour?"

"Half an hour! More like four minutes, literally. And then, brutal – and I mean brutal – arrest. Victor, forgot his name, they knocked his teeth out, and didn't drag him to court, bad optics. Instead, they sentenced him to incarceration in an asylum. Four or five minutes! But they did manage to get out their picket signs: "For Your Freedom and Ours!" And that says it all."

"But weren't they a bit naive? The risks and all?"

Sasha flared up with indignation. "No, they weren't naive! They knew perfectly well the price they'd have to pay for those minutes. Years of gulag, psychiatric prison, exile. The difference between them and somebody like me is that they were prepared to pay that price."

"Did they really think they could stop the Soviet tanks?"

"I told you, Emma, they had no illusions whatsoever! They went in with their eyes wide open."

Sasha burst into baffling sobs. I'd never seen her crying, and I felt confused and embarrassed.

"What is it, Sasha? Did I say something?"

"No. I guess I'm just getting old. Sentimental. The Czech government made them all honorary citizens of Prague later."

"And that's why you're crying?"

"I don't know. I mean, we've always been silent. And they found the courage to break that silence. And their sacrifice wasn't in vein. The world found out. The Czechs were grateful. Maybe that's why."

I put my arm around her and was struck by the sensation: no flesh on her frail shoulders, just raw bones. I wanted to steer our conversation away from the painful past. "But life in Russia has changed for the better, Sasha, right? What do you think? People here have never been so well off."

"Some, in big cities. But travel two hundred kilometres outside Moscow. Still, yes, generally speaking, it's much better. And then, I don't know. People have been leaving. I miss Annie and her little boys, of course. I thought at one point about moving to the United States. But, you know, somebody has to stay here. In the past, we couldn't do much. But now we can. Next year, Medvedev will leave, and I'm sure Putin will rig the election. If he gets into power again, we'll end up with a disaster."

"What do you mean by that?"

"He's a KGB colonel. He'll...well...he'll build the country in his image. Terrible things will happen... with no point of return. I can feel it. It's in the air."

"But you said things are better. And you, personally, what can you do? Protest in Bolotnya Square? I didn't really think you had an activist gene in your body."

"I don't. And I'm not a fighter. How to put it? See, this is a unique moment in history. We can't let it slip through our fingers. We've built the rudiments of civic society. It's fragile. But it's there!

To let it go would be an awful, awful mistake!"

For some reason, this kind of talk made me nervous. She must be over sixty now. She'd never been involved in politics. She was a poet, a scholar, not a political activist.

"How is Annie doing, by the way? Happy with her life in the United States?"

"I think so. She lucked out with her husband. I like him a lot, by the way. They have two small boys, twins. I don't get a chance to see them often, unfortunately. They've come to Russia twice, since the boys were born. The boys started chatting in Russian right away."

2

I knew Sasha had raised her daughter on her own, just like her mother had raised her. Who was Annie's father? In spite of our closeness, I never dared to ask. Nor did I ever hear Sasha talk of an unquenchable desire to have a baby, typical of many women reaching a certain age. I was surprised when I noticed her pregnancy. She turned out to be not a bad mother. But the domestic chores that multiply with the arrival of a child bewildered her. She looked at her little daughter from a certain distance, as something separate from herself, the attitude rare in most mothers of very young children.

"How did you manage after you lost your job?" I asked.

"Like everyone else. Some tutoring. Some translations. Book reviews. Also, Vera helped. She's a strange bird, but she's not unkind. Those special parcels from secret distribution centres for the privileged, she didn't touch them, saved them all for us. Buckwheat, coffee, sausages, sometimes salami. It did help. And...well...you remember Max, my neighbour? He was helping too. A lot. He and his wife. When I taught evening courses for factory workers, I had that stint once, they looked after Annie. We somehow managed."

3

I met Max in the late seventies at Sasha's. Before that, through an accidentally open door, I would catch a glimpse of canvasses leaning against the walls of the room he shared with his wife, abstract art in bright colours. The smell of oil escaping the room, I remember that too. Though Max was a member of the artists' union, this didn't put bread on his table. Selling art or organizing exhibitions that bypassed the state was illegal. Max's main source of income came from clandestine business on the side. A book *bariga,* a hukster, a *spiv* was an essential profession in a country of readers, as the USSR was known to be. Though books in the Soviet Union were published with Gargantuan runs of millions of copies, these were not the books that interested sophisticated readers in the big metropolises. What they wanted could be obtained only from under the flap of a *bariga's* coat. Shivering in a blizzard or in the rain, the collar of his coat up, a stooping emaciated figure, the *bariga* would circle the bookshops of Kuznetsly Most, waiting for his clients. Each *bariga* would cater to his own clientele. Mark's had high-brow interests. The full collection of World Library Editions or Literary Monuments were connoisseurs' objects of desire. They were published in small quantities that couldn't meet the demand. Hunting for them could take months. A quarter of a monthly salary for one volume of *life of the Twelve Caesars,* for example, wouldn't be considered an unfair price. Discerning clients requested a volume of Virgil in the Literary Monuments Series, but only if it had the introduction by Shervinsky, no other. And there were collectors who wouldn't hesitate to pay half their salary for the first autographed edition of Pasternak or Mandelstam. Nabokov or Brodsky, published abroad and forbidden in the USSR, were equally difficult to get. The *bariga's* profession was not without danger. *Barigi* had to trust their clients, who could easily rat on them. A respected *bariga* would not deal in pornography, nor in the works of dissidents like Solzhenitsyn or Varlamov. Those had their own channels of transmission, usually by way of complicated relays, from trusted hands to trusted hands to trusted hands. The starting point could be some diplomat or a North American or European PhD student whose love of Russian culture, language, and literature exceeded the risks at the border.

For Slavists and scholars from the West, the camaraderie, the high-brow conversations at midnight; the easy access to writers, poets, painters, filmmakers (everybody was either one or the other, and everybody seemed to know everybody else); the easy, almost immediate familiarity, heartfelt, family-like connections forged in tiny kitchens and communal apartments – all of this would seem so unique as not to be matched by anything back home. The combination of this genuine warmth, the insider knowledge they sought, and a tinge of danger were all irresistible magnets for Western students, scholars, and journalists. They'd come to Russia at every opportunity, and bring from their land of plenty clothing, food, bottles, and pacifiers for babies as well as shirts, sweaters, and Russian books published in the West for adults. Their friends paid them back in the intangible currency of erudite conversations and camaraderie.

Max looked nothing like a typical *bariga*. With his big head on his powerful torso, his shock of greyish-red hair, and his dishevelled red beard, he could easily pass for an epic hero of Russian ballads or a mighty Viking, were it not for his short statute. Yet, his body, his small but powerful hands, exuded a sense of great physical prowess. His easy laugh, deep baritone, and sincere warmth quickly put you at ease. Max's smile, though, never quite reached his eyes, of a rare bright green. Like many painters, he had a particular way of looking at the people he talked to, quickly summing up the face of his interlocutor, cannibalizing their features with his shrewd gaze. Max, a gentle giant of a short statute, seemed to be one of those people around whom life wasn't a chain of battles but a thrilling adventure on a sunny, breezy day. And Sasha visibly changed in his presence. Her eyes mellowed every time she turned them to Max, a barely perceptible smile touching her lips. The restrained tension you sensed in her melted away, and her proud and flinty demeanour softened. I saw them together for the first time as they were leaning over the books he'd just brought, their heads almost touching. What a contrast, I thought, between austere Sasha, with her long thin limbs, dark eyes, and hair and jovial, laid-back, full-lipped, light-skinned Max, half a head shorter than her.

"You wanted Robert Herrick? The last time he was published was in 1841, in Odoevsky's translation. I suppose I could get you that, if I really look."

"Oh, Odoyevsky I've got. I was looking for the original."

"I'll put a word in with one collector I know. Sasha, of all my customers, you saddle me with the most difficult tasks!"

And then they'd both lean back and take a puff, she on her usual cigarettes, he on a pipe with an amber mouthpiece, the likes of which I'd never seen. While they were smoking, my attention shifted to my daughter. I brought her along for little Annie to have a playmate for the evening. But I had to be on the watch. Rita thrived on the noisy dramas she'd stage with one goal in mind, as far as I could tell: to watch helpless adults go bonkers. I brought along a bag full of Rita's clothing that she'd grown out of. They might fit Annie, I thought, a big and chubby baby who, though younger than my daughter by two years, was almost as tall. I warned Sasha not to look at Rita's clothing in front of her, a possessive and jealous kid.

Her hands on her hips, lips pressed tight, Rita looked around. Not finding anything to entertain herself with, she focused on shy Annie. "You like my doll?" Then she quickly withdrew the bait and hid it behind her back. Annie stretched out one hand for the doll, the index of her other hand lodged in her mouth, her eyes wide open in anticipation. Rita twirled the doll in front of the perplexed girl, stuck out her tongue as far as it went, then quickly hid the doll behind her back again. Annie silently endured several rounds of sadistic teasing before finally her pink, milky cheeks folded into a mask of utter suffering. Her trembling lips released a heart-wrenching scream. But not even that could soften the heart of my little monster. Triumphantly, she watched Annie turning crimson, her screams alternating with spasmodic sobs. At this moment, Max stood up from the table, lifted Annie up, and took her in his powerful arms. She cuddled against his chest while he stroked her reddish curls, gently rocking her. Soon, Annie stopped sobbing, and peace was restored. I hurried to say goodbye and took my unperturbed troublemaker away.

4

It was Max who came up with the idea that would change Sasha's life. On the outskirts of Moscow, Boris Krivin, Max's acquaintance, was organizing poetry readings in his studio apartment. Boris worked in an obscure research institute penning articles on the history of Soviet technology. That, however, couldn't satisfy the ambitions of a young man whose dream was to edge himself somehow into the vaunted circles of writers and poets.

This is how Sasha described to me what happened next. "My first impression of Boris," she said, "was of somebody tall and lanky, with colourless, albino-pale hair and skin, closely set eyes, and thin lips, He was easily excitable. I remember watching his Adam's apple travelling up and down his ostrich neck as he dramatically flung his arms up in the air, his high-pitched, metallic voice shifting into a falsetto at the end of each sentence."

"Alexandra, darling!" Sasha mimicked the man, "Our young people thirst for poetry! We've had two readings already, and they were incredible. You won't believe this, but Tarkovsky himself promised to come."

"Which Tarkovsky?" asked Sasha with incredulity. "The son or the father?"

"Arseny Tarkovsky himself, the greatest poet of our times, the father of the greatest filmmaker of our time. Promised to read his unpublished stuff. And by the way, I had to work hard for that. He'll bring his wife too. You should see her. An absolute beauty, even at her age."

"How do you know?"

"I was invited. Saw her as I see you now."

"You mean...Tarkovsky invited you to his home?" asked Max, silent until now. "How did you manage that?"

"A trade secret, I'm afraid. Wonderful people, these Tarkovskys. Old stock, you know. Had tea with them. He's on crutches, of course. Hops around on one leg like a pro. Must be used to it since the war. You have to come, Alexandra. I'll dedicate the evening to you."

"But what can I offer?" Sasha asked, throwing a sidelong glance at Max.

"Max told me you've done some seventeenth century Brits, right? What are they called, Cavalier? How about that? We never heard of them. It could be fun."

But Sasha hesitated. "I doubt that'll be of interest to the general public. Robert Herrick, Richard Lovelace, they're pretty difficult... more for specialists."

"Is Shervinsky good enough for you? He's coming."

"I didn't think he was alive."

"He's still kicking. You wouldn't believe it. He just churned out a new translation of *The Iliad*, at eighty-three! Max, tell her we need her. Time to get your stuff out of your desk, sweetheart. Time to let the people hear you."

"Don't push her," said Max, his eyes scrutinizing Boris.

"Oh, we want you, Alexandra, we do. But you know what? Have you got something more contemporary? You translate modern American stuff, Max told me?"

"Yes. Twentieth century. Wallace Stevens. William Carlos Williams. Others."

"Great! We just have to make sure that there's nothing...well, you know what I mean."

"Of course, not to worry."

"Well, what do they write about, then? In two words? Just so I know."

"I told you, nothing ideological. The usual poetic themes: the human condition, love, death, nature. Some poets are whimsical. A very different sensibility from what we're used to. A poem about a blackbird is a good example."

"A blackbird? My God, such trivia. No, no, I didn't mean it like that, but you know, I like that naive quality about Americans. I really do. Russians would never avail themselves to writing about a bird."

"Oh, Boris, come on! Is Pushkin trivial? 'Godly birdie knows neither labour, nor concerns.' A quote from a Bible of course, but it's a lovely poem."

"Okay. You win. If it has to be blackbird, we'll have a blackbird. I'm not going to argue with an expert here. I'll have to put you down after Pasternak though. He tentatively agreed to come as well."

Max chuckled. "You do get out much, do you?"

"Actually, I have to. Evgeny Borisovich said he'd read some

of his father's poems, and then excerpts from the new biography on his father. He's working on it now. Do you know that he has all his father's archives? Keep your fingers crossed. We might be lucky enough to be the first to hear them!"

"Wait!" Sasha shook her head in disbelief. "How do you know Evgeny Pasternak?"

"As the proverb goes: The head on my shoulders is not just for wearing a hat. Speaking of hats, last winter Pasternak was giving a talk in the Literary Museum. At the end, I, by mistake, grabbed his fur hat from the rack in the lobby. It looked exactly like mine, exactly! So we met, exchanged the hats. I swear, he looks like the spitting image of his father. And I go, 'Evgeny Borisovich, I know how busy you are. Your contribution to Russian letters is incalculable! The young people of this city are dying to meet you. Would you kindly...' And so on. By the way, do you mind if I call you Sasha or even Sashenka?"

"Call me whatever you like."

"My sweet Sasha! I want you to know why I'm doing all this. In case you're still wondering."

"Yes?"

"In a hundred years from now, somebody will ask, 'What was the literary process like in Moscow of the seventies and eighties? What did Pasternak's son sound like? Or the famous Tarkovsky? Or Levik, with his wreaths of sonnets?' And we'll have their voices. On tape."

"You're going to record them?"

"That's the whole idea! We'll make two copies. I'll keep one suitcase with tapes at my place, and somebody else should keep the duplicates. Just in case. For posterity." There was a pause. Then Boris broke the silence."Max, I would have asked you as a friend, but, on the other hand..."

"Don't ask Max!" Sasha interrupted. "You know his line of work!"

Max said, "Well, I don't mind if..."

"No, Max, no!" Sasha stretched her arm toward him in agitation.

"Sashenka is right. Just to be on the safe side, you shouldn't. Who will get all our books for us? Mind you, there's absolutely no risk involved. No fools there, you understand, in terms of content. Marya Ivanovna will, I'm sure, send a couple homing pigeons. To spare us any trouble." He laughed in his breezy manner. Marya Ivanovna was code for KGB homing pigeons, for the bureau's clandestine agents.

"I'll do it," Sasha said."I'll keep the suitcase with the copies."

5

Boris was lucky to have his own place, a one-room apartment serving him as a bedroom, dining room, and study. One wall of the living room was lined with bookshelves, but Sasha couldn't identify a single title: every book was wrapped in white paper and put on the shelf backward, with the binding to the wall. A white shower curtain covering the shelves from floor to the ceiling provided the final degree of separation from the greedy eyes and hands of any potential predator.

Twenty or thirty lovers of poetry sat on a bed, or nabbed a spot around the window. The lucky ones occupied two rows of chairs borrowed from the neighbours and arrayed at the front of the room, where a poet would overlook the audience. When Sasha's turn came, she lowered her eyes, collected her thoughts, and looked around: mostly young faces, some older. She started with her translations of Robert Frost, the ones that she'd managed to get published in poetry journals. She preserved the rhymes where Frost had composed them. It went well: descriptions of nature, depictions of rural life – her audience could relate to those. But Wallace Stevens' "Thirteen Ways of Looking at a Blackbird" was met with silence. The abstract non-rhyming poem was totally alien to a Russian ear. The two girls sitting in the middle of the first row struck Sasha with expressions of undisguised boredom. They looked strangely alike these two: both blond, starry eyed, and in pretty but discreet dresses. At the end of the evening, the girls disappeared. Nobody knew their names. The homing pigeons, thought Sasha. The girls were the homing pigeons.

6

For six months, Sasha regularly took long rides on two buses to Boris's place. Every once in a while, Max would be there to keep her company. Introspective by nature, she didn't make other friends, but she was grateful that her work, her craft, carried out in solitude before, had finally found an audience. And Boris Krivin proved to be a better person than she initially thought. His bubbling, high-pitched enthusiasm attracted more and more people. Through "grapevine radio", half of Moscow now knew about Krivin's poetry evenings, which opened doors for him that had been tightly shut before. He now seemed to know everybody of importance in literary circles. Boris was prone to telling jokes and being the first to laugh at them, but he was a good sport once you got to know him better. He even lent Sasha a volume of Tsvetaeva from his shower-curtain shelf. It was obvious he liked her.

It was in the morning, already in the fall, Annie at school and the neighbours gone to work, when four men rang the doorbell of Sasha's communal apartment. One was wearing a uniform, the other three in plainclothes. Once inside her room, the shortest, pudding-faced one, opened the flap of his jacket, quickly flicked the KGB ID in front of Sasha's nose, and then closed the flap. Another, totally bald, also in plainclothes, showed her a warrant to search the premises. They seemed to know what they were looking for and quickly extracted a suitcase with tapes from under Annie's bed. They browsed through her papers and books, but didn't seem to find anything of interest, except a volume of Tzvetaeva poetry, which they confiscated. They also took her typewriter and, after a couple of hours, left. After, Sasha's first instinct was to knock on Max's door, but she thought better of it. She sat, pressing her hands against her temples, trying to calm the onslaught of a headache. From her small fridge, she extracted an onion and started munching on it without being aware of what she was doing, an old habit from a postwar hungry childhood, when her mother attempted to save her from scurvy. In the evening, she went out and called Krivin from a telephone booth. Nobody answered.

When she got a phone call summoning her to the KGB for interrogation, her first thought was to grab Annie and disappear. She didn't sleep all night, and in the morning, she went to Lubyanka, the infamous KGB quarters.

7

Sasha couldn't tell the rank of the uniformed woman sitting behind the desk, under the portrait of Dzerzinsky, the founder of the KGB, on the wall.

"Please sit down,"said her interrogator, fixing Sasha with the unblinking, KGB eyes, which Sasha determined to be typical of their ilk: light steel, shrewd yet impenetrable.

Dropping her gaze, Sasha kept her own down while trying to collect herself. A clandestine booklet that had been circulating Moscow in the seventies, at the peak of the arrests, instructed potential victims how to behave during interrogations. Avoid eye contact with the interrogator, it said, you may not be able to withstand it. But now Sasha quickly raised her eyes. She'd met this woman before, but where? And then she knew: no other but Alyona Lebedeva was presiding over a massive oak table. But was it really her? Not much was left of the ephemeral beauty Sasha had failed at the exams. The braid was gone, replaced by a bleached perm. Her then large and luminescent eyes were now barely visible within the cushions of her sockets. Her high cheekbones had become the most prominent features of her face. The hefty woman in front of her had spread in width, and was almost obese, and though still young, she looked like a typical middle-aged woman in the lower echelons of a bureaucracy, with a stiff, pompous expression on her fat face, bland like an udder. Women on party committees, and unions, in the city halls, and passport-issue offices, anywhere where they could and would say "no," wielding power over hopeless mortals at whim.

"Well, well! Nice to see you, Alexandra Markovna! Talk about coincidences in this life. You probably don't remember me? But I remember you very clearly. Entrance exams to law school? No? Still don't recall?"

Sasha didn't break her silence.

"Not a problem!" exclaimed Lebedeva, rubbing her hands together. "We are old acquaintances, but this, of course, has no bearing on things we need to discuss here. You were summoned here, why?" She shot the question across the table, her joviality extinguished in a blink.

"You'd know more than me," Sasha replied curtly. "You summoned me. I didn't summon myself."

An expression of surprise flickered across Lebedeva's face, but she quickly suppressed it. "Fair enough. We'll find out in a jiff. But before we begin, please sign this."

"What is it? A non-disclosure?" Sasha leaned over the document. She remembered the clandestine instructional booklet: Don't sign any non-disclosure papers. You have no secrets from yourself. How the KGB keep its secrets is its business. Refuse to give any evidence that can incriminate you, your family, or your friends.

You have a legal right to do so.

"I'm not going to sign anything," Sasha said calmly.

"Well, I have to warn you that confrontation is not in your best interests, Alexandra Markovna." Lebedeva shook her head in distressed empathy, then opened a file sitting on her desk. "Yours is a serious case, I'm sorry to tell you: participation in anti-Soviet propaganda. That's number one. Aiding and abetting the CIA. That's number two. You understand what's at stake for you, don't you?"

Sasha felt blood rushing into her face, a familiar throbbing in her temple, the harbinger of a migraine. She collected herself, assuming a tone of total indifference. "A mistake. It has nothing to do with me."

"I wish, I wish! But we have facts, Alexantra Markovna, and facts, as you know, are very stubborn things."

"I repeat. This is a mistake."

"Ah! Here we go again! I can't tell you how many times I hear that same phrase: 'It's a mistake, it's not me.' But we don't make mistakes, here and we don't interrogate innocent people. You took part in those gatherings, those so-called poetry parties, didn't you?"

"No, I didn't," said Sasha, and immediately regretted her words. They have your suitcase, idiot.

"I need to warn you," Lebedeva noted calmly, "giving false statements is a criminal offence."

"You misunderstood me. What I meant is that I didn't participate in anything remotely political. Anything that can qualify as involvement in any illegal activity. Poetry readings don't."

"That's fine," said Lebedeva, as if the answer had suddenly satisfied her. "At least you don't deny you've been there. By the way, are you the member of the Communist Party?"

"No."

"And yet you teach at the school of journalism? In Moscow State University? The vanguard of our ideological front. Interesting!"

"I'm a lab technician. That's my official title."

"I see. And what kind of music you like? Do you love Wagner?"

"Why?"

"You didn't answer my question."

"I don't care one way or another. Maybe some Wagner, sure."

"Maybe? Hitler loved him too." She paused, then said in a softened voice: "You may not believe me, but I'm worried about you. Your case doesn't look good, and I'm willing to help you. But you have to help the investigation in return, Alexandra Markovna. Now, going back to your so-called poetry meetings. In case you've forgotten, which you tend to do, unfortunately, let me remind you that you went to Boris Krivin's apartment twice in February, twice in March, and three times in April. In fact, over a six-month period, you went about nineteen times. A real dedication to poetry, isn't it?"

"It's my profession. I translate poetry from English, French, and Spanish."

"So what did you do at Krivin's apartment, exactly?"

"Read my translations."

"What's your relationship to him?"

"An acquaintance."

"And here we are again. But why? Why? We're not innocent children, are we? Have a look at this picture. Here's Boris Krivin on the left, another man on the right, and you, right in the middle. All three smiling. Their arms around your shoulders. Good friends, eh? And by the way, this man on the right. What's his name? Oh? Can't remember again? Let me remind you. It's your neighbour, Max Ruben. The man you have a more than neighbourly relationship with, by the way, much more."

Instantly drenched in sweat, Sasha lost all her composure and half-rose from her chair. "Lies! All lies!"

"Why are you so upset all of a sudden?"

"You're blackmailing me! Who told you this?"

"Ruben himself did. We have his written testimony."

"I don't believe you! Show me!"

"In a minute. You didn't answer my question. If it's not true, why such agitation?"

"Because...because you have no right. I mean, nobody has the right to meddle in...my...in people's private lives!"

"And you do? Comrade Rubin is married. You don't consider your actions to constitute an immoral intrusion, to put it mildly? Your relationship with him – you don't think it constitutes the disruption of a married couple's peaceful life? And not only that. You exploited them. You took advantage of their kindness. You'd happily leave your daughter in their care and take off at night to engage in some dubious activities in the city. It's remarkable how Comrade Rubin was always ready to come to your rescue. Even more surprising, his wife co-operated. Extraordinary generosity on her part."

Sasha scoffed. "I don't know who your informants are. But...I refuse to have you teach me morality. I remember you well, Alyona

Lebedeva. Not a word of English, and yet you insisted, you begged for good marks! You couldn't make it to the university, but you made a spectacular career in this despicable organization. I presume you don't need much education to work here!"

Lebedeva's face grew ashy, and she sat back in the chair, mouth agape. But she quickly regained her composure. "You'll regret your words, Luntz! Regret them bitterly. I have some news for you. Max Rubin is implicated as much as you are, but he turned out much more co-operative. He's the one who described your relationship in full detail."

"Provocation!" exclaimed Sasha. "He couldn't have. I don't believe a word of it."

"That's your right. But let's move on. Boris Krivin told us – we have his written statements as well – that initially you wanted to read some...cava...cavalier poems, correct?"

"Cavalier poets," Sasha said dismissively.

"He tried to talk you out of that, didn't he? Thinking it's not appropriate for young people. Correct?"

"He thought the poems were too archaic."

"Cavalier? Were they horse riders or what?"

"Those poets belonged to the circle of King Charles I. I'm sure they could ride horses too."

"In other words, they were monarchists? King's lapdogs?"

"Loyal to the king, yes, not to Cromwell."

"Who's Cromwell?"

"You can look him up in history textbooks."

Lebedeva raised her voice. "And you decided to translate the filthy propaganda of these lackeys! You, to whom our government entrusted the future warriors of our ideological front!"

"This has nothing to do with propaganda. These poets celebrated love, nature, and the joys of life."

"Joys of life? What makes you think these monarchists, these pests on the back of proletariat, can be of the slightest interest to Soviet youth? What can they offer to our builders of communism? Nostalgia for monarchy? You personally, do you hope to replace our system by a monarchy? Is that what you long for?"

"Ridiculous!"

"I suggest you chose your words more carefully. If it's ridiculous, why do you bother to translate these poems?"

"Don't distort my words. I didn't call this poetry ridiculous. I translate it out of professional interest."

"Namely?"

"You want me to explain technical challenges that I try to..."

"Challenges! Sneaking in hostile bourgeois ideology under the disguise of debauchery you call love and the joy of life! However, as we have established already, Krivin tried to dissuade you. Tried to prevent you from harming our youth, as he wrote in his statement. Initially, you agreed. But what did you do next? Something much worse! You chose "Thirteen Ways of Looking at a Blackbird" by some American spy. What was his name?"

"Wallace Stevens."

"Yes, that CIA agent."

"This is absurd! He was a poet! He died in the fifties!"

"Don't be naive. The CIA constantly uses the names of the

dead. It's clear as day that the piece you read was their secret code: 'The only moving thing is the eye of the blackbird.' Meaning that a CIA agent under the code name Blackbird has already crossed our borders and is now doing what his master tasked him with: subversion. And further: 'The blackbird is a small part of a pantomime.' Obviously, the poem implies that the Blackbird is not acting alone. He's part of a cell. And here again, clear as day: they have already recruited you. 'A man and a woman are one.' Obviously, 'a man' stands for the CIA. 'Blackbird' stands for an agent operating in our country. What's left? A woman. And who is that woman? You. Working in cohort, conspiring.'A man and a woman and a blackbird are one.'" Lebedeva took a deep breath and suddenly lowed her voice: "How much have you been paid for betraying your country?"

"What?" Sasha knew then, with perfect clarity, that she was going underwater again. The same familiar sensation: squeamish disgust and scorn. No panic this time, no fear, just apathy. Exhaustion and resignation. You hit the wall: there is no reasoning with them. The only thing you can do for yourself is get out of here... by agreeing. With an enormous effort, she shook off her stupor, put her elbows on Lebedeva's desk and leaned forward. Then cleared her throat. Looking straight into the eyes of her tormentor, she said in a low and measured voice: "You know it's bullshit. All of it. I know it too. You make it up as you go. And I'm telling you this: I'm not going to sign any of this nonsense. Not now, not ever. My father was a close friend of Stalin. And if you do anything to me or Max Rubin, then my father's friends will immediately take all the necessary measures. You career will be finished."

"Your father – who?"

"My father, Cheburidze. The right hand of Comrade Stalin in Georgia. Awarded three medals. Fell as a hero at war. We have powerful relatives. They won't allow you to blackmail the daughter of a hero. They won't! You're seriously jeopardizing your career, Comrade Lebedeva."

8

That blatant lie about her father was not a calculated move. It came to Sasha instinctively, as an act of total desperation, and the very last resort. It'll take them some time to discover her lie, and then, well, come what may. But in the meantime, in the meantime she'd get some respite. Three weeks have passed and just when Sasha thought she was off the hook, the interrogations have resumed.

Different officers filled in behind the oak table, but Lebedeva didn't come back. Usually, Sasha was summoned to Lubyanka late in the evening, and she returned home at dawn, on the first subway train. In the morning, she'd get Annie ready for school, then go to job she was still miraculously holding. After several visits to Lubyanka, her hair turned totally white, and she started cutting it short. After the first encounter with Lebedeva, she knocked on Max's door. His wife, Elena, opened it a crack: "He's out of town. Back? No, he didn't tell." Sasha tried to call Krivin again, from different telephone booths, with no luck.

She finally took the long, familiar subway ride to Zuzino, where

Krivin lived, and she knocked on his door. No answer. She waited. A
door to the right opened, and a woman in a chintz housecoat came out
holding a bucket with garbage. She threw a quick glance at Sasha and
hurried downstairs, her slippers padding off each step.

Finally, in early winter, she ran into Krivin. The first snowfall
had powdered the trees along Gogolevsky Boulevard. The benches,
occupied in summer by grandmothers with their young charges, were
now empty. A crow walked around with an air of importance, leaving
next little footprints on the seat of bench. Sasha noticed Krivin's lanky
figure in a long, black coat and fashionable grey cap, thick mohair
muffler wrapped around his throat in a knot, the way the French
used to do. He seemed to be waiting for somebody near Gogol's
monument, a pigeon perched on a great writer's snow-powdered head.
Krivin shifted from foot to foot, shivering in the cold wind. Sasha was
suddenly overtaken by fear, but she approached him anyway. When
he saw her, the icicles melted in his eyes, and his small, almost lipless
mouth stretched into a tentative smile.

"Sasha, darling! How fortunate! Of all people, you're the one
I've most needed to see. And here you materialized out of thin air."

Lying, flashed through Sasha's mind. Every word is a lie. "I
called you several times," she said coldly. "Never any answer. I even
knocked at your door."

Krivin glanced at his watch."You know what, I did want to
talk to you...but right now, well, I have a few minutes. Where are you
going?"

"To Kropotkinskaya."

"I'll walk you there."

Doesn't want me to see who he's waiting for, Sasha thought.

They went along the boulevard, toward the subway station. As they walked, Krivin was the first to break the silence. "I know what happened to you. It's unfortunate, but you're not the only one. They searched my place too. Confiscated my typewriter. What am I going to do without it? Obviously, we've put a moratorium on the whole thing for now. Till the dust settles. But the main thing, the suitcase is safe. Yours, they took away, you're saying, but there were duplicates. The originals are in a safe place. I'd already taken care of that. And you know what? We have fulfilled our historical mission. Future generations will thank us."

Sasha stopped short. "Are you serious, or are you making fun of me? They threatened me with jail! I have a young child! But of course you don't care petty little trifles like that. You're a snitch for them!"

Boris stopped and turned his face to Sasha. His thin, bloodless lips quivered. "What did you just say?"

"You heard me."

"Is that what you think of me, Alexandra?"

"Convinced."

"You're wrong!"

"Why would I believe you?"

"I swear to you on..."

"Don't!" She detested the way his voice raised to falsetto. "Don't swear on anything."

She started walking away from him, but he quickly caught up with her.

"Listen, Sasha, you said you knocked at my door, and I wasn't there. That's because I tried to escape. Got to Podolsk. The moment I stepped out of the train, they were already there, on the platform waiting for me. In a way, I'm glad. It was better that way. After all, I'm responsible for the whole thing. It was my idea. Sooner or later, I had to face them. And I now know what they want."

"You do, do you? And what is it, exactly?"

"Trust me, it has nothing to do with you. You personally have nothing to be afraid of. You were summoned as a witness, not as a defendant. They're collecting *compromat* on three people, and you're not one of them."

"Who are they?"

"Listen, the less we know, the better."

Krivin quickly looked around, then, putting both hands on Sasha's shoulders, he pulled her close and looked imploringly into her eyes. "I want to tell you something. Who knows when we'll meet again and under what circumstances. You're the most beautiful woman I've ever seen. I've always admired you. Beauty and talent in one package, that's rare! I would've gone for you like that!" He snapped his fingers. "But I would never cross a friend's path. For me, friendship is sacred. And remember: I never ratted on anybody. Never!" He quickly pecked her on her cheek and was gone.

That was the last time she saw him.

9

I took a sip from my third cup of tea. "Do you think Krivin was the KGB stooge?"

Sasha sat silently, her immobile gaze fixed at something only she could see. "Max thought he was." She said. "Maybe the KGB tasked him with starting poetry parties so he could trawl in as many writers as possible. Or maybe initially it was his idea, but at some point he got entangled in the very net he helped cast. Nobody can tell now."

"But after all these terrible things, why did they let you go?"

"I lucked out," Sasha responded. "See, there was a period in the seventies and eighties when the KGB would avoid arresting artists, writers, dissidents. In case they had access to Western journalists. The KGB didn't want the West to find out. Instead, they tried to break us through interrogation."

But it was only a matter of time before she was fired from the university. And though this time she wasn't arrested, the threat of arrest didn't disappear. Soviet law stipulated that to be out of work for more than four months was a criminal offence, officially called "parasitism," punished by five years in jail. At the same time, the KGB made sure that "parasites sucking blood out of the proletariat" would be denied work anywhere they might turn. Suspected of disloyalty, physicists, mathematicians, doctors, biologists, linguists, professors, writers, scholars, and artists could no longer hope to find their habitual refuges as street sweepers or janitors or boiler room attendants. Some "categories of citizens," like women on maternity leave, handicapped, pensioners, and underage children, were exempt.

And then, at the beginning of the eighties, newly installed KGB Chief Andropov turned the whole city of Moscow on its head by orchestrating raids and ambushes on the parasites who happened to be out and about in full daylight. These slackers were snatched out of long lines, an ever-present feature of Moscow's landscape. They were plucked from bus stops and train stations, parks and subways. Luckily, Russians are ingenious. Enduring. Adjustable. Wonderfully patient. In no time, bread-and-butter queues started looking like kindergartens or nursing homes, full of pensioners and young children. The huge anthill of a city seemed suddenly abandoned, its inhabitants deep in hiding, hunkering down in their attics, their junk rooms, their crawl spaces, barricaded behind their Ficus plants and bottles of moonshine. All you could hear from their crooks and crannies were muted stirrings.

It was at this time that I, a young, freshly divorced, mother of two (my son was born when Rita was four years old) decided to venture outdoors. I don't recall now what exactly I needed: a bottle of milk, a loaf of bread at a corner store? It had to be a very quick sortie, while Rita was in a kindergarten and her eight-month-old brother was having a nap.

"Your passport!" barked a policeman, who was the first to spot me. "No?"

He detained me and brought me to a station to be identified. Without any documents or personal belongings, I could've been a lawless hobo, for sure, a parasite.

"I'm a breast feeding mother!" I protested.

"Prove it!" shouted a policeman.

I began to unbutton my blouse.

"Stop this outrage! Or I'll arrest you for pornography."

Both of my children were gifted with boisterous vitality. Baby Alex was a little giant. I imagined the screams that would come out of his mighty lungs the moment he woke up and realized his mommy was gone. The power of those screams could collapse the walls of our apartment as easily as the trumpets of the ancient Hebrews collapsed the walls of Jericho. After three hours of interrogation, the policeman finally let me go. This event marked the first time Alex made an attempt to walk. When I returned, I found him, his face redder than the Soviet flag, next to the front door, on his way to raid the city in search of his stray mother.

It would've been wrong to assume that Vera Petrovna's worldview prevented her from noble deeds. Grumbling and rumbling, she called her friend Galina, and Galina called Tamara, and Tamara called Sergey Michailovich, who couldn't say no Tamara, his former lover during his first and present – his third – marriages. Being at the same time the head of a trauma department in a central hospital, Sergey Michailovich agreed to look at Sasha's left leg, the one that was slightly shorter than the right one. He warned her, though, that the shorter leg wasn't short enough for him to issue her a disability certificate of the first degree, which could shield her from parasitism and provide her with a minuscule pension. Instead, he promised her a piece of paper that she could keep in her pocket when out and about.

"How did you manage?" I asked.

"As I said, Max helped a lot. Also, on Sundays, Vera would take Annie to the zoo sometimes. When her husband was still alive, they'd bring Annie to their dacha for a weekend. There was a lake there, and Annie loved to swim. See, Annie was an easy, accommodating child. You'd give her toys, and she'd sit quietly and play with them. Since childhood, she loved to draw. I think she has a real talent for art. It's too bad that now, with two kids, she doesn't touch a brush. Vera had no children of her own, and she had a soft spot in her heart for my daughter. When Annie married an American and left, Vera was distraught. It didn't sit right with her at all, the American part."

Thinking about my life in Moscow in the 70s and 80s, I realize how lucky I was. Apart from being once detained by the police for trying to buy milk for my children in the middle of the day, I was able to avoid direct encounters with the KGB. But those who got in the KGB clutches and survived the experience to tell the story...well, they were leery of telling it partly because they had been forced to sign a non-disclosure agreement, partly out of fear. But now, almost forty years later, I wanted to ask Sasha how it was all possible? How did they manage to rule and subjugate the whole nation? My friend gave me a strange look and ruffled her short hair, her new habit. "I'm not sure I have any special insights," she said. "When I came face to face with Lebedeva...well...but even then, you're inside a puzzle of which you only see one piece. Did I tell you I've been volunteering for Memorial for several years now? I went through thousands of files on the executed, looking at faces that aren't around anymore. That's when the puzzle started coming together. You read the interrogation protocols, and you know what struck me most? That it was such an ordinary, commonplace affair..."

"How do you mean?"

"The KGB was us! It was part of the society, not separate from it. Same five-year plans, same socialist competitions, like in a plant, say, producing tires or bricks. You fulfill the plan, you get promotions, you get bonuses. The KGB worked on a schedule, like everybody else. It had to uncover a certain number of plots by certain deadlines. Some had to involve the CIA and who knows what else. Once the goal was determined, the fabricators get down to work. They'd come up with fantastical scripts. Then investigation simply followed them. Like in Aleshkovsky's *Kangaroo*, remember? No? Well, it's a funny book! The interrogator is an accommodating guy: 'Let's just get this over with.' He lays out several scenarios. 'If you want the lightest sentence, I strongly recommend the Kangaroo script. Confess that on July 14, 1789, you cruelly and violently raped the oldest kangaroo in the zoo.'"

"It would've been funny," I remarked, "if it hadn't been so sad, as the saying goes. But why did they go to such lengths? Extracting confessions, guilty pleas. If they knew perfectly well the outcome: jail, labour camps, executions – why? Why did they play at legitimacy? Why pretend to observe 'legal procedures'? Why follow their profane constitution? It all took a whole army of agents, investigates, prison guards, camp guards, executioners, thousands of people. Why?"

"Millions, not thousands. And look at the result! As a tool of intimidation, it worked wonders. It's one thing to have some kind of criminal or rogue accusing you. It's another thing when it's the State, with the capital "S," with all the trappings of legitimacy.

"But you know, Sasha, the fact that we can talk about it openly, that to me is mind-boggling! I never thought I'd live long enough to see this!" I exclaimed.

"Yes, as I said, we managed to plant the seeds of the civil society. But just the seeds...because the KGB is back...I mean, it has never really left, it just holed up for a while."

Sasha's pessimism irked me, but who was I to argue with her?

"You know," she continued," there are certain axioms in physics: If you jump from the tenth floor, gravity will send you to your death. Same with moral laws, laws of the human psyche. Some things are possible, others inconceivable. But they created the lobotomized reality where the inconceivable becomes real. Take Stalin's show trials from the thirties. Heroes of the revolution, Lenin's closest allies. Suddenly they all plead guilty to most hideous crimes. You watch, you read it in every newspaper, and whom would you believe? Your own eyes and the government of your great country that you've been taught to love more than yourself? Or do you believe those traitors? How can you make sense and reconcile the irreconcilable? If even such great leaders turned out to be saboteurs and turncoats, then every man, including me, could be accused of any crime. I'll deflect the danger by spying and denouncing my neighbour, on the slim chance that it'll save me. Suspicion, mistrust, paranoia, and betrayal on a national scale, exactly what the state was after. My image of hell is not the frying pans, no, but the world where lies, fabrications, and slander are indistinguishable from the truth."

"Surely, that's now all in the past? And surely not everybody would confess and incriminate oneself?"

"Most would. It's a matter of time and a method of torture. It occurred to me once that the Soviet jurisprudence used the same methods as Medieval Europe."

Well, that was too far fetched, I thought. "How can you compare a modern industrial state with feudal societies?"

"I'll tell you. Take *Spanish boots* and manuals about torture. Why were they so widely spread in the Middle Ages? Because crime investigation in the Middle Ages didn't have much to do with collecting evidence. Evidence and a proof of the crime were all tied up in confessions from a suspect. And the USSR revived that practice. The Soviets didn't use the *Spanish boot* or maybe they did, but how about this: one interrogator, with a fecund imagination, put a gas mask on his victim, gradually reducing oxygen before cutting it off, then turning it on again. You just have to do that half a dozen times before the victim will sign anything you put in front of him. Of beatings and sleep deprivation, I won't even talk. They were routine. But there were simpler measures, no less efficient. Your stand your victim facing the wall for five days, not hours but days. And of course, you promise a pardon as soon as the accused confesses and signs. If that doesn't help, they'll arrest your children and torture them in front of you. Who wouldn't break then? Except that signing your confession meant signing your death sentence, especially, in Stalin's times. There'll come a time when death will look like an unbelievable gift. That's what they tell you.

"But what happened to Max, then? He was the one who implicated you."

"How can you say that?" Sasha exclaimed, her voice trembling.

"Didn't he introduce you to Krivin?"

"Yes, but Max isn't to blame! The choice was totally mine. And in any case, he suffered much more than me."

10

I remembered how Max once invited me, Rita, and little Annie to his place. He was alone. As he was showing me some of his canvasses, the girls studied, in shy bewilderment, the riot of bright colours on display. Where was Sasha then? I don't recall. But I remember how Max put both girls at ease, amusing them with funny faces he quickly sketched on a piece of paper.

In a voice choked with emotion, Sasha told me what had happened when she was interrogated. At the beginning, the KGB was concocting a group case against her and the other poetry reading participants, including Max, even though he hardly ever attended the events. But at some point, the KGB decided to drop the CIA angle and make up different scenarios to prosecute each person individually. Max was accused of several crimes. One was selling books outside bookstores, a "speculation," punished by three to seven years in jail, with the confiscation of property, in many cases. Another was much more serious. Max had published abroad, in the United States, in *Ardis,* a catalogue of non-conformist Soviet artists. He wrote an introduction, comments, and a biography of each artist. Now, the KGB had all the names of these dissident artists in their official records. They went on a rampage arresting them and confiscating their art.

"It was terrible for Max," Sasha told me, "he had unwittingly betrayed all his friends."

That was bad enough, but then the worst of all crimes surfaced: his contact with foreigners. Max knew art collectors in the United States, people who were keen on buying the Soviet underground work. Once, when they came to Moscow, he was their liaison, and he negotiated prices on behalf of the artists for a small commission. What would've been a perfectly legitimate activity in the West, was a serious multi-faceted crime in the Soviet Union. Direct contact with foreigners? Receiving dollars that bypassed the state? Hard currency belonged to the state. Not one sketch, one painting could leave the Soviet borders without the state permission. The KGB couldn't have dreamt of a better case.

"By the way," Sasha added. "I knew nothing about this part of his activities. Max had never told me."

"You think Max confessed?"

Sasha gave me a sidelong look. "You never ask people questions like that, do you? They must have been tracking him for a long time, and finally they pieced things together. And of course, there was a catalogue, which was material evidence. Max got the most terrifying punishment of all: they locked him up in a psychiatric asylum. 'Schizophrenia of a sluggish flow.' A diagnoses invented specifically for dissidents."

"Did they keep him there for a long time?"

"What constitutes a long time? Is six months long, or short? For Max, well, he returned a ruined man. Almost a vegetable."

11

The dissidents who survived both the gulags and the psychiatric asylums reported that the latter were much more horrific: they could ruin people faster and irrevocably. When sentenced to a gulag, the accused was told their term. Even though it could be repeated or increased for no reason, at least there were some numbers involved, arbitrary as they were. Psychiatric asylums meant indefinite incarceration. You could be kept in one for twenty years, or all your life, with no way to appeal the conclusions of the so-called medical experts. If you survived and were released, the victims of the treatment would be stripped of the basic civil rights: they were never allowed to work, to study, to drive a car. The advantage of this punishment for the state was obvious: The medical cases didn't have to be tried in court; the signature of a "doctor" was enough. That way, the state avoided bad rap in the West.

How did Max spend his days? Better not to think about it, Sasha said without looking at me. Punitive medicine was no different from a prison: guards with dogs, electric fencing. The orderlies were formerly convicted criminals who got sadistic pleasure from beating their patients. The wards were so full that many patients slept under beds. The injected neuroleptics would leave victims without the ability to talk for several days. Those who resisted the injections would be tied to a bed – arms and legs – and left in that position for several days. Whoever tried to complain to authorities would be tightly wrapped in wet sheets and placed near a radiator. As the sheets dried up, they'd squeeze the body, causing excruciating pain. Apart from physical damage to the body, the constant injection of neuroleptics into healthy people erased their personality. It turned victims into indifferent shadows of their former selves, with only a twilight of consciousness left.

After Max's arrest, his wife also seemed to vanish. Or at least, Sasha didn't see her in the usual places where neighbours used to bump into each other: neither in the kitchen nor at the sink in the corridor. But one evening, Sasha noticed a narrow streak of light coming from under Elena's door. She listened in, then quietly knocked. The person who had opened the door just a crack was barely recognizable. Against the wan light of a desk lamp, coming from inside, stood an old bedraggled woman, her voice but a whisper. "What is it you want? My husband is...he's not here. Please go. Nothing here for you now."

For a moment, Sasha was motionless, lost for words. "I see you haven't eaten," she finally said. "I can bring you some bread... some potatoes."

"I don't need anything, thank you. Leave us alone. Please!"

"Elena, let me come in. For one minute. I have something to tell you."

Sasha had no inkling of what, in this situation, could be said or done. It was just a spontaneous reaction to the sight of a wasted, shrivelled figure, her face in dark shadows. Elena stepped back, and Sasha squeezed in, then quietly closed the door behind her. The musty smell of an unaired room hit her nostrils. One of the paintings stacked against the bookcase began to slide down to the floor. Sasha quickly bent over to pick it up. Elena, with the movement of a scared bird, and unexpected agility, dashed forward.

"Don't touch, don't!"

Sasha retreated. "I'm sorry," she said. "I just wanted to tell you that...that.... I know what happened to your husband. I've been there. They let me go. They'll let him go too, you'll see."

A sharp, sob-like sound emerged from Elena's throat. "Then... then...you must have some connections there?"

"No. None. I'm sorry."

Elena's lips twitched."I don't know if you're telling me the truth. Why would you? You were always deceitful, sneaky. But it doesn't matter to me now. Nothing matters anymore..." Then all of a sudden she dropped to her knees and groped for the hem of Sasha's skirt. "I beg you, Alexandra! In the name of God the Merciful! Help us! Save Max! We have some money left. Take it all, take any painting you want, only bring him back!"

Sasha was stunned. "Money? How can you even...I know I have no right to say it, but I'm not what you think. If only I could help, I would!"

But Elena wouldn't let go of Sasha's dress, getting on her knees so she could hug Sasha's legs. Then she raised her pleading eyes to Sasha's face: "I know you can do anything you put your mind to. You always get your way. I'm weak. I could never compete with you. But now I'm begging you. Bring him back alive. He won't survive there. You know Max. You know him as well as I do. He only looks strong, but he's an artist, a gentle soul, and he won't...he won't withstand it."

Sasha put her arms around Elena, trying to lift her up, but with unexpected strength, Elena resisted.

"I know you love him," she bawled."If he comes back, he'll be yours, I promise. I'll pray for you two for the rest of my life! Everything that is dear to you, your daughter Annie, your late mother, in their names, save him! I beg you!"

12

"So what did you do?" I lowered my head to conceal my quivering lips.

"I promised her."

"Promised? What could you possibly do for her, in reality?"

"In reality, nothing. I myself was walking on a razor's edge."

"Oh, Sasha, Sasha."

"Divine powers interfered. A chance encounter."

That chance encounter happened during the prestigious International Tchaikovsky competition that once every four years attracted gifted young musicians from all over the world to Moscow. Sasha's friend, working as an official interpreter for the festival, called her with an urgent request. Her child got sick. Could Sasha substitute for her interpreting the deliberations of the jury? An informal arrangement, without letting the "Intourist" know? Two days only. Sasha said "yes" to this first case of divine interference.

Waiting for deliberations to start, Sasha leaned on a wide marble windowsill, watching a crowd mill around the vestibule of the Tchaikovsky Conservatory. "Not allowed! Don't you know the rules?" She heard the voice of a fat, middle-aged female attendant. A divine messenger in the disguise of a nagging hag, as Sasha told herself later. That was the second case of divine interference, because right after, Sasha left the vestibule and went to the entrance for a bit of peace and some fresh air. There, on top of the stairs, leading to a small square with a Tchaikovsky monument in the centre, stood a young man with a tape recorder and a badge: "Press. The Voice of America."

Sasha quickly approached him and said in English, "I'm working here as an interpreter. I have very important information. Can you spare me five minutes?"

The man looked her over."Sorry. I'm busy right now. Interviewing a pianist in a minute or two."

"I see. I'll be busy for the next two hours as well. Interpreting for a jury. But after that? Can we meet after?"

"I'm not sure," the young man said evasively. "I'll be busy till late tonight."

"How about tomorrow?"

"I'll be here the whole day," the man said decisively turning away. "You'll find me somewhere."

It's at this point that Sasha switched to Russian. "My name is Alexandra. And you? Ed? Ed, sweetheart, this is really urgent.

Somebody needs your help. Just give me a minute. Don't leave. Just wait."

She quickly descended the stairs to the square and sat on one of the benches encircling Tchaikovsky's monument. She tore a page out of her notepad and jotted down in English and Russian: "Max Rubin, a well-known Russian painter, is locked in a psychiatric prison on false political charges. He won't survive if the world doesn't interfere. Please save Max Rubin! *Ardis* in Ann Arbour, Michigan, have recently published his book. They'll have all the information."

Without signing her name, she put her note inside the festival program and handed it over to Alex, who was still waiting on the stairs for his interviewee. She watched him open the program and glance at the note. Going back to conservatory, she stopped on the stairs and, in passing, quickly whispered to Alex in English, "Thank you Ed. I know you'll help."

Five day later, the Voice of America, Radio Free Europe, and the BBC were telling the world about the plight of Max Ruben. After spending six months in the asylum, Max was released.

That was the third case of divine intervention.

13

Sasha's chain-smoking made my head swirl. Maybe she sensed it, or maybe she was just finished with this particular cigarette, extinguishing the butt alongside another ten or so, then walking over to the window. There, hidden in the jungle of potted plants, was a bowl of water with a gold fish inside. I'd never associated Sasha with ordinary domestic hobbies.

"They say the blood pressure goes down when you gaze at fish. That's why," she added, as if apologizing. "I should quit smoking. I'm sure the fish hates smoke, though it fails to complain."

"When I worked with the archives," she said, "I was looking for one file, my mother's. No, nothing had happened to her, though she came close. When they were both third-year students, she had a buddy, a close friend, apparently, exceptionally talented: the young man wrote poetry in three languages; was at home with world literature, philosophy, history; also interested in theology, a forbidden topic at the time. Then one day his own wife denounced him. The reason? Jealousy. The fact that they had a one-year-old child didn't stop her. The KGB searched their home, confiscated a Bible. That same night, Alexander, the young man's name, knocked at my mother's window pane, and standing under her window – she lived on the first floor of the hostel – he whispered to her that he expected to be arrested any moment now. He gave her his word that no matter what happened to him, he'd never mention her name. Alexander died in the uranium mines. My mother was lucky to have stayed alive. I saw his written testimony in his file. Detailed conversations with my mother. The report said the testimony was obtained under 'usage of physical impact.' Their standard euphemism for torture. I've seen so many accounts like that. My mother hoped to have a boy and call him Alexander. She had me instead, hence my name."

"Alexander has a little son, you said."

"Yes, my mother tried to find him later. But didn't find a trace."

"And the wife who betrayed her husband?"

"She quickly left the city. Nobody knew where to. Friends found out and ostracized her."

"Did I tell you what helped me cope later on? The Memorial. Getting access to the archives, talking to the relatives of the executed. We're getting queries from all over the country now. People want to know. It was easier in the early 1990s than it is now. The KGB had given access to certain archives then, although by far not all. They'd managed to destroy all the Leningrad archives, nothing left. With the Moscow archives, things are slightly better, especially the federal ones. That myth sculpted in Soviet films and books of the noble ardour of the intelligence offices, their staunch principles in the KGB – it's vile of course. They knew they were criminals. Otherwise, why would they put so much efforts into covering up their tracks and destroying the evidence?"

"Like the Nazis."

"Exactly! Except the KGB did it to their own people. We managed to identify three million victims. That's just the tip of the iceberg. Organized financial help to the victims' families. Put up the plaques with their names and last addresses, where they'd been taken away in *a Black Mary, a*s those vans for transporting the arrested were called."

"Yes, that infamous name." I said. "Another drink or maybe a cup of tea?"

"Oh, I've had enough," Sasha said, pacing her small room in

agitation. "When I started, I didn't know how important 'Memorial' would be for me. We were all so excited during the Gorbachev reforms. Our usual apathy, our fears cracked like a shell and fell off. We were free. We breathed! There was so much energy, so much enthusiasm in people. How many people? It's never been a large number. Mainly intelligentsia. Mostly in central cities. Moscow, Leningrad. Five percent maybe? Out of one hundred and fifty million. I myself was never a dissident, as you know. I don't have what it takes."

"Well, one has to have the right temperament," I noted vaguely.

"That too. But the main thing, you have to be a Buddhist, in a way."

"How do you mean?"

"No attachments. Be prepared to lose all you have. Then they can't do anything with you. But in reality, everybody has something they can't live without. I'm attached to my daughter, to my desk, my dictionaries, my poets. I sometimes felt they were waiting for me, depending on me to give them a second life in this remote, snow-clad land, Russia. I felt I couldn't let them down by disappearing."

For as long as I'd known Sasha, she'd never been in the habit of talking about herself in such a manner.

"But," she continued, "then I met Raginsky, the chairman of the Memorial. He knew my story. His father, an engineer, had been executed as an enemy of people. He himself had spent four years in a gulag. And he said to me, 'Alexandra Markovna, I want you on our team.' I accepted without a second thought. Then he said something I'd never forget: 'Memory had been banned to all of us. Oblivion has spanned generations and enveloped the whole country. Unless we return memory to our nation,' he said, 'the country can't move forward.' And then this: 'Each of us is either a victim or an executioner. There are no people in our society who wouldn't fall into one of these two categories. But now children and grandchildren want to know how their parents and grandparents had died. It's our duty to find out and tell them the truth.'" Sasha shook her head. Does all this sound too highfalutin to you? Am I boring you?"

I didn't have the nerve to tell her how disturbed I felt. It was with a sort of horror that I watched her slash open the wounds of my country, puss dripping. "Oh, no, no, of course not!" I hurried to assure her. "True, I haven't been thinking much about these things since I left Russia. Had no time, really. I was down on my luck for a long time, as you know...with two kids and all that...till I met Edwin. Then I totally immersed myself in his life, his needs. Started working for him. He's s a wonderful man, you know."

Sasha gave me a surprised look. "I thought he was an engineer. Not your line of work, or is it?"

How to explain that my hands were full with a job she would neither understand nor appreciate? Edwin designed parking lots, and I did all the administrative work. Getting the permits from the city, coordinating the work of urban planners, architects, engineers, builders – my God! Plus, we had four kids, two his and two of mine. It was hard work all around, but it finally paid off! All four have grown up; they have their own families. We could now afford travel, have a beautiful home, an apartment in Paris, a place in the Bahamas.

Life was good. None of it, though, I could share with my friend.

Not to look too boorish, I said apologetically, "You know, you're right. It's a bit boring. Kind of an ordinary, mundane life. I even suggested to Edwin, half-jokingly, but still: 'Why don't you design roads instead of parking lots? That would be way more fun. Parking is sort of a dead end, right? You've arrived and are now facing a cement wall. But with the road, you just go. Anywhere you want. One road turns into another, and it never ends.' And you know, Sasha, I would really like to do something exciting, useful in life, like you do."

"Like what?"

"Something to help Russia, maybe? You have connections."

Sasha didn't respond. She ruffled her hair and then lifted her elbows almost parallel to her shoulders, a new and awkward gesture, like a bird with clipped wings, trying to fly. I asked her if she was still translating poetry. She wasn't. There was simply no time.

"See this?" She pointed to a ragged stack of paper sitting on her small, round night table, next to a pyramid of books, an ashtray, and several bottles of medication, some standing, some lying on their sides. "Out of seven hundred submissions, I have to choose fifty. Memorial's joint project with Ulitskaya. Though it's really her idea, her baby."

I confessed I'd never heard the name.

"You've never read Ulitskaya? Then I really envy you!" Sasha rubbed her palms together, giving me a knowing smile. "I'll tell you something. No joke, it really happened. An exam in Russian literature. A student tells Professor Makagon that he has no idea who Anna Karenina was because he's never read the novel. And the professor goes, 'Well, young man, I envy you the pleasure of reading it for the first time. Come back when you have.'"

"Is Ulitskaya such a great writer?" I asked timidly.

"Not as great as Tolstoy, of course, but I'd say she's one of the leading writers in our literature, yes. Wait." Sasha walked over to her bookshelves. "I have extra copies of two of her novels. You want them? Where are they? I'll find them for you later. Anyhow, it was Ulitskaya's idea to collect the childhood memories of people who grew up roughly from 1945 to 1953, before Stalin's death. My time as well. I thought it was a great idea. Especially because Ulitskaya was interested in the ordinary: what kind of food kids had, even though most didn't have any; the clothes they wore; the games they played; what was it like to grow up in a village versus the city; their relationship with their parents, siblings, and school teachers. The response was overwhelming. Stories poured in from all over the country. One woman's most vivid memories – she's from Leningrad – was her parents' regular visits to what she calls 'Paradise.' Of the hundreds of toys sitting on the shelves of Paradise, she could choose any number for free, and her parents, likewise, could pick carpets, beautiful vases or mirrors in intricate frames. Her father's personal driver would load a truck with furniture of their choice. Though their apartment was filled to the brim, her parents continued their weekly trips to Paradise, which became a kind of hunting grounds for them. It took the author decades before she discovered the truth: her Paradise was a storage room filled with belongings confiscated from those arrested, imprisoned, or executed. Turned out her father was some big fish in the Polit Bureau. The spacious apartment they lived in, and the similar apartments of her father's friends, came fully furnished and fitted out. Paradise has stopped providing. Are you listening to me?"

"Of course. I'm just overwhelmed. Little did we know that they'd already built their Communism. I hope you'll include that one in your collection."

"Not sure I'll have space. There are so many other excellent stories. Hard to choose. Like this one, for example. The man who sent it to me was born in 1940, just before the war. His father was killed in the first year at the front. By the way, most kids of that generation didn't have fathers: wars, labour camps, arrests. Not many had mothers either. Many were raised by remote relatives. If they were lucky to have any. But this boy, he and his mother somehow survived. Hunger, unimaginable hardships, but they did survive. The mother was a nurse, by the way. After the war, in 1947, a woman, a total stranger, comes to see the boy's mother. She brings along her mentally retarded daughter. The daughter is now pregnant, raped at fifteen. The woman begs the nurse to help. But Stalin has banned abortions. The Happy Motherhood law – Stalin's usual travesty – guaranteed at least three years of gulag to both a woman and a doctor. But the nurse takes pity on the poor girl and agrees. What happens next is...well...the retarded girl lets the cat out of the bag, and the boy's mother is arrested. But here's the crux of the story. The man who sent me that story remembers how he, a small child then, was standing in front of the courthouse alone – children weren't allowed in, of course – while his mother was being sentenced to the labour camps. After the sentence, she was whisked off to prison right away. No good bye to her son. Everybody quickly left, away from trouble! The seven-year-old was standing alone, in the empty street. He had no relatives. His great country didn't care how he was going to survive or if he survived at all. But suddenly, his life was saved by somebody only slightly older than he was. Another boy came up to him and said, 'I can gift you half a street. One half is mine, the other half is yours. For begging.' That's how this little boy survived. But you know what's truly amazing when you read these stories, one after the other? An inexorable belief in happiness! You have the state that humiliates, brutalizes, takes everything away from you, tortures, executes, makes you afraid of your own shadow. And you have people who, in spite of everything, believe in happiness to come! Arriving tomorrow! I belong to the same generation, so I remember that feeling vividly. Tomorrow the sun of communism will shine over our heads. A different tomorrow from Macbeth's, I'd say."

She shook her head as if not believing her own words.

"Well, I think it's natural," I wedged in. "How can you live without hope?"

"Natural! Is living with blinkers natural? I had them too, but I had to give them up. And then – what? Then for years you linger in the land of despair. There's a painting of an old master, Breugel, I think. Depicting hope as a woman standing on an anchor. Well, I'd lost my anchor. I drifted in the open seas, untethered. But then, the USSR imploded, and the intelligentsia finally said its word and was heard. Difficult times, yes. People lost all their meagre savings in the nineties. There was no food, but we had hopes. Think of it. For the first time in almost hundred years, since 1917, history has given us this chance. No more noose around our neck. Free at last. Can we now squander this opportunity? No and no."

I looked at my friend in amazement. A flame was burning inside her frail and aged body, a flame I hadn't seen in Alexandra before. Yet something bothered me. A contrast between her heroic words and the mournful wrinkles around her eyes and lips, her wistful eyes, with their abstract glare. I thought about her loneliness in this abandoned communal apartment, rooms that used to teem with strange, often grotesque life, now empty and locked.

"Please don't think I'm that naïve," she continued excitedly, starting to pace her room. "I'll be the first to say hope takes strength. It takes courage! There's always the danger of backsliding. But Russia has talented people in every field. Huge resources. What a wonderful country it will be one day. But if we don't actively work toward our future now, there won't be one. Down with our usual passivity, down with fear. With our servile docility, veneration of a Daddy figure on the throne. Down with this poisonous, deadly mixture that flows in our veins." She stopped, breathing heavily, her eyes unfocused.

"What do you mean, mixture?" I dared to insert, but timidly.

"You don't see it? It's everywhere! Inferiority complex will be our peril. We love the West and we hate the West. And we resent the West because we envy the West. We're sitting on a powder keg!"

"Sasha, are you okay?"

"I'm fine, fine! You wanted to know."

"But I think you exaggerate. You yourself told me that there is...how did you put it? There's a civil society. Freedoms. Russia is part of the West. It belongs to Europe culturally, historically, and also..."

"Sure, I'll give you that. But ask yourself a simple question: Why does Russia never vilify, say Latin America or Africa? It's always the West, that stinging in the Russian eye. Because Latin America is relatively poor. But the West is rich, and Russia envies it!"

Her voice grew peevish. She ruffled her hair again and made that funny gesture with her elbows. I turned my eyes away. I felt I needed to pacify her as one pacified a child.

"Well, you know," I said, "I'm just thinking out loud here. Maybe I can help you with this book or something. Going through stories. Choosing the ones for publication. Maybe even doing some work for Memorial? What do you think?"

She reached for a pack of cigarettes, then put it back, possibly remembering I didn't like the smoke. "Yes, but you're in Canada. How can we make it work, practically speaking?"

"True. That's true. You know, I talked to Edwin. He's such a homebody. Not a movable feast. The place we have in the Bahamas. I usually go there alone. In Paris? Alone. But maybe I can talk him into spending three months in Russia every year. What do you think?"

It was already two o'clock in the morning when we finally parted. I promised I'd visit her again before returning to Canada.

14

That night I couldn't fall asleep. I wasn't just exhausted. I felt confusion and a terrible void inside me. I couldn't relate to my friend's loud enthusiasm or to her prophetic angst. On the surface, she was right, she certainly spoke the truth. Why my misgivings, then? Was it her assured, not to say frenzied, tone of voice that embarrassed me? A certain awkwardness in her gestures? Instead of the elegant femininity of her youth, she had a rough boyish angularity and this...well...strange chicken flapping of chicken wings?

I remembered that magical day we'd spent in Abramtsevo more than thirty years ago. How lovely she was. I noticed then, for the first time, that her eyes were not all velvety dark, the way I'd thought, but had green specks around the irises, and when she looked at the blue sky or water, the reflected light made her eyes look liquid green. Nothing seemed to be left of that Alexandra, except pain and suffering. No doubt the past of our country was tragic. But it's gone, never to be repeated. After the Soviet Union collapsed, a new generation of modern, Westernized, dynamic, worldly, well-travelled kids was born. These new players of history had nothing to do with the old Soviet ways. Didn't she see it? Sasha's fears for the future of the country, I came to believe, were simply the reflections of her personal wounds, still raw, the wounds that prevented her from noticing the new reality. Traumatized people can't let go of the very things that have traumatized them. They need to massage their wounds constantly, as some way of making sense of their painful past. Seeking acknowledgement, validation, even empathy. But who was seeking validation here? Could it be that I envied her? Great things had been happening right under my nose, and I'd missed them all. History was being made here, now, and I was standing on the sidelines, facing the cement walls of the parking lots. I asked her she'd go to Bolotnaya Square to protest against Putin's possible return, but would I? Is that what I really wanted, instead of my peaceful pleasant life? The life I clawed out of my destiny? I felt somehow unprotected, terribly vulnerable now. I tried to call Edwin in Toronto. No answer. He must have been at one of his morning meetings.

When I finally dozed off, strange shapes and intimidating presences, all bearing Sasha's face, besieged me. For an eternity, the whole length of my nightmare, I desperately tried to escape her. Morning came. To shake off the night's shackles, I put on a fluffy white housecoat provided by the hotel and took the elevator to the twentieth floor. A pleasantly smiling woman checked my room number and gave me two fresh towels, and I immersed myself in a large swimming pool with a glass bottom. I felt like a fish in a bowl. Though swimming refreshed me somewhat, the nagging feeling left by the dream didn't disappear. I needed to get out, into the fresh air. The city was already awake. To regain my equilibrium, I took a leisurely walk through the centre of Moscow. I couldn't recognize it, so impeccably clean it was. Paris – I'd stayed there for a week before boarding a plane to Moscow – looked like a messy place in comparison. Since the oligarchs had appropriated Moscow's historical centre, the old seventeenth and eighteenth mansions, drab and forlorn for lack of repairs during the communism era, were unrecognizable under their new coats of paint. As if throughout all the years of the Soviet rule, they'd used their sordid facades for mimicry, to weather seventy some years, but now, finally, came out of hiding transformed. Painted, renovated, refurbished, they shone with all the colours of a rainbow, their stucco mouldings accentuated with red and white and pink against the bright yellow plaster of the walls. And the window shopping. Neither in Paris, Milan, nor London had I seen such opulence, such abundance. What elegance, ingenuity, and wit in these window displays. With Armani, Dior, Luis Vuitton right there to compel all who saw. I wanted to buy an Armani tie for Ryan. A clerk in a perfectly tailored suit, with impeccable English and an even more impeccable smile, showed me several pieces, more than a thousand dollars each. A folly, of course, but I did buy a couple of dresses and blouses for myself, the beautiful European brands we never see in Canada. Some very fine lingerie, wonderful cosmetics, Italian and French creams, two pairs of Italian shoes, as well as nice presents for the family. I must admit, I felt a bit guilty, but as I said, in Canada, I wouldn't get this quality, this fine feel. After indulging myself, I felt a little better – much better, to be honest.

It was time to get some coffee. I noticed that anywhere I went, the cafes were full of beautiful, slim, carefree young people. Moscovites were stylish now. They knew how to dress. No sloppy, oversized hoodies, torn pants, or flip-flops. A thought flickered through my mind: Where do these kids get time and money to spend a day in a cafe? Rich parents?

Outside one of the restaurants, I watched a beautiful scene. A man carrying a bunch of snow-white pigeons perched on large hoop approached the customers on the patio. He proclaimed, "Peace and grace to you all, the great Russian nation!" The pigeons took flight, and then alighted on the customers' shoulders and tables, walking between the dishes. Lots of joyful screaming, as you can imagine. The man then approached each table, bowed, and pressed his palms together. "Long live the great Russian people! Peace and blessings to you all!" The moment he uttered this incantation, the pigeons hopped right back on to the hoop, and off he went.

Speaking of restaurants, what a variety of sophisticated cuisines. With an elaborate presentation I really appreciated. And the quality? Excellent! Top marks. And the decor of restaurants' interiors. One place I walked into – the Pushkin café – magically immersed me in a bygone era. Waitresses dressed up as high society ladies from the St. Petersburg salons of Pushkin's times. The interior made up as parlours, the recipes of the time period. Fascinating. All I was missing was Pushkin himself.

By evening, my mood had considerably improved. And it was the time for the theatre. Moscow was now full of art galleries, theatres, and concert halls. In two weeks, I saw ten performances. Moscovites had become great theatre-goers. They say there are about one hundred stationary theatres in Moscow alone. I can't be certain about that number, but I know that tickets are hard to get. I saw some of the finest productions, from Stoppard to Ionesco to Euripides. And I didn't want to miss famous Ariane Mnouchkine, with her Théâtre du Soleil, while she was in Moscow. Russians had become big on avantgarde. London and New York faded in comparison, so daring and innovative Moscow art directors had become. Now, I wasn't big on the Renaissance, but there was a whole retrospective of Raphael from every Italian museum. If my Canadian friends asked me, there'd be things to tell. And the bookstores: Anything I wanted. Anything worthwhile anywhere in the world was immediately translated. I'm sure Sasha wouldn't not longer need to turn to Max, poor soul.

And in the evening, the city turn into a Festival of Lights! In some places downtown, garlands of light hung horizontally across the street, connecting houses, twinkle up and down, up and down, emulating the rain. Simple, but quite original. I hadn't seen anything like it anywhere else. At night, the streets were full of people promenading leisurely, just like they would in Italian cities.

I must admit, at some point, I thought, well, Moscow didn't look like a real city, did it? It was more like a theatre set. I especially got that feeling once I came across the churches. And how could I not? There were twelve thousand of them in one city, virtually one at every intersection. Some looked like wedding cakes, their colours and architectural details running amok. Some had onion domes covered with golden leaves, some domes painted like starry skies; yet others were a combination of green and red and blue. Of course the irony of it didn't escape me: during the Soviet era, churches were blown up, priests executed, religion prohibited. Now the head of state, the former KGB head, imposed religion, professing himself to be the most pious man. But give these churches a hundred years, and the patina of time would make them less ostentatious, in better taste.

15

Three weeks passed since I'd visited Sasha. But before returning to Canada, I went back to Arbat to say goodbye to her. She looked much calmer, her intensity given way to some brooding quality. I wanted to tell her how wonderful I found Moscow, the plays I saw, but I looked at her, and something stopped me. She seemed disinclined to talk, immersed in her own world. And I decided that she would always live in the past and that there was no way of freeing her from her blindness.

I pulled out of my bag of presents I'd bought for her in Paris but forgot to give her last time. A light chiffon dress for summer and a warm, oversized sweater and a scarf for winter. She turned my presents this way and that, smiling weakly.

"Lovely things, thank you! But you shouldn't have taken all this trouble, really!" Then she held the clothing up to her body and said, "The dress is just perfect, but the sweater, I'm afraid it's too big for me. See?"

"That's the fashion now."

'Oh. Do you mind if I give it to Max? He doesn't have much winter clothing. This will fit him perfectly. He's lost a lot of weight recently. And the scarf, Elena will like it, I think. If you don't mind."

"Well, of course, of course!" I exclaimed trying to hide my consternation. "I didn't know you were in touch. I would have brought something for them too. How is Max, by the way, and Elena?"

"Not good, either of them. Elena developed MS and has

trouble walking. Yet she wouldn't see a doctor. Always a struggle for me. Max never really recovered after the asylum. When he was younger, the body compensated, but now...They almost destroyed his kidneys with injections. And the main thing, ever since then, he lost any interest in painting. I'd say in life."

"Doesn't paint at all?"

"No, nothing. Says he has tremor in his hands. But I don't think it's the main reason. Remember how engaged he was. Now he's indifferent to everything, that's the thing. Hope your sweater will give him a bit of joy."

"Do you visit them, then?"

"Tomorrow is Monday, right? Monday, Wednesday, and Sunday are my days. Helping them a bit. Groceries, laundry, cleaning, that kind of thing. Taking Elena to her church, whenever I can."

I imagined Sasha going to Tushino, the bedroom suburbs where the Rubins had been relocated. The subway, then two buses, with bags of groceries, her limp heavier with years.

"He doesn't care about living any more, Max. That's my deepest sorrow. The only thing he looks forward to is to seeing Annie and his two grandchildren. We hope they'll be able to come next May. He loves the boys. They'll be six this year."

"Oh, I see." I didn't know what else to say. I had an early flight tomorrow and still had to pack. "Let's just sit for a second," I said.

We sat down quietly, without talking, as the Russian custom proscribes to those departing. According to the custom, the youngest is supposed to get up first.

Already on my feet, I turned to Sasha, "If it weren't for Max, would you've moved to the United States to be with Annie's family?"

Sasha raised to me her calm wistful eyes. Then, after a long pause, she said, "How do I know who'll go first? I can't abandon Max, that's all know. As long as I breathe. As long as he breathes. I've never loved anybody the way I love Max. And I never will. I have to help them both, don't I?"

16

In 2012, Putin had suppressed the opposition, rigged the elections, and changed the constitution so he could stay in power until 2036. At that point, Sasha and I were still able to exchange emails without resorting to coded language, but her letters came less and less frequently, and I would learn the details of her life from her daughter, Annie, with whom, after seeing Sasha in Moscow, I forged a strong friendship. It was around that time that my life took an unexpected turn: Edwin finally retired and yielded to my yearning for travel. We were on a cruise ship hunting for Northern lights between Norwegian fjords when the news came that Putin's so-called green men—soldiers without insignia or uniform—had marched into Crimea and annexed it. But that felt like a world away, and when I remembered the fun I had in Moscow after parting ways with Sasha, I, like many in the West, didn't see the development as anything too dire.

After Norway, we'd planned to visit Edwin's sister in

Boston, and since Annie and her family lived in Cambridge, a short drive across the river from Boston, we'd arranged to see them as well. I was excited—the last time I saw Annie, she was a little girl in Moscow. Now, a mother of two, Annie, with her milky complexion, the bright gaze of her light eyes, and the round, slow movements of her full, dimpled arms, Annie was a serene and delightful presence. She turned out to be a marvellous cook, and we thoroughly enjoyed her lobster pie and desserts in the company of her husband, Ron, a witty and energetic man my husband and I were meeting for the first time. As I said earlier, Ron was a professor of Slavic studies in Harvard, and one of the interesting stories he told us over dinner took me by surprise. Through his colleagues, Ron found out that Columbia University had obtained the records of poetry readings that took place in Moscow in the seventies and eighties. Krivin, it turned out, had sold them for $70,000.

After dessert, I eagerly followed Annie upstairs and watched her put her twins to bed. The boys calmed down surprisingly fast. She turned off the lights and suggested we leave our men downstairs and sit for a minute on the open balcony that hugged the upper floor of the house. She hesitated for a moment, looking askance, then said she wanted to talk to me. I felt I was breathing through viscous molasses, so hot and humid was the August night. I distracted myself from the physical discomfort by watching the fireflies corkscrew through the air above our heads.

When Annie finally spoke, I noticed how pallid she was, her features, serene before, now distorted with pain. "I know you were my mother's close friend...in her youth. Maybe you knew my father too?"

"Max? Of course! I knew him well, Annie. A nice man...I always liked your father." I glanced at her tense and anguished expression.

"Yes, I...I loved him too," said Annie quietly. "Very much, though I didn't have a chance to see him often after I got married and moved to be with Ron." Then, in a whisper, she added, "He... well, my father passed away."

"Max? Max died? When?" I couldn't think of anything else to say, overcome by a spasm in my throat.

"A month ago, from kidney failure. He'd been sick for a long time...after the asylum. And now I worry about my mother. She's, well, alone now." Annie bent her head, hands crumpling the edge of her blouse. "The reason I wanted to talk to you is, well, maybe you can convince her to move in with us? We have a nice house, as you can see. There is a suit in the basement. She will be totally independent, if she wishes. And the boys, she loves the boys!"

Annie fell silent again, her eyes fixed on the ground. Then she lifted her eyes to me with a question, as if her mother's decision totally depended on my answer. "Don't you think it's the right thing for her to do?"

"Yes, Annie. I think it's a good idea. Now that your mother's alone. But I'm not sure how I can help. I can write to her of course. Though she hasn't been all that good at responding lately."

"Oh. She answers me pretty reliably. But she doesn't want to discuss coming to live with us. I've tried. She can't move to the United States, she says, because of my father's wife – I mean, his widow, Elena. She's in bad shape, Elena, and needs help. My mother can't abandon her." Annie looked at me, her light eyes tearing up. "Do you think, it's the right thing to do, Aunt Emma?"

"What?"

"For my mother to look after my father's widow, now that my father is gone. Would you do something like that?"

That question, in its naive directness, expressed, I felt, the essence of Annie's sincere and gentle heart. At that very moment, more than before, she reminded me of her father. I hesitated. "I really don't know if I would do it or if in general it's the right thing to do. But for your mother? Yes, I can see that. For her, it's probably the right and the only thing. That's who your mother is."

Annie let go of the hem of her blouse and squeezed her head with her palms. "Ah! I wish I could convince her somehow. I told her that we all need her. Her grandchildren need her. She could help us, and I could go back to teaching. I used to teach art in high school before the boys were born. Although, believe me, that's not the primary reason." Her voice trembled. "The main reason...see, my mother has signed an open letter to Putin protesting the annexation of Crimea. Academics, students, and writers all signed it, and she did too. Now I'm afraid for her life."

17

After the visit to Cambridge, I found myself in regular contact with Annie and Ron, who, as a professional, watched closely what was happening in Eastern Europe. In 2014, Russia invaded the Donbass area in Ukraine, under the false pretext of Ukrainians mistreating the Russians living there. Ron was bewildered. "Sudetenland!" he boomed on the phone. "Putin is using the same playbook as Hitler! 'All I need is Sudetenland, to protect Germans there.' And then Hitler occupied Czechoslovakia. History repeats itself."

The most prominent opposition politician, B. Nemtsov, openly opposed the war in Donbass. The following year, he was gunned down at the Kremlin. Soon after, Sasha's beloved Memorial was denounced as a terrorist organization and banned, its offices raided and all files confiscated. Alarmed, I sent her an email: Was she all right? I got a response, now coded, detailing Elena's deteriorating health and the effects of severe winter blizzards in Moscow. At the end, Sasha asked me not to worry, as her mother's old fur coat was keeping her warm. Clearly, she was letting me know that any discussion of the political situation was now beyond the pale and that even if it was deteriorating (blizzards), she personally was out of danger (a fur coat). In the years to come, our correspondence almost fizzled out. Sasha would often leave my emails unanswered, or if she did respond, it would come much later in the form of some a disjointed missive. The main focus of one of her last emails was a detailed description of her attempts to find a wheelchair for Elena, who couldn't walk anymore. The very last email I got informed me simply that Sasha had left her room in Arbat and moved out to Tushino to live with Elena.

In February 2022, we all watched Russia's full-scale invasion of Ukraine, the endless files of tanks crawling toward

Kiev. We were both in bed, watching the news. "Well, Putin feels threatened by NATO," said my husband turning off TV. "No NATO, and there'd be no war, didn't Putin say that? He's not a fool. He's been in power for more than twenty years."

I looked at Edwin in disbelief. "Really? Is that what you think?"

"Americans probably want to build military bases in Ukraine, like they do all over the world. Of course, Putin feels threatened."

Suddenly, I totally lost my cool. "Oh, shut up! What would you know about any of this, with your parking lots!" But I was shaken, I must admit, by my own rudeness. For the first time in our life together, I was having a screaming match with my husband. But I couldn't stop myself. "How can you buy into Putin's propaganda? NATO has never been a threat to Russia! He uses it as a pretext for his goddamn war!" I grabbed a glass of water from the nightstand. My heart was racing.

"Then why is he always talking about NATO?" asked Edwin, nonplussed.

"Because...because he wants to gobble up the whole of Ukraine. That's his goal! And if Ukraine is protected by NATO, it would be harder for him to do so. Isn't it obvious?"

"How do you know?"

"Oh, what a stupid conversation! Ask Ron! He'll tell you!" I ran out of our bedroom, slamming the door behind me.

The next morning, we both felt awkward around each other, and Edwin, an easygoing and rather placid man, who'd never heard or could imagine me talking to him like that, tried to smooth out the wrinkles.

"You okay, hon? What came over you, yesterday? Watching

TV too much, that's what it was," he concluded, serving me cappuccino and putting his arm around me. "Look, let's think of something positive, shall we? You haven't told me yet: Where would you prefer to go next year, to New Zealand, then Brazil the year after, or the other way round? Pretty soon we'll have to make up our minds."

I almost screamed, but then just barely managed to control myself. But nevertheless, I was done with globe-trotting. All I wanted now was to go to Russia. Even ten years earlier, I'd felt that Russia was the place where important things were happening – important for me, important for the world – and I was missing them, enmeshed in my comfy, pleasant, but, ultimately, empty existence here. I remember hinting at that to Sasha during my last visit, asking her to include me in some meaningful projects of hers. But I was too indecisive then, not really knowing what I wanted. All of that changed when Russia invaded Ukraine. While I had been blithely shopping, theatre-going, history outran me.

Amid the sounds of sirens and falling rockets, it was pointing its finger right at me, but demanding what, precisely, I didn't know. And all I knew was that I somehow felt responsible for the horrors unfolding across the ocean. I know it sounds silly. I'd done nothing wrong. I couldn't stop what was happening. Moreover, I'd spent half of my life outside of Russia. I had no family, no relations left there, and, except for Sasha, no friends. So, why this guilt?

I kept watching the ship called Russia sinking, taking with it a million and a half Russian and Ukrainian soldiers – and counting. About fourteen million Ukrainians had fled the country or becoming displaced inside of it. Numbers! Bloody numbers! Twenty-five thousand Ukrainian children taken hostage by Russia, their Ukrainian citizenship revoked, their Ukrainian language and identity erased. It meant that the memory of a nation was being stolen in front of our eyes, that memory Sasha had talked to me about and had seen as her task to preserve at all costs. Thousands of famous writers, artists, journalists, and politicians had been forced into exile. All of that while Russians inside Russia placidly support Putin and his war.

"Look," my husband said one morning, folding and unfolding his newspaper. "Of course I want the Ukrainians to win. But they can't. Russia has more resources, more men. Ukrainians should be rational. They should yield those territories that Russians have already taken in exchange for peace."

"Peace? What peace?" I pushed my bowl of morning porridge away from me. "Putin will never stop. Don't you realize that? He's fixated on restoring the Soviet empire. If he's not pushed back, he'll move on to the Baltics, to Poland, to Moldova, and on and on. Look at the map! Why do you think Russia is the largest country in the world? Because that's what Putin's predecessors have been doing for centuries: conquering their neighbours! Unfortunately, we're surrounded by cowards. The United States, Europe, all cowards, covering their own asses."

"Emma, what's got into you? Can I at least eat breakfast in peace, please?"

"Listen, were you ever attacked by bullies when you were a kid? No? I was, many times. You know what a bully does? What a criminal does? He tests you, how far you'll let him go. And the only way, I repeat, the only way to stop a bully is to push back. To smack him in his stinking face. What you're talking about is appeasement. It'll never work!" My blood was boiling. I couldn't stop. "What are you doing under the table?" I almost screamed.

But Edwin didn't react, now immune to my rage. Instead, he was contemplating his bare foot, moving his toes up and down as if they were independent creatures that he'd only just now noticed. He had that habit, which had always annoyed me, of slipping one slipper off one foot, never both, and then looking for it everywhere. Right now, he was fishing for the missing one under the table. "Emma, please stop shouting at me," he said in his monotonous voice, satisfied at having both slippers on his feet now.

"I'm not shouting! Enough of that fuss under the table already! You're talking of giving away territories, that's why. But do you know what Russians are actually doing in the very territories they took? Have you heard about a twenty-seven-year-old Ukrainian journalist, Victoria Roshina? She was tortured, raped, beaten, and electrocuted, her ribs broken. To cover up traces of torture, the Russians returned her body with her brain missing, and her eyes and other organs. What was her crime? Interviewing civilians in the territories occupied by Russians! You can imagine—actually, no, you can't, and that's our problem: that we don't see further than our own yard. But I'll tell you what they do with prisoners of war, because we now have some first-hand accounts. They starve them, beat, gang-rape them, break their bones, and electrocute their genitals—that's what they're doing! They force them to stay immobile in a crouching position, head touching the ground, toes touching toes, for seventeen hours during the day and two hours at the night! And if their feet went apart, they beat them, usually for three to four hours, breaking their bones, tearing their ligaments and tendons. And that's not all!"

"Emma?"

"I have to finish! At night, they force them to do two thousand squats while beating them again. They force them to drink urine mixed with feces and to take as many gulps as they are years old. They pull out their healthy teeth, and they seal their jaws with nails."

Edwin lifted his heavy bulk off the seat, looming over the table, breathing heavily. "Enough! Enough already! It's not my fault!"

"I didn't imply it was."

"Then why are you telling me all this? What do you want me to do? To go and fight at the Ukrainian front at the age of sixty-six?"

"Don't be ridiculous! I just wanted to tell you because... because this is exactly what the Soviets, the KGB did to their own, in the seventies, when I lived there, and now it's the same story again. When Sasha was telling me about it, years ago, when she was interrogated, like you I had that squeamish feeling, and I didn't want to hear about it either. How could she be so...so...I thought it was her sickness or something. It was almost perverse to be talking about it, and now...now, I'm sorry, I just feel so weak myself, I didn't mean to scream, but I feel like my head is going to burst. It's like I'm going to die, and maybe when I say it, just say it, I feel a bit better, and maybe we let the world know and the world will finally do something about it. I'm sorry I'm crying. I don't want to, but I have to tell you! I have to tell somebody! The Russian guards invented a torture called 'fly paper.' Ukrainians have to squat, sweeping insects and worms off the floor with their hanging intestines. And those who survive these tortures will die from the electric shocks. Applied to...I can't even say it...to their tongues and nipples and testicles. To women's vaginas. They tortured women too."

"Calm down, darling. Enough. Enough already. You said what you wanted to say, and I understand. Now you calm down, hon." Edwin reached for a Kleenex and wiped away my tears, talking to me as if I were a little girl. "Look at you. You're all warm. You're going to get sick tomorrow, the way it goes with you. I'll get you vitamin C, just in case. Are you going to get sick? Tell me! No, we're not going to get sick. Come up to the bedroom. You need to rest. I'll lie down with you."

We undressed. He put me under the covers as I was shivering. He stroked my cheeks and my hair.

"Oh, not now, please," I sobbed.

"See?" he said. "See what you've driven yourself to? Enough, don't cry. I'm here with you, with my silly little girl. You thought I was indifferent? That's not fair, honey. I feel sorry for the Ukrainians. Of course I do! Remember, we gave money to the Ukrainian church for the refugees? But when you know you can't help those poor prisoners in Russian cells, you don't want to hear about those things, right? Because what's the point? In the last year, even more, you seem to be totally fixated on Russia and Ukraine. And I get that, I really do. But it's not good for your nerves. I don't want you to get sick. So let's not talk about it in the future, okay? Agreed? Now you try to get some sleep. I'm going to walk

Charlie before he pees in the house. Poor thing."

My husband knew me well. I did come down with a fever and was sick for almost three weeks. I remember lying in bed, convalescing and browsing through my emails on my laptop, reading the one from Ron: "This is the most remarkable document I have seen. Please share it with Edwin. In 2022, shortly before invading Ukraine, Putin issued an executive order stipulating the principles of his state policies. They mandated 'the preservation and strengthening of traditional Russian spiritual and moral values, which include: life, dignity, rights and freedoms of human beings; patriotism, civic consciousness, service to the Fatherland and the responsibility for its fate; high moral ideals, strong families, creative labour, the priority of the spiritual over materialistic, humanism, mercy and compassion; justice, collectivism, mutual assistance and mutual respect; historical memory; intergenerational continuity and the unity of the peoples of Russia!"

Of course, I didn't show it to Edwin. What would've been the point?

The dates are all getting mixed up in my head. I remember Putin's edict not so much for its content (nothing can surprise me anymore), but rather for the news that I received shortly after reading it.

Annie could barely talk when she told me over the phone that her mother had been arrested. "Up to fifteen years in jail," I heard her saying.

"Wait, wait, I don't understand," I said breaking into sweat again. "Fifteen years for what? Sasha is an old woman, right? She must be seventy-five now. What could she have possibly done?"

Ann wasn't sure, but it looked like Sasha, on her Facebook page, had expressed solidarity and sympathy with a friend, a poet, living in Kiev. The charge brought against her was for discrediting the Russian army.

I didn't mention this to Edwin, as I'd promised never to bring up the subject again. But since then, I started losing sleep. Not even sleeping pills helped me now. Listening to Edwin's rhythmic snoring at my side, I was haunted by one idea: I had to go to Russia to save Sasha. I had to find out where, in what prison, they were keeping her. To bribe the guards. To bribe the whole prison administration, if need be. To write a letter to Putin personally. If that didn't work, to wake up the world community. With a placard in front of each Russian embassy in every country! Free Sasha! Prevent her torture and death! Free Alexandra Luntz, a brilliant poet, translator, and teacher! And then I would go to Russia.

Except I was too afraid to do that. I could be arrested.

So I decided I wouldn't go. Not now anyway. But one day, maybe. Yes, one day, I'd overcome my fear. I will.

Like those seven did in Red Square, in 1968.

Acknowledgements

My deep gratitude to Włodzimierz Milewski, the publisher and the designer of this book, whose unfailing support and encouragement I have been lucky enough to have while working on this book.

My thanks go to my excellent editor Paul Carlucci for his insights and meticulous work.

www.ingramcontent.com/pod-product-compliance
Lightning Source LLC
Chambersburg PA
CBHW050119030726
47505CB00007B/1946